MR. HATE

Terry L. Vinson

MR. HATE

DOUBLE DRAGON

Chapter One
Ruthlessness Personified/Supply Meets Demand

TIME: 1946 HOURS
DATE: 13 MAY 1988
LOCATION: Undisclosed

"This guy is pathetic, Earl. I mean…were the pickings *that* slim?" the man grumbled, his eyes transfixed on a nearby monitor.

His oily, slicked black hair was ruffled in the back, a tiny coif curled into a perfect semi-hook. His tie hung loose from his unbuttoned collar as he reached to wipe the building perspiration from his forehead. He paused briefly before turning to the older man standing only a few feet away, waiting impatiently for a response to his rather curt query.

The older man was concentrating on a separate monitor that displayed a similar scene as the other, but from a slightly altered angle. He nonchalantly brushed a tiny spec of lint off his right shirt sleeve and adjusted his glasses before bothering to reply. His thick, wavy hair was grayed at the temples; his meticulously groomed mustache pitch-black by comparison, giving it the look of a fuzzy black caterpillar lying beneath his rather prominent nose. "Calm yourself, Aaron. My god, you're the highest-strung young man I have *ever* met. Nothing to go catatonic over, my boy. The clock at the bottom of the screen is reading a bit over twelve minutes, is it not?"

The younger man glanced back over his shoulder at the monitor he'd been screening, his face frozen in a sour scowl. "Twelve minutes, forty-three seconds, but *damn* it, Earl."

Leaning back in the comfort of the padded leather chair he had sunken into, the older man waived him off with a hand displaying a bulky, pear shaped diamond ring on the index finger and a wrist sporting a Gold Rolex watch "Three more minutes of footage is all we need, Aaron. We can pad the rest of the tape with additional footage from past skirmishes. You know, kind of a 'greatest kills 'snippet. Sit, Aaron. Drink some bottled water and by all means lay off of the caffeine for a bit."

Grunting his displeasure, Aaron Kyle sidestepped over to the chair fronting his monitor and plopped down with a huff. He was going to have someone's ass from the hiring department later that afternoon, *no* doubt, and it wouldn't be the first time.

This was the third straight 'dud' they had thrown to the wolf in the past five matches. They were either going to have to find more suitable combatants, or begin to consider placing some sort of handicap on Dr. Ruthless out there. Aaron tired of shifting through old footage to pad the product, and knew eventually the audience would feel the same about purchasing inferior entertainment. They were a fickle bunch, as most of their ilk were, and would quickly grow bored and find new, increasingly perverted ways to spend their seemingly endless supply of capitol.

Aaron sipped his warming bottled water and observed the man on the screen crouch and walk behind a row of lined metal barrels. As the man's head slowly scanned a darkened alley to his immediate left, Aaron could see the fear in the subject's spastic, darting eyes. *Jesus, soon as Parks finds this guy, he's buttered toast. Hell, I believe I'd have a better chance of walking away intact than this clown.*

The subject remained crouched between what had been two one-floor barracks buildings from back in the days when the base was fully manned. The two-foot long machete he held in his left hand shook visibly and Aaron couldn't help but smirk after shooting the older man a dismayed glare.

"The son of a bitch is going to piss his combat fatigues, Earl. Wasn't this guy a Green Beret in another life?"

Earl Barron didn't respond for a full thirty seconds, an annoying trait that frustrated Aaron to no end. He realized and accepted the entire project as being the old man's offspring right from the beginning, and that the twenty million that had been spent to renovate the ramshackle base had come from Barren's deep pockets-- but being subjected to playing second banana to *anyone* was something he could not, and *would* not, ever grow accustomed to.

"One more minute, Aaron. And yes, he did possess all the necessary credentials.

Military training...no family to speak of. He simply desired the magical payday. Wanted to become the next in line to the throne, as so many of them do."

Scratching a light growth of stubble on his otherwise flawless, smooth face, Aaron Kyle scoffed. "Next in line for a body bag's more like it. Parks is gonna hand him his liver on a plate."

Earl Barron nodded in silent agreement, his mind already locked on the matter of business at hand, such as number of VHS tapes (the majority) to produce as opposed to Beta (a definite minority), and exactly how much to charge for each since production values had been on the increase of late.

***

His bladder threatening to release its content s with each frantic movement, Bobby Kane wished with every fiber of his existence that he hadn't taken the double-hit of speed an hour earlier. In Grenada, Puerto Rico, and countless other stressful, wartime scenarios, he'd found the practice of popping a beanie or two actually settled his mind and honed his senses.

This time, however, with a cool million dollars on the line, as well as opportunities for larger paychecks in the near future, it was having the reverse effect. Every wind-blown leaf or piece of loose gravel that fell underneath his steel-toed boots caused him to leap back like a spooked grade-schooler. That, coupled with the primal fear he felt for his opposition, a man he had been told was responsible for over sixty deaths via hand-to-hand combat, was causing his hands and legs to tremor uncontrollably.

It was a feeling he wasn't used to, nor a damned bit comfortable *with*, especially under the present circumstances.

Kane wasn't a physically imposing man by any means. At first glance, one might even label him a bit scrawny in appearance. He was six-two but only carried one-hundred seventy-five pounds on a tightly muscled, immaculately toned body.

His face was gaunt; his complexion as pasty as dried dap. He wore bushy eyebrows, thick-framed glasses and a constant expression of grim weariness. Many times he had used these less-than-intimidating features against his opponent with undeniable success.

Troubled by violent outbursts as a child and juvenile, he had been trained as a weapons expert by the Army , and took to it like he'd been born and bred to the expertise that had come so naturally.

Sliding his way forward between two of the empty steel barrels, he cursed himself for wasting the limited ammo he'd been allowed. Three lousy shots from a .38 hadn't exactly been his count *or* weapon of choice, but then again, he hadn't been given one . He'd told himself before the dance had ever started not to waste them, since he would only have the blade and billy club left in a woefully limited arsenal.

Regardless of his own self-warnings, he had fired all three rounds at his large but shockingly swift quarry just moments after the klaxon horn had sounded to initiate the skirmish . The first two rounds had ricocheted harmlessly off of the paved roadway just inches from his target's scrambling boots, the third whistling off the side of a stone building just as his opponent had leapt and then rolled behind its eastern-most wall.

Kane cursed silently under his breath while scanning the rooftops of the buildings he'd slithered between. He felt his neck muscles begin to cramp from both the twisting movement and also the unbearable stress sweeping over him like a viral infection.

Big SOB has got to be strong as an ox. Biceps the size of an anaconda's midsection. Fists like twin goddamned wrecking balls. (inhales deeply) I've got to keep my cool when he comes out of hiding. Use the blade like I've been trained to do. Can't let him get those meat-hooks on me. That's the main thing.

Less than two dozen feet away, a thick shadow

paused, its barrel-shaped chest as still as the surrounding structure it occupied. Eyes that burned with a night vision not in-bred but trained as such remained glued to its prey's ever-shifting line of sight. A thick-handled yet sleekly designed machete lay propped against its left leg, held ever-so gently and without a touch of anxiety.

Although his prey was relatively small in stature, at least frame wise, the man knew through experience not to take anything for granted. He recalled a bar fight in Manila with an individual a foot shorter and at least sixty pounds lighter than himself. A broken rib, separated shoulder and full-blown concussion later, a hard, painful lesson in underestimation had been duly noted for future reference.

It would have been no problem to simply step out and spear his opponent with a quick toss aimed at the midsection or upper chest, especially from the relatively short distance between them. He had once split a man's skull from thirty yards with a similar toss and weapon, the velocity of the toss thrown with such force that the victim barely had time to blink before his head had exploded in bone-splintered fragments.

Such routine action wasn't to be allowed, however. The suits desired hand-to-hand combat if at all possible. Long distance disposals were frowned upon by their buyers, who supposedly paid a king's ransom for each new episode. The filthy rich were nothing if not bored to tears by anything other than extreme excesses. He'd heard that each cassette went for as much as two grand a copy, and that they were producing up to one hundred thousand per episode, *not* counting the overseas markets.

Small wonder the suits could afford his extravagant services, bowing to each new request, no matter how ridiculous, as if doing nothing more than tipping a loyal servant.

Peeking around the side of the concrete wall, a metal light pole positioned at the front of the building that shielded his presence even further, he watched the smaller man shuffle forward to the last of the barrels he'd been using as cover.

The man's head whirled about constantly, scanning all sides like a lighthouse beam into stormy waters, grasping the club in his right hand and the combat knife in his left. Both weapons shook visibly, and were awkwardly positioned, as if he was a complete novice in how to use either.

The smallest of smiles cracked the larger man's grim visage. He was equally elated and sickened by the lack of quality competition in recent matches. Still, better them than him, regardless of the ease in which the deed was done.

Waiting for the man to break for an opening between the barracks buildings and a stretch of grassy flatlands which led to a vacant hanger across the way, Mason Parks lingered without a hint of apprehension.

The breezeless, dead air was unable to provide the slightest hint as to his quarry's whereabouts. Bobby Kane prepped his unsteady gait for a mad sprint towards the open hanger a few hundred feet ahead. He'd come to such a tactical decision due to two distinct points; he felt like a sitting duck with a target pasted between his shoulder blades out in the open, *and* there was a damn good chance that if his opponent wasn't already using the building as a hiding place, he could utilize its spacious darkness to rethink a suitable plan of attack.

Besides, at the moment he found himself scared

shitless, and understood that such men could literally smell fear in an opponent.

Sucking in a lungful of the humid night air, he shoved himself forward in a sprawling lurch, leaving clouds of dust and flying clods of dirt swirling like swamp mist in his path.

Kane hadn't run thirty feet when his left ear detected a series of heavy thumping noises. By the time he attempted a duck and roll an instant later, leaving him in a classic crouched fighting stance, he found himself staring at a field of matted grass patted down by his own boot prints. The only sounds present were that of his own harsh breathing, his pulse pounding frantically.

"W-what the? I know I heard somet-- " he whispered through gritted teeth, the knife and club held up on each side of his sweat-soaked face as if he were attempting to assist a plane in landing on an invisible runway. He rose to his feet, blowing out a lengthy sigh of relief before casually swinging about towards the hanger.

The machete blade entered his throat just below the Adams apple, penetrating with such force that the wooden handle ended where the perfectly horizontal wound began.

Parks had pursued him with the quickness of an Olympic sprinter, carefully tracing the other man's steps through the dust and adjoining grass that led to the hanger . He'd been less than two feet away when Kane had performed the pitifully predictable roll. Parks had leaped completely over the man's spinning frame, landing on his feet after a single bounce atop the shag-carpet thick grass surface.

He had positioned the machete for the strike a mere millisecond before the other man had turned. Despite the complete incursion of the blade through the man's throat, Parks had actually held back to some extent on the torque of his jab in case the man somehow found a way to slip the blow, thereby leaving himself off-balance and open for a counter-attack.

The tip of Kane's boots hardly scraped the ground as he hung semi-airborne from the inserted weapon like a prize fish being displayed from an open pier. His body shook in a series of death spasms, simultaneously defecating and urinating into his camouflaged pants.

Sneering in disgust, Parks jerked the weapon free in a single lightning-quick movement, allowing the body to fall backward as a gush of crimson flew forward in a wide spray.

Leaning down after all movements had apparently ceased, Parks gripped the man roughly by the hair and lifted his upper body forward until it appeared the man was attempting an impromptu yoga movement, his legs splayed out to form a perfect 'V' shape.

Raising the machete shoulder length high with his free hand, Parks paused for dramatic effect before lashing the blade across the man's exposed, bloodied neck.

He held the detached head into the air for a few moments, his bare arm firmly flexed and as thick as an average man's thigh.

Walking back towards the East Side of the base camp, Parks permitted the grotesque trophy to swing freely at his side.

Certain the hidden cameras had obtained ample useable footage, he let Kane's detached skull drop into the grass like a discarded melon shell. "Shit's getting too easy," he mumbled in a deep, humorless tone that sounded as if croaked through a voice box hindered by waves of static.

***

Switching off the monitor, Aaron Kyle strolled stiffly over to where Earl Barron sat deep in thought, and was barely able to refrain from giggling in sarcastic glee. "Not exactly Oscar material in the 'warrior snuff-film' category, boss, and I thought the *previous* bout was crap. But by comparison to this travesty, it was the *Gone with the Wind* of the series. Only some seriously fantastic padding scenes are going to save us from intense bitching and moaning from certain clients who expect a superior product."

With an expression of complete tranquility, Earl Barron inhaled deeply from the unfiltered cigarette he'd lit just moments after his own monitor's screen had gone blank. "Nonsense, Aaron. I will agree it ended quite swiftly and without benefit of an actual tussle, but did you see the move our eliminator made to set up the kill? That poor bastard never even knew he was there. I have never seen a man that large be capable of such speed and agility. Professional athletes *pale* in comparison. He's almost…bionic."

Aaron didn't respond, just sat for a moment nodding his head in disbelief at the older man's overly casual demeanor before he rose to depart the tiny viewing room. "I'll get with the tech nerds about the editing process as soon as we debrief Chuckles there and get him prepared for departure," he said somewhat depressingly.

Whirling around in the bulky chair, Barron spoke sternly, his right eyebrow arched as his right hand arose in a halting gesture. "Aaron, I must tell you that your

14

pessimistic attitude is growing increasingly tiresome. Do our enterprise a favor by not spreading such poisonous opinions amongst the work force."

Kyle stiffened as he reached for the door handle, only speaking as the door was gradually closing behind him. "Whatever you say, Chief."

Sitting in relative silence in the dimly lit room, Earl Barron began to compute numbers in his head. Numbers that held dollars signs at the lead.

He glanced at his Rolex before putting out his smoke in a nearby ashtray.

Aaron Kyle was fast becoming more of a liability than an asset, he deduced. He felt a twinge of sorrow at what he realized might have to be done to resolve the problem in the near future.

***

The chopper landed on the long-abandoned but recently refurbished pad one hour later. The three-man team that greeted Mason Parks was disgustingly familiar to him in both their bland facial expressions and mechanical body movements.

Parks had peeled off the blood-stained T-shirt and grass-stained parachute pants from the taping and now sported a black tee and jeans, a thin blue jacket covering the former. As was standard operating procedure, he carried nothing off the post with him since he'd carried nothing on. He had showered off the light sweat and spatters of blood from his body, his scent no longer of battle but of cheap cologne as he stood stoically, allowing the warm air from the chopper blades to pelt him as if completing the purging process.

Mr. Smiley, as he liked to call the man leading the trio towards him-- all three walking in step like a robotic version of the 'Three Stooges'-- was easily the one that grated on his nerves the most. The man wore a frozen smirk on his thin, pale face, his lanky form suggesting someone who had been raised on bread and water since birth. He was a tall man, at least six-four, although his knees barely bent when he took the long, gliding strides that covered more ground than they probably should have.

The remaining two individuals were your standard muscle-for-hire thugs, each equipped with matching beer guts and sour dispositions.

As Mr. Smiley ever-so-gently placed the vinyl-smelling, Velcro encased blindfold over Parks' eyes, the aroma of the man's foul-smelling breath overwhelmed all others. It never ceased to amaze Parks how the air leaving a human's mouth could literally stink like a freshly deposited turd. "Been brushin' your teeth with dog shit again, Smiley?" Parks bellowed in order to be heard over the chopper.

As was the norm, no response was forthcoming. In fact, in the fourteen months that he had been making the mysterious flight from the post's hidden locale to his ranch in Conquest and vice versa, not a single word had ever been spoken within the confines of the chopper. "Ever hear of *Scope*? Aqua-Fresh? Lighter fluid maybe? Ya might also try flossing every five years or so while you 're at it, old buddy. Helps to keep the flies from landing on your tongue when ya sleep."

He was led slowly to the waiting bird, half-expecting to be shoved into the swirling blades instead of beneath them.

16

Attempting to time the flight was a waste, since he realized from past trips that each time the duration was substantially different, no doubt made purposely so. The suits were nothing if not cautious about keeping the exact location of the post top secret.

Parks' massively thick frame was given all the room it needed to stretch out once inside, and he spent the flight both breaking down the most recent battle, and mentally prepping for the next.

As per normal, he was dropped off in a paved clearing approximately fifty yards from the backdoor of his ranch house. The suits had provided the one-story brick; complete with two bedrooms; full gym with sauna; specially designed 'combat readiness room' and two-car garage.

The black Pontiac Firebird had come with the house; the brand-spanking new, glossily waxed Chevy Z28 was a fairly new addition to the growing list of perks he enjoyed as reward for being the best in his particular field.

No doubt about it, it was *good* to be King. Damn good.

"Great job if you can get it" was Mason Parks' catch phrase when questioned about his 'line of work' by strangers, although that particular query didn't surface very often due to the fact that travels away from the ranch were becoming increasingly infrequent.

Parks had discovered over the past year that there wasn't anything he desired or needed that couldn't be obtained with nothing more than a polite (or otherwise) request (ditto, a *demand*).

The ranch itself was located twelve miles from the insignificantly placed, desolate and scantily populated

17

township of Conquest, New Mexico, surrounded by a seemingly endless desert landscape; sandy dry hills sprinkled with cacti, ancient boulders and hideously deformed shrubbery that gave the area the look of a landscape ravaged by nuclear weapons testing.

Parks didn't mind the lack of a picturesque, panoramic view. In fact, the only semblance of peace he had found in a life filled with constant images of violent death and dismemberment were the week to two week-long sabbaticals spent in and around the ranch between hunts. This was how he defined them--*hunts*. Not contests or matches; nor bouts or brawls He hunted and he exterminated, plain and simple. Cut and dry.

It was the single task Mason Parks had been placed on God's green earth to accomplish, a fact he not only accepted and embraced as his personal, undeniable fate, but had also learned to savor as the victories mounted; relishing in both the act itself and the inevitable aftermath, wherein he would bathe himself in the carnal 'spoils' of his chosen trade.

After Mr. Smiley had removed and retrieved the blinding apparatus, Parks shot him a playful wink and placed his scarred right hand on the much leaner man's shoulder.

"See ya next month, Grins. Inform Mr. X of my displeasure with his staff's choice of opposition of late, will ya?"

The man turned away from him without response, his gait like that of the walking dead. He was about to re-board the chopper, ducking down comically as he walked underneath the swirling, howling blades, just as Parks cupped his hands and bellowed one parting salutation.

"Hey Smiley! Next time you bring the beer and I'll

18

bring the Listerine!"

The unmarked, yellow striped chopper sailed off into the gusting desert winds moments later, leaving Parks standing at the edge of the landing site, waving like a maniac with both arms, his lips stretched in maniacal, animated glee.

"Screw you too, ya creepy bastard," he whispered through a wide, mocking smirk while using one scarred finger to massage the bushy, dark brown Fu Manchu mustache he was cultivating.

Empty handed, he waltzed towards the fully furnished abode, secretly wondering how long such extravagancies would be tolerated until someone in upper management decided a new, fresher face was called for in the cut-throat world of bootleg combat snuff films.

The notion didn't exactly worry him, at least not in the sense that he felt even the slightest twinge of fear, but the thought of being systematically discarded like a worn-out combat boot by some pencil-pushing geek sitting behind a desk made his blood pressure rise to the point of impending implosion.

In Mason Parks' less-than-humble opinion, the one and only way he should lose his position as the primary eradicator in their little underground video gold mine was by dying at the hands of the opposition. He realized there was probably a subtle yet growing concern at the top that certain deep pocketed clients would begin to think the battles were staged, thus new meat would have to be brought in to inject a renewed interest. If sales waned, he alone would be held accountable.

Tossing his clothes haphazardly onto the king sized waterbed that fronted a large screen TV and a ten-thousand dollar stereo/entertainment center in the home's spacious main bedroom, Parks scooped a cellular phone from a nearby dresser and began to casually dial.

"Level one priority. Password is 'seventy -eight *cold*. 'Gotcha…'"

As he waited, standing naked except for the semi-white socks adorning his size twelve feet, Parks hummed an old rock tune he believed to have been sung by Bad Company. *Feel like Making Love* it had been called.

His smile beamed as the other party came on the line, restlessly rubbing the prickly short hair that adorned his rotund skull.

"Yes, my location is cleared. I would like to place an order, my good man. Alright, I believe I feel like a little Mexican tonight…"

***

TIME: 0913 HOURS
DATE: 14 MAY 1988
LOCATION: 14th Floor, Office Complex District, Seattle, Wash.

Leaving a thick cloud exhuming the aroma of Dakkar cologne in his wake, Aaron Kyle strode purposely past the unoccupied secretary's desk and entered the office marked *E.BARRON* – **President** – *World-Wide Video Corp* without bothering to knock.

Earl Barron sat behind a tiny PC monitor sitting on one corner of a massive rollaway desk that was typically immaculate in its tidiness and meticulous organization.

Kyle sat down hard in a soft leather couch positioned across from the heavy oak desk, the length of which was comparable to a sizeable conference table.

20

Barron did not look up, instead continuing to peck away at the minuscule keypad with his manicured fingernails. Large gold and silver framed photos with scenic, almost 3D country settings adorned each wall.

"Yes, Aaron. Good morning to you, as well. Ah yes, things are going remarkably well, how about yourself this fine sunny morning in the city of rain?"

Releasing a chuckle that was devoid of humor but coated in sarcasm, Kyle slapped both of his *Calvin Klein Casuals* covered knees.

"I take it by your cheery disposition that Mr. Happy's late night exploits have not as yet been divulged?"

Peering over the miniscule lenses of his bifocals at the other man, Barron nodded negatively.

"Ah, then allow me to give you the rundown, chief. This is better than chocolate covered tits on your favorite mistress."

Despite his building anger at his subordinates obvious insolence and sour demeanor, Barron maintained the stoic self-control that was his trademark. "Go on, Aaron, although I have no... favorite mistress to speak of."

His initial cockiness rapidly transformed into a squirming unease that wiped the crooked leer from his face. Kyle cleared his throat and continued, reading from a computer printout he held in both hands like a sacred stone tablet. "Credit line over-extension, incident number *one;* not ten minutes after being dropped off at the Conquest location, he contacts Mr. Conway on our entertainment line and orders not one but two ladies of the evening, both of which were delivered to the location at approximately eleven-ten PM by private chopper.

21

"The ladies were provided by City Lights Escort service in Vegas, and each charged him, make that charged *us*, for a *full* nights service.

"That's five thousand dollars, Earl, not counting the two grand for transportation costs."

When the older man didn't elaborate, Kyle wiped his wet brow with a chalky-white handkerchief while huffing like a man twenty years his senior following a ten-mile marathon. "Credit line over-extension, incident number *two* : Parks ordered two cases of ten year old scotch from Bailey's Fine Spirits in Sin City. Had them flown in by stump-jumper aircraft to Conquest and then driven out to him by courier. The scotch was twelve hundred bucks, plus the thousand-eight-hundred for direct service to his ...to *our* drop off location."

His eyes wide and reddened with rage, Kyle again paused to gauge the older man's reaction. Met with a mellow indifference, he again returned to the slightly crinkled sheet. " Credit line over-extension, incident number *three*: Jesus, if this doesn't make you piss thunder and shit lightening, sir, I'm going to have you checked for a pulse. It wasn't enough that he took it upon himself to order the most expensive hookers in Nevada...*oh no*. The ruthless, pin-headed brute had to initiate bodily injury before sending them packing. It seems he had requested two Hispanic ladies of the evening, and received one Hispanic and one black instead. The bill from St. James Medical Center in Vegas is pending, but the black hooker had a broken nose and the Hispanic a broken hand. The chopper that picked them up took them straight to the hospital after leaving his...*our* drop off point. We're looking at a minimum of five grand, possibly more. They won't press charges or

22

sue, of course, if they *are* taken care of financially. Can you believe this shit?"

Scooting his high-back chair forward as to place his elbows on the edge of the desk, Barron flashed the younger man a mystified glance. "Parks *beat* the women? My god…that is a shock, to say the le--"

Kyle waived him off with one flailing hand while again wiping his forehead vigorously with the other. "No, sir He didn't exactly…that is to say, the physical harm done was not by his hands. He…forced the women to…fight *each other*. Added a little to their tip…you might say, for doing so. At least, that's the info Conway got from the hookers themselves."

Leaning back, his chin cupped gently in his right hand, Barron fought off an unrelenting urge to giggle. "Boys will be boys, Aaron, as *you* know better than anyone, I suspect."

Kyle began to speak, his eyes wide with shock, but was quickly cut off before any coherent words could form.

"Your own past is checkered with assaults on your first wife, a porn star of growing popularity these days I hear, and then there was that…unfortunate, quite messy scenario in Hawthorne a few years back in that rat-trap hotel. Two kilos of Columbia's finest and the daughter of a record executive wasn't it? I hear the girl is fine now, just slightly brain damaged from the overdose."

His hands shaking like a junkie awaiting the day's first injection into a throbbing, craving vein, Kyle's lips quivered, then pursed together as if sewn shut.

Barron turned back to his keyboard, his expression bland and entirely void of all emotion. "The paid escorts have no case, Aaron. The punishment they inflicted upon

23

themselves was by their own free will and no more than an additional form of entertainment for which they were amply compensated. Parks is no boy scout…that fact was established eons ago. Let's get on to more substantial matters, what do you say?"

Slowly crunching the print-out between his long, slender fingers, Kyle's flesh radiated an anger that was made obvious by the thick, cord-like veins standing out on his neck and forehead. "By all means, Sir. Money, after all, *is* the bottom line here. Regardless of how much this cretin is allowed to piss away on his own perverse brand of jollies, I'm sure the company will remain comfortably in the black when all is said and done."

His mastery of the keypad reminiscent of a piano maestro fronting a Baby Grand, Barron typed briskly for a full three minutes before pausing with his squinting eyes transfixed onto the brightly glowing monitor. " To this point, our staff has confirmed an initial order of fifty-six thousand copies, the majority of which are VHS requests. Our man in Phoenix has an overseas client out of Brazil that wants a thousand copies of the newest, and five hundred of all past volumes. Looks like *Eradicator VOL XV* is an unqualified hit, Aaron."

Unceremoniously sticking the wadded paper in his inside suit pocket, Kyle sighed heavily, his shoulders slowly beginning to lose their tenseness. "Pricing still the same? Seven-fifty stateside, one thousand overseas plus shipping?"

His fingers again riding over the keys with the blurring swiftness of a speed-typist, the older man paused for thirty more seconds before responding. "No change there, but we are planning a substantial hike next month. The iron that was once red hot is losing some steam, I'm afraid. Speaking of next month, have you completed the screening process?"

"We're down to two candidates, both of which have great qualifications on paper at least. Then again, so did *Kane*. Final interviews take place day after tomorrow at the Holiday Inn in Denver. I'm flying out tomorrow at nine a.m."

"Any problems in the editing room or at the base?"

Kyle stood laboriously, his knees popping sharply. "Base sustained no damage. Honestly, it hardly lasted long enough to dent the compound grass. Lighting was a problem in a few shots, but it's being cleaned up. We can view the finished product this evening around four-thirty according to Wilt in processing. Earl, we might seriously consider attempting to set up an inside kill. The last three have been outdoors and they seem to be getting blurrier; darker, and increasingly more difficult for the boys to clear up."

His hand now resting on an open folder spread out beside the computer, Earl Barron nodded in agreement. "That's something we'll look into before next taping. Is Sarah flying with you to Denver?"

Wringing his hands nervously, Kyle looked almost apologetic. "Well...uh, yeah, if it's okay with you. I can fill out the voucher before she goes, if you'd like."

The older man waived both of his callous-free hands palm up in a gesture of surrender. "No, no, Aaron. That isn't necessary. I'm just glad to see you two are still together. This being marriage number three for you, it must be the charm. Tell Sarah I said hello."

Kyle grew noticeably more relaxed just before turning to depart. "I will, Earl. As a matter of fact, I was thinking about taking her to Hawaii next summer, if our production schedule permits."

"I foresee no problems in that regard, Aaron. She still think s you're in the mainstream video business, does she?"

Kyle stood with the door semi-opened. "Most definitely, Earl. If the wife discovered our distribution was this far out of 'Blockbuster' range, I'd be asking you for another raise to cover additional alimony," he said through a wide grin.

Barron's face grew instantly grim, a visage of stone. His eyes narrowed just as his nostrils flared. "I'm afraid it would be a tad bit *more* serious than that, Aaron I don't need to remind you of the confidentiality of our situation, do I? These are *serious* felonies, my boy. Very steep prices must be paid for any slip up in terms of security."

Aaron Kyle felt the blood surging through his veins grow instantly cooler. "I understand, Earl. Good *lord*, man. I've been in the biz as long as you remember?"

He walked out of the older man's office a moment later, giving the buxom redheaded secretary, now back at her post with a fresh, steaming cup of coffee in hand, a quick wink.

Sitting in his own smaller, openly cluttered office a few minutes later, Kyle poured himself a quick shot from a half-empty pint bottle of Jim Beam he had retrieved from a bottom desk drawer. He gulped it down and relished the burning sensation in his chest. "Aaron my man, you've gotta find another line of work No fucking doubt about it."

***

TIME: 1124 HOURS

26

DATE: 14 MAY 1988
LOCATION: Park's ranch, Conquest, New Mexico.

The clanging retort of metal slamming against metal could have been heard for miles around, if there had actually been anyone present in the surrounding desert to witness such a clamor.

"Son…of…a…*BITCH*!" Mason Parks bellowed, dropping the heavy bar onto the reinforced bench he lay upon. The bar, which presently held a total of five-hundred sixty-five pound s of cast iron, shimmied and shook as he jerked himself upright with a loud groan.

Shaking a torrent of fresh sweat from his face and exposed arms, he blew out a generous portion of air before standing to perform a series of upper body stretches. "Those whores must'a weakened my arms and knees, after all. Regardless, I *will* clear six hundred pounds before this day is over."

The room he occupied would have put most paying gyms to shame in both square footage and available machinery. On one side sat various Nautilus machines used for specific body parts; legs, chest and upper back. The opposite side held a free weight rack that contained over eleven-hundred pounds in metal plates, along with two multi-exercise benches, a squat rack designed to hold up to a thousand pounds, and two heavy-duty hard bags that hung from thick-linked chains from the studded ceiling.

In an adjoining room, smaller in length and width but with a roof that set a full four feet higher, rested a series of machines that resembled automatic tennis-ball feeders. Four of the machines were situated two feet apart on a perfectly spaced horizontal line.

27

Fronting them was a fifteen foot long, three feet wide sandpit that looked to have been bulldozed through the floor from the outside in. Above the sandpit were a series of four gymnastic rings that hung from the unusually high roof, hitched to wooden studs identical to the ones that braced the heavy bags in the weight room.

The machines fired colored ammunition, but not the type that harmlessly bounced off the intended target, leaving only a rainbow-like swirl of shades in their wake. These were designed to fire rubber bullets that left not only a smear of dye on whatever it struck, but also a rather nasty welt from the force of impact.

Three times a week Parks would don a bulky zip-up suit similar to that worn by house painters, strap on a back pack that held fifty pounds of free weights, and play a potentially painful game of 'dodge the bullet 'to enhance his reflexes. He had often left these sessions cursing under his breath with welts the size of quarters coating his back, thighs or chest.

Setting the machines on auto, he would have a full minute to prepare before being fired upon by random bursts along a pre-set line of fire. He utilized the rings to avoid ground shots, and the pit was simply to hamper his foot speed.

Parks had guffawed at the notion when first approached by the suits to endure such unconventional training regimens, but had discovered over time that becoming skilled at dodging live fire was a talent one wasn't exactly *born* with.

Nineteen hunts, and not a single bullet wound to show for it. Practice definitely made perfect. Practice and the added advantage of facing men whose aim was hampered by the prospect of impending death.

He had decided to make the '*Duck and Jive*' room, as he had come to refer to it, a seven-day-a -week exercise beginning later that afternoon. The reason was simple; he had a gut feeling the suits were going to up the ante. His hunts had been far too easy of late. His opposition was going to see a bigger, better choice of weapons soon, and invariably more ammo to stock said weapons with.

No doubt his dying on film was going to be an instant 'bestseller' amongst the loyal clients. He had decided he wasn't going to make it easy on either the suits or his future opponents. If he was going down, they were going to damn sure earn it the *hard* way.

Falling back onto the sweat coated, heavily cushioned bench, Parks barked out a series of grunts before hefting the bar upward. Ten seconds and two strained reps later, he allowed it to fall downward with enough force to shake the entire bench. "*OH HELL YEAH!* Six- hundred-fifteen pounds!

All this without a single shot of magic muscle juice. Damn, I *am* the man. Even so, I believe I'll brew me up a glass of government-banned energy booster ."

The brown liquid was premixed and kept in unlabeled, sixteen ounce clear plastic bottles that lined the top shelf of his walk-in freezer sized fridge. After swallowing a handful of pills, everything from multi-vitamins and herbal supplements to amino acid tablets the size of ping-pong balls with a full bottle of the dark, glutinous drink, he paused before ricocheting an earsplitting belch into the cool air of the vacant structure.

"Ah, Mother's milk. A few more hours in the hell room, then a quick shower and a TV dinner. After that, I do believe another order of takeout is on the agenda. Got one hell of a hankering for *Chinese* ."

Cranking the gym's built-in stereo system until the free weights virtually jiggled in their racks, Parks began a torturous session of squats that ended with every available weight placed on either side of the sagging bar. His bellowing shrieks failed to find a human receiver in the adjacent area, but half a mile into the engulfing darkness of the desolate desert landscape, a lone wolf howled its disapproval.

Chapter Two
Sheriff Dan/A Building Storm

August 27th, 2006 Elm Hill, Alabama

"Daniel, pleeeeeaaasssse…" the girl pleaded, playfully covering her ears in mock disgust.

The man kept his eyes focused on the narrow two-lane ahead while bobbing his head in comical rhythm to the music blaring from the cruiser's back speakers.

"But Kara-syrup my dear, this is a true classic. Cheap Trick's *Surrender*…circa 1979 I do believe. Just listen to this guitar riff coming up. It just don't get *no* better," he bellowed over the thundering racket, beating his palms against the wheel as to stay in time with the tune's drum solo.

Rolling the passenger side window down, the young girl stuck her head out as if to avoid a horrid odor inside the vehicle. "Help! Somebody! Anybody! My father is abusing me musically! Help!" she whined into the passing forest, oak and elm tree limbs hanging into the road like outstretched tentacles.

Daniel Whitlock reached over and playfully pinched his fourteen-year old daughter on one knee before turning the volume knob down to a barely audible level.

"I'm the Sheriff here, Kara-cake, remember? No one will ever believe *you*." He grinned, waving with his free hand as a black Chevy S-150 greeted the cruiser at the bottom of a steep grade. She was far too old for the cutesy nicknames, he knew, but found it provided him with a parental sense of closeness. Similarly, he figured she felt a similar connection by referring to him as

'Daniel' instead of 'Dad.'

After poking her head back inside, Kara Whitlock began rummaging through the cruiser's glove box, tossing cassette tapes out onto the front seat by the handful.

" Molly Hatchet? Bob Seger? Thirty...Eight Spectacle? Who *are* these people, Constable? Any of 'em still living?" she queried without a hint of humor.

"That's .38 *Special,* my young and uninformed offspring. Don 't you kids know *any* of the classics?" he replied while slowing for a right turn onto a gravel road marked by a rusty sign that read *Elm Hill School – 2 miles* .

His daughter continued to frantically dig through the overflowing compartment, her face set in a tight grimace of antipathy. "Of course we do, Daniel, but I have yet to discover a single Black-Eyed Peas, Destiny's Child or Pussycat Dolls cassette in this hideous collection of ice-age relics. By the way, Daniel, there are these new things on the market called compact discs. Check into it when you get time."

The aging cruiser, a '97 model Ford Taurus that had seen its prime at least six years earlier, rattled and coughed along the pot-hole ravaged trail. Daniel smirked at the pitiful display, thankful for the fact that 'high speed chases 'were few and far between in his jurisdiction.

"Did you really just say...*Pussycat Dolls*? And what exactly does ice-age mean? Just for that, young lady, you'll be forced to eat my cooking again tonight, understand?"

Kara's expression instantly transformed to one of pure, primal horror, her hands dropping limply onto either side of the car seat. " Ah, a fate substantially *worse* than death," she croaked.

Daniel pulled slowly past a line of off-loading sedans and mini-vans and parked just to the side of the school's breezeway entrance. "I'll pick up a couple of frozen specials at Piggly Wiggly. They're not too tasty, but make up for it by being at least somewhat edible. 'Sides, you'll only have band practice once or twice a week soon. I 'll gladly re-hand you the keys to the kitchen at that time."

Combing her fingers through the long blonde locks that lay atop her slim shoulders, Kara grinned at her father mischievously. Despite the lengthy, narrow nose that had forever been the Whitlock curse, Daniel's only child was quickly transforming into a quite attractive young woman, much to his undeniable chagrin. She had her mother's slim, lanky build and dark brown eyes, details he was hardly thrilled to observe. It seemed inevitable that he would be cursed to watch his daughter slowly but surely transform into the one woman on the planet Daniel *least* desired to be reminded of. Molly had l eft them four years earlier for a life 'outside the sticks' as she had so eloquently phrased it. The letters his ex-wife wrote to Kara (rarely since the magic of *email* had entered the Whitlock household last Christmas in the form of a new Dell computer) were addressed from Las Vegas. Molly had never been one for small town living, having never forgiven Daniel for separating from the Army , and had long talked of moving from a town she had dubbed 'Elm Dull' for brighter lights. The day she actually found the courage to do so had shocked no one, least of all her haggard husband, who had felt nothing but soothing relief at her abrupt absence. Kara visited her once a year for two weeks, and that seemed to satisfy

33

both of them.

"I bet you *will,* Constable Whitlock. You've probably involuntarily dropped a few pounds off of that beer gut of yours in the past few days. Not to worry. I'll have you back to your former cheery, chubby self in no time flat."

"Chubby? I was never anything other than pleasantly stout. Changing the subject, you get that Economics report done last night? I saw you peckin' away on the Internet last night."

Rolling her eyes in apparent disgust, Kara peered over at her father as if he had just emerged from a space pod. "Yes, father. I wasn't surfing the porn sites or researching the best way to assemble a pipe bomb, if that's what you mean."

He quickly raised a hand in mock surrender. "Hokay, just asking, future valedictorian of the University of Alabama graduating class of 2014. It's just that, in your old pop's day, we had these ancient scrolls we called 'Encyclopedias.' The first d ot-com was still decades away."

Kara giggled like a girl five years her junior before flashing a smile that was the definition of youthful radiance. "You old timers did have it tough, alright. Didn't you say your favorite pastime as a boy was hitting rocks with a broken tree limb?"

"Hey…*hey*…I'll have you know that hittin' rocks was a true sport, an artful test of skill lost on today's spoiled millionaire athletes. I had my own leagues, stats, and World Series, all played within my personal backyard stadium," he proclaimed with exaggerated glee. 'Ah, I recall it as if it were just yesterday. The oak trees were the center field wall, the briar thicket a spitting image of Fenway Parks' Green Monster. I would find a perfectly round rock and uppercut that sucker three hundred feet every time. Why, your dear old dad led the league in hitting, homers and RBI's every summer for five or six years."

Covering her mouth with one hand while hugging herself with the other, Kara was giddily unsuccessful in wiping the smile from her lips.

Daniel returned his child's smile, shooting her a playful wink just as the cruiser's com radio squelched loudly, easily overwhelming the opening cords of Cheap Trick's *Dream Police* .

"Peepers is checking in already? Must be a regular crime wave," Kara said, pulling a comically overfilled backpack from the back seat.

Reaching for the mike, Daniel shot her a grave look. "Don't call her *Peepers*. It's Deputy Morton. Respect your elders, Kara. You'll be one someday yourself, you know, and sooner than you'd ever want to believe."

The passenger door creaked loudly as she began to exit, a low mumble of reluctant acknowledgement crossing her still-upturned lips.

Daniel replaced the mike without ever responding to its incessant buzzing. "Have a good one, Kara-Berry. Good luck on that Algebra test. And remember…"

"…*your* future is in *my* hands. I know, Daniel, I know. See ya," she quipped, her eyes rolling as the door shut and she jogged away towards the entrance, which was blanketed by kids of various ages and physical dimensions.

Pulling from the lot, Daniel first spotted and then waived at Marge Williams, who had been teaching high school English at Elm Hill High since long before he had attended her classes. Stern but caring--that was Marge. Came close to failing him on several occasions, if he recalled correctly.

He also noticed young Milton Krause jogging across the mostly dead grass fronting the school's gymnasium and couldn't help but snarl a bit.

Milton was a ninth grader, a year ahead of Kara, a bookish type that kids in Daniel 's time would have labeled a 'nerd.' All elbows and knees, and about as graceful as a drunken rooster. He had also been a consistent caller to the Whitlock residence since the new school year had begun a few weeks before Kara giggled like a hyena on helium each time the boy called. Daniel still saw his skinny, coltish, baby-faced daughter as a six-year- old, and realized with a sudden pang of bemused guilt that he most likely always would.

As he neared the left turn that would lead him back onto highway six and into town, the radio sounded off once again, this time accompanied by the less than genteel voice of his lone deputy, Tracy Morton. "Sheriff, you ignorin' me or asleep at the wheel again? Over."

Daniel groaned aloud, bringing the mike to his lips after donning a pair of wraparound sunglasses to block the bright morning sunlight. " I told you to never wake me while I've driving, Trace. What's up? Over."

"What else could it be at seven-forty-two in the a.m., Sheriff? Have yet to pour a fresh cup'a joe into my system, and old 'hollow-leg' Wilson is reported to be stumblin' out in front of the newspaper office, drunk as a skunk and twice as ornery. This time he's reportedly armed with a rather large red brick. Over. "

"Hoyt on another 'Evan Williams' rampage, is he? Well, it *is* that time of the month. Must have gotten his

36

retirement check a few days early. Over," Daniel replied somewhat grimly. He had hoped to swing back by the house for another cup of coffee before heading to the office. His deputy of four years made the worst coffee in the county, perhaps even the whole blamed state, but he was far too polite to ever say so within her earshot. Tracy was tough as nails on most matters, but accepting criticism wasn't exactly her strong suit. It had taken Daniel years and several hard lessons to finally understand that his deputy's toes were both overly tender and extremely sensitive. The townspeople had jokingly nicknamed her 'Miss Peepers' upon her assignment as Daniel's deputy, due to the thick, black rimmed glasses she wore, the lenses of which were literally the thickness of old Coke bottles from an era long past. She spoke often of corrective surgery, having repeated several thousand times (to anyone unfortunate enough to be within the general vicinity) that contacts were 'a bigger pain than glasses, with double the upkeep .'

"What's your twenty, Sheriff? Over."

"Pulling onto H number six right now. Meet you on main in five. Over."

"Gotcha, Sheriff. I'm hoofin' it over as we speak. Coffee's made by the way, but

I guess it'll have to wait. Over and out."

Daniel pushed the accelerator a bit harder, the cruiser's engine moaning in obvious disapproval. He couldn't help but laugh at the coffee remark, despite the shadow of sincere dread that accompanied it. "We'll have an extra cup for our troubles, Trace. Over and out."

Highway six ran directly into Main Street from the eastside of town, and Daniel discovered the roads depressingly desolate for what would have been considered 'rush hour' in a larger township.

He had heard that both Remar's Printing shop and Winslow's Apparel plant had laid off quite a few folks in the last several weeks. Such news would matter very little to a more populated area, but Elm Hill could hardly afford many similar scenarios if they were to maintain the current head count of just over two-thousand residents.

Sitting at the first of two red lights balanced across Main Street (there was another light on Oak Street, but it was a flasher only), Daniel waived outside his open driver's window as Carolyn Peters crossed the street on her way to the Rexall Pharmacy. She flashed a brief, shy smile his way and then proceeded across, her flower design dress instantly reminding Daniel of something once worn by June Cleaver. Rubbing his eyes vigorously, Daniel briefly pondered how much longer he could continue to function on less than four hours sleep per night. The last good night's slumber he could recall had long since slipped his weary mind, although he figured the specific day count was fast climbing towards the hundred-day point.

As the light turned green, Daniel glimpsed into his rear view mirror and caught the image of Pete Henley sitting behind the wheel of his shiny new Expedition. Pete lifted a finger in acknowledgement just before turning left into the Bank One parking lot.

"Doing okay, aren't you, Petey? Bank managers do quite well even in small towns, I take it," Daniel whispered as he shot through red light number two and directly between and underneath the town's most recognizable monuments; giant twin elm trees that adorned each side of the street like swaying bookends.

The main street had been constructed *around* them during the summer of 1854, the city of Elm Hill officially christened shortly thereafter.

Parking slowly alongside the mostly empty parking lot that fronted the *Elm Hill Times* building (actually a small one room office no larger than an average 'one hour photo' stand), Daniel observed his subordinate standing stiffly at the office's oak door entrance. Deputy Morton held her black handled billy club in one hand, as if standing guard over an exiting celebrity, her thick arms and muscular legs spread wide in a classic blocking stance.

Suppressing a wide smile by tightly pursing his lips, Daniel exited the dust coated cruiser and stepped onto the badly cracked curb, keeping his eyes trained on the wobbling, swaying man just to his left. Hoyt Wilson was a slightly chunky, big-boned, white haired man in his mid-fifties, but whose weathered, line-creased face resembled a man at least a decade older. He had spent over twenty years in the Navy before retiring in the mid-nineties and taking up permanent residence in the old Wilson farm just outside the city limits. Prone to weeks of heavy drinking that mostly tied to the loneliness (Hoyt had supposedly never married and had no known living kin) of living alone on a thirty-plus acre farmstead, his frequent visits to the town newspaper office had become irritatingly commonplace.

"Alright Hoyt, drop the brick," Daniel said calmly as he took a relaxed stance directly in front of his poised deputy. At six-two and a tightly wound (except for a slightly swollen midsection that had developed within the past two or three years) two-hundred ten pounds, Daniel stood perfectly eye-level with the older man, who stumbled back a step from the sudden intrusion on his space.

Lurching hard to the left, Hoyt came dangerously close to tipping over before eventually righting his balance, the square red brick almost dropping clumsily from his curled right hand. "Sheriff...I've had it...up to..." he babbled, pausing only to raise an outstretched hand to his forehead in a spastic salute, "here with the state. Th-they need to p-pave my driveway 'fore I kill myself...drivin' through the gopher h-holes near my bux...uh, box...mailbox. I want an ad...art. .article wrote up to tell everybody...how the state is puttin' the screws to a local."

Deputy Morton stepped forward and whispered into Daniel's right ear, although still loud enough for the hopelessly inebriated subject to easily comprehend.

Several early morning commuters passed by, none of whom bothered to slow for a closer look at what had become an all-too familiar scenario the past several years.

"I say let 'im shatter the window this time. Maybe havin' to foot out the bill for a new one will help break him of pulling this crap."

"He doesn't have the five or six hundred bucks it would cost for a replacement, Tracy. Besides, he wouldn't even recall *doing* it. Let's just drive him home and put 'im to bed."

Stepping forward with both his hands held up shoulder level with the palms up, Daniel spoke in the tone of a scolding parent. "We'll talk about it later, Hoyt. I understand your problem, and I'm sure Mayor Jenkins will be willing to listen as well."

His face suddenly contorted in a mixture of rage and

disgust, Hoyt reared back in a classic baseball pitcher's half wind-up. "Jenkins? He's on the damn payroll, D-Dan...Sheriff Dan. The cheap SOBs own half the driveway...they should at least pay for half the pavin'. They're just m...m...pissed 'cause I wouldn't...s-sell 'em those other ac-acres...a d-deca...ten years back."

Halting only a few feet from where Hoyt alternated staggering first side to side and then front to back, Daniel felt like a politician on the final stop of a ten city campaign junket, each word he delivered almost verbatim to ones he had repeated mere weeks earlier. "Like I said, Hoyt, we'll discuss it through and through and figure out a solution. Maybe the state will finally let you buy that thirty-foot stretch, possibly at a real bargain. Now, put down the brick and we'll jaw on it, okay?"

"I still say let the old souse toss away, I..." Deputy Morton began, cut off mid-gripe as the brick fell to the pavement with a loud thump. Hoyt quickly followed suit, falling onto his hands and knees, then proceeding to toss his cookies in a series of violent, jerking heaves.

Daniel was forced to leap back as if he had been bee-stung to prevent having his newly shined boots soiled by the sour-smelling onslaught.

"Oh Jeez Louise,' Deputy Morton spat, turning away as briskly as her bulky frame would allow, 'smells like a mix of Jim Beam and buttermilk."

Betty McBride, the editor/publisher and lone employee of Elm Hill's bi-weekly periodical, stepped cautiously from the office entrance just as Daniel bent to assist Hoyt to his shaky feet.

"Is it over, Daniel?" she croaked in a bored tone, blocking the morning sun with a liver-spot covered hand.

"We'll take him home, Betty," Daniel replied

41

without looking back, forced to practically carry the slumping, heavy set man to the cruiser a dozen feet away.

"Mark your calendar for two weeks from today, Mrs. McBride, and give us a call when he actually shows up," Deputy Morton added with a friendly nod, tugging on the form-fitting blue uniform pants she sported.

Shooting the deputy a final, somewhat dubious look, Betty McBride's only reply was a low grunt as she casually reentered the cramped office.

After laying the semi-conscious man in the cruiser's back seat, Daniel stood at the driver's door and nodded at his deputy as she strolled sourly by. "Shouldn't take more than thirty minutes, there and back. See you at the office. Keep that java warm for me," he said wearily.

Deputy Morton just shook her head apathetically.

"How much longer you gonna play Sheriff Andy of Mayberry to his 'Otis Campbell, the town drunk', Dan? Doesn't it get old?"

Daniel paused for a moment, glancing into the bright blue sky beaming down onto a mostly deserted main street as a gentle morning breeze massaged his rugged face. "It's part of what they pay me for, Trace. You know, like breaking up major drug rings, busting Mafia bosses, or...straightening out bent stop signs. Check total's the same every week, regardless. Besides, at least the man *is* a Crimson Tide fan. If he rooted for those pig-farmers from the plains instead, I'd toss his hide *under* the jail."

Tracy Morton grinned the wry, 'that's my boss' smile that Daniel had grown so lovingly accustomed to, then walked briskly away as Daniel began the U-turn that would eventually lead him towards the county line.

A few moments into the peaceful, scenic drive that

42

led to Hoyt's badly neglected farmhouse, Daniel was bombarded by the man's usual drunken rants and raves, a series of mostly incoherent mumbling that normally made little sense.

"...noises, Sheriff. Weird ones...weird racket. H-heard...similar a few...months b-back. W-what you...gonna do about...it?"

Passing by the old Alexander farm, a fifty acre spread that had been deserted for at least a decade, Daniel was taken back by Hoyt's latest string of psychobabble, a surprisingly fair amount of which had been partially rational. With little else to do but kill time along the picturesque trail, Daniel decided to inquire further, although he hardly expected a sensible reply for his efforts. "What noise you talking about, Hoyt? Those wild dogs out at your place again?"

The man gargled for a moment--Daniel figured his back seat was in for a warm drenching --then managed to clear his raspy throat without heaving.

"I...dunno f-for sure. Comes from...d-down in the v-valley, near M-Matson's... place..."

Passing a hay truck that was managing to lose a large majority of its load along the cracked pavement, Daniel started to reply before noticing that Hoyt's reflection was no longer visible in the rear view mirror. Just seconds later, as he swerved onto the deep clay ruts that led towards the man's red brick abode, he heard the reverberating sounds of drunken snoring rise up from the back seat.

"Typical Hoyt. Just *couldn't* wait another ten seconds to drift into la-la land, could you?"

As had become the sad ritual within the past year and a half, Daniel piled the older man onto his back, openly

43

straining to half-step along the dirt and gravel drive leading up to the house, subsequently lying him on an aged sectional couch in the center of the trash-strewn living room.

As he departed the single story brick dwelling, the echoes of Hoyt's slumbering snorts cutting rudely into the forest's surrounding tranquility, Daniel couldn't help but ponder the old man's last mumbling sentence inside the cruiser.

Lighting up a fresh Marlboro (a habit Susie never could stomach during their short-lived marriage, and more than likely the *so ul* reason he refused to give it up), he strolled unceremoniously past a large two story barn at the west side of the homestead, it's once shiny red finish now faded a grungy pink from countless years of exposure from the merciless Alabama sun.

At the far edge of the partially rotted, long-abandoned structure, Daniel peered past several acres of overgrown pastureland that split the Wilson and Matson homes. Only the very tip of Douglas Matson's angled roof could be viewed through a break in the thick foliage encircling it.

Doug was a retired pharmacist from Birmingham that had moved into the old Varney house in the late eighties, Daniel recalled, about the same time he himself had been finishing up a tour of duty at Fort Campbell, Kentucky. Matson was one of many middle-aged or senior citizens of Elm Hill who fell into the category of 'resident hermit', folks who had moved from the hustle and bustle of city life for the peace and tranquility of small town America. A large man whose physical appearance could best be categorized as 'thick', with thinning gray and white hair and a wide, barrel chest,

Daniel had only spoken to the man twice in the nine years he had served as sheriff of Elm Hill. Two or three times a year Daniel would spot Matson at the Piggly Wiggly or Dollar General stores, but rarely anywhere else about town.

Taking a final, drawn out drag from the cigarette, Daniel ran his free hand through the thick, wavy hair hanging above the deep grooves of his forehead.

Checking his Timex Sports watch, which read eight-thirty-three a.m. , he briefly considered paying Mr. Matson a friendly, unofficial visit. As he turned back towards his vehicle, he stepped into a deep, uneven rut in the driveway and barely avoiding tripping. "Hoyt old buddy, you just *might* have a valid case against the state at that," he grumbled just before the two-way sounded off noisily inside the cruiser.

"Sheriff Dan, come back," Deputy Morton barked.

Piling slowly into the driver's seat, Daniel purposely waited a moment before grabbing the mike.

"Sheriff, you sharin' a bottle of Boone's Farm with ol' hollow foot or what? Come back."

"Just sippin' some shine and chewing on Moon Pies, Trace. Over," he replied between low chuckles.

"You on your way back, Dan? Over."

"That I am. Rip Van Wilson has been safely delivered and I'm just pulling out from the minefield he calls a driveway. A driveway that is very close to impassable, I might add. The man might be a lush, but he has a justifiable gripe. What's up? Over."

The pause that ensued sent a shiver up Daniel's spine, although at the time he didn't have the slightest notion why.

"Um, I'm...I'll fill you in when you get here, Sheriff.

No emergency, just somethin' that came over the wire you might be interested in. Over."

"Ah, suspense *and* mystery. All this and I still haven't had anything resembling breakfast. See you in fifteen, Trace. Over," he replied, just a hint of nervous apprehension coating his normally cool tone.

The radio sounded off one final time. "There's a steaming cup of Joe waitin' on you, along with a Danish that can't be over three or four days old. I stopped by Lindy's Bakery on the way back. Poor woman needed the business. Main Street sure is getting that 'ghost town' look about it. Over and out. "

Accelerating as he pulled back onto the main highway, Daniel nodded in grim acknowledgement.

***

Squinting at the brightly lit monitor as her fingers glided effortlessly over the computer keypad, Deputy Morton sighed nervously as Daniel peered over her shoulder.

"Here's the email from Hal over at the Probie office," she said, leaning back to allow her supervisor a better view.

The message was brief and concise, as was normally the case when originating from the Birmingham Parole office. Daniel read the words as if they were being displayed a syllable at a time solely for his personal consumption. He felt his face grow instantly flush as the meaning sank in, and straightened up with an expression of pure befuddlement.

"Well, ain't that a solid kick in the pants," he said, peering out of the front office window at the sparse traffic winding down Main Street.

Deputy Morton reached over and retrieved a large black coffee mug that read " Auburn War Eagles" in faded b lack lettering, and sipped slowly before responding. "How can a man only serve eighteen years for first degree murder? How is that even possible?"

Daniel slid into the brown leather chair behind his cluttered desk and shrugged his shoulders, then scooped u p a manila folder and began casually flipping through it without actually reading the contents. "Prison system is packed, Trace. They could build 'em on every corner and still be cutting sentences in half just to make room for the next generation of thugs. Last time I talked to Hal, he said his case load had tripled since the mid-eighties, drug offenders being the main culprit."

Placing her hands behind her head, where her thick black hair was tied into a tight, circular knot, Deputy Morton flexed the thick, bulky biceps she so proudly displayed at every opportunity. Daniel always pondered what Pete, Tracy's rail-thin, downright frail looking better half, thought of his wife's over-enthusiastic gym habits. Pete worked as a supply clerk at Wainbrook's Feed N'Seed a few miles to the east of the Sheriff's office, and was the definition of 'mild mannered milquetoast.' In the handful of instances in which Daniel had shared company with the Morton's as a couple, he couldn't recall Pete uttering more than a few mumbled sentences in his wife's presence.

"Sorry, boss, but that's BS to the extreme. By *all* means, pack the Penal units with pot smokers and coke-heads but release all the rapists and psychos. That just ain't right."

"No disagreement here, Trace It's the times we live

47

in, unfortunately," he said with a distant, faraway look.

Deputy Morton stood and donned her cap, pulling down the bill until it barely left room to peek underneath, then strolled towards the front door before pausing at the edge of Daniel's desk. "Yeah, I guess. It's kinda like 'Bama's pigskin program being on probation every other year these days. It's sad. Downright *pathetic,* in fact, but life goes on. Right, Sheriff?" she smirked while adjusting her gun belt and simultaneously tilting her head towards a framed newspaper article adorning the edge of her desk. The headline was dated November 1 8th from the Birmingham News, and read, in thick black lettering--
IRON BOWL 2005: Make it Four Straight. Tigers clip Tide 28 -18

"Yeah, well, now that Don Shula's baby boy has a firm grip on the reigns down at the capstone, we'll see who laughs last. Probation or not, the *King* of the state reigns on and on," he quipped, winking slyly. "The dark cloud is slowly lifting, and it's only gonna get better."

Deputy Morton pulled the door open with an annoyed grunt, then paused again before exiting. " Yeah, yeah. I guess when livin' in the past is all you've got, I can't begrudge ya too much outta sheer pity, Sheriff 'Bear' Bryant. 'Sides, at least we *can* beat those toothless hillbillies from Tennessee more than *once* every ten years. "

"Maybe, but you ain't even the best team in your own *state* ! How many national titles them War Eagles won again, Trace? Refresh my foggy memory. *One* wasn't it? Eleven more and we can seriously talk some football!" he bellowed just after the door closed noisily behind her.

"Goin' on patrol, Mister Memory Lane!" she barked

before vanishing around the corner.

Daniel's good-natured grin faded just seconds later, as the contents of the PO's latest email reappeared in his mind's eye like a re-wound videotape:

FROM THE OFFICE OF HAL MOBLEY, LICENSED PAROLE OFFICER, STATE OF ALABAMA, COUNTY OF JEFFERSON, CITY OF BIRMINGHAM:

ATTN: Sheriff Daniel J. Whitlock, City of Elm Hill

SUBJ: Announced Intention of Parolee to Reside Within Your Jurisdiction SUBJ NAME: Curtis Lee Barber

AGE: Thirty-Seven years, five months. DOB: March 11th, 1969 HEIGHT: Six-Feet, Two Inches

WEIGHT: Two-Hundred Seventy- Five Pounds

RELEASED FROM: Vines Unit, Cullman, Al RELEASE DATE: August 29th, 2006

NOTE: Former resident of Elm Hill community. Felony conviction originated from incident within city limits during time period: May 1987. State Incarceration date: September 9th, 1988.

SUBJECT HAS BEEN INSTRUCTED TO CONTACT SHERIFF'S OFFICE ON DAY OF ARRIVAL.

"Why *here*, Curt, of all places to show your face again?" he whispered solemnly, standing to adjust his own belt, his right hand unconsciously stroking the holster that held his .38 revolver.

Staring out onto Main from the office window a moment later, Daniel resigned to undoubtedly knowing the answer to his own query.

"Looks like I may finally get a chance to actually *earn* this badge," he said after a deep sigh, his eyes narrowed and jaw set tight, like a man preparing for intense physical pain.

As he walked behind the small communications console, consisting of a two-way radio set up and a single line phone, Daniel was force d to clear his throat several times to clear the nervous tone he knew would be evident to his ever-perceptive deputy. It was barely nine-thirty, but his stomach was already growling a mean mealtime concerto.

"Tracy, come back," he finally managed, removing a cigarette from his shirt pocket without really thinking.

"Got'cha, Sheriff. You miss me already? Over," she replied in a stoic monotone. "Just wondering about lunch. Over."

"How 'bout the diner, Goob? I hear the special this week is creamed chicken, " she began excitedly, only to be cut off in mid transmission.

"But, Deputy, you know I just happen to *hate* my main course concealed in a heavy sauce. Over," Daniel concluded cheerily.

He awaited her response wearing a broad smile.

"Unreal. It's on me, oh great trivia master. Over," she blurted in apparent irritation.

"Four years, Trace. Four long years as my gun hand and you still think you can stump me with Mayberry references? *Gilligan's Island* maybe, *Green Acres* a possibility, but never, *ever* Mayberry. Can...not... be done. How many days in a row now? Five? Seven? Again, please refresh my aged memory Over."

"Next time I'll depart TVLand altogether and hit you

50

with a *Will & Grace* question. Over."

"I'll have a chicken salad sandwich and small fries, Deputy, and say hey to Beverly for me. Over."

"Got it, boss. Jeez, I swear I'm gonna start bringin' peanut butter and jelly sandwiches one of these days. Over and out," she concluded depressingly.

As with most days, they consumed their lunch in near total silence within the confines of the office, only the occasional screeching of bad breaks or echoing of an elderly muffler piercing the tranquility.

"I'll take lake patrol," Daniel announced once a last sip of soda had been slurped.

His deputy glared at him gravely, her shoulders instantly tensed.

"I knew you'd do this, Dan. Already worryin' yourself a new ulcer, ain't ya?" she began, tossing the trash from her meal into a nearby wastebasket.

"Don't start, Trace. I just need to gather my thoughts, that's all."

Walking over with her arms crossed defiantly, Tracy Morton's stare was intense. "You mean you need time to brood, Sheriff. Brooding that leads to nowhere but a state of depression."

Laying her hands on the sparse clearing the front of his desk provided, she purposely left no room for interruption until her point was clearly laid out and subsequently understood. Dan leaned back and stared at the tiled ceiling, having learned long ago that attempts to interrupt were pointless.

"Depression over a two decade old homicide that you could never have stopped 'cause there was no way to see it comin'. You might as well take the blame for not jumpin' in front of the bullets that took out Abe Lincoln

51

and JFK. We knew the murderin' jackass was up for parole. Knew it for the past three months. I've got to think you also knew there was at least a chance he'd be hot-footin' his size thirteen boots back here if released. I've noticed the edginess in your voice lately, boss. I know you better'n you think."

Cocking an eyebrow, Daniel leaned forward and finally met his subordinate's intrusive glare. "You going somewhere with this, Trace? It's gonna take me a good twenty minutes to get up to Mann Lake, and I've got to gas up the cruiser fir—"

The palms of her hands slapping against the oak desk caused him to wince back as if electrically shocked. "*Damn* right I do, Daniel! You're preppin' for a showdown with an ex-con that murdered an old girlfriend, and I'm just selfish enough to admit I really, really have no desire whatsoever to be appointed the new sheriff of Elm Hill once said facedown is over. You're either gonna end up in jail or dead, Dan, and I'll do everything I can possibly do to prevent either. If nothin' else, think of your daughter. It's been hard enough on her to live without a mom all these years. Don't think losin' a father at this stage will do much for her overall well-being."

Daniel paused with his mouth agape before ending the staring contest between them by glancing down at the leathery skin covering the back of his own hands. When he looked back up, his deputy's stoic expression and matching stance were unchanged. "Tracy, I appreciate your concern. I really…I mean, you know I do. Can't say I understand where you caught the vibe that I was planning on *facing down* Curtis Barber in some old west gun fight at the Elm Hill Corral, but it just…*ain't*…so, okay?"

"You hearing me? It's not that way at all."

Her eyes narrowing to fine slits, her thick lips pouting like a scorned child, Deputy Morton's heavy sigh was born more in frustration than relief . "Then why are you so eager to tromp up to Mann Lake so soon after hearing of Barber's release, Dan? As memory serves, you've handed that particular lake patrol to me twice a week for the past two years. Suddenly feel like takin' a stroll down murderin' lane?"

"Trace, I won't deny the man rejoining our community concerns me," he began, now eyeing the blackened computer screen that revealed his somewhat fractured reflection back into his own eyes. Daniel studied his own facial movements and hand gestures while speaking, as if secretly evaluating the sincerity of his own words . "But your tale of 'vengeance for an old flame' is way off base, alright? I 'm more worried about Debbie's uncle, old Stan Basham, and his reaction to the news that the killer of his niece is back in town. There are others that won't be driving the welcome wagon either Sandra Williams for one. Debbie's best friend in high school, Williams had been quoted as saying that if she ever saw the man released from prison, there was a savings account put aside solely for the purpose of hiring a hit man to take Curt out. *That's* what I'm cultivating an ulcer over and need to sort out in my mind. How to keep a man, a citizen of Elm Hill whose paid his debt to society, safe in his own hometown, even when there is a part of me that definitely wants to turn my head the other way."

Finally, it was Deputy Morton's turn to look away,

her shoulders visually relaxing several notches.

Daniel stood slowly, joining her at the com console, where she carefully poured herself a cup of coffee that was the color of decade old motor oil and nearly as thick. "Don't fret, Trace. I promise you there are only two ways this boy's leaving this high office. One is death by natural causes. The other is a sex scandal involving a bus load of Playboy Playmates and a gooey vat of semi-melted butter."

As if on cue in a staged comedy skit, Deputy Morton spat a wavy mist of hot java into the air before bending over in raucous laughter. Daniel leaped back from the oily onslaught, managing to dodge all but a single drop that landed just above his sewn-in nametag. He sincerely loved the sound of his deputy's howling merriment, a deep, hearty laugh with just a touch of sexiness, and rarely missed an opportunity to draw it from her. He considered his subordinate not only a loyal, trusted friend, but the closest he would ever come to comprehending the big brother-younger sister relationship.

"Oh, gawd, that hurt. I almost swallowed a filling," she blurted, finally gaining a semblance of self-control.

"Cruiser keys, Deputy Morton?" he asked with an outstretched hand.

She slapped them forcefully into his palm, her tongue stuck out like a panting dog.

" I think I burned a crater into my tongue, you miserable..."

"Just being honest, Trace. See you in a few hours If you get bored, think up some Mayberry trivia and fire away. It's a long, boring drive up there, if I recall correctly."

54

Leaning down to wipe the saturation from the console's outer edges with a large white napkin, Deputy Morton's replied with little of the good humor of a moment earlier. "Don't get lost up there, Dan. I ain't just talkin' about directions, neither."

"Yes, Mother."

The sheriff departed with an amiable nod, his mind's eye already focusing in on future matters, and the foreboding sense of overwhelming dread slowly enveloping his very soul.

***

Mann Lake was located seven miles to the west of town, a wide body of tranquil water that had served as a haven for fisherman and campers since the town had been established. It rested peacefully at the bottom of a mountainous valley engulfed in ancient elm, oak and pines, the tops of which seemed to literally be interwoven with the low hanging clouds that permeated the area on a year round basis.

Daniel was forced to detour onto three separate dirt and gravel roads, each a bit narrower than the one before, to reach the outer edges of the lake. Various shrubbery, tree limbs and weedy overgrowth seemed to reach out toward the cruiser as he ascended further into the dense forest that served as the lake's perimeter, the effect noticeably more ominous than comforting.

Regardless of the cool breeze of the air conditioning beating against his upper body and face, a fine layer of perspiration had formed on his forehead, cheeks and neck. The partly cloudy conditions hovering above brought little chance of actual rain, but did manage to assist in raising the humidity level to the high seventies, hardly unusual in the dog days of an Alabama summer. This coupled with an afternoon high temperature that threatened triple digits had Daniel's sweat glands working some serious overtime despite the chilled air within the vehicle's interior.

Passing several clearings that served as boat docks along the lake's flatter edges, Daniel slowed the cruiser to less than twenty miles per hour due to the deep, rock solid ruts dominating the constricted trail.

As he neared a steep, U-shaped turn just past the base of a thick, aged willow tree, he felt the infestation of countless goose bumps coat his sweaty frame. He had last visualized what he and his generation of Elm Hill teens had called 'The Carnal Circle' back in the summer of 1987, some nineteen seasons passed . As he parked the cruiser at the cusp of the wide clearing, Daniel noted the dramatic *lack* of change in the nearly two decades since his last visit. Other than the understandable weed growth on the lake bank itself and a jagged stump where a large, crooked oak once rested, it was amazingly unaltered.

'The Carnal Circle' had once served as an unofficial 'lovers lane' in Daniel's time, although at initial glance it was obvious that today's Elm Hill teens had moved on to greener, less snake-infested pastures. The clearing itself was at least twenty-five or thirty yards wide and fifteen to twenty from the edge of the roadway to the banks of the lake itself.

Departing the vehicle, Daniel stepped into the awaiting mugginess with a loud groan as he sucked in a preliminary wave of summer heat.

Varied visions of a youth and innocence long expired sailed through his mind as he trudged cautiously through the tall, dry brush towards the bank. Many of life's 'firsts' had been experienced along the same trail he now occupied. His first drink of beer; an icy cold Coors handed to him by Carl 'Scooter' McCloud during the summer of '84, the majority of which had ended up barfed into the back seat of Jimbo Green's rusty Buick LeSabre later that same evening (along with the other four bottles he had subsequently ingested). His first real kiss; a predictably clumsy but nonetheless passion-fueled smooch that had practically burst his upper lip in the process (Carol Oates, his date for the evening, had giggled endlessly as the swelling increased until his lip resembled a bulging slug on the verge of exploding). His first 'feel' of a budding female breast (that belonging to Wanda Carlyle, who had been excessively drunk on vodka and orange juice that particular spring evening); his hand buried deep within the snug confines of the girl's T-shirt and bra. His first (and only) taste of a marijuana cigarette; a single inhalation that had been followed by choking, hacking coughs that had literally brought him to his knees, much to the hilarity of Todd Platt, the owner/roller of said joint. His first fistfight as an adult (legal age of eighteen *anyway)*; a Budweiser/wacky weed induced, combination wrestling/boxing match with the same Todd Platt, whose raucous laughter at his expense had not been appreciated in the least. The comical non-event had concluded with both young men rolling into the nearby lake, howling in joyful, chemically enhanced glee.

Good memories, Daniel smiled, cherishing days of reckless youth that only those raised in the rural Southern United States could truly identify with. Summer days spent fishing, playing pick-up baseball and basketball.

Summer night s spent cruising town (either by ten-speed bike as a pre-teen or via a borrowed car in later years) and secretly visiting the local bootlegger. Falls spent rooting for the local boys on the gridiron while following the Crimson Tide's annual ascent up the AP and UPI polls, usually on their way to challenging for a national title. Good-natured ribbing slowly transforming to primal hatred as the *Iron Bowl* versus hated Auburn University neared in late November. Fine memories one and all. All, that is, save *one.* A single dose of tragedy that overshadowed all that had come before it in a town woefully unacquainted with such grisly, vile scenarios-- the day that Debra Lee Rainer had been found dead on the same grounds Daniel now walked upon. She'd been found bound to a tree with a jagged section of barbed wire fence, her slim throat slashed from ear to ear until her head lolled grotesquely to one side like a mutilated rag doll.

As he drew to within a dozen feet of the pine's thick trunk, Daniel nervously paused to inhale deeply, the midday sun now blazing onto his exposed neck, his shoulders searing beneath the dark shade of his uniform. At that moment, an insane desire to lie down in the tall weeds and simply fall sleep was almost overpowering in scope.

No, he hadn't loved Debra Lee, as was the popular rumor, one that had grown in mythological incorrectness over the decades. True enough, he *had* dated her several times during their senior year at Elm Hill. Also true, they did seem to be growing closer just before the incident occurred, that much he couldn't deny, least of all to himself.

Now the man convicted of performing the

unspeakable act that left an entire community shell-shocked and horrified was coming home.

Daniel kneeled down onto a single knee and looked to the semi-cloudy sky as if for advice. A single breeze, hot and steamy beyond description, blew into his upturned face, as if to deny such a foolish, unreasonable request.

"Calm and collected, Dan old buddy. Whatever comes to pass, remain above all…calm and collected," he muttered, removing his cap and wiping the sweat free from his reddened forehead with an equally moist forearm.

Somewhere within the dense forest, a crow shrieked just instants before a distant thunderclap echoed through the valley. Daniel felt a storm brewing at his back, a churning, building mass that had little to do with meteorology and *everything* to do with the human condition. A human condition that knew kindness and understanding, but was capable of growing dark, coldly callous, and unforgiving when in the presence of true evil.

Lowering his head into his hands, Sheriff Daniel Whitlock felt hot tears fill the corners of both eyes.

It was going to be a trying week ahead, to say the very least.

Chapter Three
Contestants/Legacy of Hate

TIME: 1517 HOURS
DATE: 15 MAY 1988
LOCATION: Warehouse District, Denver, Colorado

"You do understand the contract the way it is written, Mr. Eastmon?" Aaron asked, placing the freshly signed forms into a bright blue folder.

The tall black man sitting across from him at the conference table adjusted the toothpick dangling from his mouth before responding indifferently. His shaved head reflected off of the high fluorescent lighting in ultra-bright waves with even the most miniscule of movements. His hands lay flat on the table, all but the thumb and pinky of each sporting rings of various shapes and sizes. Kyle deduced they were easily the largest hands he had ever seen, almost shovel-like.

"Understood, man. Play the game with only two outcomes. Win, get rich and infamous. Lose, you get buried as the unknown soldier. Do I have the gist?" he replied in a low, humorless tone.

Clearly taken back by the man's lack of emotion, Kyle glanced over at Myron Scott, a fifty -ish man with a large round gut and full beard, and who at the moment seemed to be intensely studying the back of his own left hand. "Mr. S? You have anything to add here?" Kyle asked sourly, feeling his blood pressure begin to shimmy slowly up the charts. Sitting in on the interviews had been his own decision, his intent being to upgrade the quality of the combatants from the less than impressive clients that had been thrown into the wolf's den a s of late. Upon visualizing Scott's nonchalant, " don't give a rat's ass" attitude during the process, he was beginning to understand why such combat-meek individuals had slipped through the cracks.

"Yes, uh, Mr. Eastmon, your resume here says you spent some time in the Army as an infantryman. What weapons were you trained on during that time?" Scott asked in a flat tone that screamed disinterest.

TC Eastmon, former soldier, state penitentiary inmate and present day member in good standing of the Dark Aces street gang based in Little Rock, began to tap his impossibly long, slender fingers impatiently onto the table top. "That has been a few years back, but I do recall firin' the M-16 rifle on a regular basis, and maybe the .38 revolver. These days I prefer a 9mm or .45. Don't leave home without it, you dig?" he answered without making eye contact, instead leaning his head back in a gesture of irritated boredom. When next he leaned forward, TC glanced blandly over at Aaron. "How about hand-to-hand combat? Have you studied the martial arts at all?"

Kyle injected, ignoring the interviewee's baiting mannerisms. Eastmon spoke each word in a slow, rap-like cadence, each syllable stretched out to the breaking point.

"Never needed any fancy moves to bring somebody down, no. I've been scrapin' since I was old enough to make a fist. I have boxed, was the light-heavyweight champ at Fort Sill for two years runnin'. Still, didn't *really* know what a brawl was 'til I spent time in Leavenworth and then Riker's Island. That, my boys, was when I discovered I had a real god-given talent for not

61

only survivin', but for exterminatin' as well."

"How long were you incarcerated at each location?" Scott said with what seemed like a twinge of actual curiosity.

"Spent two years in Leavenworth for deckin' an officer. Three more at Riker's for stabbin' a worthless piece of rat-shit that was tryin 'to pinch my ride. Boy was hot wirin' the Town Car when I strolled up. I then proceeded to pull him outta the car and carve my initials into his chest. Like I said, the real clashes didn't start until I was locked up. It was just a slightly altered version of your little game here, you see. Fight to live, gents. Fight to live."

Shuffling the papers one last time before tucking the folder underneath his arm, Kyle forced himself to display a neutral, wooden smile. "Mr. Eastmon, we will contact you within the week at the number you furnished . The only further information we require to complete this session is the main reason you have applied for this unmistakably dangerous venture."

The man sneered, revealing a top row of teeth layered in gold. "Why the hell you think, man? My boys and I need the money, plain and simple. It was either one of us do this thing, or keep knockin' off local pushers and robbin' dime stores. Once I take the crown, the *Aces* are comin' out of the dark and into the light of day. I'm doin' this not only for myself, but for all brothers and sisters of the cause. Can't do anything legal in the white man's world that nets any worthwhile gain. I know your kind don't get it and probably don't really give a good goddamn, but it's cut and dry as to why." Kyle pushed back the wooden chair nosily, extending his open right hand at the center of the table. "Remember, Mr. Eastmon, secrecy is of utmost importance here. Once you signed that contract, you agreed to the provisions of confidentiality. This of course, includes your fellow…associates. We will be in touch that I *can* guarantee."

Rising from the chair with the speed of a sloth on Quaaludes, Eastmon more slapped than shook the outstretched hand. "My lips be sealed, Mr. Man. I'll be waitin' for my car phone to sound off."

Moments later, the man Mason Parks referred to as "Mr. Smiley" silently entered the spacious warehouse from an open dock door and with little more than a token nod, escorted TC Eastmon out of the building.

With briefcase in hand, Kyle was readying to depart the mostly empty warehouse himself, barely acknowledging the dazed presence of his fellow interviewer, when the familiar buzz-like ring of his cellular phone stopped him cold just a few feet from the exit.

"Yeah?" he paused, feeling the blood rush into his face as he fought the urge to interrupt the caller.

"Jesus, Earl, you have to be kidding…" he managed to insert with a scowl, placing his free hand at his side after setting the briefcase on the dusty concrete floor.

A full minute later, his expression unchanged, his response was strained but still cautiously polite. Shoving the bulky phone back into his inside jacket pocket, Kyle noticed Scott standing just a few feet away, displaying a bland, mildly confused expression.

"Might as well sit your fat butt back down, Myron. We have one more interview," Kyle blurted, scooping up the briefcase with a heavy sigh.

Seemingly unfazed, Scott checked his watch, then

joined Kyle back at the conference table.

The gusty winds that blew in through the cracked, shattered windows of the abandoned warehouse howled a gloomy symphony echoing Aaron's present state of frustration.

"But, I thought Shaft there was in like flint as the new client for this month 's taping. Aren't we getting ahead of schedule here? I mean, we've already agreed in principle to this man. If we choose someone else, that means he'd have to be eliminated, you know that. I don't want to be a party to *another* mur—"

Kyle suddenly slammed his left palm down on the wooden table, the echo careening throughout the mostly empty building like a gunshot.

"Damn it, Myron, do me a favor and take a deep breath before you blow a gasket. East LA or Eastmon or whatever his name was *is* in. He's under contract. Mr. Barron just informed me of a major format change that was requested by one of our most generous overseas customers. There will be two combatants going toe-to-toe with Sergeant Sunshine next taping. Also let me clear up something for you, buddy-boy. You *are* a party to murder, every damn time we interview somebody and okay them to travel to that reprehensible compound. Don't try to underplay what we do here just to justify your paycheck or your conscience. You and I might as well be shooting the poor sons of bitches ourselves just to save Parks the trouble of butchering them on film."

Ignoring the majority of Kyle's rant, having obviously sat through a number of similar tirades in the past, Scott sat back down in his still warm chair and began running his chubby fingers over his mostly balding head.

"Two contestants, huh? Looks like customer demand might be the undoing of the reigning champ. Who is this mystery man we're waiting on, anyway?" he asked wearily.

Kyle flipped open the case and stared into it like a man looking into an endless chasm. "The 'guy', Myron, has a first name of Kayla. Kayla Lee. Asian female, age twenty-eight. That's all I know, so please refrain from attempting further interrogation. Her arrival is imminent."

"*Her* name? Holy crow," Scott murmured, starry and wide-eyed for the first time that afternoon.

***

TIME: 1531 HOURS
DATE: 15 MAY 1988
LOCATION: Parks ranch, Conquest, New Mexico

With an unsteady, wobbling gait, he stepped at a snail's pace through the ransacked living room. He could feel his pulse pounding like a trip-hammer at his temples, his short, cropped hair warped on all sides and besieged by various shaped indentations *Damn, son. Somebody's gonna be extremely pissed off 'bout this. Oh well, such is life. What do they expect from a man whose been diagnosed as deranged and a touch psychotic. Shouldn't keep such maniacs on your payroll, I say.*

The Toshiba big screen had a splintered portion of what *had been* a wooden chair protruding like a spear from its shattered screen, the occasional thin tendril of smoke still visible from the wreckage. The thick marble

65

table that had been positioned in front of the TV had been broken neatly in half, so precise the split it was as if it had been measured and cut.

Don't even recall that little number. Must have been after that speaker got mysteriously lodged in the dry wall over there. Mason old buddy old salt, you gotta lay off the J&B. I was better off back in the days when I guzzled Beam like Kool-Aid. The quality booze messes with my mind, no doubt.

Wearing only a pair of boxer shorts that were a size too small for his trim, rock-solid waist, he glanced down groggily at his bare chest and caught sight of the deep red scratches there for the first time. Rubbing them with a bare hand, Mason Parks grimaced at the fresh stinging sensation.

Must have been the chink. She had some long ass fingernails. It's a damn wonder two or three of 'em aren't lodged in my back like tiny mosquito wings. I really should have held back on the forearm I almost feel bad for the gook, though. Her arm looked kinda gruesome twisted completely out of its socket that way. Looked like it got stitched on backwards by some doped-up mad scientist.

All I wanted was some back-door action. White chick stares at my johnson like it was a Louisville Slugger and screams "I ain't about to take that thing." Thought the chink was gonna scream at the sight of it. What's the big deal, anyhow? Ain't eleven inches about average, for Jake's sake?

Side-stepping a pile of shattered ceramic from what had once been the bottom portion of a lamp he slumped into the kitchen and poured a tall glass of orange juice, topping it off with a full shot of vodka. He gulped it down in three long swallows and belched cheerfully.

"Ah, another carefree day here at the raunchy ranch. Think I'll lay off the broads. At least for a few days, anyhow. Another night like last, the suits are liable to seize up in their high-backed leather chairs."

Genuine laughter, deep and full, rang out in Celtic waves, the man responsible realizing fully that the edges of such maniacal guffaws were lined with an undeniable layer of lunacy. A lunacy he had not only grown to accept, but willingly *invite* without reservation.

Following a breakfast/brunch that consisted of six eggs (over-easy), five large slabs of ham, four pieces of toast and three extra strong cups of coffee, Parks dodged the carnage that enveloped the living room and scooped up the cordless phone he had stashed in the bedroom.

The suits were going to fume, he knew, over this latest, rather dicey scenario. Second one in as many days, at that. He reveled in their squirming over his excesses, truth be told.

The phone rang twice before being answered in code. Mason Parks was practically ecstatic.

***

TIME: 1540 HOURS
DATE: 15 MAY 1988
LOCATION: Warehouse district, Denver, Colorado

Kayla Lee was gorgeous. There wasn't another word in any chosen language that better described or defined her. She had informed Kyle and Scott (both of whom were equally distracted and mildly shocked by the outward appearance of a woman applying basically to *die*

67

) that she was of Korean descent, twenty-eight years of age; five feet three, an even one hundred ten pounds. She was a naturalized citizen, having been born and raised in the DC area.

It took Kyle a full thirty seconds to compose himself before managing the first coherent query He found it extremely hard to concentrate while staring into her dark brown eyes. Her lips were full, her small but perfectly chiseled face surrounded by long locks of pitch black hair which seemed almost fluorescent, even within the dull dimness of the warehouse. She was wearing a simple, pocketless black T-shirt and faded blue jeans, her tiny feet, the toenails of which were painted dark red, cupped snugly inside a pair of strapped high heels.

His throat cleared and his daze at least partially broken, Kyle eventually found the 'on' button for his vocal cords. "Ms...uh, Mrs," he fumbled.

"Miss Lee. Never married, never will," she injected with a devilish smile. "Miss Lee then. Let me lay this on the line for you as simply and in the most straightforward way that I possibly can. What we do is a federal offense to the *extreme*. You would be a combatant in a fight to the death with a man who, from what I 've witnessed, is more animal than human. The weapons you are allowed to utilize against this individual are exceedingly limited, and it normally comes down to a hand to hand situation to determine who wins and who loses. Miss Lee...the loser isn't patted on the back and given a door prize Instead they are placed in a body bag and shipped to an undisclosed location for immediate disposal. Their death is never disclosed, nor is the event that led to it. Knowing this, are you still unwavering in the response given in our company's initial interview last month?"

Her glare was intense, and Kyle felt his face grow hot at its intrusion.

"I am perfectly willing to die for the money offered in this venture, yes," she finally replied in a husky, sexy whisper that served to label her a combination of temptress and a cunningly dangerous predator.

Scott fell back in his chair, clearly impressed by more than just her obvious beauty, and gave Kyle a 'What now?' look.

"Okay then. Let's go over your credentials one last time then," Kyle resumed with an amiable nod.

"Let's," she replied curtly.

Kyle kept his eyes glued to the forms lying about the table. "We have copies of your certification as a second degree black belt in Tae Kwon Do and a first degree in Karate. Date of completion on the latter is June of last year. How long have you studied the arts?"

"Began classes at age sixteen, so a little over twelve years. I plan on opening my own studio as soon as I collect the generous check you folks offer."

Kyle cleared his throat and began to ask for additional information when Scott blurted out a query of his own, the raw excitement apparent in his high pitched tone.

"How much *real-world* combat experience?"

In Kyle's opinion, Scott asked the question with the same boyhood fervor as if he had been asking for a peek at her titties.

"I've participated in kick-boxing and martial arts tournaments from North Texas to Thailand. Some legalized with KBA rules, televised on cable, the whole bit. Some others… not so organized, with very few rules, if you get my drift. Fought in a tournament in Manila just

69

last year. To advance, you had to, at the very *least*, cripple your opponent. Needless to say, I walked away without a limp and with the winner's check in hand. I like a good scrap, the worse the odds, the better. In the end, it's all about the prize money, gentlemen."

"Says here you are an expert marksman with a cross bow," Kyle asked, taking in her exquisitely thin neck and perfectly rounded shoulders while still managing to avoid her searing eyes.

"I am certified with both a Rhino Quad and a Barnett Quad, one-hundred sixty pound draw weight. If I say so myself, I am very proficient with each. *Deadly* proficient."

"I've already made a note of that, Miss Lee, although I will not guarantee that your weapon of choice will be accessible. Let me ask you this…in these tournaments did you encounter any male opposition, or strictly female?" Scott managed in between nervous swallows.

Kayla Lee's expression bore disgust, her teeth evidently gritted behind her pursed lips. "They were *all* men, sir. I don't waste my time with pussy, unless it's spread eagle on my bed and I find I have a sudden craving."

Both men instantly felt the oxygen stick in their throats like badly burnt toast.

***

TIME: 1012 HOURS
DATE: 17 MAY 1988
LOCATION: Holiday Inn, two miles outside of Reno, Nevada

70

Mason Parks' intense scowl became more animated the further down the printout he read, his free hand pulling at the bottom portion of the brown, wiry hair that made up his caterpillar-like mustache. Moments later he let the sheet fall freely from his still positioned hand, then began to giggle as if hearing the punch-line of a particularly hilarious joke that only he could fully comprehend.

Standing at the third story hotel window, his back to the laughter, Aaron Kyle winced at the sarcastic tone being administered.

"This is excellent, Slick. I enjoy a good gag as much as the next murderin', whore-hoppin' psycho, and this is some prime, grade-A shit."

Mr. Smiley stood by the hotel room entrance, facing both men. His gaze was hidden underneath his ever-present dark shades, his arms crossed defiantly over his chest. Parks turned and shot him a lighthearted wink.

"Ya hearin' this, Smiley? They not only want me to fight two at once, but play 'dress-up' to boot. Ain't that a knee-slapping, boot-scootin' hoot?"

The other man showed no indication he had even been spoken to, inducing Parks into a comical shrug.

"Guess not. Who came up this happy horseshit, Slick? Was this one of your bright, sell-the-product-at-*any* -cost schemes?"

Kyle turned with his face red with rage, but smartly kept his distance from the minuscule hotel desk the larger man sat behind.

"No, Parks. It wasn't *my* idea. For your information, not that it should matter to a born mercenary such as yourself, a very substantial buyer from the Middle East requested the medieval scenario. When I say substantial,

I'm talking a man wealthy enough to keep you in healthy whores to slap around and houses to trash for *decades*. Money talks, as you should know better than anyone."

Effortlessly shoving the desk to one side, momentarily sending it completely airborne, Parks stood with his oversized fists clinched tightly. Cord-like veins covered his swollen biceps, the bulkiness of which was pronounced by the short-sleeved muscle T-shirt he donned.

Kyle practically leaped back a step, almost tripping into the closed sliding glass door that led out onto the sparse balcony.

"Son, I can insult myself, but I don't recall giving *you* permission to do the same.

I know the old saying is 'don't bite the hand that feeds you', but you need to realize that at this point and time, this particular dog has enough money to live comfortably for the rest of his life, and he's just itching to chow down on some raw preppy meat."

Parks felt a bony hand land on his right shoulder with a light tap.

"Mr. Smiley, I suggest you remove that skeletal meat hook from my person posthaste, unless you wanna be known as 'lefty' for the rest of your days," he whispered harshly.

Regaining an air of dignity, Kyle waived the other man away.

"It's okay, Mandrake, I'm fine. Mr. Parks just got a little...excited for a minute." Parks howled, turning to the taller man as he back-stepped away.

"Mandrake? Did he call you *Mandrake*? Either that's a code name or you were once one helluva magician, bones my boy."

72

Leaning an elbow against the mini-fridge that sat in the far corner of the dimly lit room, Kyle had managed to regain a small portion of composure. "Let's get back to the subject at hand, Mason, if you don't mind."

Parks sat down on the bed closest to Kyle, his expression one of mock interest. "Okay, then. You will don the gear listed; cloth shorts torn as to appear like a warrior of old, perhaps from the seventeenth century; padded mukluks; leather strapped black headband with skull emblem made from marble sewn into the center of the forehead. Your lone combat weapon will be a single ball mace, spiked with elk bone and a heavy steel chain. Total weight of weapon is seven pounds."

"And my opposition will be supplied with what…grenade launchers? Maybe a small nuclear device or two?" Parks grumbled while rubbing the virgin growth of rigid stubble on his square, scarred chin.

"Not quite. Contestant number one, black male, code name *Shadow Panther*, will be equipped with a forty-four inch bladed rapier. Contestant two, Asian female, code name *Dragon Fly* , will be supplied with a wooden handled, twelve inch bladed scythe along with a crossbow of ancient design. Both will be wearing warrior gear similar to yours, except that-- "

"Hold it, Slick." His face bitterly contorted, Parks stood up from the creaky, moldy-smelling bed and placed his hands on his wide hips. "Did you say Asian f*emale?* Let me pull the corncobs outta my ears so you can repeat that little nugget in a clearer, more *manly* tone."

Maintaining an even keel, despite the fact that holding his anger at bay was becoming increasingly difficult in the face of constant scorn, Kyle nodded pleasantly and repeated the words he had somehow

73

known Parks would greet with a healthy dose of sarcastic disdain. "Yes, she is female, but one who has proven herself in combat situations against well-trained males on numerous occasions. Now, the scenario that we envision is--"

Whirling toward the bare wall between the room's separate twin beds, Parks threw a rapid, viscous overhand right that connected with the part wood, part stucco barrier with a stifled thud, his wrist covered in a white powdery substance as he jerked it free from the basketball-sized hole his punch had created. He stood back and jeered, a small line of spittle running onto his chin. "Slick, I can bench press six-hundred fifty pounds and squat damned near a half-ton. I run the hundred in ten seconds flat. I can decapitate a full-grown man with a single backhand…hell, I've *accomplished* that very feat on several occasions, in fact. Recall volume three in the series? You pinheads actually believe a female of any species stands a snowball's chance in hell against me? Talk to me, son. What's the real purpose of such a set up? Are sales that far into the shitter? Goin' for the skirt crowd now, are we, as in chick *snuff* flicks?"

Holding his hands out palms up as if begging for aid, Kyle tossed the folder he had been gripping onto the top of the small color TV a few feet away. "I did not write or even assist in creating this particular screenplay, Mason. It was dreamed up by a man with tons of assets and little to spend it on that doesn't bore him to tears. *He* requested a female join the party. *He* requested two opponents. *He* holds the cards because he holds unlimited potential for incoming funds into our company. *He* also pays a large chunk of your massive salary. It's cut and dry, nothing overtly complicated. May I set the scene for you now,

74

please?"

Bowing with one sweeping arm stopping at his midsection, Parks grew silent, although the now-familiar sneer never left his rugged visage.

"Actually, once your hear this you may have a reversal in attitude. The wooded area of the island is being fenced off to use in this particular battle. No buildings or concrete blockades will be utilized this time around. It's you, your opponents, and the elements of darkness and self-concealment. Cameras with special lenses that adapt to the dark have already been placed in the grounds, which covers roughly seven acres of rocky terrain dominated by trees and overgrown vegetation.

" Your opponents will attempt to search you out from different locations, and although they both have been informed that there are two of them combating yourself, they've been instructed not to treat each other as members of a team. Each will provide you a one-on-one challenge. If one does manage to eliminate you and the other also survives, a championship match between them will then be scheduled for a later date. Your mission remains the same. Terminate with extreme prejudice, with one *major* exception…"

Parks didn't reply, just continued to smirk while ringing his hands together impatiently.

"It is advisable you take out the Panther first, due to the fact that the higher ups desire an added bonus once you have the female under control. They want you to…rap e her before the kill, and they want you to look like you're savoring…every moment of the act."

The transformation from ill, non-compliant malcontent to just-happy-to-be-there, well-adjusted employee was easily the scariest Kyle had ever witnessed by a man he'd ever considered to be *less* than a sadistic psychopath. "So tell me…she a nice looking chink, Slick?" Parks queried with a quick wink.

Haphazardly tossing a yellow manila folder onto the bed, Kyle feigned disgust. "One of the unspoken benefits of being the producer of your work is witnessing the unbridled glee with which you size up your victims, Mason."

Ignoring all but the glossy black and white photos contained in the folder taken during the initial interview process, Parks eyes grew wide with maniacal excitement as he scanned the image of the pretty, petite Asian glowering into the camera.

"Va-va-va-*voom* ! Slick, I cannot express my appreciation for such a fine prize without hugging you 'til your ribs crack. She might even put up a decent struggle, from the looks of her. She a martial arts junkie or what?"

Kyle began dialing onto the cellular he had pulled from a coat pocket. "Two separate black belts. Combat savvy. The works."

Parks nodded, his gaze again turning to the photo. "*Always* with these gooks. The spook won't last ten seconds, Slick. He looks like nothing more than a street punk-bad ass wannabe. What the hell does he bring to the table besides gold teeth and a sneer?"

Kyle waived him off for a moment before turning towards the balcony doors with the phone stuck tightly to his left ear. "Do we have clearance? Fine. We'll be exiting out front in five minutes."

The folder was shoved gently back into his chest just as he whirled back around. His face a mask of microscopic grooves and scars, Parks stood only a foot away, looming over Kyle like a ravenous vulture. "Don't get me wrong, Slick old pal. I generally get a good feeling about wipin' up the floor with any jig-a-boo I can lay my mitts on, but there is the question of healthy competition here. What's he gonna do, throw *basketballs* at me?"

"There's more to the Panther than meets the eye, Mason," Kyle replied, backing away until the nearest wall halted his reversal in direction. "He's perfect for this scenario, actually. He's a street fighter with a mean streak a mile long. Don't make the mistake of underestimating him. We would hate to lose our champion to simple carelessness."

"Put that tiny preppy brain to rest, Slick. Won't, *cannot* happen. 'Sides, you'd love nothing better than to observe my head on the end of a spear, so don't bother with the sappy horseshit . Anyway, what's the agenda on the rape scene? How many positions you want before the money shot? Looking at the Dragon Lady there, I figure I can cover half the Kama Sutra before the deed is done."

In all his years of dealing with the dregs and morally bankrupt, Kyle had developed a thick skin; a threshold for vulgarity and immoral behavior beyond most of his ilk . That said, sharing space with Mason Parks never failed to turn his stomach.

"Use your own…judgment, Mason. You're the artist. Paint the landscape as you deem fit."

Parks shrugged, then began stretching his massive arms over his head as if warming up for impending combat. "How about the kill? Should I just snap her neck or do they expect something more dramatic?"

"I believe using the girl's scythe or the black man's sword would be more…appropriate, Mason. The

77

bloodlust factor, you know. A car will arrive to take you to the airport within the hour. Keep up your training and await our call. And Mason…"

His glare like that of a cautious parent preparing to scold a misbehaving child, Kyle's tone was more reverent than he had intended. Parks lay b ack onto the bed with his massive hands propped behind his neck.

"…please try to refrain from totally dismantling the entire ranch in the meantime, what say? The bill for broken furniture and appliances, along with medical dons for bruised and battered hookers, got a bit…out of hand last week."

"Hey, I'm in training, Slick. Gotta indulge just to keep my spirits up. Speaking of spirits, I believe I'll jog on down to the hotel bar and have a belt or twelve while awaiting my chariot."

The response Kyle had considered stuck in his throat once he deduced that if verbally spoken he would most likely lose the use of his legs soon afterwards. "We'll…be in touch, Mason," he grumbled weakly as he exited in front of the stoic bodyguard who followed closely behind.

" See ya, Slick. Hey, take a shower, Mandrake the Great, and invest in some floss while you're at it. Your teeth are the same yellow tint as my underwear!" Parks bellowed through cupped hands.

As they stepped into a quietly idling Astro-Van across from the hotel entrance, the man named Mandrake spoke for the first time since their arrival, his tone as mechanical as his stride. "Recall your own words mere weeks ago, Mr. Kyle. When and if the decision is made to eliminate Mr. Parks, I still have dibs, correct?"

Leaning back in the cushioned high back chair as the

78

driver pulled away, the cool fan air slapping his pale face, Kyle reached over and patted the other man gently on the shoulder. "Mr. Mandrake, the pleasure will be all yours. I only hope to be in the cheering section at the time."

The other man's smile was closer to a pain-induced grimace as they pulled onto an interstate ramp, the reflection on the inside of his sunglasses revealing a lunatic's gaze.

***

TIME: 1145 HOURS
DATE: 29 MAY, 1988
LOCATION: 14TH Floor, Office Complex, Seattle, Washington

The nerdy, bookish young man sat hunched before the VCR/Big Screen set up, waiting for the VHS tape to rewind completely. Behind him, two men sat side by side in matching leather love seats, a lengthy oak conference table at their backs.

The man sitting in the chair closest to the conference room door was rubbing through his perfectly groomed, solid black bread. He was heavy set, possibly in his mid-forties, his skin a dark olive shade, obviously of Middle Eastern descent. " Mr. Barron, I have to say that this particular volume is the least impressive I've seen produced by your company. There is only fourteen minutes of actual combat footage, and the majority of that is stalking and hiding. Only the kill itself was of any real interest. The imagery that remained has all been seen before in earlier editions. I have to tell you, it may be difficult for my distribution people to coax the usual

79

buyers into donating the preset amount per copy. Your recent line of pornography-based volumes might actually outsell this pale rendition of what once was a gripping series."

Earl Barron, wearing a dark black suit with a purple tie that was almost fluorescent in the faint light, reached over and patted the other man gently on the hand. His smile was kind, understanding, almost grandfatherly in nature. "We have taken extra care to ensure that this volume, while low on actual combat action, will eventually surpass all previous sales of earlier volumes."

The other man, his accent barely noticeable until his voice grew agitated, leaned back while pulling a long, thick cigar from his front suit pocket. He lit it while eyeballing Barron with careful scrutiny. "How do you propose to back up such an intriguing boast, Mr. Barron?"

Barron gestured to the young man stationed at the VCR, who in turn removed the tape just viewed and plugged in a new, seemingly unmarked tape in its place. "You can go now, Lawrence. Thank you," Barron said politely.

After the man's hasty departure, Barron stood up and began to pace slowly from one side of the spacious room to another, his arms positioned behind his back in a 'parade rest' stance. "We are going to distribute this latest edition together with a twin brother, so to speak. Two tapes for the price of one, actually."

Fresh cigar smoke engulfing his face, the other man's interest was noticeably piqued . "What exactly is contained in this second volume, sir?"

Still pacing although his eyes never left his guests, Barron's chest seemed to inflate with self-pride. "My own idea, actually. Came to me as I was supervising the padding process of this latest combat scenario. Over a year ago, before his first combat kill was ever filmed, we did an extensive interview with the man known to you only as the *Eradicator*. We kept this interview, one I personally consider the most personalized, most in-depth, ever conducted with someone with his…let's be polite and just say 'behavioral difficulties', on tape and in the archives. It's never been viewed by anyone other than myself and one other in the company. The man hired to perform the interview in person was… well, I'll let you see for yourself."

Barron retrieved the remote from its grooved slot on the wide entertainment center and returned to his seat just as his client was reaching over and putting out the remainder of his smoke.

"What is the duration of the interview?" he asked, unable to hide the excitement in his tone.

Barron clicked on the play button, and the screen began to lighten almost immediately. " A little over two hours, but trust me when I tell you, sir, there isn't a single boring moment. Let me know if you desire a drink or a restroom break during the showing."

Moments later, a man easily recognizable as the centerpiece of World Wide Distribution Video faded into view, the intimidating, menacing looks still evident, but less so in a white dress shirt than in combat gear. He was seated with his elbows resting atop a mahogany desk, the wall behind him a faded shade of green. No windows were visible, nor daylight streaming in from any direction. Wherever the filming had taken place, great pains had been taken to ensure absolute privacy.

The interviewer stayed out of sight of the camera, his

voice a bit muffled in the background. Mason Parks' expression was calm, almost frighteningly so, his eyes unblinking and unrelenting in their icy coolness.

***

"Mr Parks, I have the results of the psyche exam you were given at the conclusion of your first interview. I must say, if you did answer each question honestly as per instructed, you are either the bravest man I've ever come into contact with, or easily the most disturbed."

His fingers intertwined on the tabletop, Parks only reaction was the slight rising of his left eyebrow. "I would say it's a lethal combination of both, sir, and thank you."

A quick giggle could be heard from the interviewer before he again spoke. " So if given the opportunity, you would actually relish being the only survivor of a depleted, desolate earth?"

"Let me clear up the whole shebang in layman's terms. I don't give a rat's ass about anyone but myself. I learned from an early age to take care of number one, 'cause their ain't no number two that's worth dying for. People in general sicken me, period. What they *do*, what they *say*, how they *live*. Their so-called beliefs and everything they stand for. Survival is all that matters in the late 20th century, man. I'm gonna be like old Mister Roach when it all comes down. The best have tried to take me out, but here I still sit, a bit scarred but stronger for it."

While he spoke, Parks' upper body seemed to tremble just slightly, although his neck and head remained strangely unaffected.

82

"I…see. Mr. Parks, I have a series of questions I am tasked to ask, per my superiors.

They will delve into personal matters regarding your life. Very personal matters, as a matter of fact."

Parks nodded amiably but did not speak.

"You spent time in both county and state penitentiaries, is this correct?"

"Juvie jail when I was thirteen for bashing my step-brother over the head with a brick. Was given three months and served six. Had a slight problem with the faculty. Kicking the assistant director in the balls didn't help my cause a hell of a lot, looking back on it. Spent time in county lock-ups in three different states once I turned legal age. Nappy-headed spear-chucker was mouthing off one particular night in Austin and I commenced to snap a pool cue over his head. Got six months for that little maneuver, but that sorry asshole won't ever chew another LifeSaver. Got another four months for putting my fist through the windshield of a local banker's T-Bird in 'Orleans. Jew bastard was tailgating me in on Bourbon Street late one evening. I had belted down about a quart of Jimmy Beam and got a tad annoyed. Heard he lost his right eye. Lucky that was *all* he lost. My first trip to the state pen was up in West Virginia, the Myers Unit just outside Wheeling."

Parks took a breather, stretching his massive arms into the air and yawning as if awakening from a long, restful nap.

"Continue, Mr. Parks. I am enthralled," the interviewer said without a hint of insincerity.

"It's real bestseller material, alright. Anyhow, I was bopping this little spic whore in an alleyway, behind a bar I'd become a regular at. I was just shoving her into

83

position for a little backdoor action when two guys pull me outta my Grand Torino head first with my jeans still wrapped around my ankles.

"One of 'em claimed to be her husband, although I couldn't understand but about half of what the worthless beaner was babblin' about. His buddy was a white guy that must have tipped the scales at four hundred pounds. First time I nailed him in the gut, it was like popping a helium balloon. I shoved the greasers head into the pavement, then propped it against the curb and proceeded to remove most of his burrito-chewin' choppers with my size thirteen Wolverines. Cops got there just in time to see me toss the whore into a garbage dump, head first. She'd climbed onto my back while I was stomping on her common-law hubby, and had just about scratched my right eye out before I broke her ribs with a quick elbow shot. I got sentenced to eight years in Myers for basically defending myself against a couple of illegals and their lard-ass acquaintance. Lard-ass damn near croaked and the beaner had his mouth wired shut for the better part of six months, I heard"

The interviewer broke in just as Parks final word had been uttered, and the irritation at being interrupted, however unintentionally, was visibly detectable in the large man's searing, squinting eyes. "Where you employed when this incident transpired, Mr. Parks? The work history we have uncovered, other than the two years you spent in the Army when you were in your late teens, was…spotty to say the least. Please inject more detail on this subject if possible."

Taking an anger-driven hiatus before replying, Parks began to carefully roll up the sleeves of his button up dress shirt, revealing immaculately toned forearms. "Did some construction and warehouse work, basically just to keep myself in food, booze, and the occasional woman. I discovered at an early age that I wasn't meant to be anyone's nigger. Working was an annoyance I had little patience for, 'specially after the Army. I recall working on a road crew for the city at the time of the arrest I just described. Is that detailed enough?"

The interviewer's tone remained pleasant but unapologetic. "Fine. Please continue."

Leaning back in a chair that seemed painfully small to hold his bulky frame, Parks'voice lost its earlier edge. He fell into a steady, continuous monotone, not unlike an instructor settling down for a lengthy lecture. " I was only twenty-six when I was driven through the main sally port at the Myers unit eleven long years ago.

Thought I was the toughest hombre walking the planet. Hell, *convinced* of it in fact. Well, it was in between those concrete walls that I first got tested on that self-theory. I mean *sincerely* tested. I had been fightin 'and scrapin' all my life up until that point, but it had always been my own temper that had led to the breaking of man's laws. In the state pen I got to stand face-to-face with some of my true peers, the genuine article. It was at Myers that I learned my *true* calling on this hunk of clay called Earth."

Mason Parks' words flowed freely and without a single pause from that point, forming a screenplay for the listener's ears that was almost visible in its panoramic description.

***

MYERS UNIT, Barton, West Virginia

"Might as well drop the linens, and I ain't just talkin' bout those sheets in your hands, boy."

Parks wheeled around, tossing the tied up bundle of bed coverings to one side, his hands clinched and positioned in the classic boxer's pose. "Not this horseshit *again*, Sarge. I told your boy Mack just before I sent his happy ass packing to the infirmary with a broken jaw that my butt cheeks are off limits . I'm sick and tired of repeating myself to you perverted bastards."

His naked arms a map of homemade and parlor tattoos consisting of every color in the rainbow, Jonah 'Sarge' Miller took a cautious step forward, his ample gut leading the way. He gestured with a quick jerk of his thick neck to the two men standing a few feet to his left. The far end of the laundry room had seen its fair share of gang-rape scenarios in the decade long history of the Myers Unit, most of which went uninvestigated or completely ignored by the unit staff. Parks had smelled a rather large rat a few days earlier as he'd read off his assigned duties and the location of each, but as a rookie inmate with only two months served under his belt, he had sorely lacked the leverage to have anything done about it.

"I told ya the day you got here I'd have your cherry, Parks. It don't have to be this way if you reconsider my earlier offer. Join the *Aryan* cause and I'll even think about usin' a dab of Vaseline. If not, Jonesy, Wilton and I are gonna take turns riding you dry."

Jonesy, a scrawny kid with a shaved head and a chin full of peach fuzz, side steppe d over until he had cut off the pathway that led to the front entrance of the facility.

Despite the tattooed swastika embedded on the pink skin of his forehead, the kid looked absolutely petrified.

His long, hairy arms almost dragging the floor at his sides, Milton 'Kong' Gilmore flanked the other side, fronting one of the large laundry presses Gilmore had thick, muscled arms that were in stark contrast to his otherwise lanky frame, each covered in a thick layer of black hair that resembled glued-on carpet. Long strands, like snaky tendrils, also protruded from where his partially torn T-shirt ended on either side of his neck. His teeth were piranha-like, filed and manicured to a fine point.

Parks could smell his rotten, putrid breath from six feet away.

"Kong, if I'm you and Mr. Teenage Bad-Ass over there, I'm making tracks back to D block. I got no quarrel with you two. On the other hand, I'm gonna thoroughly enjoy providing a little free dental work to your boss."

Keeping his gaze locked straight ahead, Parks allowed his left leg to scoot back six inches, bent only slightly. A fine layer of sweat was forming on his slim but tightly muscled biceps and forearms. Young Mason Parks could smell s pilled blood even before it was extracted. The sensation thrilled him beyond even the anticipation of impending sex.

For sixty seconds, only the loud hum of machinery could be heard. "I guess not, then. Don't say I didn't warn ya."

The man known as Sarge , an eight year vet at Myers and a relatively unchallenged mouthpiece of Block D for the last six of those threw his head back and howled in raucous laughter, his tubby gut wriggling like half-formed pudding.

87

"Damn, ain't you the tough one, now. Son, just because you managed to cold-cock Mack a few days back does not entitle you to a free pass in my block. You got lucky, kid. Now you're gonna get steamed and reamed."

Jonesy sprinted forward in a clumsy lurch, his arms held high in what at first resembled a frantic gesture of surrender. Just before the kid's left arm fell forward in the general direction of his right shoulder, Parks caught a glimpse of the tiny metallic object making a bee line towards his flesh.

Ducking down onto his right knee, he flung his right fist upwards in a perfectly executed uppercut. Just as the punch landed with a squashing sound at Jonesy's groin, Parks rose and launched his upper body forward with his left arm thrust out, connecting just underneath the other man's pointy chin. The small, rusty shank wind-milled into air just as Jonesy's skull cracked against the cement floor with enough force to cause three shattered teeth to fly free and land casually onto his bony chest. Momentarily wide-eyed, Jonesy shot them a quick, comical look before drifting off into a pain induced mid-morning nap.

Catching the shank in mid-air upon its descent, Parks then whirled around in a blur, sweeping his left leg around floor level while positioning the weapon between the index and forefinger of his right hand. The leg sweep caught 'Kong' Gilmore just above the ankles, using the large man's momentum against him as he had dived forward with his upper body's weight in the lead. Sprawling to the ground, Gilmore executed three complete rolls before regaining his shaky footing.

Jonah Miller stood his ground, his sarcastic grin

growing a bit strained. "Take 'im, Kong. Just watch his feet. Little fairy fights like a damned skirt."

A stifled growl on his puffed lips , Kong rushed forward, then stopped a foot and a half from Parks, his furry, mammoth fists poised at his chest.

Parks kept his eyes on Kong while directing his words at the Sarge. "How exactly you train this ape, Sarge? Ya feed him peanuts by the pound? Maybe it's the sexual favors you give 'im, huh? You packin' the Sarge's fudge on a regular basis, Tarzan?"

Kong Gilmore's eyes widened and quickly turned a dark shade of raging crimson. He lurched forward, throwing a wild, sweeping left hook which Parks easily ducked.

A quick series of jabs to Gilmore's exposed ribs bent the man's head forward into position for the knee that crunched his nose, sending him pin-wheeling backwards, eventually landing atop a rolling laundry bin, blood gushing through the trembling hands clutching his face.

His arms crossed out in front of his chest, the weapon protruding from his fingers like an extra appendage, Parks faced the Sarge with an expression that could only be defined as lustful. It wasn't sexual in nature, but the bloodlust he had grown accustomed to and learned to savor in such situations.

" Looks like the last dance is ours, Sarge old buddy. Jonesy has bowed out with a severe migraine and Kong is currently taking inventory on the unbroken portions of his face. What'll it be, tubby, a slow, romantic polka or some hard rock butt-quaking?"

Reaching back like a man with a sudden itch between his shoulder blades, the Sarge brought the blade forward, displaying it like a prize trophy. The flat blade was serrated near the tip, its wide base leading into the crude wooden handle gripped loosely within the Sarge's chubby left fist.

"Ya like this one, kid? Been working on it for months. Hell to hide from the bulls, but I've managed. It's my masterpiece. It's a virgin to human flesh, boy, and I promise you it will not be gentle nor timid with its first insertion."

Holding his bulging arms out wide in an obvious invitation, Parks whistled through gritted teeth. " Come and get it, dimple cheeks. My hard on is growin' limp."

With a speed belied by his bulk, the Sarge rambled ahead, swinging the blade from side to side as if slashing through a bamboo forest with a dull machete.

Parks calmly stood his ground, his face a mask of bemusement.

The first swipe of the blade opened up Park's shirt at the breastbone and a few layers of skin underneath. The second came back across and nicked his unshaven chin. The third never fully materialized as Parks ducked under its arc and firmly planted the shank under the lowest roll of fat on the man's hanging underbelly. He pulled the short blade viciously from right to left after feeling it puncture the Sarge's soft gut, his entire fist submerged in a wad of coiled intestine. Rolling swiftly to one side, Parks flung himself up in time to brace just before his wounded opponent's last gasp effort at retaliation.

Jonah 'Sarge' Miller was permanently demoted a moment later, his weapon spilling helplessly from his weakened grip. Parks had easily evaded his final swing, then threw two quick jabs forward with the shank pointed forward between his fingers. The first ribbed a three inch gash in the man's bloated double chin. The second took out his right eye with a sound resembling a grape being popped beneath the weight of a heavy work-boot.

Parks backed away, studying with wry amusement the helplessness and frustration of his soon to be deceased opposition, who stumbled clumsily to the center of the room, waving his arms madly. Blood poured like wine from an uncorked barrel from the crimson hole that now served as his right eye socket.

"You...son of a...bitch! My e-eye..." the Sarge croaked in a voice shrill with rage and fear. His abdomen and groin were soaked from the torrent of fluids escaping the deep slashes there, a small portion of lower intestine jutting out like a snake crawling free from its nesting place.

"Quit sniveling like a woman, Sarge. You're tarnishing your image as the tough, veteran con," Parks smirked, reaching down to pick up the homemade machete lying to his left. Its end was smeared with his own blood, and he fought the urge to lick the remains clean before strolling ahead a few feet.

The Sarge's remaining gaze grew wide with terror just before the blade connected with the left side of his skull, just above the ear. A moist chunk of scalp hung in the air like a pulpy cloud before splattering the nearby tile flooring. What remained of the Sarge's face looked to have been repeatedly ran through an industrial grinder.

Removing his badly stained shirt, Parks wiped the blade clean and placed it neatly into the oversized hands of the semi-conscious 'Kong. 'He pulled a clean shirt from a pile of linen, pressurized his own wounds until the bleeding ceased, and sauntered away from the laundry facility as nonchalantly as possible.

When questioned about the incident hours later, he

informed Warden Walker, a thick- necked, burly looking man with a walrus mustache, that he had heard an argument in the rear of the facility that morning, but ignored it in fear of his own safety. The cut on his chin he explained away as a 'shaving mishap'. He was released without further interrogation and listed as 'witness' on the incident report that was filed to the state.

Mysteriously, Jonesy and Kong didn't rat him out, but instead pinned the murder on a gang of Hispanics that had attacked them without provocation, slaughtering the Sarge in the process. They stated the attack had been swift, ensuring recognition of the attackers to be virtually impossible. Obviously the fear of retaliation had prevented them from regaling the true events, not just from the other cons, but from the man who would come to be known to snuff film buffs everywhere as the *Eradicator*.

The inmate population knew the truth, however, and Mason Parks was labeled as untouchable from that point forward, at least by the older cons.

Over the years that followed, several new arrivals had tried their hand at 'dethroning the king 'while attempting to establish their own reps. A black man named Lucas Batch, AKA *The Widow Maker*, a member in good standing of the Little Rock Bloods gang, had the misfortune of cornering Parks in the showers less than a week after hopping off the county lockup bus. He had been instructed to do so by the rather well-represented Bloods spending their days and nights incarcerated in the Myers Unit, the attack considered the ultimate 'test' of Luca's loyalty to his fellow brothers.

Mason Parks had remained a neutral Army of one in the years after the laundry killing, spending his yard time pounding weights and molding a physique that was simultaneously bulky in mass and impeccably carved. He began acquiring steroids from C block's main scrounger, and within weeks his entire body had sprouted layers of tightly wound muscle. In a span of mere months, it looked as if he were wearing a muscle suit underneath his prison garb. Mason Parks spoke rarely, instead utilizing glares, glances, and scowls to get his point across. Inmates and COs alike feared and respected him, and rarely was his personal space invaded. When such occurrences arose, rare as they were, he was forced to reiterate his stance as a man who allowed actions alone to speak volumes.

Lucas Batch, a giant of a black man who stood six-eight and owned a chest as wide as the grille of a Mack truck, had been one such instigator. Transferred from Joliet, he meant to make himself a name at Myers almost immediately upon arrival. He was quickly informed of the quickest way to do so. Challenge the king of the block, none other than Mason Parks.

Lucas had managed to break Park's nose with a ten-inch long roll of rod iron (later found lodged deep into Lucas 's lower colon via his anus) before falling victim to a series of quick jabs to the ribs, groin, and forehead. A vicious backhand across the bridge of his nose had sent a shard of bone into his brain, thus ending the skirmish in just under two minutes from its inception.

Departing the unit eleven years to the day of his arrival, Mason Parks had undergone a physical transformation that a movie special effects team would have strained to equal. He had entered the unit at a lean one-hundred ninety pounds, a clean shaven and relatively scar-free complexion, with shoulder length hair that hung down into his eyes. On the dreary, rainy morning he had re-entered society, the weight was two-fifty five, his face was sporting a thick Fu Manchu mustache and pointy goatee which covered a recently carved crevice that ran from just underneath his chin horizontally towards his lower lip. That specific relic had been chiseled out weeks before by a Puerto Rican gang-banger utilizing a razorblade melted inside a toothbrush (a gang-banger later discovered tucked inside a dumpster outside the mess hall with his head twisted completely around until his chin rested *between* his shoulder blades). His hair was short cropped in boot camp style.

Most impressively, he had departed the dehumanizing confines of a maximum security facility with his anal cavity undamaged, probably the one single achievement he considered uniquely impressive.

Mason Parks had killed eight men in his eleven year stay, and crippled at least a half dozen others. He was released with a thin yellow folder that was to be turned over to his parole officer. This file had labeled him a 'model inmate.'

The power of intimidation and the brute force to back such power had been a raw, unproven mystery to him outside the walls of the Myers unit. It had never truly been harnessed in his early twenties. He had been a street punk; a ruffian; no more. The day he escaped forced incarceration and strolled back into the maddening circus known as free society, he had entered it as a fearless, ruthless, compassionless warrior. Not exactly what the state had intended by way of rehabilitation.

Only weeks after release, while putting in ten excruciating hours a day loading heavy pallets of dried goods into truck trailers, Parks received an offer for employment elsewhere . An offer that was far from legal, and layered in pure malice; a temptation he found, predictably, impossible to resist.

***

Sperryville, Virginia Date: 19 MAY 1986

Juan Garcia had not been a happy camper the day he called Mason at the trailer park in Barton. Juan was the stereotypical Hispanic immigrant (at least in Mason's totally biased, wholly *bigoted* opinion); he carried a tubby, two-hundred plus pounds on a five-foot three frame; had lived in the U.S. for over twelve years and spent at least half of that incarcerated. The man spoke badly broken English and wasn't the least bit interested in broadening his vocabulary. And he thought bathing was no more than a *semi-annual* task. Juan had also suffered both the fortune and misfortune of spending two plus years as Mason's cellmate at Myers.

Fortunate for the protection it provided against roving predators; unfortunate for the bullying (both mentally and physically) he was forced to endure as such.

Juan had somehow finagled Mason's number from someone at the parole office, and had practically been weeping on the afternoon they spoke.

A member of Juan's family had been wronged, and he was offering Mason a substantial payday to help assist in gaining a measure of revenge against the responsible party. The offer was substantial enough that Mason didn't hesitate to pack his meager belongings, 'borrow' the first available vehicle, and make the two hour trek to Sperryville, leaving both his parole officer and the state's charity job behind without a second thought.

He met Juan at a flea bag motel ten miles out of town, along with a man named Manny Rivera, the morning after their phone conversation. Juan had introduced Manny as his 'cousin', a useless bit of information Mason nonetheless found infinitely humorous. To him, spics were like niggers and chinks. They were *all* related somewhere down the line.

Manny Rivera was a stocky, muscular man in his late twenties or early thirties. He sported a scruffy-loo king goatee that hung almost onto his upper chest, and was a walking illustration of cheap, faded tattoos that engulfed his arms, hands, and neck. Displayed over his left eye and onto his lower forehead was a deep, grooved scar shaped eerily like a horseshoe.

Mason felt instant distrust in the man's presence, even more so than with most people of such questionable ilk. He had decided from their initial meeting that a close eye was to be kept on Mr. Rivera at all times.

As they sat in the dimly lit, roach infested room that smelled of stale urine and a cheap whore's perfume, each sucking down their fair share of brew, Juan laid out the plan to Mason in his usual whiny, slightly nasal tone.

His heavy accent and broken English were handicaps Mason had grown accustomed to hearing and translating long ago, though being forced to put forth the effort never failed to grate on his ever-sensitive nerves.

Manny, who had been briefed on the situation days earlier, had sat in front of an ancient thirteen inch color set and viewed a free porno channel the fifteen buck a night room provided, his expression never transformed beyond that of a heavily sedated Zombie. Juan regaled the story behind the plan in less than five minutes, his already dark complexion increased two-fold as his blood pressure rose at least as high as his squeaking, irritating voice.

His sister, Maria Brava (again, Mason couldn't help but smirk. He never understood why it was that spics, despite being siblings, seemed to *never* share the same last name) had been employed, until recently, at the home of Scott D. Markum of Sperryville, as a domestic, Mr. Markum owned a company in Washington, D.C that created and manufactured computer video games. His business had started out modestly enough some five years earlier, but had rode the wave of new technology and customer demand to a net worth of somewhere in the neighborhood of six million dollars.

Juan spoke with a sour grimace covering his pudgy, moistened face when speaking of Markum, as if the idea of becoming a self-made millionaire was a lifestyle he would personally *reject* for himself. Markum, according to Juan, was barely twenty-five but owned a two story brick with double garage, indoor and outdoor pools, a fully equipped weight room, and a bar and lounge that could easily serve thirty to forty individuals.

Markum, according to Juan's sister Maria, was also a sadistic, egotistical, bigoted pervert who took out his many varied and warped aggressions on his domestic staff. The young man, also according to Maria, badgered and degraded all servants whenever possible. A month earlier, Markum had begun to physically touch some of the maids and cooks. She explained that at first the contact had been brief and harmless; a pat on the shoulder or a quick rub between the shoulder blades or on the back of the neck. Markum was admittedly gay, and Maria had told Juan many times of the large circle of male 'companions' that frequented the mansion on the weekends. Still, the touchy-feely episodes escalated until the light pats were fast becoming lingering massages.

Fearful of losing her position, which was substantially higher paying than similar jobs in the city, Maria endured the increasingly bothersome, borderline harassing behavior until one evening just two weeks prior.

Maria and the regular cook, a young black woman named Venus, were the last servants on duty and were in the process of finishing up when Markum entered the kitchen area for what he had called 'an after dinner appetizer'. Maria said Markum, who she described as 'a repulsive little boy', was wearing only a pair of boxer shorts and black socks, and had obviously been dipping into the mansion's plentiful liquor supply earlier that evening. Maria reported that he began to openly fondle Venus's breasts, then playfully kiss the nape of her neck. Venus became enraged after a few moments of his groping, eventually whirling around to shove him away. When he again reached to touch her breasts, she slapped him hard across the right side of the face, then grabbed her purse and ran out the back kitchen exit with tears streaming down her cheeks.

Maria, who had been standing in a far corner of the spacious kitchen in complete shock, reported that Markum showed no change in expression in wake of the physical rebuff, but instead turned toward her wearing a smile born of pure malevolence.

She said he began running his hands over her neck and shoulders, the overwhelming stench of scotch on his breath She said she tried to push his wandering hands away, but that he practically pulled her down onto the

98

tiled kitchen floor and began to 'finger' her vagina roughly through her panties.

Juan had paused at that point in the story, his hands shaking and his face crimson red with rage. After gulping down the majority of a fresh beer, he seemed to calm down a notch, at least enough to conclude the story.

Maria had fought her way out of Markum's drunken grip, kicking him in the groin in the process. She had positioned herself behind the kitchen's lengthy cutting table, and informed Markum in no uncertain terms that 'her lawyer would be in touch'. She later told Juan that Markum stood across from her sporting a wolfish, predatory grin, and spoke in a harsh whisper. The words he'd spoken were pronounced with the simplicity and conciseness that one might expect from a parent warning a young child of an impending spanking. Maria said she recalled each venomous word, and understood with complete clarity that Scott Markum, respected yuppie computer geek millionaire and proud member of the Fortune 500, wouldn't hesitate to carry them out to the letter. The words had been "Fuck with me, woman, and there won't be enough left of you to spoon into a coffin."

Needless to say, Maria had wisely decided *not* to test such a threat. People such as Juan and Maria knew how dangerous white men with access to unlimited wealth could be--especially men as inherently evil as Scott Markum.

Maria had been forced into working low paying menial jobs in the meantime, her anger at Markum's assault turning her bitter and incommunicable. Maria, divorced with three small children, had turned to her older brother for support. The secret she divulged from her year and a half of being on Markum's payroll

99

spawned the plan that Mason had been brought in to help carry out.

Scott Markum had cash in upwards of *at least* a quarter-million dollars stashed away in his bedroom Maria had cleaned the man 's room for over a year before noticing the foot high, foot wide cabinet that was built into the bed's headboard. She had been instructed by Markum himself on the morning of the discovery to "clean behind the Lions head, if you will. It has been awhile and I believe there might be a dead mouse lodged between it and the wall." The 'Lions Head' was the design of the headboard itself, which was constructed of solid oak with the marble Lions head built in. The head was at least three feet high and two feet wide, and was lined in silver plating. The cabinet was located on the back side of the head, and was more or less invisible to the naked eye. Maria had found its tiny combination lock dial by complete accident while dusting.

Although wary to do so initially, Maria eventually tested the handle and found it to be unlocked. She told Juan the contents were bundles of cash, mostly fifties from what she had seen, and clear glass containers filled with gold and diamond jewelry of all shapes and dimensions . She hadn't previously mentioned the cabinet to anyone, neither co-worker nor family member. The reasons for her caution were the vibes she felt each day she neared the headboard and stared into the blank yet somehow watchful eyes of the marble Lion's head. Markum was *testing* her. A sick little rich kid playing sick little rich kid games-a game of 'bust the spic maid and then blackmail her into perverse sexual favors'. She had always heard how the high and mighty enjoyed keeping 'her kind' down; how they never missed an opportunity to unveil their superiority to what they deemed the 'weaker links' of society. Markum was capable of such, she knew. She had witnessed his arrogance, even towards his peers. In his ruthless eyes, she was less than dog shit on his Gucci Loafers, and she knew it.

Maria was certain the stash still existed, probably maintained as a test for all present and future employees. A cruel trap set by a man always in search of an edge on anyone he deemed unworthy of his divine presence. She didn't have to drop any subtle hints to her big brother about the opportunity lying before them. That treasure was theirs for the taking, but only if they acquired the right helps to map out the logistics of such a potentially dangerous undertaking. Dangerous for two very large and distinct reasons. Their names were Jake and Lyle, Markum's paid muscle and eternally present bodyguards. Both had been weapons specialists in the military (Marines and Army , respectively), and rumor had it they had both spent time in South America as paid assassins before hooking up with young master Markum. Maria had reported to Juan that only on those specific evenings that Markum was feeling particularly 'froggy' and was in the mood to dish out his own special brand of cruelty towards the staff were the 'Brute Brothers'(as they were referred to by the domestics) *not* present at his bony-framed side. Young master Markum had made a number of enemies in his rapid rise to the top, and rarely left the grounds of his estate without suitable protection.

Hence, Mason Parks suddenly understood why he'd been recruited into the mix.

Maria had told her big brother that the security provided to the home was modest at best; coded security for every door and window in the main house and a single guard stationed at the entrance to the grounds themselves; an eight foot high brick fence surrounding the entire two acre perimeter. Guards worked twelve-hour shifts in the diminutive wooden shack that fronted the main gate entrance, usually older men already collecting a pension following retirement from active law enforcement.

Mason knew the type; soft gutted, drowsy and only half-coherent, there to collect a weekly check and nothing more.

According to Maria, a former co-worker who was still employed on the grounds as a part-time cook had provided her with Markum's home security code in return for a small cash fee once the job was completed. Maria recalled Markum changing the code on a monthly basis or whenever an employee quit or was fired.

His steely eyes seemingly unaffected by the substantial alcohol consumption of the previous twenty-four hours, Mason sucked down the remainder of his brew and calmly rolled the empty bottle across the table until it clanked against Juan's half-full container. He could guarantee Juan of two things; the night watchman at the front entrance would provide *little* resistance; the bodyguards of one Scott Markum would be dealt with accordingly and with a minimum of fireworks.

In return, Mason requested a single guarantee from Juan; *half* of whatever was taken from the lock box in the man's bedroom.

A bit shakily, and ignoring a stern, disapproving glare from Manny, Juan ever so reluctantly agreed to the terms.

Approximately twenty hours later, Manny leisurely

pulled onto a rain-soaked grassy shoulder fronting the paved driveway belonging to one Scott Markum. The late model Monte Carlo had been borrowed from one of Juan's dope-dealing contemporaries, its glossy red paint job and chromed rims reflecting its just-off-the floor room look. Juan's badly rusted Mustang, its tires as bald as any sports ball manufactured by Spalding, wouldn't have fit into the elegant surroundings as comfortably, nor would have Manny's bullet-hole pockmarked late eighties Cutlass Supreme.

Mason had remained vehicle-less (at least from a *legal* standpoint) since his release, only because he realized it was much easier to drop out of the parole office's sight when the paper trail one left behind was as limited as possible.

Juan was curled into the Chevy's spacious trunk, while Mason tucked his bulky frame onto the back floorboard. The Monte Carlo's windows were as darkly tinted as the law allowed, so staying out of the guard's view wouldn't be a problem until Manny rolled down the driver's side window. By the time the unfortunate soul took the time to peek past Manny to check the contents of the rear seat, remaining hidden would be a pointless task.

Manny quickly mounted the *Rocco's Pizza* sign onto the vehicle's roof, the letters lit up in true Vegas strip style by tiny, built-in tube lights. He re-entered the vehicle, shaking fresh droplets of rain from his shaggy mane, and Mason nodded agreeably before slumping back down as far as his broad shoulders and V -shaped back would allow.

It had been agreed, after a lengthy argument on the part of Manny, that no firearms of any kind would be taken onto the grounds. Mason had refused the Beretta

9mm that Juan had offered, as well as the pearl handled .44 Magnum. He had then explained, rather explicitly and in no uncertain terms, that if such weapons were to be utilized, he would no longer be offering his assistance.

Mason's reason was both logical and sensible, factors which made convincing Manny an even harder task. If there was no gun, there was no bullet. No bullet, no ballistics involved. No ballistics involved cut the odds of ever being placed at the scene easily in half. Mason had survived dozens of viscous attacks within prison yards and showers without benefit of such weapons, and saw little need to fall into their seductive trap on his initial mission in the outside world. Mason assured them both that regardless of the fact that the entrance guard as well as Markum's bodyguards would more than likely be strapped to the gills, it wasn't necessary to out firepower them, thus leaving behind a crime scene loaded with shell casings, empty clips, and slug holes.

Thus, each was given an assault weapon specifically designed for the task they were assigned. Each wore leather gloves pulled over a set of rubber ones, thus eliminating prints. Avoiding on-site wounds was a must, as leaving spatters of blood was frowned upon for obvious reasons. All three men were tucked away in the FBI's files as former felons. It wouldn't take more than a few well-placed clues and an hour of work by the Feds before their collective faces would be plastered on every TV set in the eastern U.S.

Tucked underneath the driver's side seat was an eight inch bladed wooden handled stiletto that Manny had handpicked from Mason's personal stock, a variable plethora of instruments created for the sole purpose of instituting the age-old art of inflicting pain upon another.

Juan had decided upon the marble handled Bowie with the serrated seven inch blade, strapped onto his belt like a miniature version of a pirate's broadsword. Mason stuck with an old standby that had served him well in several past skirmishes; the six inch bladed Jungle King combat knife, complete with a camouflaged handle that fit his grip as if it had been sewn into place. He kept it strapped on the inside of his left ankle, the blade itself submerged into a homemade pocket in the side of his steel toed boot.

He would only use the blade as a last resort, however, choosing an eighteen inch long baton as his main source of offense for the evening. Less mess, same result if used correctly. The pitch-black baton seemed weightless in his hands, but could crack a man's skull like an eggshell if swung with enough force and at the correct angle. This he knew not from hearsay, but from personal experience.

Manny exited onto a two-lane road marked 'Basehart Avenue' and drove cautiously up the thickly forested, immaculately paved trail, which seemed void of even the tiniest of clearings. Tall, ancient oaks, maples and elm trees lined the otherwise well-manicured shoulders, and it appeared Markum had bought up the surrounding acreage to prevent other potential builders from homesteading anywhere near his perfectly manicured grounds.

After topping a steep grade between two rocky hillsides, the Markum estate swam clearly into view. Manny had remarked "Welcome to Disneyland" in an almost incomprehensible Spanish accent as he slowly braked on the rain slicked two-lane.

Mason arose and peered out from the passenger's window. Head-high, impeccably pruned shrubbery lined the football-field sized yard that led to the diminutive guard shack. The home itself stood out like a lighthouse beacon in the shadowed background of the surrounding countryside. It was a two story brick constructed in Mexican ranch style, with a glass-domed breezeway leading from one section to the next, and a double garage that could effortlessly hold twin RVs. The entire front section, including the aforementioned breezeway, was lit up like a Fourth of July fireworks display, a disturbing fact not entirely lost on Mason, but one that did little to alter his confidence concerning the mission's eventual outcome.

With the vehicle's windshield wipers set to the swiftest setting, Manny had whispered "Showtime, Holmes" and turned toward the entrance, which was positioned no more than a hundred feet from the highway turnoff. Mason scrunched down awkwardly with the baton held snugly against his chest, the circular tip rubbing the stubble on his scarred chin.

The guard emerged from the shack wearing a rain smock that covered his entire face save the chin. His voice was gravelly and harsh, sure signs of a lifetime smoker. The guard placed his liver-spotted hands onto the driver's side door just as Manny rolled down the window, and Mason heard the words "Pizza delivery, huh? I don't envy your job on this nasty night, son.. ." followed by a grisly gurgling noise as Manny planted the stiletto deep into the man's exposed throat. Mason departed the back seat and assisted in tossing the man's convulsing body back into the guard shack. Blood was spattered onto the roof, hood and driver's door in a fine, perfectly horizontal line, the falling rain quickly washing away the majority as seconds passed.

Maria had assured big brother Juan that Markum's

security measures did *not* include mounted cameras. After quickly scanning the perimeter fence, Mason saw nothing that would indicate otherwise. Other than the baseball caps each sported, their faces would have been clearly visible that night, but it was a chance Mason deemed worth taking. He had worn masks for concealment in past jobs, and found them not only a distraction, but at times dangerously crippling in the way they reduced one's overall line of sight. Mason wanted to ensure they all walked into the situation with clear, unblocked vision. He had a feeling they were going to need all their collective senses working at maximum effectiveness if they planned on driving away from the Markum estate with their skin intact.

It took only two and a half minutes from the time the car had braked at the guard shack to tuck the body away and then proceed to the home's main entrance.

Manny didn't seriously consider turning off the vehicle's headlights as they drove the hundred yards to the front drive, since the grounds were lit up so brightly it would've been a moot point even bothering.

A short concrete stairway encased in black rod-iron railing led to the front entrance; a set of double oak doors that looked practically tank-proof. As per the plan, Manny paused for a full minute with the lights on and engine running before shutting down and departing the vehicle with an empty pizza box held high in his left palm. The vehicle sat at a side angle to the entrance with at least a fifty-foot distance to the front doors. Through the tinted glass, Mason observed Manny stroll through the falling rain and halt just to the right of the entrance, casually shaking the water buildup from the bill of his cap.

Manny glanced back at the vehicle and then side stepped until he was positioned directly in front of where the security code box hung, approximately shoulder length high and to the left of the doorframe. Mason took a deep breath as he watched Manny punch in the code that had been provided by Maria's mole. Despite knowing the possibility of the situation turning nasty very quickly if the code didn't match, Mason didn't feel anything resembling nervousness or apprehension. He had discovered those specific states of mind weren't part of his emotional being since his years spent at the Myers Unit. Anxiety had simply ceased to exist within his permanently scarred mind-frame.

As Manny stepped back over to the double doors and grasped the right's shiny chrome handle, Mason reached over the front seat and popped the trunk release through the glove compartment. Within two minutes, the trio stood inside the foyer leading into a living room roughly the size of a regulation basketball court. Mason gestured for all to cease movement once they had tiptoed halfway to the room's center, the faint sound of classical music being played in a faraway room the only noticeable distraction.

Juan had shot him a look equally relieved yet openly frustrated; one that mirrored his own thoughts: the place might well be deserted; Mr. Markum and his twin tower bodyguards having flown the coop for the evening.

All three took a moment to revel in the outrageous lavishness of the objects surrounding them. A black leather couch, the length of which seemed to equal a semi-truck and it's adjoined trailer, sat to their immediate right, surrounded by lamp tables which looked to be constructed of marble and *layered* in pure silver. A colossal crystal chandelier hung from the vaulted ceiling, its thick shiny spears ending only a scant seven feet from the thickly carpeted floors below. On each side of the room, in all four corners which held exits, stood statues which were similar in their grandiose theme but utterly opposite in the style's they represented.

Mason Parks had never claimed to be an expert on interior decorating; a few nudie posters and ample closet space to hang his duds had always been sufficient. That said, even he could recognize the tell-tale markings of a rich, young *flake* when he saw them.

The statues were of mid-evil knights, their poses as diverse as the combat gear they donned, but similar in that all were frozen in mid-swing with their mighty sabers. Coate d in silver, Mason approximated each of them at a weight of at least a thousand pounds, for it was a foregone conclusion that none were hollow on the inside and more than likely welded from solid steel. Mason held back a sarcastic snicker at the thought of a preppy, pretty boy fag millionaire fantasizing himself as the first gay *knight of the round table*.

After a brief but thorough walk-through of the massive first floor, including the kitchen and living room areas, all three met back at the foot of the stairs leading to the second. There was little chance that the thickly carpeted stairway was capable of even the slightest creak as they ascended, even as the music blaring from above ceased in between tunes.

Following the origin of the music, they found Mr. Markum behind bedroom door number three to the left. The second floor hallway itself had been so dimly lit it had taken their eyes a few moments to adjust, only the sparse illumination lining the bottom of the bedroom door itself preventing total darkness.

Mason had swung the unlocked door open without impact of any kind, leaving the occupants comically dumbfounded as the trio leaped inside.

After spending over a decade inside a maximum security prison, Mason Parks considered himself utterly 'shock-proof' by any scene of depravity man could create. He had watched men sodomize one another ad nauseam, and usually less than passionately. He had committed murders and had his own life threatened by the same numerous times. In his lifetime he'd been a party or witness to stabbings, shootings, strangulations, chokings, beatings, and all other variations to end a man's life.

Despite the cold, calculating and unfeeling monster he freely admitted becoming through the years, the picture filling his eyes on that fateful night would flash into his subconscious for the rest of his days, somehow providing a sense of surreal security in knowing there indeed *was* a higher plain of evil than the one he himself resided within.

Manny had laughed aloud, albeit a bit nervously. Juan had simply uttered "You sick little fuck" before charging forward in reckless abandon.

A painting that might well have been put on display amongst the sickest of the elite at an underground art exhibit would have revealed a snapshot definition of unbridled decadence. Markum had the Bo and Luke brothers, both buck naked and oiled up like sunbathers on a Caribbean beachhead, tied to adjoining high back chairs, a thin, knotted rope encircling their ankles, waists, chests, and necks. Both were gagged with leather straps tied snugly around their chin and skulls, something dark, round and immensely large protruding from their overstuffed mouths. For a moment Mason mistakenly identified the lengthy red stripes drawn across their chests as paint. He realized upon taking a step forward that they were instead fresh wounds inflicted in the name of some kinky, violent sex act. The pair's eyes grew wide with rage at the site of the intruders, both struggling madly against the binds that held them Mason noticed that the enormous erections each had displayed upon entry were now slowly dissipating as seconds ticked away.

On the far corner of the eloquently furnished room, complete with a fully stocked wet bar, mirrored walls and ceiling, and a big screen TV that took up a full wall all its own, sat a noticeably underage Asian girl, also hopelessly bound. Her mouth was gagged with an adhesive tape of some kind, and her eyes were covered with a maroon shaded blind fold. Her arms, which wriggled and strained weakly, were bound behind a diminutive metal chair, though her thin, badly bruised legs remained strangely unbound and sat splayed apart and unmoving as if paralyzed. Her shirt and bra had been removed, and fresh circular burn marks could be seen just above the tiny, grape-like nipples of each pre-teen sized breast. The torn white panties that hung from her left ankle were spattered in blood, as was her right thigh just above the knee. Tears flowed down her reddened cheeks from underneath the confinement of the blindfold. Even in the faint mood lighting, Mason realized the girl had obviously suffered some major league molestation, and definitely *not* of her own free will.

Young master Scott Markum sat atop the colossal bed, a pitch black canopy swooping over its space like a

111

giant bat wing, and met their intrusion with a snarl one would associate with a rabid, cornered predator guarding a fresh kill. As pathetically scrawny and sickly looking as Markum appeared, for a split second Mason had felt a small twinge of fear when their eyes locked and the young man's growl seemed to increase in its animalistic intensity.

Markum had been grasping separate items in each hand upon the unexpected trio's arrival upon the grisly scene, a double-headed dildo at least fifteen inches in length in his right and a whip of some type in the left; its loose, flowing straps seemingly encased in hard, worn leather. The latter of these two objects at least help explain the raw wounds across the bodyguard's chests. The young millionaire was also nude except for the knee high, white panty hose he sported, and the dark purple lipstick that looked to have been applied to his pouting lips with a spatula.

Mason's eyes departed the gruesome yet undeniably fascinating stage for only a moment until they landed upon their true objective. The headboard was just as described, the gleaming lion head standing out like a silver plated talisman in clear, blue seawater.

Markum had blurted out something along the lines of "I'll have your collective balls stuffed and mounted" just as Juan had leapt towards him.

The kid had been surprisingly fast, jumping from the bed and dodging Juan's initial stab attempt, the stiletto slicing nothing but air. Mason had averted his attention solely to the headboard by that time, while Manny had decided to pay the steroid twins a visit.

None had expected Markum to actually be *prepared* for such a hit, and later Mason cursed his own carelessness.

Markum stuck his left hand inside the bottom drawer of a colossal, solid oak dresser, and in one quick, fluid motion removed a pearl handled, snub-nosed .38 . Mason had just begun to peak behind the headboard for the desired hidden treasure when the first retort of the revolver sounded off, temporarily lighting up the room like a shot from a flare gun. Instinctively ducking down into a shooter's crouch, his upper back hugging the wall, Mason pee ked cautiously around the headboard and saw Manny laying face down on the shag carpet just a few feet away.

The kid had evidently spent some time on a range, as his first shot having sheared away the front portion of Juan's nose and sending him reeling back against a rear bedpost. Darting behind the wide, circular mahogany bar, Markum fired another round that neatly removed Juan's index finger from his left hand and sent it sailing against a nearby globe lamp, leaving a bloody outline on the glass before plopping onto the carpet with a muffled thump.

Juan had shrieked first in rage, then in immense pain as the numbness of his wounds began to wear off. Meanwhile, Mason had ducked behind the mattress sometime between the first shot and its sequel, joining Manny in a frantic session of carpet munching.

Juan had begun to laugh like a rabid Hyena once the fireworks had begun, and Mason recognized the evil cackle as the initial hairline crack in the man's already suspect sanity. Following his sentence at the Myers Unit, it was a sound he was frighteningly familiar with.

Looking past Juan, who continued his banshee-howl concerto, Mason saw that Manny had already sliced one of the bodyguard's throats just beneath the Adams apple. The man's entire chest and abdomen resembled a crimson waterfall, his stony, deadened eyes only half opened. The other was struggling valiantly against the bonds, attempting to scream out but managing only a wad of leaky spittle at the corner of his outstretched lips. His straining ended a moment later, as Markum's third retort tore through the palm of Juan's upraised right hand, passed clean through, and ricocheted into the guard's right eye, the sound at impact not unlike a light slap of flesh against flesh.

Mason rolled over the rambling, mostly incoherent clown that Manny had transformed into, and fell behind a large oak dresser (Markum's secret gun cabinet) that stood almost to his shoulders in height. He had caught a brief glimpse of Juan along the way. The man had made a final charge towards the bar, his blade held in the bloody pulp of his right hand in a high, 'stab downward' arc. Mason heard Juan *rebel yell* something in Spanish, then grow instantly quiet in mid-scream, like some inner 'mute' button had been pressed.

Things grew eerily still and silent for a full thirty seconds, only Beethoven's Fifth humming along in the background like elevator music piped in directly from the pits of Hell.

As Mason was reaching to pull the combat knife from his boot, he heard Manny's heavy footsteps as they charged ahead like a raging bull elephant towards a lone desert watering hole. As idiotic as the bullish effort was, Mason conceded to himself later that without such a reckless act from his lunatic partner, his own chances of walking out of Markum's mansion that fateful night would have been slim to none. It seemed Scott D.

Markum, mad yuppie at large, was much more than just your everyday Joe with a gun firing off 'lucky shots.' The young man was obviously an expert marksman whose aim seemed to actually *improve* under stress.

Mason gripped each weapon loosely while crossing his massive forearms over his face in an 'X' shape, then sprang from behind the dresser and practically ran up Manny's back towards the bar.

Juan lay at the bound Asian girl's feet, the majority of his scalp blown into red, mucus-like chunks. The girl's legs were splattered in his blood, although in her comatose state she seemed mercifully oblivious.

Manny leaped the waist high bar like a track hurdle, shattering shot glasses, varied bottles of spirits, and a crystal ice holder in the process, all the while screaming a warrior-like cry that would've drowned out an approaching ambulance.

Mason had been using Manny's torso as a shield before the leap, and utilized the outside of the bar for the same afterwards, again crouching low with the weapons held almost flush against the flesh of his forehead.

Another moment of unexpected silence followed before he heard Manny curse out in agonized frustration. Mason joined him behind the bar's wide counter, noting a small, hatch-like door still partially opened and swinging slightly on its hinges.

Markum had obviously felt the need to insert an elaborate escape hatch for just such a situation. There was little doubt the mystery portal led to a portion of the mansion hidden away from any and all outside guests.

Gladly allowing Manny to lead the way, Mason secretly wished he'd brought along adequate firepower, damn the rules of 'safe' engagement. He'd never expected a blood bath with Markum as the instigator. After all, the bodyguards had been the main concern, now both dead and stiffening in their binds a few dozen feet away.

Ducking into the narrow void, both men were forced to duck-walk down a narrow, box-shaped hall that was void of light other than a thin, ivory line shining beneath the door it led to, which sat at least thirty feet in the distance.

Being careful to ensure Manny's body was completely blocking his own, Mason stayed a scant foot behind as they neared the mystery room. It was like crawling through an amusement park haunted house where the only scare tactic afforded was forcing it's patrons to tread pitch-black, square shaped hallways, never leaving a clue as to what lay ahead.

Manny shoved the door open with a single push and hurled himself inside, and both men were instantly blinded by a rush of bright light not unlike the fiery beam of a stage spotlight. It took a full five seconds for either man to regain enough composure to even *begin* to define the odd shaped objects dominating the room like posed statues.

Manny began to laugh anew, although some of the maniacal edge had apparently wilted away, replaced by a layer of good old-fashioned, gut-crunching fear.

Mason leaned against a multi-colored wall dripping in psychedelic imagery and studied the surroundings with schoolboy-like fascination.

He was beginning to understand why the medieval statues graced the first floor.

Markum's blue-blood surroundings were simply a portion of the innocent façade the youthful, filthy rich and obviously mentally disturbed young man created for his potential lovers just before introducing them into his own personal pit of degeneracy.

Bottom line: Scott D. Markum was one astonishingly *sick* pup.

The enclosure resembled the prop room from the movie *Hellraiser*. Chained ropes hung from the ceiling with fishhook ends. An entire wall was composed of hand-held torture devices, some sexual in nature and others for the single purpose of inflicting immense pain *without* the accompanying pleasure. There were circular straps on the wall to bind the victim motionless, as well as what appeared to be three separate flat racks also supplied with leather tie-down straps. One resembled something out of old pirate films, used to stretch the human body to its breaking point.

Mason noticed more than a few dried bloodstains on the tiled floor as he pushed himself away from the wall with slow-motion cautiousness.

Several feet away, Manny was fronting what bore a striking resemblance to a cello case, constructed in a hard leather casing and at least six feet high and three wide. It was propped in the rear by two thick iron rods, while no handle of any kind was visible on its slick sided front. Manny was running his right hand along its top, the stiletto held lazily at his left side. Before he could even manage a grunt of warning, Mason jerked back as a hole the size of a softball blasted open at the center of the case, the smoke from the firearm's detonation filling the air around it in a thick, sweeping fog.

Just before rolling behind the nearest object, a flat metal table that displayed trays filled with sex toys both familiar and weirdly surreal in nature, Mason had

117

watched Manny sail across one of the flat racks, a ragged, almost perfectly circular hole blown out from between his shoulder blades.

Realizing his lower body would be fully exposed by the meager cover provided by the rolling table, Mason waited to act until the smoke cleared just enough to see movement from within the torture case. The case door flew open swiftly, and Markum stepped out with a sawed off shotgun literally strapped to his bony, heaving chest. His grin was hideous upon viewing Manny's battered corpse lying sprawled out a few scant feet away. Thin tendrils of smoke spewed from the sawed barrel as Markum scanned the room, blinking rapidly through the misty haze the weapon's blast had created.

As he crept towards the exit on his hands and knees, Mason managed to roll quietly to the opposite side of the rack without giving away his position. He knew he had to keep Markum trapped within the confines of the relatively closed space to avoid authorities being contacted, as he'd spotted a cell phone lying on one of the numerous bedroom lamp tables before the fireworks had commenced.

Peering over the flat padding of the rack, he saw Markum had turned back towards the hallway, evidently thinking the kink room now deserted. Without a single wasted movement, Mason sprang to his feet and threw the baton end over end with all the force he could muster. He then leapt the rack in a single bounce with the combat knife held by the blade tip and cocked slightly behind his head, his legs pumping in a rhythmic blur. Markum heard neither the baton nor the man who had thrown it, his concentration frozen in a tunnel vision view of the hallway entrance mere feet ahead. The baton struck him on the meat of his left calf, the yelp that escaped his lips born from both shock and intense pain. He fell back, the sawed shotgun flying from his grasping fingers to land with a loud thump against a forward wall, just inches from the hallway itself.

Mason reached him a millisecond later, just as he was attempting to roll to his feet by reaching for a pair of leather straps hanging from a nearby wall. Aborting the earlier idea of actually throwing the blade at his fallen prey, Ma son instead re-gripped the weapon by its pearl handle and drove it forward in a straight arc with the precision of a striking Cobra. The blade penetrated effortlessly through the pasty flesh of Markum's right hand, dead center at the palm. Mason shoved the handle forward with his own palm while simultaneously body blocking the smaller man, pinning him against the wall. With only the handle of the blade visible from Markum's punctured, spasm racked hand, Mason gave it a final, forceful shove and felt the blade slide easily through the wall's thin paneling and then into a two by four stud beneath.

Satisfied that the man was significantly pinned, Mason leaned back a step and then thrust forward with a series of short, powerful jabs that connected with jaw and forehead, leaving Markum dazed, battered and hanging from the wall like a mounted trophy.

Mason could have simply cut the man's throat or beat him into a pulpy mass with the baton, but recalling the tales of cruelty and passionless spite regaled by the sister of a man lying shot full of holes a room away, he came to the conclusion that a more *punishment fits the crime* type of fate was in order.

Approximately five minutes later, Mason re-entered

119

the blood splattered rubble of the bedroom, a space that had more than likely served as Markum's personal torture chamber since the day he'd first exceeded his first cool million in assets, and had become aware of how much power a man with unlimited funds can not only acquire, but subsequently utilize for his own vile self-gratification.

Mason had momentarily studied the bound and ravaged husks of Markum's former bodyguards/ sex-toys and secretly pondered their roles in the young millionaires' grand scheme. He felt no pity for such men. They had been nothing more than well-paid mercenaries for whom moral boundaries did not exist. Sadly, men of his own ilk in many ways. Mason realized he could very easily be viewing his own future if certain steps down the wrong highway were ever taken.

He untied the comatose girl, removing her blindfold without hesitation, although the prospect of being identified to the authorities became an instant concern until he looked deep into her dark brown, slightly slanted, and utterly lifeless eyes. The girl had long since drifted into her own inner universe, no doubt to escape the unimaginable horrors previously endured. Mason had seriously considered killing her, but instead left her lying on the bed, tucking her in like a father would an exhausted child.

Shoving his bulky frame behind the thick headboard, he found the lock box exactly how and where Maria had described it. The small, metal-levered door was slightly agape, and swung open noiselessly. He gave the insides a quick study for possible booby traps, then casually reached inside and removed the contents with gore splattered rubber gloves. After retrieving a nearby pillow and removing the white-laced pillowcase that encased it, he hurriedly stuffed the contents inside with only the briefest glimpse at a select few items.

Mason left the shell-shocked Asian teen staring unblinking at the canopy above, only the barely distinguishable breathing motion of her narrow chest giving away the fact she was alive at all. He again considered ending her misery, both present and future; a future sure to include dead- end stints as both teen runaway and drug-rattled prostitute, then again reconsidered and quietly departed, barely avoiding stepping on Juan's splayed, bullet riddled corpse in the process.

Before leaving the grounds of the estate, Mason re-entered the slim hallway that led to Markum's bondage room, paused once inside to recover Manny's once-used stiletto, and performed what his own demented soul truly deemed a merciful act of kindness. Before departing to claim his treasure ten minutes prior, he had systematically slashed both of Markum's Achilles heels, along with a deep, grooved slice into the upper shoulder of the man's unpinned, previously uninjured arm, thereby rendering it totally useless other than its capability to bleed profusely.

Before leisurely cutting Scott Markum's throat from ear to ear, barely avoiding being coated in crimson when the jugular released a fine, gushing spray upon the blade's intrusion, Mason had stared long and hard into the man's teary, terror-filled eyes. Although he saw a bit of himself mirrored in the image of such evil, an unfamiliar twinge tugged at his gut before metal penetrated flesh. It was a phenomenon he couldn't recall ever experiencing before that moment, and one he found impossible to define until hours later while attempting in vain to get in his usual two to three hour nightly nap. The word that came to mind was *revulsion*. Such a thought did not settle well, and it was one he realized wasn't going to fade easily or be forcefully shaken from his subconscious, not entirely anyway, for months or even years to come.

***

He read of what the media had labeled 'The Preppy Assassination' in the next day's afternoon newspaper. The local media reported that the authorities were treating it as a 'simple break-in attempt gone awry' by two local thugs.

Confident that he'd left the premises print and/or clue free, Mason loaded his meager belongings into the late model T-Bird purchased with cash earlier that morning from a local used lot and quietly departed town exactly twenty four hours from the time of the incident.

Prior to cruising onto the interstate heading north late that evening, he did make one final, nonscheduled pit-stop to tie up a loose end that had mutated from minor annoyance to major migraine in a matter of hours.

Maria's boyfriend had put up a decent enough scrap, actually connecting with more than one hard right hand as the confrontation had ensued. Mason barely avoided getting his skull opened up by the sharp end of an iron coat rack before instituting a series of jabs that shattered jawbone and a spinning side-kick that splintered a knee cap. A final, forceful blow to the throat had ended that particular dance.

Maria had been trying to dial 9-1- 1 at the time, and

was discovered, along with the valiant boyfriend, by her landlord two days later. Her face was a mask of purple, the phone cord wrapped so tightly it looked as if it had been welded into the soft flesh of her throat. It had been nothing personal, as such matters rarely were, but Mason realized with the death of her brother in Markum's home, she would eventually, if not *immediately* , spill his name without hesitation as being an involved party in such a thoroughly *FUBARed* mission. She would've reached out for a goat to blame for her brother 's involvement, possibly even fingering Mason as Juan's 'puppet master', the man who had initiated the 'master plan' that had gone so ridiculously awry.

Afterwards, it had taken him a full six months to fence the jewelry and an additional three to loiter the cash. The total value of the items removed from Scott Markum's head- board deposit box had come to around sixty-eight thousand dollars Not exactly the nest egg fortune he'd anticipated. Obviously the greedy little bastard had set it up almost entirely as a trap for his employees, just as Maria had suspected.

It was quite the disappointing haul, for sure, but enough to allow safe, comfortable travel far away from the scene of the crime, and with an ample supply of ready cash to live on for at least a year while keeping the lowest profile humanly possible.

As clean cut as his apparent getaway had been, however, the memory of Scott Markum's expression just before his malevolent term on earth expired re fused to dissipate from the back of Mason's mind. The memory was especially vivid on certain nights when much-needed downtime was fleeting and his bed sheets wrapped around his body like a cocoon from continual tossing and turning.

***

Mason Parks remained somewhat dazed, his lips parted but unmoving. The interviewer was forced to repeat his inquiry for a third time before the hulking man's eyes seemed to gradually return to his present location, like a man waking from an extended, coma-like dream sequence. " Mr. Parks, you realize you have basically just confessed to the murders of at least five individuals. You not only named places, but the names associated with the specific situations. It wouldn't take much of a detective to track and confirm such activities."

Parks yawned sheepishly, his expression never wavering from the dry, humorless mode displayed since the interview had commenced. "Do *you* realize, sir that providing such information basically shows that I do not give a rodent's hairy ass? I divulged because I *meant* to, get it? It was no slip of the tongue, by any means.

Have your crack staff investigate if you insist. Everything I 've said is the stone cold truth, so help me Satan."

Another pause ensued, followed by the sound of the interviewer clearing his throat incisively before continuing. "We will pay you to kill, Mr. Parks, or pay you *not* to die, however you wish to look at it. I take it from your biography that you are officially fine with such an agreement?"

Parks leaned forward with squinting eyes and spoke through tightly clenched teeth.

"Fucking-A, Mr. Suit, but I expect to be paid very, *very* well, and the perks I request along the way won't

124

come cheap, either. You people need to unders--"

"Um, Mr. Parks, this is not to say you've been approved as a contestant. There are other people in higher positions than I who make that decision based on several factors. I--"

Parks stood suddenly, shoved upward by rapidly bulging biceps and thickly veined forearms. The flesh of his face was flushed red. His eyes were fiery, crimson coals.

"Oh, then you're just a well-dressed peon? In that case, Mr. Suit, if you interrupt me just *once* more, I'm gonna reach over and hurt you very…very badly, do you fully comprehend my drift, sir?"

Being off camera, the interviewer's gestures could have only been guessed by viewers of the tape, but one could have assumed they were of less than a positive nature.

A muffled "Mr. Parks, I don't…" was barely audible just as Parks leapt across the table top with a quickness associated with a man half his size, his face a mask of calm, controlled rage, the tiniest of smiles crossing his pursed lips.

A brief, stifled scuffle followed off-camera, which remained unmoved and still trained on the portion of the room Parks had been occupying. A shrill, animal -like shriek was abruptly cut off as if its originator had been virtually unplugged.

A man wearing a bright blue suit, his formerly slick-backed hair now ruffled and comically displaying the world's worst cow-lick literally flew into view, his upper body slammed atop the table top like a slab of beef onto a butcher's stand. The man's hands, both of which were partially tucked underneath his gore-splattered cheeks, trembled and shook uncontrollably. His face was turned directly into the camera's lens, and a thick stream of pulpy, reddish/yellow liquid leaked from his right eye like milk from a punctured carton. A black felt-tip pen protruded from the eye at a slightly warped angle, its oval-shaped end pointing towards the overhead lighting. All but the last few inches had been driven directly through the pupil, as if it had been used as a bulls-eye for the sharp end to penetrate.

From the left side of the screen, Parks' grinning mug appeared, leaning over his bloody handy work like an abstract artist over a prize sculpture. Within seconds, there was the sound of a door being battered upon, followed quickly by hurried footsteps as others rushed to the injured man's aid. Parks spoke slowly into the lens, his chalky white, perfectly squared teeth displayed in horrid amusement, his right hand flashing a mock 'thumbs up' gesture just underneath his squared chin.

"I told worm-boy here not to interrupt me, did I *not* ? Looks like the punk got a real *eye* -full, huh?"

Bolts of static mercifully replaced the picture just as the last spoken word was completed.

***

Earl Barron clicked off the VCR and stood before his speechless guest, whose face was now a noticeably whiter shade of pale. "And a star was instantly born," Barron announced dramatically.

After coughing somewhat nervously into his hand, the other man was finally able to rediscover the power of the spoken word. "Mr. Barron, I do believe we can come to an amiable agreement concerning this newest volume.

126

I must digress from my earlier opinion. It most definitely has selling potential."

Barron nodded agreeably while slowly pacing from left to right. " I thought you might see it that way, my good man. Let's talk further over lunch."

The other man rose stiffly from the deeply cushioned chair, his eyes still wide in a mixture of excitement and shocked revulsion. "I must ask you…what happened to the man conducting the interview? Did he recover from such a grave wound?"

Barron patted him lightly on the left shoulder, much like a grandfather would a querying grandchild. " Actually, Mr. Tooms did indeed lose the eye and suffered a few cracked ribs. He works in our accounting department now. He holds no grudge, and is given credit for 'discovering' our current champion, although he refuses to ever occupy the same room as Mr. Parks again, for obvious reasons."

"When does the next segment go into the filming stage, Mr. Barron?" the man asked, his gait still a bit shaky as they made their way towards the door.

"Six days from today. We have our contestants chosen and the grounds outside the compound are in the initial prepping stages. I, along with my co-workers on the project, believe this will be the chart topper of all previous volumes."

"A new champion crowned perhaps?" the man asked, the color of his cheeks finally regaining normal tint.

"Sometimes it can be most profitable to...how do you say…bring in a fresh face?" he continued.

Barron paused before reaching for the door handle. " You have a specific scenario in mind, my good friend?"

127

he replied inquisitively, the grayish colored eyebrow above his right eye suddenly cocked with interest.

"We'll speak over lunch, Mr. Barron. I have… a proposal from my people you might want to seriously consider."

Earl Barron nodded amiably as the office door closed quietly at his back, his semi-balding scalp tingling with renewed excitement.

Chapter Four
The Prodigal Son Returns/Mysterious Visitors

Date: 28 AUGUST 2006
Time: 0739 HOURS
Location: Elm Hill, Alabama

It wasn't until he'd already parked the cruiser beside Tracy's late model Honda Accord and turned the corner to enter the office that Daniel spotted the blue Lincoln Continental with Government plates resting on Main Street.

Feeling a slight burn at the base of his neck, he sucked in a deep breath, displaying his most casual smile before twisting the doorknob and entering. Tracy was handing the man a steaming cup of coffee in a Styrofoam cup, both standing to the right of the Communications console. "Mornin', Sheriff. Just in time for a fresh cup," she said with a smile, stirring her own cup with a plastic spoon.

The man turned to face Daniel, and the Sheriff was instantly taken back by the overwhelming aroma of Old Spice cologne. "Good to meet you, Sheriff. Peter Krane, Federal Bureau of Investigation."

Daniel took the man's outstretched hand and shook it firmly. The man's voice was impossibly deep, as if he were speaking through a surgically implanted bullhorn.

He looked to be in his late forties to early fifties, thin build, short-cropped hair, with deep grooved wrinkles at the corners of his mouth and eyes. Daniel figured it was no stretch to concede that the man standing before him had seen his share of hard living. "Same here, Agent Krane. What brings the FBI to our neck of the forest?

Don't tell me it's that bootleg ring again? I told the ATF Regional Manager a few months back that the whole thing was a misunderstanding. We arrested the two sellers and they started spitting out names of innocent folks. I didn't think--"

The agent quickly waived him off, leaning against a small metal filing cabinet before taking a brief sip of coffee. "Good java," he remarked with a slight grimace. Daniel fought back a giggle at the obvious lie. "No, this isn't an ATF matter, Sheriff. I'm on a missing person junket, actually. I've got a case I wanted to run by you. Just hoping to pick up a useable lead. Got a report the missing party was headed this way, so I had to at least check it out before heading further south to Birmingham."

The man's gravelly tone seemed to ease a bit the more he spoke, although Daniel found it virtually impossible to comprehend each word as a separate entity, instead forced to wait for the entire sentence to be completed before fully comprehending its overall meaning.

The sheriff gestured for the man to sit at his desk while he and Tracy remained standing.

"We don't see many strangers in Elm Hill, Agent Krane. Not exactly a hot bed of tourism, as you've probably figured out already."

Krane again sipped his coffee before responding. Daniel had filled his own cup in the meantime and was savoring the stout aroma as an alternative to the cloud of cheap cologne filling the room. "Like I said, Deputy, it's a long shot, but I had to at least give it a fair shot."

Folding her tan, muscular arms across her chest, Deputy Morton glanced over at Daniel and shrugged, as

130

if waiting for her boss to proceed with any further inquiries.

"The missing party is?" Daniel asked while continuing to inhale the aromatic steam rising from his cup.

Pulling a small white envelope from his front suit pocket, the man then removed a three by five color photo and reached over the desk to hand it to the deputy "Clarence Owen Richardson, black male, age thirty-two His family reports he was living in Huntsville, although they could provide no specific street address. Richardson was an indigent. We've had...*several* reports from a local Huntsville hobo jungle of missing street people."

Daniel stepped next to Tracy and studied the photo. It displayed a head and shoulders shot of a large black man wearing shoulder pads and a white jersey with the number sixty-eight etched on each upper biceps in bright yellow. The man was shaved bald and wore a nasty, comical sneer.

"Clarence had played college ball at North Alabama University for two years, then dropped out of school to sign up with the fledging XFL's Birmingham Bolts franchise. He lasted only a bit longer than the league itself, cut from the squad after three games. His family had stated he had a horrendous weakness for crack cocaine and heroin. They hadn't heard from him in a month or so, later discovering he was a regular at a jungle just outside the Huntsville City limits. Local PD handed the case to us a few days ago."

A hard, straight rain suddenly thumped the roof overhead, causing the trio to pause momentarily.

"Cloud burst. Never saw that comin' on the drive in," Deputy Morton remarked, glaring into the torrential downpour now coating Main Street.

Daniel continued to study the photograph, noticing a deep scar on the right side of the black man's face, a jagged groove that ran the length of the young man 's cheek almost to the base of his neck. "What makes them think he passed through Elm Hill?" he finally asked.

Agent Krane casually rested his elbows atop the sheriff's desk, lowering his head like a man preparing for a mid-morning 'power nap.'

"One of the hobo jungle residents stated that Clarence was headed to Birmingham to look for a missing friend of his, a fellow indigent known only as 'Bow- Wow.' Supposedly this Bow-Wow fellow told Clarence he was going to 'take the scenic route' to B-town, being that he wanted to avoid the Troopers on the interstate because of some past warrants. Clarence drove a rusted out seventy-eight Nova that hadn't seen a legal tag in years. We found the vehicle broken down six miles north of Elm Hill two days ago No Clarence or Bow-Wow to be found"

The sheriff handed the photo back to the agent, who then placed it back into the tiny envelope and re-pocketed it.

"Agent Krane, I wish we were able to provide some useful info, but I can safely bet that no one in or around Elm Hill has seen or come into contact with either man. Like my deputy said, we rarely see strangers in these parts, and an unknown black male, especially one the *size* of your basic Army tank, would stand out like a cannon ball in a bowl of corn flakes."

Deputy Morton spoke just as the agent started to stand. "We can ask around, Agent, but like Dan... like the sheriff said, it's not likely. We have only a handful of

African-American citizens in Elm Hill, and all of 'em are lifelong citizens. Your man might have driven straight through with no one the wiser, but if he stopped to get gas, we only have two gas stations he could've used as a pit stop."

The agent strolled towards the office door, careful to place his empty coffee cup into a nearby trash container. Daniel noticed the man walked with a slight limp, seemingly favoring his right leg. "No need to bother, Deputy. I've already spoken to attendants at both the Shell station and the BP. They reported no sightings of *any* out-of- towners within the last few days, least of all a black male or possibly two."

"Probably thumbed his way to B-Town after breakin' down," Deputy Morton said just as the phone on her desk began ringing. She nodded to the agent and turned to retrieve it.

"Excuse me, Agent."

Daniel peered out onto Main Street as a Peterbilt semi hauling petrol sailed by, tossing thick waves of rainwater onto the nearby sidewalk and onto the office windowpane. He turned back around just as the agent was offering him a business card.

"If you do happen to hear anything, Sheriff, please call my cell number. I'm headed back to Birmingham. More than likely both men are camping out near the tracks downtown, making new friends as wine bottles and syringes are being passed around."

Deputy Morton was hanging up the phone just as Daniel began to reply and paused to adjust her glasses, an oft-performed ritual during the course of the day. "You headin' out already, Agent?"

Agent Krane turned to her and grinned. Daniel

couldn't help but compare the man's radically insincere expression to that of a used car salesman. "On my way to the Steel City, Deputy Morton. More than likely that's where the trail will end. I always feel for the families of such men. They spend lifetimes worrying over matters completely out of their control."

Daniel took the man's outstretched hand once more, as did his deputy a moment later. "Thanks for the coffee and your time, folks."

"No problem whatsoever. If we hear anything, we'll buzz you right away," Daniel said just as the man stepped through the door and walked gingerly over the wet pavement towards the waiting Continental.

With a furrowed brow and slightly squinted eyes, Daniel observed the man as he carefully scanned the block before entering the vehicle and slowly driving away.

Seconds later, Deputy Morton's light tapping on his right shoulder broke his daze. " Well, that's a first, huh Dan?"

"What's that, Trace?" he replied, his movements a bit skittish as he walked around her and back towards his desk.

"Never met an actual FBI man, that's all. I never knew they handled such mundane cases. Poor guy must'a royally pissed off his boss at the bureau, ya think?"

His chair still warm from the other man's body heat, Daniel leaned back and studied the business card momentarily before tossing it haphazardly into a desk drawer. For just a split-second, he had felt an overwhelming urge to call the Bureau Branch in Huntsville to verify not only Agent Krane's story but also the man's ID. He quickly shrugged off such a notion as

Tracy stepped up and leaned against a corner of his desk.

"That was hollow leg...uh, Hoyt Wilson on the phone," she quipped, again pushing her glasses up the bridge of her nose.

"Calling to thank yours truly for the cab ride yesterday, I take it."

"Well, that and to remind us about the noises he's been hearin' around his place."

Daniel leaned up and placed his elbows in almost the exact position as Agent Krane had minutes before. "Noises? Oh yeah, he did manage to mumble such a tale to me, as I recall, in between belches and heaves. Wasn't real specific. I guess a fifth or two of George Dickel could definitely alter one's communications skills, not to mention that of perception."

"You want me to drive out there? He sounded sober as a preacher's wife."

"I'll ride up after lunch. You've got that Founders' Day meeting at one, remember?"

Deputy Morton suddenly frowned as if pinched, her drawn out groan resembling that of a woman suffering from intense abdominal cramps.

"Aww, hell, Dan. Why *me*? Two hours of listening to those old farts talk about Tomato Queens and sack races? I'd rather clean porta-potties at the construction site with a toothbrush. If the mayor calls me 'She-Hulk' one more time, I'm gonna knee him in his shriveled up old--"

Managing to keep a straight face despite the urge to guffaw aloud, Daniel raised his hand's palms up to cut her off.

"Now, *now*, Trace. You know the mayor has always had a crush on you. Don't take it personally. Man's been

135

a widower for over a decade now. Besides, you know how important Founders' Day is to the community. We need a day set aside to reflect and forge ahead as a township."

Gripping her stomach and bowing as if to be physically ill, the deputy couldn't help but giggle as she leaned back up. "Stop. Please just stop. If you spout anything about 'civic pride' or 'duty to one's hometown' in this ramblin' speech, I'm gonna hurl sausage and eggs all over your finely polished boots, Sheriff."

" Okay, okay, but you get the picture. One of us has to be there to arrange the blocking off of main street, where the cruiser fits in, blah blah blah, and you know I don't like to pull rank, but.."

"You are."

"Darn tootin' I am. I *hate* that crap."

Deputy Morton turned to retrieve her cap before sauntering slowly towards the front door. "Going on patrol now, Boss. Get the squad car back to you before lunch," she spat indifferently, although the tight smile she displayed ruined the illusion of anger.

"No problem, and be careful out there, *She-Hulk*."

"Oh, you're hilarious. A regular Jim Carey on stilts…" she mumbled while exiting.

The phone rang a moment later, and Daniel knew before answering the subject of the call. I t was a call he'd been waiting on since the email a day before. A former citizen of Elm Hill was either in town already or was at least on his way. Rubbing his temples like a chronic migraine sufferer, Daniel reached for the phone with a shuddering dread shooting through his veins like a surging virus.

136

The car crept to a complete stop at the rear of the old homestead, having matted down the tall weeds and dried grass along the narrow, deserted trail leading to what had once served as a backyard. A badly rusted mailbox that read 'Whitmore' in faded red letters had sat at the drive entrance, the pole that it sat upon engulfed by overgrown vegetation.

From its ragged, worn appearance, it was obvious the wooden, one-story structure hadn't entertained human inhabitants in several years, if not a full decade. The front porch was rotted completely through in spots, and layers of pine-straw covered shingles hung from all corners of the home like overgrown bangs. A wide, wooden storage shed that owned barely half of its original roof sat a few dozen feet from the back door, and the man shot it a weary glance as he exited the car and cautiously began surveying his new surroundings.

He entered the dilapidated lean-to through a thick oak door that had been standing partially ajar, his right hand instinctively moving to a holster tucked near his left armpit. What had been the kitchen greeted him initially, all that remained to identify it as such being a round, dust-coated boiler stove and rotted cabinets that hung open like fossilized maws waiting for a long-overdue feeding.

He strolled into the adjoining room a bit more at ease, the set of his shoulders and upper body not quite as tense. He understood it never, *ever* paid to be careless, regardless of how tranquil a scenario appeared. The eternal guard had to be on alert at least somewhat, no matter the banality of the circumstances.

What had been the living room held only a single wooden high-back chair at its center, a portion of the ceiling's decomposing roof hanging down in thick clumps of insulation and torn, twisted wiring. The man wiped a hand over his close-cropped hair, sighed unenthusiastically and pulled an ivory colored handkerchief from his back pocket. After wiping off the seat and back portions of the still surprisingly sturdy chair, he sat with a loud huff and casually crossed his legs, looking as if he were waiting for a bus on a deserted street corner.

Even as his body grew visibly more relaxed, the only sound permeating the secluded area being that of the constantly croaking bugs in the neighboring forest, his mind began the arduous yet strangely soothing task of calculated detail processing.

There was no doubt that the tiny burg of Elm Hill was the 'Hot Zone.' The trail dead-ended within a five-mile radius on all sides of the city limits. Six men from three separate townships; Memphis, Nashville, and most recently Huntsville. All six telling friends that they'd been offered 'good paying, steady employment' south of the aforementioned cities. All six witnessed entering vehicles that none within their circle recognized (although the vehicles in question were always of a different make and model). All six never heard from again. All six with either a military or athletic background, or both.

No less than three witnesses had watched Clarence Richardson enter a dark blue Ford pickup (late 80s to early 90s model) on a Huntsville downtown street just a few hundred yards from the Hobo jungle just as dawn had broken on July 1st. Almost eight weeks later and even

138

his closest contacts, both family members and jungle associates, hadn't heard a single word from a man they all stated was apt to keep in touch no matter the hardship. Three weeks before the earth seemed to have opened up and swallowed the man whole. Similarly, a cohort of Clarence's named Will 'Bow-Wow' Jeffries, a thirty-six year old black male and one-time Green Beret, had seemingly taken the same route to permanent banishment Clarence had told friends he'd hoped to 'find' Will while working in Birmingham. As it presently stood, both men had either been abducted by aliens or fallen into a black hole somewhere down Highway 76 from Huntsville to Birmingham.

The man knew better, as did his dedicated, intelligent, yet undeniably *deranged* cohort. Eighteen years of dogged pursuit, following threadbare leads that eventually led nowhere. Almost two decades of scanning TV and newspaper reports and later Internet news sources, paying off countless government and state contacts for information that more often than not was utterly useless. Dozens of crimes, from embezzlement to simple theft, had been plotted out and committed in the name of retribution. Monies obtained both legally and (mostly) illegally spent almost as soon as it appeared to payroll the search. A search that the man and his partner had sworn to see through while laying in adjoining deathbeds eighteen years and two months ago.

Their quarry was near, he realized with a mix of apprehension and elation, his gut a swirling nest of butterflies. The man removed a small beeper from his left pants pocket just seconds before it buzzed, never ceasing to be amazed at the inner radar his mind possessed. It was a phenomenon he could only credit to the ruthless beating

139

he had endured all those years ago, for he had displayed no such talent prior to that particular incident.

Glancing at the flashing numerals, he quickly punched them into his cell p hone and gently massaged his aching right temple, the only obvious side effect to his psychic episodes.

His colleague answered before the first ring was even complete. "Aaron, you still in Oak Hill?" she asked, her tone ultra-cool as usual.

"*Elm* Hill, my dear, get your trees straight. Yes, I've taken up residence, so to speak," he replied in the thick, guttural voice that had also been a result of the same mass trauma that enabled him to 'sense' certain proceedings just moments before actual occurrence.

"You've spoken to the sheriff's department?"

"Less than half an hour ago, my dear. They didn't even ask for my official ID from the Bureau. These small-burg lawmen rarely do, I've noticed. That was certainly money well spent. Exactly how much did we shell out for the fake docu--"

"Goddamn it, Aaron, it was a necessary expense. Now, what *did* you find out? Had they seen Richardson or Jeffries?" she barked, obviously struggling to maintain her infamous cool. The man truly enjoyed pushing her buttons, although he had never managed to export true anger from the woman, a goal he couldn't help but good-naturedly strive to accomplish as the mission had proceeded.

"Hide nor nappy hair, sweets. I told them he'd dumped his car just outside the city limits and that he'd been headed into Birmingham. They punted, having stated that the presence of two unknown black males within their jurisdiction would have caused at least a few

140

residents 'gums to flap. No such talk hit the streets, I'm afraid."

There was a short pause, and the man could hear the woman's short, huffing breath as it increased in intensity. He smiled, awaiting the impending rebuttal.

"Then why exactly are you camping out in Hobokin? Get back here ASAP. I may have a new lead near Atlanta. A local junkie and former light heavyweight boxer has been reported miss-"

"Cool your jets, apple cheeks. He's *here*."

The woman's raspy breathing rapidly increased. The man grinned ever wider. "What do you mean...h-he's *there* ? Richardson and Jeffries are more than likely smoking crack in Birmingham as we speak, maybe even down in F.L.A or Louisiana. Listen, stop yanking my chain, you miserable asshole. You know I can't stand it when yo-- "

"I said he's here, woman. Those men were here, as well. *He* drove them from Huntsville. Just as he shuttled the men from Memphis last November, more than likely with the promise of a job and fresh start."

"B-but how can...you be...for certain, Aaron? If we're going on nothing but one of your infamous 'Brain Pulses', we might end up wasting time we can little afford to lose," she spat indifferently, although a barely noticeable tint of excitement coated the words.

"I'd bet my...*our* lives on it, sugar dumpling. Just departed the local sheriff's office. Their lack of useable info, although not surprising, left me not in the best of moods. I was seriously drained, body and mind. Hadn't driven but a few miles from the Main Street when it kicked in. Fingers began to tingle and burn like I'd dipped 'em in battery acid. I had to pull over near this

141

rather spacious pasture which smelled of ancient cow-droppings, my head ringing like a school bell had been implanted between my ears. Believe me when I tell ya, sweet thang, I've never felt a more intense jolt in the last fifteen years. The son of a bitch is in *or* around Elm Hill, Alabama. He's playing small town farmer Brown, but he's up to his old tricks.

No...*doubt*... about...it."

Another pause, although minus the harsh breathing.

"Has our day f-finally come, Aaron? Is...it finally here?" the woman cried quietly, the simple sound of which sent a faint tingle of exhilaration up the man's spine.

"Damn right it is, babe, and we're gonna savor it, believe you me. What's your ETA?"

"The equipment is locked and loaded and the van is lubed and ready to roll. You can direct me in on the way. Take me... no more than ten hours, max. It'd be less of course, but then most people aren't forced to make hourly pit stops, and then only to rest stops equipped with the proper handicapped facilities for one such as I, that rare breed of half-female, half- *toaster oven* who takes fifteen to twenty minutes just unhooking herself from the car seat, rolling onto the roadway like a goddamned *tin can* with a head, one working arm and half a fucking eye!" the woman ranted hysterically, a pent up release that caused the man to wince as if smelling a foul odor while holding the phone several inches from his ear.

"I want that motherfucker to suffer, Aaron. I want him to suffer for days on end--"

"Not to worry, my sweet. Mister Hate will definitely be forced to preview *hell* before he actually makes the trip."

Minutes later, Aaron Kyle sat completely motionless, staring at the stained, cracked wall in front of him as if entranced. A small droplet of spittle had formed at the right corner of his mouth, where a wry smile had frozen into place.

He had ten short hours to pinpoint the quarry's position before the boss arrived to supervise the actual termination. The temptation to jump the gun and perform the act himself would be overwhelming, he knew. The mere thought of placing a nine millimeter securely against the man's temple just seconds before jerking the trigger never failed to give Aaron the beginnings of a modest hard-on, and it was a fantasy he'd both awoken to and fallen asleep contemplating for just under two decades.

The grumbling and groaning at his midsection eventually shook him back to reality, and he arose to check the contents of the Continental's well-supplied trunk for an early evening meal.

Even as he loaded the large cooler into the kitchen area and began rummaging for just the right cold-cut to slap between bread pieces, Aaron's heart palpitated wildly as the video shoot displayed in his inner mind's eye replayed as if stuck permanently in rewind mode.

He could literally smell and taste the gun smoke, as well as the coppery stench of freshly spattered blood. He clearly saw the man's battered, lifeless face, frozen in an eternal grimace of unspeakable pain. He saw the fist-sized hole the slug had created upon exiting the man's skull. He could hear the loud clapping and howling laughter in the background as his boss released years of pent-up frustration and anger in a few short moments of unabashed celebration. Most of all, Aaron felt the knot at

143

his gut unwind. A knot he had previously thought to be unyielding; unbreakable.

Hours later, while sipping from a cool bottle of Lipton's iced tea, Aaron Kyle stared glassy-eyed as the sun gradually sank behind a thick line of pines just south of the abandoned homestead and a chorus of crickets filled the forest with its nightly concerto.

The warped, rather hideous smile had yet to completely leave his face, even as an uncontrollable tick caused the trigger finger of his right hand to curl and uncurl spasmodically.

***

Deputy Tracy Morton had re-entered the sheriff's office at exactly two-thirty that afternoon, gladly swapping ninety-degree heat for the cool air conditioning trapped within.

Sticking a yellow post-it to the notepad she had brought with her from the meeting, she had first scribbled the words *Founders 'Day Jollies* across the top sticky before placing them at the center of the sheriff's desk. Sipping from a semi-warm bottle of Evian, she groaned as her rear end settled uneasily into her own squeaky chair. Her husband's chicken-scratch writing was easily identifiable on the piece of bond paper taped to her computer monitor.

MISSED YOU AT LUNCH...SEE YOU AT DINNER, MUSCLES... SNEAKY PETE

Instinctively checking her watch, Tracy frowned at her forgetfulness and reached for the phone. She halted in mid-dial and quickly replaced the receiver, recalling Pete telling her that they were in the middle of a bi-annual inventory at the feed 'n seed, which translated to 'no personal phone calls allowed' for everyone involved. In checking her wastebasket, she noticed the wadded up clear wrap and the empty Mountain Dew can, accompanied by the faint aroma of bologna and mustard.

"Food of the gods, it ain't. Lord, I've gotta learn to cook and feed that boy right or I'm gonna lose his scrawny butt to a stiff southern breeze one of these days," she muttered, tossing the remains of her bottled water into the same basket.

The com center radio squelched to life just as she'd found a comfortable leaning position. "Deputy Morton, this is mounted patrol…checking in, over," the sheriff's voice chimed in cheerily.

"Go ahead, Sheriff. You out at Checkpoint Chickie? Over."

The sheriff paused before answering, no doubt to properly conceal his outward delight in her perfectly worded 'Andy Speak' response. Her supervisor was the self-proclaimed 'King of *The Andy Griffith Show* Trivia', a fanatical follower of the 'Mayberry Reruns Club' who once claimed to have sat through an entire 48 hour TV Land '*Andy Griffith Show* Marathon' without missing a single episode. Tracy, a novice by comparison, nevertheless rarely missed an opportunity to 'stump the king.' "That's a negative, Deputy Morton," came his openly bemused reply, "got side-tracked on my way to Hoyt's, so I'm just now heading his way. Those speeding truckers out at Checkpoint Chickie will have to wait, I'm afraid. How'd the Founders 'Day proceedings go? Over."

Adjusting her glasses with a loud sigh, Tracy then inhaled deeply, as if prepping for a deep-sea dive. "Left the detailed notes on your landfill, I mean desk. Gist is

145

this; Barbara Kyle will don the Tomato Queen Crown for the record breakin' third straight year. Also, your old school pal Todd Platt is donatin' his flatbed this year, bringin' the float count to four. Also, Wilbur Potter has agreed to supply the soft drinks and 'tater chips from the Piggly Wiggly, but flat refused to include the ice. Not to worry, though, as Claire Vincent leaped to the rescue by sayin' her meat market would be proud to do so. Over."

"And the mayor's contribution? Over," the sheriff queried. Tracy didn't have to envision his broad smile to know it was present.

"He kept us all on the edge of our seats before givin' his okie-dokie. Over."

"And…"

She sighed again through a wide grin of her own. "You'll be amused to know he referred to me as *Xena, Warrior Princess* as I departed his office. Satisfied *now?* Over."

"Xena? Oh, that's classic. I'm sure he pictures you wearing medieval garb and swinging a fifty-pound broadsword. Over."

"Sure he does, Sheriff. Probably not only thinks it, but also yearns to yell out Xena! Whenever he's chokin' his own chi—"

"Now, now, Deputy, that is our boss you speak of. Over."

"Uh, huh. You getting near Hoyt's place? Over," she said, quickly shifting gears before the subject of Mayor Jenkins turned from comedic to profane.

"Almost close enough to smell his homemade wine a'brewing. Over."

"What delayed you getting out there, Sheriff, if you don't mind my askin'?

146

Actually, I don't care if you mind or not. Over."

"Well, uh, Kara had this soccer game and I stopped by the school to watch a few minutes. Over."

Leisurely shaking her head up and down, Tracy's frown transformed into a resigned smirk. *Just* as I suspected. You seemed a bit too eager to meet up with old hollow leg."

"Well, uh...I...you see...the thing is...I...uh..." he stammered in a deliberate, mechanical monotone.

" Yeah, yeah, whatever. Hey, you want me to wait for ya or close up at four? Over."

"Lock 'em up if I ain't back. Go home and feed that toothpick of a husband. Last time I saw him, he looked like a Halloween decoration. One of those hanging skeleton chimes. Over."

"Got'cha, Chief. I'll be workin' out if you need me. Over."

"Tracy, if your arms get any bigger, Todd's gonna put you to work at his warehouse as a forklift. Over."

"Can't start slackin' now, Sheriff. I'm edgin' up to two-hundred on my bench press. By the way, while you're out in Hoyt 's neck of the woods..." she purposely hesitated in order to allow the interruption she knew was inevitable.

"...Yeah, I'll make sure to ask him, for at least the hundredth time, where he's getting the booze. Tracy, you are nothing if not doggedly persistent. Over," he replied tiredly.

"Thanks, boss. You never know, maybe he'll crack this time. There's no way Hoyt is makin' that many trips to Jefferson County to get the stuff. There's a 'legger out there we ain't nabbed yet. Over."

"Over and out. See you in the a.m. , Xena, I mean,

Tracy."

"Call me if you need me, Sheriff," she spat sourly, replacing the mike before turning her attention to the computer monitor to its left. With just over an hour left on shift, she decided to spend it surfing the net, checking prices for health supplements on GNC.com.

The front door opening a few moments later barely broke her concentration, though the looming shadow that followed coaxed her eyes from the glowing monitor and onto the unexpected visitor standing just a few feet away.

The man could only be described as massive. His bowling ball shaped shoulders and tree-trunk sized arms were attached to easily the widest chest she had ever seen, the pecs of which were perfectly defined. He wore a tight fitting white T-shirt and blue jeans that looked to have been spray-painted onto astonishingly thick thighs. Sitting up straight as if called to attention in a military formation, Tracy fought to keep the uneasiness from showing in both her tone and movements.

"Yes sir, what can I do for you today?"

The man glared at her for a moment longer before speaking, and Tracy instantly felt her face begin to blush. "Looking for the Sheriff, Dan Whitlock. I'm supposed to...check in with him personally," the man said, his thin lips barely parting as he spoke. His face was well-tanned, almost leathery in appearance. He was balding on top, with long flowing brown locks tied into a ponytail at the back. Although he was clean-shaven, Tracy couldn't help but think the man resembled an early 90s version of Hulk Hogan, even minus the Hulkster's trademark Fu Manchu mustache.

"Sheriff's on patrol right now. I'm Deputy Morton. Can I be of service to--"

148

"Nope. Got to see him face to face, I'm told. Besides, me and old Dan got some catching up to do anyhow," the man interrupted calmly, folding his hulking arms across his chest.

Tracy Morton had rarely felt apprehension in the presence of anyone, much less actual fear. It had taken her at least a year to gain the respect of most, if *not* all, of the surrounding population, although she understood that some of the town's 'older generation' of males would never truly accept a female deputy. " Twenty-First Century World, Twentieth Century Minds," Daniel always said. The behemoth towering over her desk was the exception to the 'fear factor' rule, despite his calm, non-aggressive demeanor. She had instantly known who he was, of course. She also knew of his history. That, mixed with his imposing appearance had teamed to at least place a sizeable chink in her normally unbreakable facade of coolness.

"And your name is?" she asked while shuffling papers from one side of the desk to another, breaking his steely gaze and instantly ashamed of doing so.

"Curt Barber. Tell him I'm staying out at my folk's old house off Route 9. I've decided to fix the place up after all. Won't have a phone for a week or so, or might not decide to put one in 'til things are completely settled. He can drop by in the afternoon any time after four. I start work at Stony Watts Garage tomorrow, so he can find me there from seven a.m. 'til around three-thirty. I'd *rather* he came by the house, you understand," the man said before clearing his throat loudly, his glare never wavering.

"Understood, Mr. Barber. I'll let Dan…the she riff know you're in town," Tracy managed in the friendliest

149

voice she could manufacture. She stopped just short of saying "Welcome to town," a remark she deduced could have easily been misconstrued as sarcasm.

"I appreciate it," he said, pausing to study her a bit longer, his lips parting in the tiniest of smiles. The man had only the faintest of southern drawls, unusual for a man raised in the surrounding area. She chalked up his unfamiliar accent to the state penal institution and the 'melting pot' of nationalities housed within.

"You work out, Deputy?" he finally asked, his chin now resting atop his propped right fist, which was approximately the size of a honey-dew melon.

Tracy felt her chest expand in the familiar pride that normally accompanied such recognition. She noticed the man's expression before replying, a mocking smirk that was the definition of belittlement. Tracy realized instantly that she not only feared the man, but disliked him as well.

"Yeah, I hit the weights every now and then," she remarked through slightly squinted eyes, her smile as insincere as her visitor's curiosity.

"Good deal. Should be mandatory for all in your line of work, I say. Nothing more sickening than a fat slob in a police uniform. I've seen my share of 'em, for sure."

With that, Curtis Barber turned on one boot heel and strolled away, careful to allow the front door behind him to close without slamming.

Deputy Tracy Morton spent the next minute trying to stop her hands from visibly shaking.

***

"Some weird happenstance goin' on, Sheriff. I kid

150

you not, *unnatural* happenstance."

Hoyt Wilson sat on his living room couch, a large circular fan tossing pages of yellow-tinted newspaper into various piles within the confined space.

Daniel remained standing, for want of a clean, uncluttered place to sit, and stared out from the living room's picture window, not an easy chore due to the years-old dust attached to the pane glass in thick smears. The place reeked of stale food and spilled booze. The carpet his boots rested upon held a cornucopia of various colored stains, most of which hung to the matted material like dried paste.

"Hoyt, do me a favor and be a little more specific. What kinds of disturbances are you talking about? Animal noises? Flying saucers?"

Sipping from a comically huge yellow coffee mug which read *NAVY TRAINED KILLER* in faded black letters, Hoyt Wilson paused, his forehead creased in thought.

He sat shirtless, his swollen, gray-hair coated midsection resembling an over-inflated basketball, although his arms looked surprisingly lean and well-toned. "Oh, they were human in nature, Sheriff Daniel. The screams and wails I heard were not from any critter I've ever come across."

Removing a small note pad and ballpoint pen from his left shirt pocket, Daniel stepped forward and propped his left boot on a small end table, careful to push away a moldy pizza box (*Tombstone three-cheese*, he noted) without dumping its remaining contents onto the floor. "Human screams? You're telling me you heard *people* screaming between here and Matson's place? When exactly was this, Hoyt?"

151

Vigorously scratching his stubble-covered chin, the man stared at the ceiling in deep thought. "First time was a few months back…might'a been late May or so, just turnin' hot then. The second time was…"

The pad propped on his kneecap, the Sheriff halted after briefly scribbling, shaking his head in disbelief. "Hoyt, why are you just now telling me about this? Two or three *months* have passed? You do have a working phone, correct?" he scolded, albeit mildly.

The man leaned forward in a clumsy lurch, spilling coffee onto the carpet next to his feet in the process. "Damn it, Sheriff, I did tell ya! You and that dyke-y lookin' deputy'a yours!" he bellowed angrily, coughing harshly immediately afterwards.

"Refresh my memory, Hoyt," Daniel replied, pen and pad placed back into writing position.

"You arrested me for fallin' asleep on the courthouse steps, remember? I was gonna talk with Mayor Jenkins about the god-awful postal service I was receivin'. Old Billy Hobbs wasn't deliverin' here but every other day, sometimes every three days. My bills were late by the time I received 'em…that lazy son of a--"

Daniel shook him off with a nod and a raised hand. "Alright, alright. I recall the arrest, Hoyt, but I don't remember you mentioning piercing screams in the night." The older man paused, rubbing the leathery skin beneath his square chin. "Well, I must'a told old Deputy Butch then. I'm bettin' she'll deny it, but if I didn't tell you I sure as hell *did* her."

"I'll make sure to ask her. Now, when was the last time you heard similar noises?" Daniel asked, his face and arms coated with fresh sweat. He would've bet a week's pay it was at least eighty-five degrees *inside* the house, the hot air being circulated by a floor fan that actually worsened the effect.

"Just a few weeks ago. It was a Sunday night. I 'member cause I was watchin' *X-Files* . It was a rerun, but I hadn't seen it. Some kind'a bat creature was killin' off a bunch of those Amish folks. I can't remember why it was after 'em, but it was a mean, pissed off SOB."

"Uh, Hoyt, what time was that? Early evening or later in the night?"

"Must'a been 'tween ten and midnight. Hard to recall down to the minute since I had sipped a little Southern Comfort that evening."

"Were they long, drawn out screams or short and stifled?"

"Aw, man, they were long and dragged out…like a wolf howlin' at the moon."

"Could you tell if they were male or female?"

"Pretty sure it was men both times, at least by the pitch of their hollerin'. Tell ya what though, whatever was causin' it made 'em cry out like scared females."

The sheriff finished his last few notes and leaned b ack up, pushing up his cap to rub beneath the bill. "How long did these cries go on?"

Hoyt licked his lips hungrily, patting his naked, bloated belly. "You want a sandwich, Sheriff Dan? I got some semi-fresh bologna in the fridge."

Just the thought forced Daniel to swallow his own bile just to halt its sudden ascent "No thanks, Hoyt. I…could use a glass of H- 2-O of you can spare it," he replied, tempted to add 'if you have a clean glass in the place" to close the request.

Pushing himself up from the couch with a pained scowl, Hoyt suddenly resembled a man twenty years his

153

senior.

"Oh, and the crying and howlin' only lasted a minute or two, but long enough to shake my foundation plenty. Almost sobered me up... *almost*," he smiled, wobbling off towards the adjoining kitchen.

Hoyt re-entered the living room a moment later holding a tall glass of water for Daniel and a similar glass filled with orange juice for himself.

Sipping cautiously, Daniel was surprised to find not only the glass sparking clean, but the contents cool and refreshing.

"Tell ya what though, Sheriff, even those damn rebel yells beat the crap outta all that hammerin', sawin', and dozer work from a few years back. You would have thought old man Matson was building a friggin' sports arena. If not for passin' out with a little help from my...uh...bottled associates, I would have gone the whole year of 2001 without a decent night's slumber, you know?"

"What *was* he building, Hoyt?" Daniel asked between gulps.

"Told me it was a storm cellar. I caught a glimpse of the outside door a few months later. Didn't look like much to me in comparison to all the racket he made creatin' her."

Daniel nodded, handing the glass back to Hoyt, who was still nursing his juice. "Appreciate it, Hoyt. Well, think I'm gonna pay me a little visit to Matson right now. See if he heard any of the same ruckus."

Hoyt smirked and proceeded to wipe a hairy forearm across his mouth before releasing a loud, ringing belch. "Good luck on pryin' more than five words outta that strange bird, Sheriff Dan. I've lived next to 'im for

154

almost ten years and he ain't said enough to me to complete a whole blessed paragraph."

Pocketing his pen and pad, Daniel headed towards the propped front door and paused just before exiting. He turned back around with one hand raised, as if offering his surrender. "Before I go, Hoyt, you know I gotta ask. Who's providing the happy water?"

"Aw, Sheriff, why you wanna go ruin such a cordial visit? You know I get all my stuff from the runs I make to Jefferson County."

"What I *know*, Hoyt, is that you've been spotted on several occasions cruising downtown Elm Hill with Clint Massey, and that every time we have to drag you from the main square as drunk as a monkey, your car is sitting right here in the driveway. Is Clint selling again, Hoyt?"

Turning his head to peak out into the late afternoon sun, Hoyt began to whistle the theme from *The Andy Griffith Show*. "You still Mayberry's number one fan, Sheriff Dan? Gonna defend your title at the Founders' Day trivia contest again this year?"

Wearily shrugging his shoulders, Daniel turned and walked out without responding.

"Let me know what old Grumpy Gus down there tells ya, Sheriff. If he says he didn't hear anythin', he's lyin' through his dentures!" the older man yelled at his back.

***

Curtis Barber drew many stares within the narrow aisles of the Piggly Wiggly store, the majority of which he chalked up to his physical appearance Others he could sense were gawking for a different reason. They either

155

had known him in his youth, or knew *of* him as the sole convicted violent felon the township of Elm Hill had ever produced. He checked out amid deafening silence and awkward stares, the cashier (a gaunt, gray haired man he faintly recognized) never bothered to verbally acknowledge his presence during the scanning process. The old man had croaked a pathetically insincere 'have a good'un' while handing Barber his change, although their eyes never actually met.

Loading the grocery bags into the back of his Uncle Maury's late eighties model Ford pickup (which had been 'loaned' to him for thirty bucks a week from his uncle's car lot in Birmingham), Barber could feel the eyes burning into his bulky, V-shaped back. Despite the ninety pounds of muscle added to his frame thanks mostly to the sheer boredom of incarceration, they *knew*. No matter the total baldness up top and the addition of more than a few nasty scars on or about his face, they *knew* . The passing of almost two decades did little to disguise his identity within the tightly wound perimeters of his old stomping grounds. He was in for some serious resistance, no doubt. The small town variety that started slowly, then built to a fever pitch before drastic measures were eventually attempted. He was prepared for such a shit-storm, having spent most of the last decade playing out literally hundreds of possible confrontations, both of the verbal and physical variety, and exactly how he would react to each.

Cruising back down the main drag a few moments later, Barber was again taken back at just how little had changed in the eighteen winters since his eyes had last rested on the town of his birth. It was as if he had stepped out of a time capsule of his own creation , one which had

156

dramatically accelerated his internal aging process while leaving the surrounding landscape eerily unscathed. If not for the newer model vehicles occupying the roadways, the majority of which were either SUVs or tiny, box-shaped foreign jobs, Barber could have easily convinced himself it was still 1988.

Peering over at the sheriff's office one final time before passing, he spotted the thick-bodied female deputy with her back to the street, seemingly locking up for the evening. She reminded him of a female CO back at his old prison unit, a muscled-up dyke named Rozier (nicknamed 'Razor-rooter') who rarely missed an opportunity to crack a few skulls when the need arose. Barber wondered if the deputy owned even a portion of the *inner*-toughness she seemed to revel in displaying on the outside. Elm Hill wasn't exactly a prime testing ground for measuring the grit and indomitable spirit of a trained lawman. Directing traffic at a church picnic or writing the occasional parking ticket rarely prepared one to handle a major felony. Of course, in the century-plus history of Elm Hill, there had been only *one* such scenario arise to test the local law's mettle.

Turning sharply to the right as he departed Main Street for the narrow two-lane that was highway six, Curtis Barber sported a tight smile that most would have characterized as a pained scowl. Thinking back to the jittery expressions worn by Sheriff Lance Hendricks and Deputy Bill Detmer the night of his arrest in connection with the murder of Debbie Rainer, both had failed said test *miserably*.

"Hope you're made of sterner stuff, Sheriff Dan Whitlock," he murmured just before making a left onto a dirt-gravel one lane, the pickups aged shocks creaking loudly with the effort.

"...'cause the true exam ain't long in coming."

***

Daniel held his cap in one hand while wiping the dripping sweat from his forehead with the back of the other. Standing beneath the carport 's overhang, he was grateful for the shade, although it provided little relief from the smothering humidity.

"But you did hear *something,* correct?" he asked while replacing his cap with a single, firm tug.

Doug Matson stood motionless, so much so that from a distance his frozen form could have easily been mistaken for a posed statue. His stony gray eyes rarely blinked, his forehead locked in a permanent furrow. The black, button-up shirt he wore was cut off at the shoulders, revealing muscular yet uncut biceps and forearms that were weirdly similar in girth. *Lumberjack* arms, Daniel decided.

"Wild dogs, more than likely," Matson replied stoically, his nostrils flaring as if stifling an impending yawn.

Daniel shuffled his boots from side to side and stared out onto the perfectly manicured front yard and the shining, recently waxed red Chevy Blazer parked a few dozen feet down the paved drive, resting in the wide shade of an ancient oak.

"You keep a neat place, Mr. Matson. I sure wish your neighbor to the north could develop the same habits."

When the man didn't respond, Daniel gestured to the left of the one story brick home, just past a line of

158

flawlessly pruned scrubs.

"Hoyt said you'd built yourself a grade-A twister shelter."

The older man nodded quickly, as if to dismiss the subject without any further queries.

Daniel could make out the shelter's angled entrance, a dark tinted oak door with a thick iron brace lain across the center. "Looks like a solid one, alright. Is it reinforced Texas style?" Daniel quipped, noting the man's continuing indifference that was growing increasingly irritating.

"Never been to Texas, Sheriff. I'm sure it'll withstand the worst *Alabama* has to offer, though," he replied, flashing a cursory smile that was the definition of disingenuous, and eerily similar to one Daniel had witnessed earlier that day by a certain FBI agent.

"Well, thanks for your time, Doug. If you do hear anything peculiar, don't hesitate to give me or Deputy Morton a ring."

"Take care, Sheriff," the older man replied, already having turned to re-enter the home before Daniel had even begun to walk away.

"See you at Founders' Day," Daniel blurted just as the front screen door closed with a clanging sound that effectively drummed out the last word.

Carefully backing the cruiser from the man's lengthy, winding drive, Daniel again eyed the storm cellar door as it came more clearly into view from the outer edge of the front yard.

A wide clearing covered in what resembled Kentucky bluegrass lay above and beyond the shelter, surrounded on all sides by a perimeter of young ferns that looked to have been planted within the past six months or so.

Daniel thought it resembled a green 'runway' of sorts, the grass so evenly cut and finely manicured as to look artificial. Douglas Matson had obviously invested ample amounts of time and money on such a project, a fact that was a bit perplexing considering how hidden and remote the man's home was from not only the main highway, but also from his closest (and sole) neighbor.

The house vanished from site as Daniel backed onto the gravel road that fronted it, and he couldn't help but shake his head cynically while glancing at his watch, which read four-seventeen p.m.

"A strange bird *indeed*, Hoyt old buddy. A species all his own, in fact," he whispered, the cruiser 's spinning tires created a billowy dust trail in their wake.

***

Arriving back at the sheriff's office at five-sixteen, delayed by a half-hour jawing session with Rob Hastings at the nearby BP while fueling the cruiser, Daniel discovered the first of several yellow Post-It notes Tracy had left hanging from the edge of his cluttered desktop.

It simply read: *C. Barber came by to say hey- seems like a real butt-boil to me – Trace.*

Reaching for the phone, he intended to dial Tracy's home number, but instead punched in his own. Kara answered in a sarcastic, scolding tone that never failed to amuse him. "What is it this time, Sheriff, closing in on the local bootleggers or is it that pesky double-parking problem out on Maple Street again? Must be an *extremely* serious dilemma, as you've already missed half of the 'Barney Fife, Mayberry Undercover agent' episode."

"Oh, it was, Kara-berry. Myself and Rob down at the gas station were debating the Crimson Tides chances in the SEC West this coming fall, not to mention when and if the mudcats were gonna start biting over at Mann Lake. Delay couldn't be helped, I'm afraid."

"Long as you understand, Sheriff Blabbermouth, that the chicken and dumplings that were done over an hour ago are now more aptly named 'chicken and boulders', and the accompanying rolls would be more suitable utilized as mortar shells at a National Guard artillery range."

He paused just long enough to study Tracy's hastily written note for at least the fifth time, his eyes dazed and unblinking.

"Keep that yard bird and gravel gravy warmed in the oven, my dear. I'm on my way as we speak."

"Spoken like the trained procrastinator that you truly are, father."

"Bye."

Daniel stared at the phone for just a moment longer, again contemplating a quick ring to his deputy before dismissing the idea once and for all. As his grand-pappy Dexter had always proclaimed, "Bad news can *always* wait for a later date."

As he rose to depart, clicking off the overhead lights along the way, a burning sensation similar to building indigestion racked Daniel's midsection like jagged claws across bare flesh.

Chapter Five
Changing Formats/Termination Game

DATE: 1 JUNE 1988
LOCATION: The Tranquility Motel, Denver, Colorado

TC Eastmon stood at the dust stained window of his second floor motel suite located in beautiful downtown Denver and felt the blood rush from his cheeks for at least the tenth time in the previous half hour.

TC alternated shadow boxing in front of a slightly cracked wall mirror, and taking short draws off of the second of five thick joints he'd rolled earlier in the evening. His bare chest and back were coated in sweat from the exertion, although his breathing remained fairly steady and unaffected.

Thirty minutes earlier he'd been lounging on a narrow, slightly soured couch, the TV turned to a free porn channel with the sound muted. TC realized better than anyone that the jive-talking, laid back, pimp cruising-down-the-boulevard façade he portrayed was hands down his most effective psychological weapon. The *man* had always underestimated his kind, and that was the weak underbelly he'd continue to exploit with merciless, simplistic ease.

His boys were counting on him, as he was them. They only had each other in the silent, secret war they fought, and TC had weeded through dozens upon dozens of potential soldiers through the last decade to build a crew he could trust with his own life and vice versa.

The prize the man was offering would be a decent enough haul if taken at face value. TC and his crew had ceased such small-time thinking long ago, however.

Whatever treasure existed to take from these men would be theirs. It was simply a matter of logistics and timing.

TC ran over the possible scenarios until they each had their own personal space in his subconscious, individual mental files he could pull from with just a single flash of inner imagery. Following the initial battle, he and the boys had a much larger till to raid.

He smiled happily at his own reflection before another bout of ghost sparing ensued. The gold -plated teeth reflected in his dark brown eyes were like metallic streaks of lightning caught on film.

"Kick ass, forget names, then stash the cash," he mumbled, the flesh of his mostly nude form stinging pleasurably from both the effects of the weed and the adrenaline rush of impending battle.

***

A mere three rooms down on the same exact floor, Kayla Lee carefully wrapped the palm-sized tape recorder into a small brown pouch, then placed it carefully atop a loosened ceiling tile she'd pulled free earlier. She then lowered herself onto the bed, sighing nervously.

Years of searching for a clue of the man's whereabouts; countless hours of contemplating exactly *why* she was so hopelessly obsessed with the pain of her sordid past; pubescent-based queries which begged to be answered before even a minor semblance of inner peace could be achieved. She had pumped out gallons upon gallons of perspiration over the past decade, honing her

163

physical skills and mental constitution to near perfection, or at least as near as possible in such a limited existence. Her mind was a virtual springboard of readiness, every possible hypothetical situation covered with a workable, sensible solution filed away as if on some inner hard drive within her subconscious.

Drying off after a hot, steamy shower, Kayla glared at her own glistening nakedness in the full-length mirror mounted on the outside bathroom door.

Hour-glass figure; firm, pert breasts; simmering, sumptuous hair that reached to the pit of her tightly toned buttocks. How long had it been since she'd felt the touch of another on such a goddess-like body? How long since she had even *desired* such contact? She realized her looks had been her ticket, the magic shiny key that opened doors that others weren't allowed access to simply by the plainness of their physical attributes. Her exotic looks and the thick aura of mystery which surrounding them was a lethal weapon with undeniable reach, and one she had utilized to perfection.

Kayla didn't bother to dress as she checked her alarm. Her masturbation was slow and sensual, her thoughts solely of the *man*. The man whose appearance was nothing more than a dim blur in her memory banks, but who somehow held her future in his alluringly dangerous grip. This she had always known, but until the past few weeks had never mustered the courage to envision a face to face encounter with the source of her ills.

She slept deeply, her dream the same as it had been for the past decade-plus. The man was making love to her, roughly and without consideration for her pain or discomfort. The knife he held tightly to her throat had the feel of jagged, sharp edged ice slicing ever-so-gently into the delicate flesh of her moistened throat.

As was normally the case, Kayla never awoke from such trauma. She would awake with the clock's blaring just as dawn broke to a familiar aching in her chest and upper abdomen. It would fade as the morning passed, as it always did, the virus initiated by nothing more than constant longing and the maddening loneliness she had endured for as long as memory served "Soon..." she whispered to herself convincingly while dressing in semi-darkness, "this *too* shall pass."

***

TIME: 1954 HOURS
DATE: 4 JUNE, 1988
LOCATION: 14TH Floor, Office Complex, Seattle, Washington

Aaron Kyle winced, his forehead giving the illusion of being permanently creased. It was an expression Earl Barron was growing increasingly tiresome of. "Sir, I've got to tell you with all honesty, and believe me...this isn't easy to say, but I cannot completely agree with this decision."

Barron calmly reached over and mashed out the tip of his cigar, loosening his tie with the other hand. He didn't look Kyle in the eyes, fearing not the other man's response to his reply, but his own temper, which was dangerously close to emerging full-force despite all containment efforts. "And why would that be specifically, Aaron my boy?" he asked timidly, leaning back and keeping his eyes pinned on the exquisite gothic

165

era water painting hanging on a far wall. The rushing creek water and foggy mountain setting made him instantly envious of the man who had been fortunate enough to reproduce such wonder in person.

Kyle was in mid-sentence by the time he snapped back to reality. " ...why end it *now*? Don't misunderstand me, sir, it's not like the guy makes me all warm and fuzzy inside. He's a sadistic, uncaring, unmerciful Neanderthal with absolutely no regard for human feelings or life, for that matter. Actually, those are the exact points that make him so *irreplaceable* in the grand scheme of things. I understand one of our Middle Eastern clients have dubbed him *Mister Hate*. Coming from such a vile, war-torn region, that's pretty high praise."

"Aaron, Aaron, Aaron..." the older man whispered, briskly massaging his forehead, "...you sat right here not three weeks ago and spelled out a grocery list's worth of the exact same reasons we *should have* Mason Parks eliminated. Alas, neither your pros nor cons have a place in the decision, my boy. Two recent items have come to light that serve as the core motive for updating the...plan for tomorrow's...actually later *tonight's* battle."

Kyle leaned forward and placed his elbows on the edge of the spacious desk, his eyes wide with schoolboy excitement, as if expecting to hear a juicy tidbit of gossip.

Barron sighed and rolled his eyes in response.

Kyle raised his hands palm up in exasperation, reminding Barron of a common street beggar. " *Tonight?* Well? Sir, as director of operations for tomorrow 's little skirmish, I am owed at least a reasonable explanation of why plans have been so dramatically altered."

"Fine. Number one, we have reason to believe a federal agency has been actively tracking Parks for some time, more than likely linked to the Markum case. The family has unlimited funds and has refused to let the case drop by the wayside. Not sure how close they are, but obviously if they find him...they find *us*. Number two, a very influential client has grown a bit bored with Mason, period. Just as in the world of professional sports, the man on top is loathed by as many people as he is loved and respected by. This client is responsible for almost half our company's profits thus his wish is our command, my boy. He wants us to change the format to more of a 'battle royal' wherein an entire group of combatants vie for the prize with each new taping. Kind of a 'Professional Wrestling' variation on our present theme. More on that in a moment, however."

Falling back into his chair, Kyle's disdain was plainly clear. "Jesus, sir. The logistics involved and potential problems that will arise in paying off a new winner each time, not to mention keeping them under wraps is...astronomical in nature. A thug like Parks is fairly easy to please; booze, hookers, raw meat and the occasional boat-load of steroids. What we don't need is a list of possible - make that *probable* - whistle blowers who have a sudden attack of conscience years from now. You know as well as I that--"

Barron halted the younger man with the simple raising of a finger. " Not to worry, Aaron my boy. I didn't say I was going to completely adhere to the man's every whim. Yes, my plan is to hold a single battle royal as detailed, the first and last of its kind as produced by our company. Aaron, I been thinking about this for quite a long while, and I must tell you now."

"What's that, sir?" Kyle replied somewhat cautiously, his jaws wound so tightly that the words

167

escaped only as a grim whisper. He could feel his meal ticket slipping away like shredded confetti in a monsoon.

"This business has afforded me a lifestyle like no other I could have invested so much time and effort into, but there are…factors, obstacles over the near horizon that concern me greatly. The pornography was shameful and…horrific enough, but the… future of what our clients refer to as 'termination films' is not only shaky at best, but not worth the toll its taking on my rapidly slipping health. I have never allowed the guilt of what we do to creep into my daily thoughts, nor affect my business sense. I find I can no longer separate the two worlds of gruesome, medieval violence for violence's sake, and the simple matter of financial well-being.

"The final volume in our series will chronicle the extermination of Mason Parks, period. It will be my swan song, Aaron. There will be no 'new format filmed under *my* supervision. It will be a 'battle royal' of sorts, but not in the way our number one customer expects. I have no doubts it will, however, be the record breaking 'bestseller' he hopes to purchase. Kyle, it's… become too much for my psyche to handle in the past few months. I'm a *grandfather* for Christ's sake. I have decided to act as such, as to insure the future of my family's heritage. I will not further jeopardize their lives by having my name defamed as a convicted felon."

Barron paused, finally meeting the younger man's gaze as to gauge his response.

Aaron Kyle sighed forcefully, lowering his face into the palms of his hands. His head lifted a moment later, an expression of pure, joyous relief pasted to his features like a form-fitting mask. His shoulders slumped noticeably, like a man receiving a much-needed dose of muscle-relaxers. For possibly the first time in their nearly five-year relationship, Earl Barron witnessed Aaron Kyle display a smile utterly void of insincerity. "Are we closing up shop, Sir? I m-mean, for *good?*" he finally managed, albeit a bit shakily.

"All things run their course, Aaron my boy. We're fast running out of track."

Kyle leaned up from the chair and positioned his outstretched hand over the older man's desk. "Sir...*Earl*...I can't thank you enough. Damn, this is hard to...explain. I feel almost...*reborn.*"

Shaking the younger man's hand briskly, the older man couldn't help but quench his building curiosity. "My god, Aaron, such calm acceptance was the last thing I anticipated. After all, the companies disbanding will of course mean the end of your present livelihood. There will be residual payments for a time, obviously, but..."

"To be honest, sir, I'm more than a little...shocked by my response as well. I have to admit that I've been mulling over a drastic lifestyle change for the past few months. Parks had gotten so...out of control that I had foreseen treacherous waters over the ship's bow. I have a substantial nest egg built. Think I'll give the legitimate side of the business world a go, kind of...feel out the territory, so to speak."

"Good for you, Aaron. You need...*deserve* a life that's less stressful, both for you and your budding family. I myself have grown tired of the constant worry, the persistent glancing over my own shoulder. When you deal with lowlifes and butchers, you inevitably discover that the traits of such individuals become your own over time."

Kyle fell back into his chair, his face suddenly

169

creased with worry. "What about... the clients, sir? Aren't they gonna be a tad pissed off at the end of our series? Many of the ones I've met, especially the South American and Middle Eastern spokespeople, have a mob mentality. How much of a danger do you suppose they'll pose to us once we announce the news?"

Barron rested his elbows on the desk, his chin propped on his upturned thumbs. " No such announcement will be forthcoming, my boy. Once the payments have been secured for the final volume, we 'll simply cease to exist. I believe the majority of the major customers will find themselves so, how should I say, 'blown away' by its contents and sales potential, they'll take little notice of us for months. By the time they even think to ask about a new volume, the smoke from our exit would have long drifted away. Don't fret for them, Aaron. They'll have little difficulty securing a new source for the vile entertainment they seek. The world of supply and demand involving such films won't end with our retirement. I feel we are backing away just at the right time, much like a star athlete calling it a day while still within his prime."

"What's the plan on taking out...uh, eliminating Parks?" Kyle asked with unbridled enthusiasm.

"*Mister Hate,* as you referred to him, will be paid an unscheduled visit at his ranch house early tomorrow morning. A visit that will include our two handpicked opponents, a mobile, three-man film crew to acquire the necessary shots for the taping, and a crew of efficiency experts for back-up purposes. Regardless of how it's carried out or who specifically does the honors, Mr. Parks' final breath must be captured in crystal clear clarity. I've set a release date for two weeks from today. I understand it's a bit of a rush, but the sooner the better for all concerned."

"Um, *efficiency* experts, Sir? How many men are we talking about here? I hate to be the worry wart, and I'm not doubting your ability to oversee such a project, but Parks is one mean Motherfu--"

Barron raised his left hand palms up, smiling politely.

"I've seen the tapes, Aaron. I know what the man's capable of. Not to worry.

Even unarmed and caught off-guard, I *don't* expect the two combatants to fall him. The backup crew consists of three heavily armed professionals who will surely earn the substantial fee we are providing."

Looking less than relieved, Kyle sat up as if suddenly pinched. "He's likely armed to the teeth, sir. Those cameramen are liable to film their *own* deaths--"

Barren nodded while thumbing through a thickly packed manila folder. "Surprisingly not so, Aaron. We've... kept a running tab on Parks whenever he left the ranch, airborne photo recon mostly. While he did made several stops at a local Army surplus warehouse, the only recorded purchases were that of a single combat knife and a pearl handled machete. You're familiar with Parks' attitude on firearms, Aaron. The man's ego controls and commands his warped psyche, which in turn has bought into the notion that killing in a way *other* than hand to hand combat is akin to cowardice in the extreme."

Kyle shook his head in scowling disbelief. "I have to believe the bastard has hardware stashed away somewhere in that house. Parks is a lot of things, but stone-cold *stupid* isn't one of them. He knew that there was always a possibility we'd come after him, and I can't buy the idea that he figured to hold off an assassination attempt strapped only with a knife and sword. T.C. Eastmon and the Asian girl are gonna get butchered more than likely, but…"

Placing the folder to one side, Barron began casually rummaging through a desk drawer. " The man considers himself a warrior from another time, Aaron. He does in fact 'buy into' the idea of facing such challenges with vastly limited weaponry. His mindset is brutish and prehistoric in nature. If he dies, he dies with his maniacal code of honor intact, no matter how badly outgunned, he refuses to stoop to the level of his attackers. Besides, the element of surprise would more than likely leave him little time to garner such weapons, even if he had them. The cameramen, by the way, will be donning thick Kevlar vests and protective headgear…just in case. Mr. Eastmon and Ms. Lee will be provided with the weapons earlier discussed, that being the rapier blade and crossbow. They of course, will not survive the attack, *regardless* of the outcome with Mason Parks. If everything works out as planned, our resident champion will make short work of bot h before our team steps in and provides final closure. Regardless of the structure of attack, it will surely make for fine entertainment."

Kyle started to respond, one hand partially raised, but hesitated once his eyes met the other man's.

"Something else, Aaron?"

"Sir, I kind of…promised Mr. Mandrake that if such a deal ever went down, I'd allow him the pleasure of participating. Could we…I mean, would you?"

"Mr. Mandrake has been a stellar employee within this firm. By *all* means."

"Thank you, Sir. Are you going along for the ride also?"

The older man nodded somewhat solemnly. "I feel it's my…obligation somehow, although I plan on keeping a fairly safe distance from the actual combat zone until all is clear. How about yourself, Aaron? There are still seats available if so desired."

"Sir," Aaron grinned devilishly, "wild horses couldn't drag me away."

Glancing at the shimmering Rolex adorning his right wrist, Earl Barron's eyes grew dramatically wide. "Hmm, better head on home and get a few hours rest, Aaron. We meet back here at one a.m. ETA to Conquest is three and a half hours. Thirty minutes of prep time will set mission activation at approximately four a.m."

Aaron Kyle stood stiffly after checking his own watch.

"Affirmative, sir. I'll tell the wife I'm catching a red eye to one of our southern distributors for an early morning conference."

"It's almost over, Aaron my boy. The final curtain is set to fall," the older man said, sounding a bit nostalgic.

The younger man paused before exiting into the dimly lit, deathly quiet hallway. " Sir, I personally haven't felt this psyched since my first piece of ass."

Never one to either appreciate or respond to vulgarity in any form, Earl Barron nonetheless smiled at the younger man's unrestrained eagerness. "To each his own, son. To each his own."

***

TIME: 0258 HOURS

173

DATE: 5 JUNE 1988
LOCATION: Parks Ranch, Conquest, New Mexico

After mixing his third rum and coke within the last half-hour, Mason Parks stretched out on an oversized leather couch and clicked the VCR off of 'pause' mode. Instantly, the separate piles of nude bodies on display across the large screen began to hump and grind in ritualistic rhythm, the expressions of each varying from slack boredom to a drug-induced lust brought forth solely for the benefit of a nearby camera lens.

Moments later, Parks rose from the couch and roughly ejected the tape, the plain white label reading *ORGIES GALORE, Volume Five* in large typed text. "Boring crap anyhow. I definitely have to upgrade the ol' skin flick collection," he muttered while fumbling with the TV remote, accidentally spilling a sizable portion of his drink in the process.

As was the normal practice the eve of a match, he had viewed his two favorite 'pre-game' flicks earlier that evening, *Faces of Death*, a documentary which featured horrific accidents and actual murders caught on tape, and the mid-seventies sci-fi flick, *Westworld*. Parks identified with the murderous android gunslinger played by Yul Brenner as a kindred spirit; mission-oriented, emotionless, relentless, and above all, *death* personified. Earlier that afternoon he had taken the Firebird for a leisurely ride through the surrounding canyon roads, most of which were eerily deserted once the moon arose to play the part of desert sentinel. Sucking on frosty Bud longnecks while reaching speeds up to one-ten on the mostly flat-surfaced highways, Parks had kept the stereo cranked with the likes of Black Sabbath's *Iron Man* and

174

the Fabulous Thunderbird's *Tough Enough* , anthems of unrestrained machismo from his personally recorded cassette of similarly themed tunes.

Gulping the remainder of his drink in one long swallow, he casually tossed the empty glass over his shoulder and winced as it shattered against a far wall. "Whoops. My fault. Put it on my bill, barkeep."

Clicking off the TV, wearing only a pair of cut off blue jeans, he then leaned back on the couch and belched loudly before peeking through the semi-darkness at the large clock hanging just over the set. Three-oh-eight a.m., and not even the faintest symptom of drowsiness, despite the continual barrage of booze.

Less than seven hours before the chopper arrived to shuttle him to the killing grounds, and sleep was as elusive as a virgin porn star. Normally, he slept soundly the night before a match, an almost coma-like state that prepped his senses to honed perfection for the combat to come. In analyzing the possible motives for his rare bout with insomnia, Parks first considered the new match format. Although it was obvious that the powers that be desired a more competitive product, he felt no apprehension whatsoever at the thought of simply being tossed another victim within the combat zone, regardless of the superior weaponry each would be supplied with as compared with his own. They were lambs to the slaughter, no more.

He then pondered the increasingly narcissistic attitude displayed of late by his so-called 'Superiors', meaning Mr. Slick and his creep-show sidekick, Mandrake the *turd-eater*.

Parks had a deep-seeded hunch that some seriously devious plots were being hatched behind his back, spawned in closed-door conferences between wealthy, well-dressed men puffing on expensive cigars. Men who might well have finally come to the conclusion that Mason Parks was becoming far too large of a liability to maintain on their payroll.

His midsection groaned and tingled as if to confirm such suspicions. Scanning the clock as he arose for a short jaunt to the nearest toilet, Parks was mildly surprised to see it read three-forty-eight.

Damn, must've dozed off. Better lay off the firewater for the duration of the mornin', old buddy. Keep this up and a Girl Scout could kick your ass.

Standing over the urinal with his eyes closed and head thrown back, Parks heard the faint echoing of a classic rock tune reverberating from the nearby rec room . As the second chorus of Blue Oyster Cult's *Don't Fear the Reaper* chimed through the adjoining wall, he couldn't help but dwell on the potential irony. *Now that's fuckin' prophetic. My unworthy opposition should take those lyrics to heed.*

Reaching out to pull the urinal's silver handle, he heard himself groan aloud as the dim lighting flickered several times just before the enveloping darkness ensued.

Parks fell instantly to one knee, his entire body a coiled spring.

Something tells me that wasn't a circuit breaker. Company ain't just coming...company's already here.

Seconds later, as he crawled from the bathroom entrance crouched like a stalking panther, Mason Parks heard glass shatter from the kitchen area as if struck by a swinging anvil.

He felt his entire body began to throb and pulsate in anticipation of the impending skirmish. *Well, hell Looks*

176

like that check marked 'past due' has finally arrived, old buddy. Let's see how much mercenary blood we can spill 'fore the son of a bitch gets cashed.

Duck walking down a narrow hall leading towards the workout room, Parks caught a faint glowing as he checked his flank. *Penlites more than likely. Must be the spear-chucker and the chink come to take my throne. Shirts must'a changed the taping format. Now why would they keep such a dirty little secret from their reigning champion? I get the feelin' I'm in a 'no win' situation here, at least in their eyes.*

He could just make out muffled footsteps within the vicinity of the living room area prior to leaping through the gym's open door and executing a series of combat rolls. Leaning with his naked flesh pressed against the side of a wide metal locker, he reached back with his left arm and gently pulled open the unlocked double-doors. The pearl -handled machete fit into his left palm as if designed solely for his colossal grip. The sixteen-inch blade was oily slick as he pulled it from its tight-fitting leather sheath. Backing further into the pitch-black darkness of the gymnasium, Parks crouched between a huge squat rack and multi-purpose Nautilus leg machine, his movements taunt and sure footed, despite the lingering alcohol buzz.

The dim glow of light was no longer present in the front hallway, but he could still make out the faint shuffling of footsteps in the direction of the living room.

The metallic trap that served as Mason Parks' mind in times of duress instantly created a multiple choice list of possible attack plans, quickly and meticulously breaking down each until one was ultimately chosen as superior.

177

Sprinting through the blackness with a speed that belied his massive bulk, he made a bee -line for the gym's back exit, which led into a separate hallway and eventually into the ranches largest of three bathrooms.

Halting inside a tiny foyer that lay just outside the bathroom's thick cherry wood double-doors, Parks peered upward and grinned devilishly. Just as he made his initial descent into the small metal overhang, constructed as a base for the glass ceiling above, he heard the first wave of whispering voices ricochet down from the north end of the hall.

"Better learn to keep up, man, or you're gonna miss the money shot when I lay that mother down," the first male voice spat sarcastically in a cocky, rap master tone that reeked of overconfidence.

"Hold up, Shadow Lion....I need better positioning as you enter these narrow entranceways, or I won't get *any* shot at all," the second male voice replied in a low, nervous cadence, his breathing a bit labored.

"That's Shadow *Panther*, asshole, and don't get in my way once the shit starts flyin'. My blade won't stop slicin' til I see ivory white bone shining in my flashlight's beam."

Parks watched the thin trail of light grow increasingly defined until the hand that held it broke the plain of the foyer entrance.

A split second before he released his feet and hand grips from the overhang, the machete's handle dropping from between his gritted teeth into his right hand upon dissention, he visualized a tint of metal from the rapier blade that immediately followed.

TC Eastmon's head bolted upward as the dark form swooped down like a collapsed section of ceiling.

The scream that had formed at the base of his throat froze there, never reaching his parting lips for release.

"Hiya, chuckles,' Parks screamed huskily as the machete blade led his descent like a swinging pendulum, 'Here's your fucking *money shot...* "

***

TIME: 0356 HOURS
DATE: 5 JUNE 1988
LOCATION: Hwy 453, six miles east of the Parks Ranch, Conquest, New Mexico

Carefully navigating past a rusted out Chevy Nova, careful to maintain the posted speed limit of 55 on the pothole ravaged two-lane, the man's blurred vision darted from the faded yellow lines of the road to the darkened skies above. He understood the need to change vehicles as quickly as possible, but that such a move would have to wait at least until he reached the outskirts of Las Cruces, which was a good twenty-mile trek from his present location.

He had seen the two choppers descend upon the ranch upon his abrupt departure, one from the east and another from the south. The suits had driven in, but had no doubt planned on flying out to hasten their own escapes from the fiery carnage left behind. Keeping his left hand planted firmly atop the blood-drenched field dressing wrapped around his thigh, he felt stout waves of dizziness briefly sweep over his vision before mercifully fading away. He figured the gist of the bleeding had stopped; otherwise he would've long since lost consciousness. The shoulder gash hardly bled at all,

179

despite the substantial depth of the wound. Sighing heavily as to eventually slow his labored breathing, he fought to avoid skidding off the wide gravel shoulder to his left and several times discovered he was cruising directly down the center of the deserted highway. He had wisely decided to steer clear of the interstate and any potentially prying eyes sporting New Mexico State Trooper uniforms.

Allowing his mind's eye to replay the final frantic moments before his hurried exit from the Ranch grounds, there was one particular event that simply did not adhere to logic within the final outcome. The second chopper had landed on the south side of the ranch, at least a football field's distance from the ranch house, as opposed to the first craft, which had settled to the west, no more than two dozen feet from the structure. He had parked the recently obtained (not without fevered but futile resistance, as he recalled) Jeep Cherokee at the edge of one of many nearby summits that surrounded the ranch from all sides, requisitioning a pair of night binoculars from one of the vehicle's former inhabitants to better view the newest visitors to his former homestead.

At least ten armed men had poured from the second craft, while the first seemed unoccupied save the chopper pilot. The man figured the strapped brigade to more than likely a 'second wave' of assassins, no doubt led to the festivities in his honor to ensure mission compliance. He'd heard a single blast of gunfire echo from the ranch's grounds while steering down a sandy grade leading to the highway, throwing an unexpected wrench into the proceedings that possibly involved outsiders.

It wasn't out of the question that either of his hired 'combatants' had conceived plans of their own concerning who was to get paid what in the grand scheme of things, and had somehow trailed the first chopper to the sight for an ambush.

The man's gut feeling told him it was the cocky spook nicked *Shadow Panther* , the first of many to die between the ranch's cool stone walls this night, who had organized a 'posse' of his peers in some elaborate kidnapping plot of the suits or something deviously similar. He smiled despite the throbbing pain, despite the gunshot hole in his thigh and the gaping hole in his upper shoulder--smiled despite the fainting spells that threatened to send the Jeep careening into the nearest ditch whenever the Asian girl came to mind. Shaking his head in comical disbelief at his own savagely cruel actions, he reconsidered leaving her alive as he did. The humane thing would definitely have been to seek out her shattered carcass and place a neat hole at the center of her forehead with the AK he'd pulled from one the assassins.

Unfortunately for her, the word *humane* held no meaningful definition within his admittedly demented mindset.

One thing he did understand about her with crystal clarity. She had *known* him previously. He'd seen the look in her eyes just as the hammer had fallen. It held two distinct qualities; recognition and *searing* hatred.

Mason Parks tensed as a distant light came into view over a jagged mountain range to his right; releasing a sigh of relief a moment later when it became obvious it had originated from a small commuter plane.

The money stashed behind his seat (tightly wound rolls of cash tucked inside a blood-soaked duffel) would easily suffice for the low-key lifestyle he would now be forced to endure. He had a contact in Waco who would supply a new identity within a matter of hours, complete with various forms of ID and a fabricated work history, a man who could also arrange a dramatically altered facial appearance, as well. He would play the part of one-man witness protection program, moving from town to town and state to state for the next several years or until it was felt safe to settle into a more permanent existence. Parks had long accepted such a day would come, and had prepared both financially and mentally for its arrival. Several banks, both home and abroad, held accounts in his name.

The survivors, few in number as they might be, weren't apt to forgive *or* forget the shambles he'd made of their very existence within a span of fifteen minutes inside the smoldering battlefield that had been his home for the past two years.

He would have relished finishing the job, save the Asian female, but time had been at a definite premium. Still, he found a sense of solace in the tidal wave of pain he had so expertly dueled out in such a limited time span, especially considering how woefully outgunned and outnumbered he'd been.

He would've thought they'd have known better than to underestimate his survival instinct.

As the Jeep topped a steep grade and began to drop into a flat, cacti-infested valley, void of oncoming traffic for at least the next three miles, Parks pondered the decision to keep the camera equipment --abandoning it at the scene meant leaving evidence of several homicides caught on film for the authorities to utilize in the manhunt that would've surely followed. Reaching into the Jeep's back seat, he felt the hard edge of one of the three hand-held video cameras protruding from the pillowcase he'd stuffed them into while departing. He could pull over and destroy the evidence, burying the shattered remains beneath a sandy dune. Quick, simple and easy, no sweat whatsoever. No better place to rid himself of at least one potential catastrophe in the making.

On the other hand, certain people would pay dearly for such grand drama, the same violence junkies and gore hounds that collected the previous volumes of his work. It would take years to develop and produce, but if manufactured correctly, could possibly outsell all previous tapes triple-fold. He had contacts that'd complete the task in spectacular fashion, it was simply a matter of allowing the considerable heat to cool for a few months or possibly years before initiating such an undertaking. The suits, those still breathing at least, would attempt to clean their own mess to prevent outside investigation. That would be their first priority. The second was just as easily predicted. Find and eliminate the man responsible.

Massaging the area around the shoulder wound, Parks' winced while again checking the skies for possible pursuers. If not for the presence of mind to don the first cameraman's protective vest, such undeniably painful yet tolerable wounds would have instead resembled crater holes within his chest cavity. Then again, if Aaron Kyle had simply been a better shot, all points, past and future, would have been moot.

The thigh wound would require stitches and constant supervision over the next several weeks to avoid permanent damage. Feeling the endorphins surge through his veins as his breathing finally began to regulate, Parks' mental grocery list (which already included such items as

Tylenol, hydrogen peroxide, and rubbing alcohol) expanded to include a sewing needle and strong nylon thread.

Thirty-three minutes later, he pulled into a half-empty K-Mart parking lot on the outskirts of Las Cruces. Using a pillowcase to redress his wound, Parks noted it had crusted over and no longer bled. Slumped in the shadows in between two wide metal dumpsters at the edge of the lot, he redressed in fresh jeans and a black T-shirt pulled from the duffel. He would wait until the morning rush-hour hit to choose a new mode of transportation. In the meantime, Mason Parks leaned back with closed eyes and drifted into a light slumber, the landscape of his dreams blurred and contorted, the faces of involved parties wavy and unclear, yet strangely familiar. They represented the souls of the recently slain, each groping for him, clutching at their killer in hopes of a retribution that was never to be. Mason Parks reveled at their frustrated helplessness, giggling like a tickled child as the sun began to slowly rise over the bordering desert plains.

***

TIME: 1435 HOURS
DATE: 29 OCTOBER 1996
LOCATION: Elm Hill, Alabama

The Ford F150's brakes squeaked loudly as it rolled to a rough stop on the narrow, cracked shoulder. The man backed up the vehicle until the hand-written sign was only a few feet from the driver's side door. **HOUSE/ACREAGE for Sale! Turn here for more**

Information it had read in bright red letters that looked to have been scribbled with a large crayon onto the sign's aged wooden surface.

The winding dirt road was badly rutted, the truck's springs howling their disapproval. As he pulled into the overgrown, obviously neglected drive, the man's squinty eyes scanned the surrounding landscape with great intensity, as if to make sure there were no witnesses to his presence. Large elm, oak, and pine trees permeated the front and sides of the home, a thick section of forest taking up the half acre that fronted a wide, weed infested pasture at the rear.

The man smiled broadly as he exited the still running pickup and walked casually to the front porch, already having decided that he had indeed found the perfect abode. A cardboard sign tacked to the screen door provided a point of contact for realty purposes.

Sucking in the cool fall air, the smell of distant fireplace smoke filling his nostrils, the man beat his chest like a bull Gorilla proudly marking a claim.

"Home, sweet home...once again," he bellowed triumphantly, his thick, barrel-shaped chest grotesquely pumped.

185

Chapter Six
Uneasy Reunion/In Search Of...

Time: 0830 HOURS
Date: 30 AUGUST 2006
Location: Elm Hill, Alabama

"Want me to ride along, Sheriff? Nothin' on the agenda this morning to keep me here."

Daniel peered up from the edge of his steaming coffee cup and paused a few seconds before replying, his eyebrows cocked. "Nah, you go ahead and man the phones, Trace I don't want Curtis to think we're teaming up on him on just his second day back in town I'm sure he's getting his share of questionable looks as it is."

"I hate to admit it,' Deputy Morton said, propping her highly polished black boots on the edge of her desk, 'but the man gave me a serious case of the creeps. He's big as an RV and seemed a bit on the sour side. 'Course, eighteen years in lock up might have somethin' to do with his present disposition, you think?"

Pushing up from his desk like a man suffering from a combination of raging hemorrhoids and a level five migraine, Daniel arose with a loud groan.

"If you don't mind me sayin' so, boss, you're movin' like a three-toed sloth on Quaaludes. Have a late night or did you actually share a bottle with old Hollow Leg at his place yesterday?"

After pouring himself a fresh cup of java, Daniel leaned against the edge of his subordinate's desk and managed a strained smile. A wavy, U -shaped cowlick dominated the back of his head, and even the left corner of his moustache curled up in a warped wave. "Feels like

186

the latter, although the first answer is responsible for my less than chipper appearance. Kara had a softball game that lasted until almost nine, then I had to help her research a paper on the Internet. I 'll bet my weary old head didn't the pillow until quarter 'til eleven at the earliest."

Pausing in what resembled deep thought, Deputy Morton raised a single finger as if to pause any further discussion. "Got it! The episode where Thelma Lou dates Goober to make Barney jealous!" she finally barked excitedly.

Snatching his cap from the clutter atop his desk, Daniel then took a full step outside before halting to respond. "Close, but no cigar, Trace. Right episode, I'll concede, but it was Gomer, *not* Goober. You're getting better, though Sneaky Pete must be forcing you to watch a few episodes these days."

The deputy slapped her knee in frustration, almost tipping over backward in the process.

"I'll be at the old Barber place…or I guess I should refer to it as the *new* Barber place," he said, adjusting his belt with a quick tug.

"Call me if you need me, Boss. *If* Hulk Hogan gives you any lip, let me know. I flat curled one-forty last night. Think I could take 'im."

Daniel tipped his cap playfully and departed.

Deputy Morton walked to the office window and watched the cruiser pull away onto Main, the early morning sun fast giving away to a thick line of dark, foreboding clouds building overhead. She had never seen Daniel look so weary, so doggedly haggard. He was a master of disguise when it came to hiding his emotions, a trait Tracy figured assisted in the hasty departure of his ex-wife. Tracy jokingly referred to him as 'Sheriff Spock' due to such calm, cool, almost *indifferent* behavior in times of duress. Curtis Lee Barber had resided within the city limits of Elm Hill for less than forty-eight hours, and her boss was already paying a steep mental price for the man's looming presence.

A hard, straight rain began to fall just as she turned from the window, a feeling of dread spreading through her chest and midsection like a raging virus.

Tracy Morton didn't just respect Daniel as her boss, but also considered him the best friend she had other than her husband. She had never been attracted to him in a sexual way, but thought of him in the older brother/uncle mode, thus the nagging worry she felt concerning his welfare wasn't fueled by strictly professional reasons. He had hired her despite vocal opposition from the city council, not to mention the shocked disbelief of several citizens, and had made it his personal mission to train her as his eventual successor.

Tapping her holster in nervous apprehension, she sincerely prayed that her gut feeling was unjustified. A gut feeling that screamed of serious conflict on the near horizon.

***

Daniel parked the cruiser a few dozen feet to the rear of an old Ford truck with a badly faded gray paint job. Upon exiting, he stepped onto the wet pavement, removed his cap and turned his face to the sky to allow the soft rain to slap the flesh of his face and forehead He sometimes wondered how different he might feel if only a decent night's sleep were somehow attainable; *decent*

188

defined as anything over four hours in length.

The Barbers had packed up and moved away to greener pastures a few months after their only son's conviction, unable or unwilling to tolerate the stares and innuendo certain to follow within the close-knit community. Upon returning to Elm Hill from his four year Army stint, Daniel had heard they resided somewhere in Colorado, possibly the outskirts of Denver or Colorado Springs.

The home had remained uninhabited for over seventeen years, and predictably hadn't aged well through the hot, humid summers and brief but bitter cold stretches of winter. Paint had faded and peeled from wood on the verge of complete rot, while partially torn shingles hung from the edge of the roof like overlong bangs in dire need of scissoring.

As Daniel neared the front door, which stood open within the badly rusted screen that fronted it, he heard a loud scraping sound, not unlike heavy furniture being dragged roughly across concrete.

"Hello? Curtis, you in there?" he asked politely through the screen, feeling as if he had just swallowed a lump of coal.

"Yeah?" a voice rang out from the darkened interior, followed by the sound of heavy boot steps leading to the door.

Daniel backed away a foot or so as the man stepped through, swallowing hard as the massive form moved entirely into view. Shielding his face from the sprinkling rain, Curtis Barber inhaled deeply and nodded before speaking. Daniel instantly thought of Tracy's earlier description of his old school mate. *An RV with a head* did indeed come to mind. Barber wore no shirt or shoes, just

189

a cut off pair of blue jeans, exposing each exquisitely carved section of pumped, stone-like muscle his upper body possessed.

"Son, I take it you've spent some substantial time in a gymnasium over the years?" Daniel managed somewhat shakily, forcing his eyes to maintain contact with the larger man.

"Best damn workout the state of Alabama penal system legally allowed, Dan. It helped pass the time, anyhow, and I had plenty of time to pass. So how you doing, man? Uh, excuse me, *Sheriff* Whitlock?"

Shaking the rain from his cap, Daniel gently shrugged his shoulders while attempting to shrug off the shock of his former classmate's dramatic transformation. The man was simply *colossal*. If they'd met on the street by accident, Daniel could have only recognized him solely by the center portion of his face; the eyes, nose and mouth, and even then it might have taken hours to place the name with the features. "You may call me Constable Dan, Curtis. How goes it? Getting settled in, I hear."

Stepping to one side, Barber peered into the clouds and motioned for Daniel to come inside with a single sweep of his tree trunk-sized right arm.

"Trying anyways. What kind of shitty host am I being? Get in out of the rain, man."

Moments later, both men stood inside what had been the Barber family kitchen, each at opposite ends of a horribly scratched oak table that served as the sole piece of furniture within the room. Each held frosty Dr. Peppers pulled from a nearby cooler. "Sorry I couldn't offer you a chilled brew, Dan, but I understand you're on duty and all."

"Not to mention it's still a dry county, Curtis, as you

well know, I 'm sure."

The larger man grinned mischievously, his rugged face and arms moist with a mixture of sweat and misty rain. "Never stopped us in our day, did it? I'm sure the bootlegging industry still thrives, despite you and your deputy's best efforts to slam the lid shut, am I right? Lake Mann still hosts some hellacious parties, I'm betting."

Sipping from the dripping wet can, Daniel then paused to catch his breath while tapping his fingers on the table's rough textured surface. "Why *here,* Curtis? Why put yourself through it?"

The other man's smile faded gradually as he leaned back in a narrow, high-backed chair, one hardly manufactured with a man of his size in mind "Don't you mean, put *you* through it? Or maybe, put the *town* through it? I say, why the hell *not*, Daniel? This was my home, damn it Still is, as far as I'm concerned."

Resting his elbows on the table, Daniel studied the other man for a full ten seconds before replying. " You trying to prove something, Curtis? Is that it? You've served your time, completed your debt to society."

"I'm here to live, Sheriff, period. No ulterior motives or strategic revenge plots. I'm a resident of Elm Hill, Alabama, and I want to remain as such," he calmly interrupted, leaning forward to rest on the tabletop as well.

"I've heard you've gained employment already. You might run into some… opposition at the work place. You gonna be able to handle being called 'murderer', both behind your back *and* to your face, Curtis?"

The large man's howling laughter was so sudden and out of context, so seemingly out of place in tune with the question, that Daniel cringed back involuntarily and came

191

close to tipping over his half-full soda can. "Been there, done that already, Sheriff. Our old buddy and classmate, Todd Platt, paid me a little unannounced visit last night around midnight or so. He had a snoot-full and starting screaming for me to 'get my murderin' ass' out of town or there was gonna be a second homicide in Elm Hill's history. I walked outside, wearing nothing but my socks and fruit of the looms, and kindly informed the 'Plattster' to vacate the premises or I'd be forced to call on his former best friend at Elm Hill High to toss his drunken rear end into the nearest empty cell. He had some other bearded goon with him that I didn't recognize, and both were carrying baseball bats. Well, either the mention of your name or my prison-refined physique caused 'em both to misplace their manhood real quick. They booked outta here post haste, yelling a few choice profanities along the way.

Terroristic threats I believe you call 'em these days. Anyhow, I went back inside and slept like a three-month old, Dan. Believe me, I can handle it because I have no choice in the matter. I will not be run out of my hometown by those chosen few who cannot let it go."

Daniel stood, stretching his neck from side to side while doing so. "Not to worry, I'll speak to Todd and his pal and ensure they understand the consequences of such escapades in the future. That said…they won't be the last, Curtis, not by a long shot. Stan Basham will definitely be looking you up in the near future. Bet on it. I've counseled the man about such threats 'til I was blue in the face, but it's like scolding a brick wall."

"Debra's Uncle Stan? Damn, figured that mean SOB would've kicked off years ago. I recall he looked like death warmed over at the trial. So be it. I'll be on the lookout."

Barber raised both hands in a gesture of surrender upon noticing Daniel's stern gaze. " I come in peace, Daniel. I'll avoid physical conflict at all costs."

Propping his hands on the back of the chair he now stood behind, Daniel couldn't help but sneer at the other man's gullibility, whether it be sincere or not. "In looking at you, I'd wager they'll be doing all the avoiding. If they attempt anything at all, it'll be from a distance. I'd advise you put up some outside lighting and maybe purchase a good watchdog or three."

"Appreciate the tips, Sheriff. Now, if you don't mind, I've got a new bathtub to install. The old one was a cat's whisker from falling through the flooring." Barber finished off his soda in three long swallows and stood, then followed Daniel to the front door. The rain had finally ceased, leaving the outside air thick with newly formed humidity.

"You got a cell phone?" Daniel asked while step ping onto the paved path leading to the drive.

"Picking one up tomorrow, in fact. One of those 'Cricket' deals. Figured it'd be a lot simpler than having the home lines hooked back up," Barber answered from behind the already closed screen.

"Call me with the number when you get it, okay? I want to call and check on you from time to time. See how things are at the workplace as well as out here."

"You got it, Constable Dan. Glad to hear I've got one man on my side, anyways."

Daniel looked at the man thoughtfully. "It ain't about *sides*, Curtis. It's about citizen 's rights. Take care now."

Barber waited for Daniel to turn away and complete several steps before uttering a final query. " You sleeping okay, Dan? I mean, you look a little pasty around the gills."

Turning back around, Daniel could sense the smirk covering the other man's face before actually witnessing it. "Not like I used to, Curtis. Got a kid that keeps me hopping. How about yourself?"

Holding his hands out with the palms facing upward, the toothy grin the large man displayed was nothing short of predatory. "The innocent of mind sleep deep and without guilt, Sheriff."

Not knowing exactly how to reply, Daniel simply tipped the bill of his cap and departed.

On the short drive back to town, both his hands and legs refused to stop shaking.

***

Time: 0725 HOURS
Date: 31 AUGUST 2006

"So you have his exact location pinpointed, Aaron? You've actually... *seen* him?"

"No, Kayla, not yet. Still waiting on that particular tidbit of info. It'll come, don't you fret. My flashes have been so damned... powerful, so overwhelming the past few days, maybe I'm just burnt out for now. Just need a short sabbatical to recharge the old batteries."

"To *HELL* with your low battery, Aaron! Concentrate, *meditate*...break out a fucking crystal ball if you have to! Look around, mister...we're sitting dead center in the middle of a lean-to that's liable to fall down around our ears any minute, and we aren't getting any younger in the meantime. Personally, I believe this

194

goddamned heat and humidity is going to eventually *liquefy* what's left of this old yellow carcass," she cried, banging her right palm forcefully against the wheelchair's padded armrest, her lengthy, straight black hair sailing out in silky waves.

Straining to refrain from breaking into a hysterical giggle at his cohorts unintentionally comical rant, Aaron Kyle covered his mouth and turned away as if mulling over a troublesome thought. "Calm down, my fiery Asian flower,' he replied once composure had been regained. " Even if we have to perform the leg work to do so, it won't take more than twenty-four hours...tops. How many fifty-ish men fitting his description can possibly reside in this horse and buggy burg? It's a sure bet that Mason Parks isn't running a day care or teaching grade school math. He 'll be a loner that resides off the beaten path, probably without a single neighbor within a five-mile radius. He needs isolation to keep his...hobby intact without fear of discovery. More than likely he's passing himself off as a retiree whose a bit 'eccentric' but basically harmless to the local community-t he kind of silent, grumpy looking middle-aged man that school kids label a flake, but don't dare mess with."

The wheelchair hummed loudly as she steered it forward in a wild lurch, her head jarred back roughly as she braked. As usual, Aaron felt a sudden surge of gut-wrenching pity at the mere sight of her. The irony was almost incomprehensible. Kayla Lee's face was flawless, her perfectly shaped cheekbones a sculptured masterpiece, her skin both wrinkle and blemish free. Her eyes were twin beams of exquisite beauty that shone with the youthful exuberance of a woman fifteen years her junior. As had been the case when they had first met over

195

eighteen years earlier, Aaron still considered Kayla's the most strikingly gorgeous face he had ever seen.

Unfortunately, the body which accompanied it was nothing more than a quivering mass of dead tissue and rotting vessels, void of any free range of movement save her right arm and the muscles of her neck and face. Even from a distance of over six feet, he could smell the reeking odor of her colostomy bag, which hung from her left side like a bungled growth of putrid, swollen flesh.

"So you're just going to roam about the town, asking about Mister Hate as if he were a lost puppy? The local authorities might grow a bit curious about the motives of such behavior, might they not, *Agent* Krane of the FBI?" she asked sourly, the natural slant to her eyes growing even narrower as her brow furrowed.

"I'll stick to the back roads, my dear Kayla, which is where the majority of the town resides as it is, and also utilize my briefcase full of tricks just in case I do happen upon Sheriff Redneck or his She-Male deputy," he said calmly, almost whispering.

Kayla Lee rolled her eyes and groaned, tossing her head to one side as if slapped. "What this time, health insurance or pamphlets from the Church of Latter Day Saints? Tell me you're not going to wear that horrendous putty nose and felt hat."

Bowing dramatically, Aaron arose just in time to see the faintest flicker of a smile appear, albeit briefly, on her normally frowning visage. "I doubt it'll win me any Oscars, but such an act will surely suffice for the good folk of Hooterville, USA. For your information, Dragon Lady, I'll be offering the townspeople a much needed service, that being supplemental life insurance."

Kayla fell silent, then used her remaining working

196

limb to guide the chair to what had been the living room's 'picture' window.

Aaron joined her a moment later, trying not to grimace at the sour scent emanating from her slumped form. They both stared into the overgrown front yard, the grass of which resembled the surface of a sparkling lake from the sun's early morning reflection.

Aaron broke the silence after a brief respite.

"Don't you just *loathe* the silence? Damn, I'd rather run a straight razor across my jugular than put up with this crap for more than a few days."

"You and me both, city boy,' she replied in between huffing breaths. Aaron hadn't seen her in over two weeks, and was shocked at how horrible she sounded, like a locomotive engine in desperate need of fresh coal.

"New chair? Nice," he said apathetically.

"All the bells and whistles for today's modern crip. It's a Quantum Jazzy 1470. Cost me more than we made on that Savings & Loan haul in KC last year. Worth every red cent, I must say. Adjustable seats, optimum weight distribution, active-track suspension. It reaches speeds up to six miles per hour even on rough terrain, and the damned thing is even equipped with its own battery charger. Impressive, huh?"

Aaron's chosen reply never reached his lips.

"Revved up baby can carry this stinking, rotting pus pod I call a body up to twenty five miles before I have to plug the charger in. I usually spend such time draining the crimson colored feces from my bodily fluids satchel or strapping on a new piss bag. So much to do, so *little* time, you know?"

"Um, what did the doctor say last we…" he began before she cut in as if he hadn't spoken at all, her voice

197

growing more shrill by the word.

"My arm itches like the dickens, Aaron. You know...the arm *he* broke in three places. The arm secured by pins, wires, and for all I know, fucking bobby pins and paper clips. It itches like mad, but I 'm afraid that if I dig my nails into it, the skin will peel away like wet confetti. My chest aches whenever I try to sleep, not sure if it's the scar tissue where he caved in my rib cage, or possibly the damage around the missing kidney from where he snapped my back over his fucking knee."

Aaron backed away a step, the smell of her intensifying as her good arm began to shake and gesture. "Kayla, I'm going out to make sure the van is secured...be right back..."

"My stomach rumbles and groans like a chorus of tortured maniacs and feels like a pile of mushy mashed potatoes smothered in diarrhea gravy. My ass is void of all flesh now... nothing but brittle bones and broken vessels."

"...do a quick inventory on the tools you brought..."

"Even my *FUCKING CUNT* hurts, Aaron, and it hasn't seen any action since the night that bastard raped me!" she bellowed, her face coated in beads of sweat which ran down her jaw line in thin streams. Her chin collapsed onto her chest, her breathing coming in quick, harsh gasps.

Aaron placed a gentle hand on her emaciated shoulder.

"He'll *die*, Kayla. He'll die a death that will easily surpass all the pain he's initiated. That I promise you without a moment's hesitation or a flash of self-doubt. We've waited far too long to see it slip away now. He's here. He's *ours.*"

Her neck and head shook and shimmied from the tears mixing with the sweat on her cheeks.

After a short pause, she placed her one serviceable hand on top his. They watched the sun break through the adjacent tree line in a comfortable silence.

***

Time: 0835 HOURS
Date: SAME DAY

"Boss, you sleepin' okay?" Deputy Morton queried, peering beneath the cruiser's raised hood, the morning sun reflecting off the lenses of her glasses like twin laser beams.

Daniel stepped back from the vehicle, wiping the cruiser's oil stick with a handkerchief pulled from his back pocket. "Needs a quart. Well, to be honest, Mr. Sandman and I haven't exactly been on speaking terms lately. Too much afternoon caffeine, I guess."

"Pop a couple of Tylenol PM right before you hit the sack. Knocks me for a loop every time, and I don't wake up groggy neither."

Snapping the hood shut with a single shove, Daniel rested his hands on his belt loop and scanned Main Street, which was conspicuously quiet for a weekday morning. "Might just do that. Hate to depend on pills for shuteye, but I'm about at the end of my rope," he replied, reaching to massage his sagging, bloodshot orbs.

"It's the Barber thing, right? He got to you, didn't he?" she asked once they'd entered the office, her tone a bit guarded and hesitant.

Daniel tossed his cap on atop his desktop and walked

199

straight towards the half-filled coffee pot. "Just a man trying to start over, Trace. He's already met with some resistance."

"Don't tell me. Stan Basham."

He sipped twice before responding, grimacing painfully in between gulps. "Nope. Todd Platt and a buddy, more than likely Charlie Farris. I've heard they've been bending elbows together the past few months. Paid Curtis a little midnight visit and spouted a few threats, that is until he came outside and they got an eyeful of 'im."

"Want me to bring Platt in for terroristic threatening?"

Daniel nodded wearily, running a hand through his thick, wavy bangs. " Gonna drop by the plant this morning and jaw with Todd myself. He's a stubborn, hard-headed individual, has been since our grade school days. The constant boozing seems to intensify his bull-headedness these days. He never did like Curtis. Had a running feud with each other since tenth grade, about the time Curtis dropped out of school, although for the life of me I can't remember what the argument was all about."

"Barber was a real juvenile delinquent in those days, huh? The Arthur Fonzerelli of the Elm Hill High?" she asked while casually scanning the computer monitor at the center of her immaculately neat desktop.

"More like Ernest T. Bass on uppers. Curtis was the stereotypical small town bully, short on brains and short *of* fuse when it came to how he dealt with the general public. Once he quit school he harvested and sold dope full time, while also helping a few local bootleggers run their merchandise from the county line. Real charmer with the ladies, as well," he replied while refilling his cup for the fourth time in an hour.

"Obviously. Charmed Debra Lee Rainer right into an early grave."

Plucking his cap from the desk, Daniel shot his deputy a half-hearted salute and lumbered towards the door. "Catch ya later, *Xena*. Off to see an old schoolmate gone to seed."

"*War Eagle* right back at ya, Sheriff," she replied without removing her gaze from the glowing screen.

Just as he started to lean down into the cruiser, Daniel spotted Cliff Peterson crossing the street ahead and waived to catch the other man's attention. "Hey Cliff, need to bring ol' faithful here by the station and get a quart of thirty weight poured into 'er."

Cliff Peterson, a thin, slightly hunched back man in his early sixties, nodded back without speaking. The man had worked as the town's most respected auto mechanic as far back as Daniel could recall. *A man of very few words and consistently greasy hands*, Tracy always quipped of Cliff, and a man who hardly spoke in anything more elaborate than two to three word sentences.

Pulling onto the Street after allowing an ancient dump truck to pass, Daniel's cloudy thoughts instantly turned to Doug Matson, another member in good standing in the 'Middle Aged Men Who Refuse to Speak Their Mind' Club. He wondered if men such as Cliff and Douglas were lifelong member s of the stilted speech minority, or had been transformed into such by some traumatic tragedy somewhere down the rocky, winding highway that served as life on planet Earth. It only took one such scenario to dramatically alter one's course, he knew all too well.

201

Turning from Main onto Bell road, a wide stretch of newly paved asphalt that eventually led to the town's second largest employer, the J. Bartlett Canning Plant, Daniel could feel his body aches begin to wane a bit, although his head still throbbed like an open wound.

Two hours of sleep did little but magnify a person's daily aches and pains, while simultaneously dulling the senses to a perfectly flat nub. He couldn't recall the last decent night's slumber he'd experienced, but the situation had quickly mutated from bad to worse in the past few days. Every home remedy known to man had been attempted over the years, from warm milk right before bed to steamy hot baths. He drank no coffee after ten a.m., and rarely drank soda at all. He jogged five nights a week (eight round trips to the small creek behind the house and back equaled exactly two miles) and performed nightly sets of push-ups and crunches (at least two-hundred each). Never able to either fall or *remain* asleep despite being surrounded by tranquil countryside, he kept a fan running inside his bedroom during the warm months and a 'noise' simulator during the fall and winter. All to no avail, it seemed. After years of sleepwalking through the daylight hours in a hazy stupor and spending the majority of his nights tumbling like tossed dice at a crap table, he had finally broken down and spoke to Dr. Griffin. Over eight months had passed since the Doc's diagnosis of *Chronic Insomnia* had been rendered. Various sleep aids, first weak and hardly helpful and later much stronger and *equally* ineffective, had passed through the Whitlock medicine cabinet without fanfare. The doctor had tried to point the finger of blame at the usual suspects, that being job-related stress or a fairly recent divorce, even the coming of age that Kara was beginning to experience right before her dotting father's worrisome eyes.

Regardless of the reasons why, Daniel often felt lost in a sea of surreal obscurity that threatened to blur the line between reality and fantasy, a condition that served to enhance feelings of worry and paranoia to dangerous extremes.

Through the years, he prided himself at being a master of cloaking the physical and mental toll being taken, refusing to allow his job performance or, more importantly, his relationship with Kara to suffer.

Pulling into the mostly empty parking lot that served as a perimeter for the plant, Daniel realized that such an ingenious disguise was growing increasingly difficult to maintain. He felt the tell-tale cracks in his persona beginning to tear and split with every waking moment spent beneath the sizzling summer sun and while aimlessly rolling between his own bed sheets for hours on end. Walking unsteadily towards the plant entrance, he pondered how much longer before the mask was permanently torn away to reveal the true misery beneath.

***

Time: 1315 HOURS
Date: SAME DAY

"Ham and swiss on rye, my dear?" Aaron Kyle beamed, holding the still wrapped sandwich airborne. The bridge of his nose still bore the remnants of recently removed elastic, and was just a shade lighter in color than his actual flesh.

Kayla waived him off, sipping from a frosty bottle of

203

chocolate milk gripped tightly in her right hand.

"Portable unit kicks butt, huh?" he queried between small bites of his own sandwich.

Rolling her breathtakingly striking eyes in lieu of a shoulder shrug, Kayla glanced over at the small AC unit sitting directly to her left at the center of the dimly lit living room. A slightly larger generator unit sat just to its right, the intertwining cords running between each resembling coiled, black snakes.

"I wouldn't dare allow my Asian Cherry Blossom to wilt in the southern heat," he boasted while still chewing a mouthful of turkey club on wheat.

"Not exactly the Embassy Suites, smart-ass, but I guess keeping out of sight from the locals is for the best, especially considering what's to follow," she replied curtly, a tiny droplet of milk propped on her upper lip.

"So you have the list of possible suspects narrowed down to six?" she continued, the cool air cascading through her long, sumptuous hair, forcing her to whip her head to one side to clear her line of sight.

"That I have, sweets. Rural folk are so remarkably kind to out of town salesmen, although I believe in most cases it's simply a way to 'pass the buck' to one's neighbor. I have exact addresses on three of them, and general directions to find the others. Only three of the men actually reside within the city limits. The remaining trio is spread out within a five- mile radius of Elm Hill. All are single or widowed and live alone, with estimated ages of fifty to sixty. Physical descriptions were vague, but the townsfolk were eager enough to provide general overviews of each man, especially after Mark Owens of United Southern Life reiterated the importance of *older* men near or past retirement age needing supplemental

204

insurance to prevent an unnecessary burden on their family in later years."

"Mark Owens? Wasn't that the name of the banker we fleeced in Eureka a few years ago?" she asked with a wicked sneer before reaching down to adjust her chair's angle and height.

"Damn, you're right. I knew I pulled that name from somewhere. Kayla my dear, you were obviously blessed with a photographic memory bank of unlimited disk space."

"In some areas, blessed, but in others, I believe the word *cursed* to be far more accurate," she replied, retrieving the milk from the chair's built-in cup holder and taking a final sip.

"How so?" he asked, shoving the remainder of the sandwich between his teeth before taking a long swallow from a chilled Mountain Dew retrieved from a nearby cooler.

"Well, blessed in that I can recall names and situations from years, make that *decades*, gone by. Cursed that I can also reel in such nasty little items as the last time I took a healthy crap on my own. That date, by the way, was August 5th, 1988 in Denver, Colorado."

Aaron turned towards the kitchen to retrieve a plastic trash bag from the supplies he'd stashed from the van. "Sorry I asked," he whispered just low enough to be drowned out by both the generator's gentle hum and the AC's constant whine.

Upon re-entering the room, he began gathering the plastic and paper wrap from their meals, evoking a look of comical disbelief from his erstwhile partner. "Cleanliness is next to godliness, so say those who believe in such myth," he said smiling, "'sides, a trail of

205

evidence leading back to us would be a tragic thing, indeed."

"Did you check out the equipment?" she asked, her head cock ed quizzically to one side.

"Yep. Everything on the checklist seemed present and accounted for, per plan A. Hard to believe how lightweight most of it is. That table looks like it weighs a ton folded like that, but it's damn easy to transport and set up. The shed out back should serve our purposes perfectly, don't you think?"

"As long as we can keep him silenced, yes, it should do."

Aaron grinned, kneeling down to pull a fresh soda from the ice-packed cooler. " Kayla my delicate Korean beauty, such irritating noises such as screams and wails won't be a problem, least the *initial* extraction be the bastard's decidedly forked tongue."

Kayla beamed, nodding up and down rhythmically as if entranced.

"I brought an extra bone saw as well, just in case we get the urge to carve simultaneously."

Bowing down until the full force of the AC's chilly output coated his forehead and face, Aaron couldn't help but giggle at the thought.

"It's really gonna be a bitch to be him, no doubt. By the way, the syringes have been filled. Those babies are locked and fully loaded for a bear, enough to down a bull elephant and keep it comatose for many a day."

"I even brought my new Nikon and tri-pod set up,' she blurted, seemingly unaware of her partner's presence. "Going to fill an entire roll of twenty-seven and then re-load for more."

"*Yeah*. Put together a photo album and label it *Mister*

Hate's Autopsy, performed while the unfortunate SOB was still alive. By the way, I noticed enough tape, gauze and bandages stuffed in that suitcase to supply an LA Emergency room for a month."

Her eyes tightly squinted, Kayla whirled her head about to meet his gaze. " Half the battle will be keeping the demon a live to prolong the procedure, Aaron. I want at least three hours, four if we can manage it, before the final amputation is completed."

Downing the remainder of his latest drink in two lengthy swallows, Aaron belched loudly and shoved the can into the trash bag, then yawned and stretched his arms before strolling back towards the kitchen. " Your plan is my command, my oriental goddess. Allow me to go get my face back on and depart for the open road. I've got a few farmhouses to visit and limited daylight left to sell my wares."

"What if...he recognizes you upon first contact, Aaron? You won't...stand a chance. I don't care how much *older* he is, Mason Parks isn't remotely human. He still kills for sport, for...kicks. If he even *suspects*..." she said, her voice beginning to crack as the words trailed off.

"Not to worry, cherry blossom. The spring-loaded syringe is locked in place beneath my right cuff. I may sweat like a pig upon presentation, but if the bastard reaches for me, he'll lose both consciousness and most likely an eye as well. The device acts like a miniature rocket launcher upon the sudden, upward arch of my wrist. He'll never know what hit him until it's far too late. Best hundred bucks we've ever spent on this little venture, 'cause you can't put a price on piece of mind," he replied from the next room, already in the process of reattaching the putty nose, to be followed by a bushy brown mustache and dark brown eyebrows.

Kayla gracefully steered her chair to the kitchen's entrance, where her partner scrunched over a small makeup mirror, his back painfully bowed. "I pray we actually get to initiate plan B this time, Aaron. I pray to whatever cruel, heartless God that's directing this shitty little drama. I 'm not sure I can handle many more false alarms. I'm pudding in a chair as it is. A few more months of traveling might well spell the end of the road for my decomposing carcass."

"Relax, Kayla. Plan B is in the bag. It feels like somebody implanted an electrode at the back of my skull. As the tingling grows, so grows our chances of nabbing the intended prey."

Staring at her partner's back with a mix of emotions that ran the gamut from childhood excitement to immeasurable fear, Kayla Lee swallowed hard, closed her eyes, and prayed anew.

***

Time: 1454 HOURS
Date: SAME DAY

"You'll need to purchase your supplies elsewhere, Mr. Barber."

Curtis Barber placed the palms of his hands on the surface of the checkout counter and sighed heavily, his lips curled in a sarcastic smirk. The heavyset, grim-looking woman stationed behind the counter turned and began stocking on a nearby display as if to utterly dismiss his continued presence. "Uh, miss? Ma'am? I bought

208

nails and bathroom fixtures, around two hundred dollars' worth, in this same establishment just yesterday. Paid cash, in fact. My money suddenly not *good* enough?" he asked calmly, much more so than he would have ever thought possible given the circumstances.

"I'm sorry, Mr. Barber. I do what I'm told, and I was told to refuse your business. Mr. Mack was runnin' the show yesterday. He...didn't know any better," she mumbled without turning around, each word spoken in a thick, southern drawl that forced Barber's mind to translate several times before the full gist was understood.

"I...see. Um, Mr. Garrison still owns this place?"

"Passed away 'bout four years back. Stanley Basham is the owner and manager at the present time."

The shrill giggle that escaped Barber's lips caused the woman to jump slightly, as if goosed. "Stan Basham, huh? Well, *that* sure as hell explains a lot. Thank you for your time, Miss. Please inform your boss that I'll fully respect his wishes and purchase my household goods elsewhere."

As he whirled around to exit, he caught movement out of his left eye before detecting the sound of heavy boots growing closer from a nearby a isle.

"Do yourself a favor and stay the hell off my property, you murderin' som' bitch.

I see you in here again I'll have ya arrested for criminal trespassing," the man practically yelled as he appeared from between a isles packed with garden tools and lawnmower displays. He had lost the majority of his hair and cultivated a massive beer gut, but Barber had no problem instantly recognizing Stanley Basham. The man was holding a pair of pruning shears in one hand and a small hatchet in the other, each of which shook as badly as his trembling lips.

"*Damn* , Stan... you planning on tree surgery or should I consider this a general threat to my person?" Barber quipped, feeling his blood pressure skyrocket but somehow able to maintain the guise of stability under stress that had served him so well within prison walls.

The older man waived the hatchet as if rallying invisible troops into battle. " *Leave*, asshole, or I'll do more than threaten."

Barber watched the woman behind the counter cover her mouth as if to suppress a scream, her eyes as big as dinner plates.

Unable to completely reel in his emotions, Barber pointed a finger at the older man before spinning around swiftly to depart. He could feel his biceps begin to swell, the thumping at his temples intensifying by the second. "I'm going, Stan...you're *gone*."

He heard portions of the older man's rant as he strolled towards his truck, the soul vehicle occupying the pothole ravaged *ELM HILL HARDWARE & SUPPLY* parking lot.

"...it'll be your ass, killer. I'll be seein' ya around, buddy-boy!"

Pulling back onto a virtually empty main drag, Barber felt the raging anger gradually subside. He had a long drive ahead to Cullman to get supplies, and didn't need a speeding or reckless speeding ticket adding to the misery.

Fifteen minutes and four miles outside the city limits later, he spotted a Black Ford F150 in his rear-view mirror. As it topped a steep hill he'd passed some thirty seconds before, it became a surging dark blur, leaving little doubt of the driver's intent. Curtis Barber knew he was being chased, and had little or no chance of either outrunning or out-driving his pursuer.

"Hell's Bells, Stan. That sure didn't take long, now did it?" he whispered, preparing to pull onto a wide dirt clearing a few hundred feet ahead. As he slowed, the large pickup drew to within fifty yards, and the sound of rubber burning across asphalt filled the air as it squealed to a sliding stop.

***

Time: 1529 HOURS
Date: SAME DAY

"Yes, sir, they'd be ours. I'll inform the Sheriff. Yeah, see you in a few. Bye." Deputy Morton hung up the phone gently, as if handling delicate China.

Daniel looked up from the folded report card he'd been studying, then to his daughter, who had just re-entered the office from a holding area at the rear of the building. "What's up, Trace?" he asked, sweeping his feet from the top of the desk in a single, fluid movement.

"State Trooper…uh, Williams I think he said his name was. He's bringin' in Curtis Barber, along with Will Basham and Charlie Farris," she replied, hitching her belt as if prepping for an Old West gunfight.

Kara ran up to her and whistled loudly, her face a living portrait of teenaged curiosity. "What did he…did he *kill* somebody else?" she blurted, waiving her thin arms frantically.

Wincing as he rose from his chair, Daniel took a stance between the two and gently gripped his young

211

daughter by the shoulders. "Kara, you *know* better. This is police business. Go down the street and ask Marge Powell if she'll give you a ride home. Her place will be closing up in half an hour. I'm gonna be tied up here for a while, I'm sure."

Rolling her eyes in disgust, Kara grunted as if slapped, then turned and headed for the office door. " You'd think I'd be privy to at least *some* of the good stuff, rare that it is in this town..." she pouted just before the door shut behind her.

"Now," he continued upon ensuring his daughter's absence, "what happened and where?"

"Well, it seems the trooper interrupted a major WWE event on highway six, just a rock's toss from Wiley Jackson's place," she replied, cleaning her glasses thick lens with a facial napkin. "Trooper Williams reports that upon his arrival, Curtis had pretty well beaten Charlie to a bloody pulp, and had Stan Basham 's teenaged son pinned to the ground with his knees propped on the kid's chest. Jeez, talk about your ridiculous mismatches...I'll bet Barber outweighs Will by a hundred pounds easy."

Rubbing his stubble coated cheeks, Daniel lowered his head for a moment, his entire being racked with exhaustion of both the mental and physical variety. "He's transporting them here, I take it," he finally managed in a weary croak.

"Should be here in ten minutes or so, Chief. In Barber's case, I guess this falls under the headin' of 'breaking parole' with a capital '*B*', am I right?" she inquired, nodding her head in amazement after replacing her glasses.

"Depends on the circumstances. If Stan's son was

212

involved, there's little doubt about who instigated the brawl. Charlie Farris loves a scrap, period, regardless of who ignites it. They probably baited Curtis in town, then chased him down once he didn't respond. I guess it's a good thing I had my little talk with Todd this morning, or he probably would've been mixing it up as well."

Deputy Morton walked around to the back of her desk and began anxiously digging through a lower drawer. " As long as it gets Barber outta our hair, I could care less who started it. I've got a PO guidelines book in here somewhere. They mailed us one from the Parole Office last year, remember?"

Daniel shuffled over to the office door and peered out into the street, his somnolent mind flooded by jumbled thoughts and blurred flashes, none of which were cohesive enough to gain useful insight from. "Sure didn't take long for the levy to crack, did it?" he asked aloud, although unaware of doing so.

Flashing her boss a worrisome look, Deputy Morton saw him back away from the door just as it flung open violently She heard Daniel say 'Now, calm *down..*,' while taking another step back, the form that had just entered the office still blocked from her view as she rose, her right hand parked instinctively on the 38 's cool handle that hung from her side.

***

Time: 1541 HOURS
Date: SAME DAY

Kayla Lee dozed in and out, her eyelids fluttering periodically. As was normally the case, the smattering of

213

psychedelic dreams that flooded her fevered mind had common threads tied to each. The first was the ability to run on legs that seemed inhumanly powerful. Legs that never tired, pumping in harmonic rhythm in a rambling sprint towards an unknown destination. The second, and easily most unsettling, of the common threads was of a sexual nature. The man lay atop her, his massive weight pinning her to what felt literally like a bed constructed of nails and jagged glass. He entered her slowly at first, then gradually increased the speed of his wild humping until his lower body was nothing more than a wavy blur. The face still belonged to Mason Parks, but a mutated, wickedly updated version complete with demon horns and pointy ears, his teeth razor sharp as if filed at the tips. A tongue at least a foot in length but hardly as wide as an earthworm would emerge from his grotesquely wide maw, the forked tips made up of several varieties of snake heads, each with bared fangs that seem to reach for her eyes.

The back door cracking open awoke her, the scream that had built in her chest fading without release at the base of her parched throat. She had parked her chair just a few feet from the portable AC unit, the cold air turning the flesh of her face chillingly numb.

The sunlight had faded from outside the cracked blinds of the living room window, replaced by dusk 's welcome (at least in her mind) intrusion.

"Lucy, I'm hooooome..," Aaron barked, already in the process of removing his disguise as he entered the room.

Wiping the collective drool from the left corner of her mouth and lower jaw, Kayla whirled the chair around to face him as he reached for the cooler's lift-top.

"So? Did you strike pay dirt or what?" she asked in a horse, congested voice.

Aaron consumed half the Dr. Pepper in three long swallows, then paused to burp with a single finger raised in the air. A moist belch ensued, followed by a playful wink and a 'thumbs up' gesture. "The list of viable candidates currently stands at two, each of which will receive a house call early in the a.m., that is if my rubber nose and walrus mustache hold out that long."

Snorting loudly to clear her clogged throat, Kayla strained to swallow the build-up before attempting a response. Aaron felt his stomach churn at both the sight and sound.

"How can you be so sure, so damned cocky?" she finally blurted, her tone somewhat normalized.

Finishing off the soda, Aaron tossed the empty aside and took position directly in front of the AC unit, spreading his arms as if readying to take flight. The scent of stale Brute cologne filled the air. " Because, my dear, none of the others faintly resembled our beloved Mister Hate in neither physical stature nor personality. Also, and most convincingly, the skin of my scalp is tingling ever harder as time passes. It's like a game of *hot and cold*, and rest assured, I'm heating up considerably. Not only that, but the most likely of the two suspects seems obvious, therefore I'll visit him last Just want to cover all the bases. A man, even one as inherently evil as our Mister Hate, can change quite a bit in almost twenty years. I'm not just talking losing or gaining a few pounds, either. If he's been putting on the *Farmer Brown* act for quite a few years, I'm sure he has it down pat."

"I just hope your tingling isn't tumor related. I just can't completely buy into his sixth sense bullshit..." she

215

began, whipping long black tendrils of hair from her face with a single flip of her head.

"Spoken like a true cynic,' he said, turning to face her while loosening his shirt and tie. "Listen, Ms. *Former FBI Agent,* I realize it's hard for the layman to understand my…gift, and it's beyond me to explain something I don't quite understand myself, but it's not the result of an overactive imagination or cancerous growth. I want the buzzing between my ears to cease, and there's only *one* way that's gonna happen. Mason Parks is going down. I'll mark him in the morning…we'll take him out tomorrow at dusk and transport him here. After sufficient jollies are obtained, we dispose of the remains accordingly, and depart without a trace of proof that we ever set foot within a hundred miles of Podunk, Alabama."

Huffing loudly, Kayla spun the chair around until she no longer faced him. "You act as if we're dealing with a crazed ballet dancer, Aaron. I sincerely hope you're not as overconfident as you sound."

His face rapidly growing beat red, Aaron sprinted around her chair to front her, his lips tightly pursed. "*Damn it,* woman! Do you think you're the only one the son of a bitch damaged? I lost my job, my wife…damn near my mind. I've tasted the barrel end of a loaded, cocked revolver more times than I'd like to admit, just never had the balls to seal the deal."

Kayla's head began to dip to her narrow chest as his vocal volume increased. His hand gestures grew more animated, like a church-tent preacher at a Sunday morning revival.

"Can you believe I actually said *didn't have the balls?*... ain't that a hoot? Ain't that a fucking scream?"

216

he yelled, breaking into a spastic, impromptu dancing jig. *"Oh, here comes Johnny with his pecker in his hand, he's a one ball-man and he's off to the rodeo.."* he sang, slapping his knees forcefully to end the performance, then crouching down to stare into her moistened eyes.

"He took my *manhood* away, Kayla, just as he stole your very essence as a woman. I'm *not* taking him lightly, regardless of the act I portray. Understand?" he whispered calmly, placing a cupped hand gently beneath her trembling chin, the soured, rank smell of her filling his nostrils. "Okay?"

"Better get some rest, Aaron Tomorrow's D-Day," she whimpered, clasping his hand as tightly as she could manage.

"I'll go get your bed and set it up in here, right next to my sleeping bag," he said, patting her hand a final time before rising to depart.

Kayla heard the back door open and close, a chorus of crickets and other unidentified residents of the surrounding forests insect life in the beginning stages of their nightly concerto.

Tomorrow was to be Christmas, New Years, and countless lost birthdays all rolled into one neat, albeit undeniably grisly, package. She swore with what remained of her fading, flickering soul that such an occasion would not only be reveled in, but equally cherished as a final highlight reel for the pathetic existence she'd endured since that fateful night in the New Mexico desert.

Kayla Lee slept dreamless for the first time in countless years that night, wrapped in a warm, comforting blanket made up of equal parts revenge and retribution.

***

"I'm following the law as it's stated, Stan. Your boy pulled a tire iron from the back of his truck and attempted to wrap it around the man's skull. That constitutes aggravated assault."

Danie l stood over the seated man, his hands hanging from his drooping utility belt. From her viewpoint across the office, Deputy Morton thought the two resembled a teacher scolding a misbehaving child.

"I won't even go into the fact that he and Chucky Farris over there were loaded to the gills at the time, which constitutes driving while intoxicated. Look at the bright side, Stan, Will's got some bruises and a nasty gash across his forehead. The Doc said it could've been much worse considering the individual he decided to pick a fight with. I whole -heartedly agree with that diagnosis."

Stan Basham's entire face resembled a ripe plum on the verge of bursting from within. Veins as thick as cable cord ran from his forehead to the sides of his stubby, almost non-existent neck. His fists were clinched atop his knees, which visibly shook from a fit of rage he was just beginning to control.

"You know what Barber is, Sheriff! He don't belong here. He's laughin' at us all for allowin' it, don'cha see that? Mockin' us all to hell and back…"

Daniel placed his left hand on the older man's left shoulder and gripped it firmly.

218

When he spoke, his eyes were securely locked on the other man's; his words utterly void of the good-natured tone that was his trademark within the community. "Listen, Stan. You came dangerously close to sharing a cell with your son when you came storming in here like Sergeant Rock hitting the beaches at Normandy. Heed my advice on this, all right? Leave Curtis Barber *be*. The man has every *right* to live here if he so chooses, you got that?"

After initially opening his mouth to respond, Stan Basham ultimately chose a wiser course, dropping his eyes to the floor at his feet and falling silent as the Sheriff strolled away.

Will Basham and Charles Farris had been bloodied and dazed upon their arrival, and Deputy Morton had immediately called Doctor Griffin, who dropped by and administered a quick once-over to each. Deputy Morton had placed the two together in a cell, while saving the remaining space for the man responsible for their wounds.

The only portion of Curtis Barber's person that bled had been his knuckles from punishment *inflicted*, along with a small scrape on the end of his right elbow.

To his credit, Will Basham had freely admitted to chasing Barber down and initiating the ruckus, although the stories varied a bit as to exactly why such a situation had arisen. Stan Basham had apparently told his usually cool-headed son that Barber had 'threatened to kick all our asses', meaning the entire Basham clan, once Stan had told him to vacate the hardware store. Will, who'd been stocking supplies in the back of the store at the time of the confrontation, hadn't questioned his father's words before taking action. He had apparently recruited Charlie

219

F arris from his usual corner spot on Elm and Main and took off after Barber (the two sharing a half-pint of Old Granddad along the way) while Stan stood by and did little to halt the proceedings.

Once the actual scraping had commenced, it had taken less than a minute and a half for the two predators to become cowering, whimpering prey. It had literally been a case of a single man against boys, Barber explaining to Daniel that he had "pulled his punches, otherwise bones would've snapped."

"How they doing back there, Trace?" Daniel asked, already on his way to the holding area.

"Not a peep. I told Will and Charlie that if they even started flappin' their jaws at Barber, I'd put all three of 'em in the same cell," she replied without looking up from her computer.

Daniel smiled despite the intense fatigue. His bones seemed to ache to the very marrow. "Good deal. I bet those two are scared to pass wind about now. You try calling the PO office yet?"

"They must close up shop at four or four-thirty. Couldn't find Hal Mobley's home phone in our Rolodex. I'm emailin' him now."

Looking up from the monitor, the size of her eyes magnified two-fold by the bulky lens, Deputy Morton hesitated before speaking as if dreading the expected response. "What's the plan, Chief? You...we um... ettin' *him* go?"

His jaw set tight, Daniel combed the edges of his mustache with a thumb and forefinger. "The man was merely defending himself, Trace, that's obvious. Ms. Pratt called in a few minutes ago and said she saw the whole thing from her front porch. Personally, I think

220

Curtis showed great restraint in not doing some serious bodily injury to those two."

Returning her gaze to the glowing monitor, the deputy wore an expression of mild disgust. "I take it that's a yes."

With an exasperated groan, Daniel pushed himself away from the filing cabinet he'd been leaning against. He gave Stan a final look before strolling away. The man still sat with his head bowed, pouting like a scolded grade-schooler. "No choice, Tracy. Besides, I'd rather have those three separated by more than just a few metal bars anyhow."

"I still need to report this to Hal, correct? I mean, for future reference purposes, right?"

Ignoring the underlying sarcasm in his subordinate's tone, Daniel's didn't respond until he was a step away from exiting the office for the cell area. He felt his ire rise like a thermometer dipped in hot lava for at least the third time that day. "It's mandatory to do so, *yes*."

His feet and lower legs tingling with a lethal mix of numbness and fatigue, Daniel didn't bother acknowledging either Will Basham or Charlie Farris lying about in the first cell while making a beeline towards the second.

Curtis Barber sat upright on the sagging bunk, one thickly muscled leg crossed over the other. His overall demeanor could only be described as tranquil, giving the impression of a man relaxing inside his own living room with a remote tucked inside one palm.

"You're free to go, Curtis. I'll give you a ride out to your truck."

Stretching as he rose from the bunk, Barber suppressed a yawn as Daniel keyed the door and slid the cell door open.

"Appreciate it, Sheriff Dan. I've got wallpaper to put up and a ton of overgrown weeds to slash, and being that I'm forced to drive twenty-plus miles to get the needed supplies, my schedule's been pretty well derailed for today." Barber winked at the sheriff as he brushed by, the lightly taped knuckles he displayed the only visible evidence of his involvement in the skirmish. "The price you pay for your past around these parts, huh? It's enough to make a soul feel downright unwanted."

As he pulled the cell door shut and prepared to follow the larger man through the office, Daniel felt the pounding at his temple's increase two-fold.

Stan Basham snapped from his self-imposed daze as Daniel caught up to and then led Barber out the front door.

"Be seein' you around, psycho," Basham snarled, both fists clinched tightly at his sides.

Deputy Morton practically leaped from her chair to provide a human buffer between the two men, although it seemed highly unlikely that Stan Basham was up to attempting an assault. He cringed back like a slapped pup at her unexpected arrival. "You might wanna refrain from such macho horse manure in my presence, Stanley. In case ya didn't notice, a cell space *just* opened up. It was your attitude *and* big mouth that started this mess to begin with," she barked, her lips just inches from the shorter man's scarred, pug nose.

"Back in a few, Deputy Morton. Don't hesitate to radio me if the need arises, though I hope with every frazzled fiber in this worn-out body that it don't," Daniel croaked weakly while holding the door open for Barber, who hadn't even bothered to acknowledge the other

222

man's threat.

Deputy Morton returned to her desk only after Stan Basham had retaken his seat, his head again bowed and his rounded shoulders pitifully slumped. " Just sit still and keep a lid on it for a few, will ya, Stan? I've gotta call the county seat about getting a judge to set bail for your boy."

She looked up from her computer monitor only long enough to see Curtis Barber slide into the passenger side of the cruiser, followed by Daniel standing at the driver's side, a look of utter misery coating his frighteningly pale visage like a form-fitted face plate.

Scooping up the receiver, she began slowly punching in numbers, her thoughts dominated by a growing, gnawing concern for a supervisor and friend who seemed dangerously close to a complete, rather inexplicable meltdown.

Despite the cruiser's AC set on high, Daniel felt streams of lukewarm sweat roll down his cheeks, his chest hair matted to the flesh there as if pasted on. "You realize this is only the tip of the 'burg, don't you, Curtis?" he asked, removing his cap and wiping the soaked bangs from his forehead.

"I wasn't expecting a welcome wagon. Rest assured, Sheriff, the man you once referred to as *Chainsaw Barber* is the proud owner of an emotional constitution constructed of the strongest titanium steel. I can take it…*without* necessarily having to dish it out," he replied, staring out the passenger window at a young, well-endowed strawberry blonde crossing Main in high heels that looked at least three inches high.

"How's the love-life, Daniel? You getting any of the local trim or do you prefer the out of town menu? Heard you been divorced for a few ye…"

"Let's stick to the subject at hand, Curtis, alright?" Daniel snapped, smelling his own pungent body odor mixed with the other man's heavy coating of cologne.

"Wanna hear 'bout mine? It's a bit on the sordid side, but hey, it *was* state prison after all. Humans crave the touch no matter what the situation, you know? Don't get me wrong, I wasn't a butt bandit, but after a few years the old pecker starts to ache for some action, I was…"

"Put a sock in it, Curtis..," the Sheriff replied sternly, passing a slow-moving tractor as they exited Main for the highway. "Never tried that myself, but I did see some guys stash shanks in socks. I'm talking six to seven inch blades crammed into the old fudge factory. Man, that *had* to hurt, you think? Now, back to *sexual confessions of the incarcerated…"*

"Shut up, *DAMN IT*!" Daniel screamed, accidentally pulling the car half onto the soft shoulder before righting their path.

Raising his hands in mock surrender, Barber nodded and fell silent, his lips frozen in a comical sneer.

"Heard you spent some time in the Army," he finally said, turning to study Daniel 's reaction.

"Six years, two months, fourteen days."

The larger mouth laughed, turning his sights to the sparse oncoming traffic greeting them on the narrow two-lane. "You mean you didn't count minutes *and* seconds? What was that like? I mean, back in high school you didn't seem like the soldier type. You were a pretty decent tight end, if I recall correctly. Decide you weren't the preppy, college type or were you just a glutton for punishment?"

Daniel sighed heavily, motivating the cruiser past an

ancient Chevy pickup which was leaving a thick, black vapor trail of smoke in its chugging wake. He lowered his window and stuck his left arm out, waving at the driver as he passed.

"Lester Mays. A one man ozone layer demolition crew."

"Must be weird to *know* everybody. Anyhow, when did you start the Army hitch?"

"A month or so after Debra's funeral," Daniel replied, his hands visibly tensing atop the steering wheel.

Barber twisted his massive frame around, hooking his left arm over the seat. Daniel could feel the man's unrelenting gaze pierce his flesh like a loaded syringe. "Got'cha. Very unsettling time in Elm Hill, it was. Didn't your mother object to such a decision? I seem to recall your dad passing away when we were just kids. Her only child joining the military must have been like a lightning bolt from the clear blue sky."

"I needed to get away, Curtis. She…understood."

"Rest her soul, Daniel. I heard she passed a few years back. Lung cancer, wasn't it?"

His eyes darting from a deserted stretch of flat, recently tarred roadway to the other man for just a split-second, Daniel fought once again to reign in his building anger. He quickly refocused on the road as a large semi materialized from the opposite direction. "You planning on writing my autobiography, Curtis?"

The other man laughed, although a bit too smugly for Daniel's taste. "Received the ol' home town news the last five years of my lockup. You'd never believe what a simple pleasure it was to flip through the *Elm Hill Telegraph* every Thursday morning. Hell, it was a real highlight, sad to say. I kept up with things on the home

225

front in case I did decide to come back."

The two fell into a decidedly uncomfortable silence for a full three minutes, Daniel increasing the cruiser's speed just enough as not to become obvious. Barber spoke only when the tail end of his pickup came into view after a particularly sharp curve.

"Did you really love Debbie Lee?" he finally asked in a calm, mechanical tone one might associate with a psychiatrist querying a newly assigned patient.

Swallowing hard, Daniel did well to park the cruiser a few feet behind the truck without actually hitting it, the cruiser's passenger side tires dangerously close to the shoulders steep edge. Placing the vehicle in park, he began to respond, praying that the words didn't escape his lips in an incomprehensible stutter, but was abruptly cut off.

Barber no longer stared at him, but into the deep, rocky ravine to his right. His tone was no longer calm or robotic, but sincerely poignant and laced with an undercurrent of deep-rooted frustration. "I didn't kill her, Daniel. Never even *saw* her at the lake that night."

"Curtis, I'm not a judge or jury. I can't sanctify anyone's deeds or non-deeds, if that's what you're..."

Barber popped open the door and stepped out without speaking, then walked around to the front of the cruiser and leaned down next to the driver's window, which Daniel had rolled down half way.

"I'm not asking for forgiveness, Daniel. Just stating the facts as I know they are. Just thought...you might have a need to know. You'll either believe me or you won't. Don 't get me wrong, I'm not kissing up to the local law here. We go back a ways, you and I. Stan Basham and his type crucified me years ago. Can't really blame the family. I *won't* bother repeating the same words to them. Thanks for the ride, Daniel."

Five minutes after watching the pickup pull away and out of site, Daniel cut the cruiser's low-idling engine and got out, his gait slightly wobbly as he strolled across the pavement to an overgrown valley infested with waist high sea-grass and weeds. Peering back over his shoulder, he could see the eastern edge of Rose Pratt's brick home. Rose was a notorious 'porch gazer', but Daniel figured the ninety-degree plus temperatures would keep her safely tucked inside for at least another few hours.

Falling to his knees just as the initial heave racked his chest, he lowered his head and violently ejected what remained of a sparse lunch consumed hours earlier, the dark-tinted sunglasses he wore sailing into a nearby thicket.

Returning to the cruiser a few moments later, his legs feeling strangely detached from the rest of his body, Daniel nodded amiably at a silver Honda Civic as it whizzed by, driven by a male teen he faintly recognized but couldn't quite place a name to.

As he drove unhurriedly back towards town, he once again cranked the AC unit to its maximum level to prevent possibly nodding off behind the wheel. Checking the rear-view mirror, Daniel saw only a pasty-skinned, hollow-eyed skull staring back.

***

Time: 1824 HOURS
Date: SAME DAY

"Kara, is your dad home?"

"He left a few minutes ago, Deputy Morton, still in uniform. I couldn't even get him to eat a sandwich."

The deputy laid flat on the weight bench, the cellular phone pinned to her ear. Fresh sweat coated her face, neck and chest. The lenses of her glasses were quickly fogging over, even as her breathing normalized. "He leave you a clue to his whereabouts? Maybe he got a hot tip on a local still," she said good-naturedly, doing her best to avoid sounding negative.

"No idea, Peep...uh, Tracy. He's been a little spaced out lately, what with that man Barber back in town and all. Like, he's not sleeping very well. He's had problems on and off with that as long as I can remember, but now, it's like, magnified to a much bigger one. I told him this morning he looks like a walking advertisement for Sim's Mortuary. I kinda wish now that I hadn't said that..."

Kara Whitlock was old for her years, the deputy realized, having gone through the divorce of her parents and being handed the responsibility of maintaining a household in her mom's absence. It didn't take a seasoned law enforcement officer to detect the sincere concern in the young girl's voice. "Don't worry about it Kara, your old man is tough as nails. He's just having to deal with a lot since Barber's return to town. Hey, tell him to call me when he gets in, okay? *I'm* the one on call tonight, after all."

"Alright," Kara replied, her tone again bubbly and slightly indifferent. Deputy Morton was amazed at how flexible the teen mind could be, although she couldn't quite recall such carefree days herself. "And Kara?"

"Yeah?"

"I'm buyin' contacts next month, so you guys won't

228

be callin' me 'Peepers' anymore." Pulling herself upright, the deputy could almost feel the girl's embarrassment as the line stayed silent while a suitable reply was being pondered.

"Uh…I…well, it's like, uh…"

"Forget it, Kara. It never bothered me. In my day, I'm sure I would have thought of something *much* more insulting. Talk at ya later."

"Yeah, uh…goodnight, Deputy Tracy…uh, Tracy. I'll …um…tell Dad that you called."

Finishing her work out an hour later, the deputy strolled into the kitchen and pulled a bottle of water from the refrigerator. Her husband joined her in their cramped living room a few minutes later, clutching a partially consumed Slim Jim in one hand and the TV remote in the other.

"He still hasn't called?" he asked, taking a seat beside her on the worn sectional couch they'd purchased at a flea market six months earlier.

"Nope. I'm on call this week, and he's out playin' Marshall Dillon somewhere. It's gotta have something to do with Barber."

"Hard to believe anybody would willingly place themselves in the eye of the storm the way that guy's doin'," Pete Morton said between chews.

Tracy kneeled onto the thick shag carpet and began stretching, a familiar TV theme song being whistled out as the volume increased on the big screen set fronting her.

"Yep, it's definitely somethin' serious. Six-thirty, Andy's on, and Dan's nowhere to be found. If the daily visit to Mayberry's bein' tampered with, we might well be lookin' at a mass murder," she quipped, her husband

229

seemingly oblivious to her presence as TVLand tunnel vision swarmed his senses, his eyes blank slates of boob-tube concentration.

"Oh Lord, he's one of *them,*" she concluded humorously, although her thoughts were far less whimsical in nature. Trouble and strife had followed Curtis Barber from the state pen to Elm Hill, and seemed to be mutating into a benevolent being all its own as hours progressed into days. The man was walking a tightrope that was unraveling at breakneck speed, dragging a handful of townsfolk and her supervisor down into a black hole of as of yet *unseen* perils. A sense of overwhelming foreboding and dread floated over the city limits of Elm Hill like an overfilled, poisonous cloud waiting to release its toxic content.

Finishing a set of intense crunches, Tracy Morton felt her scalp tingle with anticipation of something ghastly looming over the distant horizon. Stranger still, she had a nagging suspicion that most, but by no means *all,* of the building conflict tied into the person of Mr. Curtis Barber. Staring at the phone on the way to get another bottle of water, she suddenly wished she had the power to *will* it to ring.

***

Time: 1917 HOURS
Date: SAME DAY

Pulling his bright red Dodge pickup through the metal gate entranceway, Daniel felt as if he were entering the grounds of a long abandoned asylum. The tall shrubbery which fronted the sharp-tipped rod iron fencing hadn't seen pruning shears in what looked like several years, while the dark red brick structure looming in the background was coated in thick waves of kudzu, enhancing the overall look of desertion. The mailbox at the corner of the narrow paved road leading up to the entrance had read *Hendricks* in badly faded white lettering, and Daniel could feel his pulse rate increase measurably as he grew closer to the wide, circled driveway.

The last he'd heard, which had been at least four to five years back, Lance Hendricks hadn't been in the best of health, the early stages of Parkinson's having already begun to take their devastating toll. A few select cells of Daniel's irrational mind hoped the man was deceased, or at least suitably incapacitated. The rational side, the fine line of which was growing admittedly thinner as days passed, he would reluctantly admit, held to the optimism that Elm Hill's former sheriff would be able to communicate well enough to provide the information he'd traveled to obtain.

If Hendricks had owned a working phone, he'd kept it unlisted. Not an uncommon practice among retired law enforcement personnel, weary of visits from old acquaintances that might just have a bitter bone or two to pick. Daniel had flipped through the county phone book regardless, the few pages that covered West Bay, Alabama, population eighty-six (or so listed in the 2000 census) conspicuously void of anyone named Hendricks. He figured the twenty-five mile trek to be worth it regardless of the outcome. At least it gave him time to think without constant interruption.

Departing his truck for the stone steps of the home's oak deck, Daniel could see a faint light shining through a front window, and could hear the faint sounds of classical music reverberate from the same space. In his tenure as Elm Hill's head keeper of justice, Daniel had heard much of Lance Hendricks, as well as the man's deputy for the final thirteen of his twenty-three year run as sheriff, Billy Detmer. Most of it had been positive, both men described as straightforward and fair if not totally squeaky clean when dealing with bribes dealt out by local bootleggers.

Adjusting his utility belt before reaching to knock on the solid oak door, Daniel suddenly felt more clearheaded than he had in days, the enormous pressure and lack of quality sleep that had been his constant enemy temporarily dismissed. Like an old Warner Brothers cartoon where a luminescent bulb glowed over a characters head once an idea or course of action became crystal clear, the proper plan revealed itself to his torn and ragged mind.

As he began to gently knock, Daniel felt a tremendous weight fall from his battered, weary soul. A *cleansing* of sorts was in order, for certain; a cleansing not only for ghostly appreciations long overdue to be laid to permanent rest, but for an entire community as a whole.

***

Time: 0908 HOURS
Date: 1 September 2006

"Good morning, Sir. Ma y I ask you one simple question?" the man blurted, his pasted on smile noticeably shaky despite his best efforts to conceal that fact. Standing in the doorway with his hat in one hand

and a shiny black briefcase in the other, he could feel his sweat-soaked T-shirt stick to the flesh beneath the sharply ironed dress shirt covering it. He had openly flinched upon viewing the man who had pulled the door ajar, coming dangerously close to swinging the arm strapped with a loaded syringe up and out in a defensive posture. His senses were assaulted by a resounding, electricity-charged vibe that lasted only until the man's face came clearly into focus, along with the stout smell of rut gut whiskey.

Aaron Kyle's felt the shock wave sting his flesh as Mason Parks stared him down, the man's appearance *exactly* as it had been that night in the New Mexico desert eighteen years earlier. His naked chest and arms were grotesquely pumped as he propped the rapier blade over his shoulder like a farmer's rake.

Aaron had stepped back as if he had been stung and began to raise his arm to properly position the syringe injector to strike, his lips stuck to his teeth as his salesman's smile hung precariously in warped limbo.

The horrid hallucination vanished as quickly as it had appeared in a matter of heartbeats, the middle aged man standing before him a pale imitation of the terrifying mirage his mind had so expertly created. The man was naked above the waist, true enough, and had vaguely similar facial features to Parks if one calculated the aging process, but was so much smaller in stature that Aaron instantly relaxed and fell into his well-rehearsed spiel without missing a beat.

Get a grip and swallow a chill pill, Aaron old buddy. And I thought I was mentally prepped for this. Almost made a Milky Way in my drawers.

"What question is that, mister? You here from the

233

state 'bout my driveway?" the man queried, rubbing his substantial waistline as if indicating hunger.

"No sir, I'm here to save yourself and your loved ones precious dollars while simultaneously providing priceless piece of mind. My question concerns your present health insurance situation," Aaron replied, using his free hand to replace his cap, a derby styled headpiece that he had found in a thrift shop near Biloxi some years earlier while putting together what Kayla sarcastically referred to as 'his Cracker Jack's disguise kit.'

The man stepped back and studied Aaron for a few moments, his mouth hanging agape. Aaron quietly held his breath to avoid the sickly sour odor of the man's breath, although he did so without compromising his painted-on grin.

"What loved ones might that be, mister?"

"Krane, United Fidelity, and *you* are?"

Pushing away from the door to re-enter the living room, the man vanished into the dimly lit space, belching loudly. The door itself stayed ajar, although Aaron couldn't tell exactly what held it into position.

"Hoyt…Hoyt R. Wilson. C-come on in, Mister Lane. I'll be right with ya. G-gotta go drain the lizard. Take a seat if you can find a clean spot."

The living room reeked of stale booze and cigar smoke. Checking his watch just as a toilet flushed in the foreground, Aaron inhaled deeply in an attempt to calm his slowly decreasing pulse. The skin of his scalp literally felt *ablaze* as the internal buzzing at his temples and base of his skull increased in intensity. By simple process of elimination, there was no longer any doubt where Mason Parks would be found. He hoped Wilson would give him the quick 'brush off', the process of 'going through the motions' no longer either necessary or viable. Eighteen years of similar charades and schemes were finally coming to a merciful end.

Pulling a badly faded *LA Raiders* tee over his head as he strolled back into the room, Wilson snorted loudly as if to clear clogged sinuses.

Damned if the old boozer doesn't favor Parks with the buzzcut, no-neck look, but the nose and mouth are all wrong. Plus, there's no way Parks would go to pot in such a dramatic way, especially if he's killing again. This poor old dude has been residing inside a bottle of Jack Black for at least a few decades.

"Now, what was you sellin' again, Mr. Baines? Dental insurance?" Hoyt asked groggily.

Aaron's smile faded a bit as he suddenly found his motivation sorely lacking.

Ho-kay, here goes. Let's make this quick but not too obvious. Even a boozehound can get suspicious if you hand him enough red herrings.

"Supplemental health, actually, and the names Krane, thank you. Uh, it actually benefits your family as well as yourself. With the outlandish costs of medical care these days, our company provides additional coverage's that will save a family unit a substantial amount over a year's time."

Wilson brushed away a pile of scattered newspaper from a nearby recliner and sat down before reaching to scratch his groin through faded purple pajama bottoms. "Sorry to waste your time, Krane, but the VA hospital in Birmingham handles all my medicines and such. Actually, I ain't seen a sawbones since a ragin' case of hemorrhoids way back in ninety-six. Y'know, they had to go in and cut those ornery little suckers out. My ass was

sore for a month afterwards, but it sure beat the itchin'
and burnin' I was livin' with at the time, I... "

His patience rapidly waning as the loud clicking of a
nearby grandfather's clock echoed inside his already
frazzled mind, Aaron held up a hand in mock surrender.

"Understood, Mister Wilson. Veterans such as you
rarely need our services Um, do you know if your
neighbor down the way might be interested in what my
company has to offer?"

Wilson frowned as if smelling his own putrid breath,
his eyes squinted to narrow slits.

"Doug Matson? *Hell* son, you'll be lucky to pry
more'n two words outta him on any subject, but I guess
he does have the ability to say yes or no. Give it a
shot...can't hurt."

Tipping his hat politely, Aaron bowed like a
theatrically trained stage actor. "Apologize for wasting
your time, Mister Wilson. You have a great day now. Try
to stay out of this heat if you can and drink lots of
liquids."

Wilson winked playfully while again scratching his
groin. "Oh, I plan on doin' just that, Mister Paine, soon
as I get sober enough to drive to the county line for a
couple'a ice-cold cases of Busch."

Aaron nodded without replying further and departed,
for once finding the steamy, breezeless outdoor air a
welcome respite. Entering his vehicle, he peered into the
valley below and caught a glimpse of the next home he
planned to visit. The final such visit in a prolonged
nightmare he had once thought would never find closure.
Only a squared edge of roof could be seen due to
surrounding trees and overgrown shrubbery. Starting the
vehicle's engine, he scooped up his cell phone and dialed

236

while slowly backing from the rut-filled driveway.

"Kayla my sweet and sour morsel? Yes, I've checked off suspect number one, a retired Navy drunkard named Wilson. His reclusive neighbor is all that remains, my dear. Goes by the name Matson. Yes, I'm headed there as our lip's flap. Yes, dear...I'll be very, very cautious. Kayla, on the outside chance you don't...hear from me in...let's say...twenty minutes, the man's address is Route eight off highway six. There are only two homes out here and Parks' sets lowest in the valley. I...thought you'd like a crack at him if...well, things go bad on my end."

He paused, his shoulders visibly tensing.

"I'm as ready as I'll ever be, Kayla. Rubber nose is firmly in place and syringe rocket is locked and loaded. Yes, Kay, it *has* to be him. My head is filled with a swarm of extremely agitated hornets and it's not letting up one iota. Call you in a few."

Listening to the vehicles tires pass over loose gravel as it descended down the winding grade, Aaron reminded himself to check the syringe rocket one last time before exiting the vehicle. His mind raced even as the high-pitched racket between his throbbing temples seemed to stabilize.

Jesus, what if I am wrong and it isn't Parks? After being so cocksure...NO, don't even start that shit! There's no way in hell. He's here, and he's waiting. If I doubt myself, I'm apt to show it...and he'll know it somehow. Then I'm meat on a hook. Just breathe deep and think of the mission ahead. Think of that sadistic Son of Satan bound to a chair and bleeding like a stuck pig. Think of the joy on Kayla Lee's face as she finally has her way with him. Think of the burden finally lifted after all these long, miserable, hellish years. Let's do it, and do it right the first time. Lord knows I'll only get one chance.

The homestead swam fully into view as he executed a sharp right turn, and Aaron Kyle felt his entire being grow horrifyingly numb.

***

Time: 0813 HOURS
Date: SAME DAY

"I gotta admit, you look positively refreshed this mornin', Boss. Don't tell me you've resorted to hittin' the bottle before bedtime," Deputy Morton said cheerily, filling her *Auburn Tigers* coffee cup to the brim with steaming black coffee.

Daniel leaned back with his hands resting at the back his neck, his spit-polished boots propped on the edge of his desk. " Just had a decent night for once, I guess. Pretty sad when you start considering six hours of sleep the best you're ever gonna get. Gotta admit though...I do feel full of vigor and vinegar this a.m. compared to the last week or so."

"I still say ya sneaked down highway six last night and had a belt or two with ol' Hoyt," she replied, grinning sheepishly.

"So Stan made bail for both of 'em, huh?" he asked between sips of his own morning nectar, a large mug of iced-down orange juice poured from a dark crimson *ROLL TIDE* mug.

"Yeah. Judge Lawson set 'em both at two grand. Little on the lenient side if you ask me, Sheriff, especially

238

for aggravated assault. You think?"

"I would have thought three to five for each, but a lot depends on what mood Lawson was in at the time, plus the fact that neither Will nor Charlie has much in the way of a criminal past other than the handful of DWI's old Chuck has accumulated over the years. Trial date set?"

"Yep. Sept 13th , 11 a.m. at the County Courthouse You gonna inform Barber or shall I?"

Massaging the sides of his neck, Daniel paused to yawn before replying. "I'll get out there sometime today. You ever hear from Hal at the PO office?"

"That I did, oh groggy lawman. Received his email response first thing this morning upon firin' up my modem. In effect he said, 'no harm, no foul', that there's no violation in bein' violated. He would like a copy of the arrest report faxed to 'im, though. I'll get on that first thing."

Both fell into a comfortable silence as they drank from their respective containers, only the periodic sound of a passing vehicle on Main Street interrupting the tranquility.

As Deputy Morton rose to refill her cup, suppressing a yawn of her own in the process, she studied her supervisor curiously. "So where'd you traipse off to last night anyhow? Kara give you the message to ring me at home?"

Daniel stood and turned to the window behind his desk and opened the blinds just enough to peer through. The early morning sun was fast fading behind a line of puffy, dark clouds. " She told me you called, but it was after ten when I got home, so I thought I might be waking you up. I thought it might be a good idea to drive back over to Todd Platt's and reiterate my earlier warning. I'd

239

heard he was having a few co-workers over, so I figured it'd be a good time to set 'em all straight on the subject of harassing of a fellow citizen."

Before his subordinate could respond, Daniel nodded apathetically and resumed, his tone noticeably graver. "Elm Hill 's on the verge of economic shutdown, Trace. I've heard more rumors about the sawmill closing for good in October. That'll be another twelve men out of work."

"We'll survive, Boss. The town was here long before we got hatched, and I doubt they'll run a 'dozer over her streets anytime within the next four or five decades.

Besides, what do we care? We'll be nothin' more than worm-dirt by then anyhow."

Daniel's laugh was deep and hardy, a welcome sound his partner hadn't witnessed with much frequency of late. "Not sure if that comment falls under the heading 'optimistic' or not, actually."

She shrugged before turning to her computer's keypad and positioning her fingers to type. "You worry too much, Sheriff. Army must have implanted a 'paranoia' chip behind your ear or somethin'."

"Paranoia? Tracy, as I've informed you ad nauseam…I'm *only* paranoid because everybody's out to get me."

"Right," she replied, her fingers sailing rapidly over the keys as the glow of the monitor coated her naturally youthful face, which held hardly a tint of make-up. "So how did Todd and the others react to your little 'dressing down' session?"

"Mostly just lowered their heads and nodded in agreement to everything I said, although how sincere any of 'em really were remains to be seen, I guess."

240

Deputy Morton leaned back and sighed, watching Daniel as he continued to stare onto the streets, his stance unnaturally rigid. From the angle she enjoyed, she could make out the haggard, worn features of her mentor, who seemed to have aged a decade in the past few weeks. Just before he turned to face her, Tracy could have sworn she noticed his right eye twitching in a spastic tick.

"Guess I'll go on patrol. Anything on the ticker this fine Central Alabama morning?" he asked in a false, overly enthusiastic tone that Tracy instantly deemed a bit *too* cheery.

"Blank slate, Chief. You goin' out to Barber's place before lunch?"

Pulling on his cap, Daniel then stood at the doorway and jingled the cruiser's keys in a loosely clinched fist. "Might as well, I reckon. I tell you though, Trace, I'm beginning to think we ought to go ahead and relocate this office next to Barber's house. Save us time *and* gas money," he said before departing into the morning humidity, leaving his deputy pondering why her gut instinct was strongly hinting that her boss wasn't being completely honest on several counts.

Later that morning, Deputy Morton happened to spot Todd Platt exiting the Rexall Drug store. After sprinting from the office to waive him down, she asked Todd point blank about his meeting with Daniel, to which the openly perturbed man had snapped " I get the message already, Deputy. I have to tell ya, it kinda pissed me off that Dan came to my workplace and called me out like that. He should'a just came by the house or phoned me, for Pete's sake." Her suspicions confirmed, the deputy had dismissed the man with a brief nod and returned to the office. Monitoring the scanner while half-heartedly

241

surfing the web, Tracy sat at her desk and contemplated a series of possibilities as to why Daniel had lied about his whereabouts the night before. Was he having a secret affair that he wished to keep just that? The man had been divorced for a number of years, so it certainly would come as no shock. In their years working together, Tracy had seen more than one of the local women set their hooks for Daniel, though he usually seemed haplessly oblivious to any fishing line ever being extended. She oft wondered how he kept his sanity remaining celibate for such a lengthy period without ultimately blowing a fuse.

The more obvious answer to his deceit involved the Curtis Barber situation, though she couldn't for the life of her figure either a problem or solution other than the obvious, that being keeping the man from being publicly lynched or stoned in the street. Daniel had always been a bit tight-lipped on the matter of Debra Rainer's death, other than to make the point that the two hadn't been as close as some townsfolk had rumored.

Maybe he had simply went for a leisurely drive in the country to mull things over, but why lie about it to her? They had always confided in each other, at least up until now.

She had waited patiently to be corrected a few moments earlier. Waited for Daniel to turn to her with that hang-dog, "Think about what you're saying, Tracy" expression that she had grown so accustomed to when she had asked if he was going to drop by Curtis Barber's *residence* before lunch. Curtis had began work at Stony Watt's garage the day before, a fact that couldn't have possibly been dismissed by her boss, unless he was either suffering the early stages of Alzheimer's or knew something she didn't regarding the man 's work schedule. Deputy Morton considered reaching over and checking Daniel's twenty via the two-way, but could think of no valid excuse to do so. Stony's shop was less than two miles to the east, as opposed to Barber's residence, which was easily a twenty-minute jaunt in the opposite direction. There was always the possibility that Daniel hadn't heard her question clearly, but that fell under the bolded category listed as 'Slim and None.' The man was nothing if not verbally observant to what was being said around him, regardless of the level of sleep depravity he might be suffering.

The phone's echoing ring shoved her rudely back into reality a moment later.

Mayor Jenkins wanted to see her as soon as possible concerning the Founders Day 'Respect for the Law Seminar' she had scheduled to present to the upcoming Elm High Hill Freshman class. It seemed a few of the parents had deemed the impromptu 'scared straight' speech she had planned not just unnecessary, but an insult to their angelic offspring.

Huffing in exasperation, she donned her cap and exited the office, careful to hang the *Back Soon – That's a Promise* sign on the outside of the door. As she strolled across the street towards the faded red brick City Hall building, which stood at the center of Main Street like an ancient, crumbling castle minus only the moors, Deputy Morton paused mid-way to allow a shiny Red Blazer to pass on its way out of town. She didn't bother to raise a hand in greeting, understanding such a sociable act was a waste of motion considering the Blazer's driver. As she continued across, she noticed the rear of Douglas Matson's vehicle was packed full of what looked like recent purchases from either the grocery or hardware

243

store, large plastic sacks of what might have been fertilizer stacked high and tight against the back glass.

"Little late in the game to be plantin' anything. Well, weird *is* as weird does, I reckon," she mumbled aloud just before exiting the already scorching outside air for the frigid coolness of the City Hall building.

A few hundred yards up the road, Douglas Matson released a nervous sigh, a trail of fresh perspiration racing down the left side of his face despite the vehicle's relatively cool interior. He'd seen the deputy's roving eyes as he passe d by, carefully studying his recent purchases before she vanished from the Blazer's driver side mirror.

Conflicting emotions gripped him in a sharp-edged vice, his thick fingers turning a light shade of purple on the sweat-slick steering wheel as his breathing became uncomfortably labored. A part of him wanted the deputy, Stan Basham at the Hardware store, or *anyone* for that matter, to act on suspicion and question such unusual purchases or such openly anti-social behavior. The other half of the undeniably confused equation wanted nothing more than their continued indifference to his plight, a small-town 'none of our business' approach that had prevailed for over a decade within his stoic presence.

Still, the ever-present fantasy refused to fade without a mental feeding, a fantasy involving extensive investigations, followed by horrific revelations and ultimately, sweet liberation from the unrelenting sense of foreboding that gripped his weary soul.

Exiting Main Street onto highway six, Matson all owed such thoughts to coat his subconscious in a wave of crushing relief, despite the cold hard reality that fought for intrusion within a mind ravaged by guilt and a feeling

244

of utter helplessness.

Arriving home approximately twelve minutes later, he temporarily dismissed the arduous task of unloading the goods for a tall glass of iced water and a quick, mid-morning nap, where he prayed for dreams void of freshly dug graves and the sour, slowly decaying smell of the recently deceased.

***

Time: 0834 HOURS
Date: SAME DAY

Daniel exited the cruiser with great deliberation, like a recently released surgery patient still reeling from the effects of pain medication. Adjusting his sunglasses to better block the effects of the mid-morning glare, he stood by the driver side door and surveyed the surrounding landscape as if conducting a geological analysis. The road at his back was deserted in both directions as far as the eye could see which was at least a few hundred yards from either side. Backing up several steps until his dust-coated heels were mere inches from the pavement, he checked to ensure complete privacy before popping the cruiser's trunk with the casual twist of a key.

Daniel felt the dryness in his throat and licked his equally parched lips in a fruitless attempt to relieve their chapped, cracked state.

He pulled the object from the trunk, careful to retain the cloth wrapping which encircled it. Almost tiptoeing forward, he moved as if toting a container filled with nitro-glycerine through a live minefield, his legs bent

245

somewhat awkwardly.

He hadn't gotten ten feet from the front of the cruiser before freezing in place as if ordered to do so at gunpoint, his head turned to the right and cocked slightly upwards. Later that evening, he would have sworn with his hand parked on a stack of Bibles that his heart had ceased beating for a full five seconds. The distant humming of an approaching engine faded abruptly, and Daniel felt his pulse throb and pound at his throat and temples as he gradually rediscovered the ability to breathe.

After a moment's further hesitation to ensure no uninvited company was forthcoming, he resumed his forward progress, his slumped, slow-moving gait comparable only to that of a man traveling towards the spot of his own execution.

***

Time: 0924 HOURS
Date: SAME DAY

Aaron Kyle's faculties refused to adhere to even his most fevered commands. He sat parked directly across from a shiny, dark blue mailbox reading MATSON.D in stained white lettering, his mind a virtual roadmap of blurred imagery and severely impaired nerve endings. Looking at his hands, which still gripped the steering wheel loosely, he was mildly surprised that neither shook nor trembled within his frantic mindset. He felt as if he had stuck all ten fingers inside a light socket and was unable to pull free.

Jesus... old man Death has made this place a regular stop on his route for quite some time now. Yes

246

sir-ree, Bob Newhart. There are some unsettled old bones rattling within this stretch of land, no doubt what-so-fucking-ever. I can...almost hear 'em scream out from the dark, moldy pit they've been tossed into. I wish Kayla were here...and could...experience what I'm feeling. Don't think she'd ever question my special sense again. I feel like somebody just punctured my spine with a live wire.

After taking a moment to inhale deeply through his nostrils and exhale from between blue-tinted lips, Aaron managed to drive the vehicle forward and park a few feet to the rear of a red Chevy Blazer with a recently applied wax job.

Welcome to Hell House. Jesus, place looks like a Farmer's Almanac book cover come to life. Poor folks around here have had no inkling what kind of monstrosity they've shared the town with these last several years Even money the evil bastard is a card carrying member of a local agriculture Chapter... Maybe Even A Member Of The City Council Or The Local school board. Mason "Mister Hate" Parks, citizen farmer...it is to laugh...or cry, depending on one's outlook, I guess.

Exiting his car on weakened legs, each seemingly transformed into foam rubber upon his arrival on the man's property, Aaron eyeballed the supplies packed so snugly into the rear of the Blazer. He could read the word *LIME* on the outside of a few of the piled bags, instantly activating a new series of alarms inside his already overtaxed brain.

Damn, how obvious is that? Unless the man has a cellar full of rotting veggies, I can think of only one other logical use.

247

Shaking his head from side to side, as if to ward off a swarm of pesky insects, Aaron reached back inside the vehicle and removed the briefcase, then took a moment to straighten his tie and ensure the stability of the stick-on mustache presently tickling his nostrils. Securing his hat and checking his belt line, he could feel his pulse begin to slow. Walking past the Blazer towards the front porch, he tucked his right hand tightly against his thigh to ensure the trigger mechanism of the syringe spring loader was locked into 'firing' mode.

He paused with his right foot posed on the bottom porch step upon noticing the cellar door to his left. The iron bar lying across its oak center looked at least two inches thick, a master lock the size of a man's fist clamping it firmly to the stone exterior outside the door itself.

As folks down here might say, that makes about as much sense as tits on a boar. If a twister's making a bee - line for your home, do you really want to take the time to search for a key to your safe haven? But then, Aaron old pal old salt, I do believe we already know the answer to that one. It's more a 'death-haven' than a safe haven, now isn't it?

He gave little notice to the perfectly manicured grass area around the shelter's perimeter, altering his focus to the task at hand. His last official act of *non*-employment, that being his 'final sales pitch' as the one and only spokesman for a fictional insurance company whose name he'd chosen from a Yellow Pages ad in New Orleans. The porch's top step creaked and groaned as his foot left it, just as a gust of hot wind blew at his back like probing fingers, shoving him forward towards a fateful meeting with destiny.

Aaron noted the lack of buzzing between his ears just before the knuckles of his right hand softly struck the metal paneling of the screen door.

To hell with marking the bastard--I'm taking him down at the first opening. Plant the needle in a neck vein and watch him squirm. We'll keep him bound and sufficiently doped up while setting up the equipment in the shed out back. I can't take the chance of him getting suspicious and bolting, not when we're this damned close to pay dirt, not when...

The front door swung open even as the knob was being twisted, and for the briefest of terrifying moments, Aaron Kyle felt his bladder scream for release.

***

Time: 0925 HOURS
Date: SAME DAY

Staring at the moisture cracked wallpaper on a far living room wall while the constant

hum of the generator served to enhance the daze she had so willingly fell into, Kayla Lee experienced her own psychic flash. Unlike her partner, it wasn't a buzzing or klaxon alarm or even a series of mental movie frames, but simply a *premonition* deep from within her slowly wilting gut.

Aaron was taking *their* set laws into his own potentially careless hands. At least a decade's worth of detailed planning shot to proverbial hell. If he failed in his one shot at capturing the beast known as Mason Parks, she would surely die without ever tasting the sweet fruit of unbridled vengeance. A low click escaped her throat, like a small child's frightened gasp, the fear in that single thought more paralyzing than all of her physical ailments combined.

Navigating the chair to sit directly in front of the AC unit, Kayla opened her mouth wide to allow the air to blow directly into her suddenly vacant lungs.

As a young FBI Agent Trainee in another life, she had made a habit of depending on what some merely referred to as *female intuition* , but what she understood to be a mental 'feeler' existing on a much larger, more complicated scale. It was a mysterious phenomenon she never took for granted, much like Aaron and his 'gift', and one that had never failed her until a certain night in Conquest, New Mexico some eighteen and a half years earlier Since that time, Kayla had experienced brief flashes, although not nearly as powerful and certainly not as breathtakingly convincing as in her youth. She made the conscious decision to simply ignore them, paying no heed to their garbled pleas or blurred forewarnings.

Whether it be from the cascading waves of adrenaline assaulting her being or the overtaxed bounds securing her once logical way of thinking tittering on the edge of decay, this specific batch of preordained messages were different. They *refused* to be ignored, despite her Herculean efforts to do just that.

She stared down at her lap, the palm-sized cell phone resting between her frail, bony thighs like a living entity; an egg made of metal, glass and plastic that she guarded with the unrestrained concern of a mother bird over a soon to be freed hatchling.

Digging the lengthy, painted fingernails of her working hand deep into the flesh of the palm, Kayla began to pray to a God she had *long* since discarded. The last time she could recall reaching such heights of spiritual decadence, it had been as a pre-teen girl, strapped naked to a bed and waiting to die within the mansion walls of a millionaire pedophile named Markum.

She trusted with every fiber of her disintegrating soul that the current prayers relay a more positive outcome. Moments later, as a single warm tear ran from the corner of her left eye onto the smoothness of her immaculate jaw line, she wheeled the chair towards the kitchen exit with renewed vigor. "The agony of waiting for something important was best spent in the art of usefulness, " her old field supervisor in the bureau used to preach. Using the chair's built-in auto-lift to raise the chair's front tires over the door's bottom framing, Kayla then crossed the gravel pathway towards the waiting van. There were, of course, limits to what she could accomplish in Aaron's absence, but certain aspects of the set-up could commence in light of the agonizing apprehension caused by the waiting. Digging through a medium-sized duffel bag marked *MEDICATIONS* in black magic marker ink, Kayla found she could actually manage the smallest of smiles without forcing the issue.

***

Time: 0925 HOURS
Date: SAME DAY

"Good morning, Sir. Name's Owens, Mark Owens, United Southern Life, and you might be?"

"Short on time, *no* thank you," the man replied, his face still half-submerged in the shadows of the living

251

room, only the hand holding the front door ajar fully visible.

The door began to swing shut just as Aaron's reply reached his lips, his voice cracking slightly. "Sir? *Sir*? If I might ask you one question, please? I promise less than two minutes of your valuable time," he said, tipping his hat politely as the door's forward progress halted and then began to gradually reopen.

"One question only, then. I'm extremely busy at the moment," the voice beckoned, the face behind the words gradually moving into view.

Aaron felt instantly nauseous, purposely squinting his eyes in a preventive measure, otherwise the wide-eyed response he fought to contain might have raised suspicion in the man posed barely two feet away.

If the individual standing before him was indeed Mason Parks, it was easily the most dramatic physical transformation ever accomplished over a span of slightly less than two decades, at least facially.

The eyes were set closer than Aaron recalled, the nose upturned a bit more so that the dark black hair protruding from each nostril stood out like an ingrown mustache. The crew cut styled hair, although obviously grayer with the passage of time, was the *single* element Aaron could trace back to the face he'd known and memorized ad nauseam, since that night in New Mexico when it faded from sight in a crimson-coated blur. The densely framed body, complete with barrel chest, bulky biceps and Popeye-like forearms, could have easily passed for a once chiseled muscle-freak killer-for-hire gone just a shade soft over time. Given Parks' recent escapades into ridding the mid-south of a select few of its homeless population, he had at least stayed moderately

252

toned for his troubles.

The man wore only a sleeveless gray shirt which read *Retired Pharmacists Do it Without Medication* in faded red letters, along with a pair of cut off blue jeans and flip-flops.

"I said... you get one question and *one* question only, Mister. I ain't buying whatever it is you're selling, just so you know right off the bat. Now, what *else* might you desire with my valuable time?"

Aaron quickly dismissed any effort to distinguish the man's voice, given the time and aging factors. Besides, he realized that the tone and speaking pattern one utilizes would more than likely be the first thing altered when forcibly relocated. "I'm sorry, sir. I guess this early morning heat is already getting to me somewhat. I just wanted to inquire about your neighbor up the hill," he said, gently sitting the briefcase on the porch as he motioned north.

"You mean Hoyt Wilson?"

"Is he the head of the family?"

"Ain't no family up there other than him, far as I know," the man replied apathetically while backing up a full step as to clear the door's path.

"How old a man is he, Mr. Uh., pardon my rudeness, but I've yet to catch your name," Aaron inquired while stroking the corners of his mustache with his left hand, vaguely aware of its gradual slippage from his upper lip.

"Matson. Now you know. Like I said, I'm kind of tied up right now..."

"Sir, might I ask who constructed that beautiful storm shelter to my right?" Aaron blurted, his upper body tensing beneath the moist interior of his V-neck T-shirt.

The man stepped forward and cautiously pushed

253

open the screen door a few inches, his face a shade paler than just seconds before. His tone was kind but stern, as if the question had offended him somehow. Aaron spotted the scar's outline, a vertical slash that was at least three inches in length but as slim as if drawn with a lead pencil. All doubt instantaneously faded, the need for further ID confirmation no longer an issue as Aaron forced himself to look away from the final, damning evidence.

"As a matter of fact, you're *speaking* to him. Designed and built it from the ground up. Why?"

Reaching for his briefcase, which had sat in the screen's path, Aaron manufactured a wholly forced grin that was pure Actor's Studio; a wide, toothy effort that, coupled with the awe-struck expression that accompanied it, was the definition of sincerity in its purest form.

"Mr. Matson, my father, God rest his soul, built such shelters for a living. A carpenter by trade until his death a few years back, I'm fairly certain that Terry Owens would have presented you with a hardy handshake upon viewing such an astonishing piece of work."

The screen cracked just an inch more as the man leaned forward. "Well, I...um..."

"May I take a closer look?"

As he turned to depart the porch in the direction of the shelter, Aaron heard the man's low, panic-stricken gasp, and felt every nerve ending he possessed flare up in a harmonic shriek. He had just turned his back on a man who, less than two decades earlier, had come to within inches of disemboweling him with a single swing of a blade. Such an ad-lib was beyond simple carelessness when dealing with such a ruthless entity, he knew, but part of him longed for a game of chance, regardless of

254

how stacked the odds. As he strolled onto the recently trimmed grass of the man's perfectly squared front lawn, Aaron cocked his right arm upwards as if adjusting his hat. The muscles in his forearm ached from tension created by his tightly clinched fist, the band holding the syringe rocket to his wrist wound as tightly as a motor vehicle's alternator belt.

"Wait up a min...hold on there, mister!" the voice bellowed nervously just as the screen door could be heard slamming shut, followed by hurried footsteps departing solid wood for soft ground.

Aaron stood at the shelter's locked threshold, the briefcase swinging freely in his left hand while the right remained upright as he feigned scratching his forehead.

From a distance, one might deduce that he was sizing up the door for a possible ramming assault.

"Absolutely gorgeous, Mister Matson. The design is *fortress*-like. Even dear old dad never created such a..." he paused, lifting his chin in an alerted stance even as the older man jogged forward, stopping short just a foot or so to his left.

"You keep aged vegetables down there, Mr. Matson? Something's reeking like clabbered milk..." he said while sniffing the air like a blood hound searching for a day old scent.

"None of your damned business, Mister. Now, would you kindly leave my property? I ain't saying it again...I'll call the sheriff and have you run off if I have to. *Two* minutes of my time, my gnarled ass. You *hearing* me, Mister? I said, are you...."

The two movements could have easily been mistaken for one, so gracefully executed and exquisitely fluid that the intended target never even saw the turn, only the arm extending out as the wrist upturned and something struck at his neck with rattlesnake quickness.

"Wha..son of a...bi..." he murmured, stumbling back while clutching at the sharp pain at his throat, the palm of his left hand penetrated by the jagged edge of the broken needle lodged just beneath his right earlobe. The older man's backside struck the thin layer of grass with a muffled thud, his legs splayed as he sat upright in a 'praying mantis' pose. While the fingers of his right hand struggled to grip the syringe protruding from his neck, his left covered his face defensively. Through the space between his fingers, the man could see Aaron standing at least a dozen feet away, the younger man's leg's bent and his arms held straight out in a classic shooter's stance. Unlike a minute earlier, the smile Aaron Kyle now displayed was filled with an uninhibited glee that was impossible to fake.

"Go ahead and dig that baby out, Parks. Let the blood begin to flow, you miserable jackass..." he barked, reaching up with one hand to tear the false mustache away with a single tug, then tossing it next to the already discarded hat.

With his thumb and forefinger tugging frantically at the moistened needle, the older man stared down the blue steel barrel pointed squarely at his chest, the briefcase that had served as its holster lying open on the nearby grass.

"Just in case you're wondering, that's one-hundred fifty milligrams of *Pentobarbital* filling your arteries, old buddy. By the time we're done with you, Parks, you're gonna wish I'd pushed enough of that shit into your veins to OD your lousy ass."

The needle was finally dislodged just as the man

scrambled clumsily to his feet, a narrow trickle of blood running down his neck and onto his shoulder. He stood with his feet wide apart, his enraged expression quickly transforming into a slack parody of such, and held the three-inch long syringe in front of his own face in dazed confusion. "Getting dizzy, Slick? Feel like your ears are starting to melt and your legs are made of tapioca? Better savor the mellow ride, pal, 'cause what's to follow is gonna be anything but," the man heard Aaron say, the words sounding as if they were spoken from a faraway distance, with each separate syllable overly emphasized in dramatic refrain.

His arms suddenly felt enormous, the weight of each collapsing them to his sides as his eyelids were being slowly pulled downward by some invisible force. The man heard a bird chirp overhead, but saw nothing as his head fell back, his drooping eyes upturned to scan a darkening, cloud-infested sky.

Facing front, he found he could no longer gauge the distance between himself and his attacker, whose body seemed to be mutating somehow, dramatically altering its shape within the blurred tunnel his vision was fast becoming. Lurching ahead, he attempted to swing his arms in a frantic series of left and right hooks, unaware that his arms never actually left his sides, swinging haplessly like overweight pendulums as he sprawled forward in a drunken stupor.

Something solid struck him just above the breastbone, halting his progress, the faint sounds of maniacal cackling filling his ears. Another sharp blow, this one landing somewhere in the general vicinity of his right temple area, sent him reeling onto his back, emptying his lungs in a violent huff.

257

Aaron stood directly over his quarry, his feet spread at either side of the man's heaving chest, the .38 revolver now hanging limp at his thigh, the tip of its silver silencer attachment tapping gently against his dress pants.

"Lay still, buddy-boy. As much as I thoroughly enjoy kicking your evil ass around, I don't want to inflict any serious damage. Kayla will have my *ball* if I haul you in all bloody and broken. Did you notice that's singular, as in... *someone slashed my other nut clean off?* Ring any bells, Sunshine?"

The man's head lifted even as the rest of his body could only manage a series of quivering spasms. He blinked rapidly, trying desperately to focus on the face hanging a few feet above his own. "...you...s-s-sick fu...fuc... ker..." he spat just as his head lolled back onto the grass.

"That's my boy. Take a nap, badass. We'll talk again real soon," Aaron beamed, leaning down to spit directly into the man's pale, lifeless face. "Actually, I digress..." he continued, straightening back up and stepping to the left of the now motionless body, ". .Kayla and I will do most of the talking. I'm afraid you'll be *far* too busy screaming and begging for mercy to add any coherent dialogue to the conversation."

His watch read nine-forty-six a.m. by the time Aaron backed from the driveway with his victim securely bound and laid across the backseat. Passing the Wilson home on his way north towards the highway, he noticed the man's front door stood ajar and was propped open by a heavy wooden chair.

"Might want to invest some of that booze allotment towards purchasing an AC unit, Hoss," he whispered, reaching over into the passenger's seat to retrieve the cell

258

phone.

Kayla answered before the first ring was complete.

"Prep the shed, my dear. I have an old friend of ours in tow. Merry Christmas and Happy New Year, Kayla. Let the celebration begin!"

The sobbing noises at the other end of the line were the most heartfelt that Aaron Kyle had ever heard.

Chapter Seven
Old Suspects/New Revelations

Time: 1018 HOURS
Date: 2 September 2006

"Typical 'Bama fan. Ain't you people supposed to have the memory of an *elephant*, Sheriff?"

Daniel tossed his cap onto the desktop and began running a comb through his wavy bangs with his back turned away from his subordinate. " Hey, the old memory chip ain't what it used to be, especially lately. On the ride back I ran into Rick Vincent out by the old Timberlake Place. Man has more flat tires than the rest of this town combined. I advised him that most of us don't attempt to ride on the same ones for *decades* at a time."

Deputy Morton tapped a ballpoint pen against the surface of her own desk, only the occasional squelching of the nearby scanner interrupting the silence between words. "So you didn't swing by the garage yet?"

Rubbing his eyes as he turned, Daniel no longer held the fresh, energetic look of a few hours earlier. It was the haggard, worn version his deputy was again witnessing, and she couldn't help but contemplate the reason for the sudden regression.

"Nope. Took me almost an hour with Rick. The lug nuts on that old Chevy of his were practically welded on. I'll get over there directly. Any earth-shattering news to report from HQ?"

"Mayor nixed my seminar to the kiddies on F-Day. Some of the parents didn't agree with the notion, apparently. Thought such a 'stern' speech wasn't necessary for their little angels to sit through," she replied sourly, tossing the ballpoint into an empty file basket.

"What do you expect, Trace? This is the era of *Time-Outs* and twice-daily doses of Ritalin."

"Yeah, well…what most of 'em need is a layer of hide taken off their backsides every now and then. As a youngster, I was well acquainted with the feel of a leather belt on my butt, and it sure didn't alter the way I came out."

She heard a resounding grunt, looking up to see Daniel raise an eyebrow in mock disagreement.

"You know what I mean, Chief. Look at that daughter of yours…she's mostly well-behaved, right? I'll bet she felt the flat side of your hand a few times as a kid, am I right?"

"Kara was forced to quit being a kid way too early, Trace. I think being mature beyond one's years has a way of naturally eliminating certain forms of discipline."

Deputy Morton nodded in agreement as they both grew contentedly silent.

The phone rang just as Daniel was in the process of refilling his coffee mug. He was grateful that his back had been turned to Tracy, thereby concealing the fact that his face had begun to drain to a pasty white complexion better suited for a mortician's concrete slab.

"Sheriff's office, Deputy Morton."

Taking refuge behind his cluttered desk, Daniel watched his Deputy's upper body tense as she stood almost at attention. As she listened, her eyes slowly rose to meet his own, the graveness they held sending a frigid shock wave down the whole of his spine. "Understood I'll pass this on to the sheriff right away. Can you fax us a copy of the report as soon as ya can? Yes…five-four-eight…eight-six-five-three. And you say the cause of death was most likely? Yes…got it. Thank you, Sheriff."

"Holy Crow," she mumbled, carefully replacing the receiver.

Daniel raised his hands palms up, his cheeks and forehead chalky-white. He felt his tongue temporarily stick to the roof of his mouth as he attempted to speak. "What's up? That didn't sound a bit good."

Deputy Morton fronted his desk in a 'parade-rest' stance, one Daniel had come to realize she only displayed during times of impending duress. "Sheriff Rocker over in Winston County says a home care nurse found Lance Hendricks dead this mornin'. They're callin' it a definite homicide, Dan."

Feeling every nerve ending in his face and scalp tingle even as the flesh of his face grew numb, Daniel inhaled deeply before replying. "On what basis?" he whispered, unconsciously tapping the fingers of both hands on a stack of dark blue folders labeled *State Reports*.

"Blunt trauma to the head. Sharp-edged, heavy object of some type."

"Sixty-eight year old man with advanced Parkinson's," Daniel said, his expression frozen in absolute disgust, his finger tapping becoming faster and increasingly frenzied, "any signs of a break-in or possible motive? Robbery maybe?"

Deputy Morton observed his hands, which were beginning to tremor madly, then averted her gaze to the partially open blinds above Daniel's head. "Rocker's faxing us the report in a few. He didn't mention anything being taken from the residence. State police are still on the scene."

"He mention what time the nurse found the body?"

262

he asked, the volume of his tone increasing, becoming decidedly shrill. His finger movement finally ceased as he gently laid both hands flat atop the folders.

"Seven-forty eight a.m. She discovered him in the kitchen."

Daniel bowed his head almost to the point of resting his chin on his chest. "I'd heard that Hendricks was in real bad shape, Dan. It had to be a home invasion of some kind. Probably some punk travelin' through West Bay lookin' for an easy mark. Cruisin' the back roads to the first secluded house he came to, am I righ…"

The outburst was so sudden, so shockingly out of character for the man responsible, that Tracy Morton's only reaction was to remain frozen in place, her lips still parted as to complete the question that had been so unexpectedly cut off.

The folders sailed airborne, shoved violently to the left, the majority of their number smacking against a nearby wall, sending various colored forms and bond paper scattering into every direction like tossed confetti. His chair was shoved back with such force that it bounded off the back wall and flipped forward, the hind rollers spinning like miniature roulette wheels as it skidded to a landing against the edge of the desk. " DAMN IT! I was either too late or too early…day late and a dollar short, old Grand-pappy Whitlock used to say!" he ranted, his a rms gesturing wildly as he began to pace from the carnage of his desk to the rear of the office and back again. " He could've still been alive, but then why wouldn't he *answer* the blasted door? I figured he was just heavily medicated and couldn't answer ."

Against her better judgment considering her boss's present state of mind, his deputy stepped forward and

263

gripped him by the upper shoulders, halting his incessant treading. His arms were steel bands, wound as tightly as if he were hanging on for dear life from a cliff's edge. "Dan! Hold up...just calm down a minute. Slow down and *talk* to me."

After a moment's struggle, Daniel seemed to refocus somewhat, his movements gradually less frantic as he met his subordinate's concerned stare. "I was *there*, Tracy. Last night. I drove up to West Bay. I was at the man's home, the murder scene... more than likely within hours of the act."

Releasing his arms, Deputy Morton frowned, her eyes squinting to narrow slits.

"His ho... you told me you were over to Todd Platt's, Dan. *Why* ...what business did you have with Lance Hendricks?" she barked in an accusing tone that she instantly regretted. She had a hand raised shoulder level, and barely refrained from pointing a critical finger directly at her mentor's face.

Daniel paused with a faraway look, strolling over to the office door to stare out onto the street, his movements deliberate and a bit mechanical. He held his chin in one hand as if in deep thought, while the other rested on his utility belt. "Lance called me at home yesterday afternoon. Said he needed to see me, but only in the strictest confidence. The man was livid, scared senseless. I hadn't spoken to him in...since my last re- election three years back. 'Course, I'd heard about his health. Figured he might be babbling nonsense, what with all the medication and all, but I couldn't *refuse* to see 'im. I owed that man a lot, and more than that, respected 'im. I wasn't going to break a promise. He was adamant that no one know of his request to see me. I 'm...sorry I lied to you, Trace, but I felt it…just wouldn't be right to mention it."

Turning back to study his Deputy's reaction, his emotional state had transformed from shocked anger to somber acceptance. His voice was calmer, and he no longer gestured or gyrated. He was the living model for a sculpture depicting total defeat at its basest level.

"What did he want, Dan? What did he say?" she asked, no longer confrontational in either her tone or body language.

"He never answered the door, Trace. I knocked for five minutes. There was soft music playing from an upstairs room, Classical or Jazz, couldn't make out which. Living room light was on, could see it through the curtains. Man doesn't have a listed phone number, so I couldn't even call inside the house. After a while, I just drove off and chalked it up to the ramblings of an ill mind. Figured I'd give Rocker a call this afternoon just to check on Lance, make sure he was okay."

Deputy Morton strolled towards him and placed a firm hand atop his right shoulder as he turned his sites back onto the mostly deserted street "You…think he was already… expired when you got there?"

"Well, it's a sure bet he wasn't out cruising the singles bars in Birmingham. If he wasn't passed out on medication, there ain't much doubt that his killer had beaten me there. Then again, unless that nurse comes by every day, which I doubt, Lance might have been dead for a quite a spell."

The fax phone rang just as the echo from Daniel's final word had ended, causing them both to openly flinch.

Deputy Morton smiled nervously, embarrassed by her own jumpiness.

"We'll find out in a minute, I reckon. Rocker said the county coroner was on the scene within an hour of the nurse's 9-1-1 call. Prelim report should say how long the ME thought he'd been...expired," she said, turning to check the machine as the initial page began to print.

"I'm... sorry, Dan. I know you always liked the man."

Joining her at the small table that held the combination copier/fax, Daniel nodded without speaking.

"Page one of three," she continued, biting her left thumbnail nervously. "Lance recommended me for the job the first time I ran. Talked me up as a former Army troop who could chew steel and crap nails, but also be sensitive to the needs of small town folks. Class act, all the way..."

Fifteen minutes later, they leaned over and studied the typed report, which was spread over her desktop like a road atlas. Daniel grunted occasionally, while his deputy waited until the final word was read before displaying any reaction at all.

"Approximate time of death between seven to ten p.m. Lord, Dan, *whatever* happened, you just missed it."

"Jesus, Trace...I *knew* it. Unbelievable..."

Straightening up so quickly that his back popped like a detonated firecracker, Daniel took three quick steps to the right and snatched his cap from the muddled trash heap his desktop had become. As he brushed silently by her on his way to the door, Deputy Morton saw the air of grim determination on his face; the tense, locked jaws and the tightly pursed lips below his slightly disheveled mustache.

"What is it, Sheriff? Where are you..."

He stopped short, the doorknob hidden in his right

266

palm. Pulling the Ray-Bans from his shirt pocket with his free hand, Daniel donned them before turning back to respond. "Got a man to see over at Stony Watt's garage, Trace. Got a man to see about a murder..."

Tracy Morton gasped aloud, utterly speechless for one of the very few times in her life.

"It ain't hard to figure, Tracy. Curtis Barber didn't come back to Elm Hill to live and prosper. He came back to dish out misery to those he holds responsible for his miserable existence these past two decades."

"Daniel, don't you want to wait on the state boys to show up? Rocker said they'd be sendin' somebody down to go over any possible suspects with us. The man was sheriff for a lotta years...probably had plenty of enemies besides Barber," she managed to croak after several hard swallows.

The sheriff pulled the door open, adjusting his sunglasses with a single, frustrated tug. " Just bringing him in for questioning, Deputy. Simple as that."

"You'll need me to back you up..." she began, checking her utility belt to ensure her cuffs were present and accounted for.

"Wait on the state boys, Trace. Back in a few."

The door shut nosily in his wake, leaving his deputy groping for thin air, her mind a virtual maze of confusion as she watched him leap into the cruiser's driver's seat and speed away.

"Mama said they'd be days like these," she mumbled almost incoherently.

***

Time: 1024 HOURS

267

"Damn it, Kayla, snap out of it! You really didn't expect him to look exactly the same, did you? Asshole probably went under the knife a half-dozen times since '88."

Aaron Kyle's hair was drenched with sweat as he worked, matted to his scalp and forehead as if pasted into place. He had removed his dress shirt, his V-necked undershirt sticking to his moist flesh like an additional layer of skin.

"B-but how could he have changed...*that* much? His face is absolutely someone *else's,* Aaron," Kayla pleaded, her chair parked a few feet ahead of the inclined table her partner kneeled beside, a perfectly horizontal ray of sunlight cutting a grove up h er back through a narrow crack providing by the partially open shed door.

After ensuring the slumbering man's legs and arms were securely bound, Aaron focused on the chest straps, which were at least twice as thick as the other binds. "I showed you the scar on his leg, Kayla. That, and what I...felt the minute I pulled onto his property were all the evidence this kid needed. Alas, for hard-line skeptics such as yourself, I did run across something in the man's house that *should* remove all doubt."

The bound man was slumped crookedly, his chin resting on his right collarbone. Aaron grabbed a handful the man's short, stubby hair and shoved his head upward, pinning it back while tying a forehead strap into place with two quick tugs.

Backing away to survey his work, Aaron watched curiously as Kayla pulled her chair as far forward as possible without actually striking the bottom of the table.

She studied the naked man's slack, reddened face, tilting her own at varying angles as if to capture every minute detail, then slowly lowered her gaze to his chest, groin and legs, pausing only momentarily when reaching the scar her partner had referred to.

Following a heavy sigh, she wheeled the chair back and nodded sternly. "Can't deny it. I can smell death all over him Recent death."

She peered up at Aaron, the corners of her mouth displaying the faint beginnings of a smile. " When can we begin?"

Aaron reached over and playfully patted her shoulder, then checked his wristwatch. "He'll be out at least another hour, my Cherry Blossom special. Have you prepared the Dexedrine injections?"

"Four separate doses, increasing the milligrams with each."

"Well then, allow me to duct tape this rat bastard's mouth in case he awakens early, and you and I can go inside and cool off for a time," he beamed, bowing dramatically.

"This does call for a drink, doesn't it?" she replied cheerfully, carefully backing the chair towards the shed door as Aaron walked ahead to clear its path. "By *all* means. I have champagne on ice chilling inside cooler number two. Clean glasses are wrapped inside the small brown satchel. If you'd be so kind to prepare the bubbly, my sweet, I'll tend to Mister Hate's needs."

Kayla giggled like a young teen as she departed the shed's rickety wooden surface for the overgrown dirt trail that led back to the house's back entrance, the chair's wheels fitting snugly into the tiny ruts that had been created on previous treks.

"Don't be long, Aaron. I don't want to have to start without you..." she blurted gleefully, waving her good hand in the air, her fist pumped in triumph.

"Put some music in the boom box, sweet thang. I'll only be a few, and then I'll reveal that little surprise I mentioned," he replied, closing the shed door behind him.

Despite the remote surroundings, he still felt uncomfortable in leaving anything to chance. The old wooden shed had obviously been used for farm implement storage in a previous decade, large enough to hold a tractor or two. It had been completely empty except for an old metal desk and chair set, which Aaron had simply shoved to the rear wall in prepping for their special guest's arrival.

The metal gurney had been a fairly cheap purchase from a Little Rock, Arkansas Hospital Supply Depot, its solid metal construction surprisingly light for its king-sized frame. According to the sticker still present at the time of purchase, it had last been used in the mental ward at a large Oklahoma City hospital, thereby explaining the accompanying leather restraints. A metallic tray s at a few feet to the right of the gurney, it's dull surface littered with instruments one might associate with an inner-city ER, although a few of the tools seemed surreally out of place with the majority. Wrapped and unwrapped syringes were piled in one corner of the tray, resembling the aftermath of a crack-house party.

The upturned gurney centered the shed's center almost perfectly, as if measured for exact precision, a select few rays of sunlight beaming down through spaces in the tin roof, painting the body held there in stripes of yellow along the face, neck and chest.

Tearing off an eight-inch strip of duct tape as he approached the gurney, Aaron felt a brief twinge of doubt before shrugging it off with a quick shake of his sweat-soaked head.

"It ends here and now, Parks. It finally...just...ends."

***

Time: 1026 HOURS
Date: SAME DAY

Deputy Morton practically leaped over to the console, spilling the majority of her coffee in the process as she reached for the two-way. "You're clear, Sheriff, over."

"Tracy, I'm heading over to Barber's residence. I checked with Stony at the garage. He said Curtis took an early lunch. Stony said he's fairly certain that Barber heads home for chow. Over."

"Dan...Sheriff, I still say you need my back up on this. You don't know how he's gonna react to being hauled in and uh...questioned. Over."

There were five moments of dead silence before a long stretch of static precluded his response. "Hold your post, Deputy Morton. Curtis won't be a problem. I don't plan on having to cuff him. He'll cooperate well enough without two of us showing up on his doorstep. Besides, we're old schoolmates. He *knows* me. Seeing you there might just spook him into trying something drastic. Over."

Despite her personal objections, Tracy had to agree with her boss's analogy.

271

Still, she would prefer to have been stationed at least fairly close by in case there was trouble.

"Wear your shoulder mike, Sheriff, just in case. Over."

"You got it, Deputy Worry-Wart. You Auburn fans sure do fret over small things, don't cha? Over."

Try as she may, she found the act of even forcing a smile utterly impossible. "What's your twenty, Sheriff? Over."

"Coming up to the cut off, ETA is about five minutes max. Any more questions, old grim one? Over."

"Let me know when your pullin' into his drive. Over."

"Those worry lines are gonna make you look old before your time, Deputy. Don't fret. Poppa will be home soon. Over and out."

Tracy looked up just as the grille of a state police vehicle rolled into view through the front door glass. "Affirmative, and let *me* worry about my wrinkles, Sheriff. By the way, state boys have just arrived. Over and out."

Frantically wiping the spilled coffee from her desk with a wad of paper napkins, Deputy Morton stood on shaky legs, feeling as though her earlier premonitions were in the initial stages of falling horrifically into place.

A moment later, she greeted the two state police officers with a nod and firm handshake, openly cringing when the first of the two men mistakenly referred to her as 'The Sheriff.'

***

Time: 1034 HOURS

Date: SAME DAY

"What say you *question* me right here and now, Sheriff Dan? As you well know, I do have a job to get back to." Casually leaning against his pickup's dust-coated grille, Curtis Barber spoke between chews of a half-eaten sandwich and sips from a can of Dr. Pepper. The faint echoes of music could be heard from the house, a guitar riff Daniel quickly identified from the Eagles classic " Hotel California."

"Curtis, I'll need you to ride back to town with me," Daniel replied curtly, adjusting the shoulder mike until it hung almost directly under the left side his chin.

Pausing to belch, Curtis sat the soda can on the truck's hood and took another small bite of the sandwich, his rugged face utterly void of emotion . "You mind telling me what this is about, Dan? I thought that shit with Todd and old man Basham 's kid was set for a court date already."

Daniel cleared his throat nervously, walking past the front of the cruiser until he stood only a few feet from the other man. He could feel the fingers of his right hand tingle numbly; the hand that hung next to his unsnapped holster. "Nothing to do with that particular situation, Curtis. This involves…a different matter altogether."

After a moment's hesitation, Barber shrugged while chewing the last of his sandwich, his expression remarkably bland considering the request. Daniel could smell the man's body odor through the green coveralls covering his massive frame. "Well? What might *that* be, Sheriff?"

"Lance Hendricks was found murdered at his home last night, Curtis. You *do* remember the man, I take it."

273

Barber took a long sip of soda, seemingly unaffected by the revelation. He forced another belch before responding. "Actually, he was found murdered in his home *this morning*. Get your shit straight before your mouth outdistances your brain, Danny-boy."

Feeling his face grow flush with anger, Daniel sighed in frustration, peering momentarily into the cloudy sky above, which was growing increasingly ominous as the morning progressed. "How exactly did you come by that information, Curtis?"

Barber laughed, crossing his arms over his chest defiantly. "It's called a *scanner,* Sheriff Dan. I heard 'em while I was sipping my java this morning. Sounded like a mighty young trooper, from the nervous hitch in his voice. Probably ain't even shaving yet. Sounded pretty damned spooked, actually."

"You've been out of stir for less than a week, and one of your first purchases is a police scanner?" Daniel asked sourly, his hands resting on each side of his utility belt.

"Hey, everybody needs a *hobby*, Danny boy," came the sardonic reply, followed by a steely glare that Daniel instantly defined as a test of his authority, displayed by a man who apparently held little respect for symbols of the law, but instead viewed such with a deep-seeded bitterness common among former convicts.

Feeling his head grow light as the skies grew ever darker overhead, Daniel broke the silence without averting his eyes. "It's just a few questions, Curtis. You understand my position in this situa..."

"I don't understand *shit* , Dan, and I have no time to have it explained to me. Sheriff, Lance Hendricks is a part of my past. A part I've flushed away never to be relived again. Means nothing to me that somebody turned out the old man's lights. Shit, means *less* than nothing."

"Get in the car, Curtis, and we'll talk about it at the..."

"Fuck you, Whitlock. You want me in that squad car, Sheriff, you go ahead and *put me* there."

Barber leaned up, his arms still crossed, his booted feet set wide apart.

Even as the shoulder mike squelched to life in a series of blasting static, Daniel remained motionless, concentrating solely on the looming figure ahead; a figure that outweighed him by at least sixty pounds; a figure who was just a simple reach away from a loaded .38.

"Sheriff, you copy? Over."

Daniel reached up to the mike in virtual slow motion, his right hand covering the .38's holster protectively. "Loud and clear, Deputy Morton. Over."

"Sheriff, Lieutenant Galvin from the state office is here to see you. What's your twenty? Over."

Daniel could easily detect the apprehension in Tracy's tone, though others, possibly even her own husband, would have found such a task impossible. "I'm with Curtis Barber at his place. Be there shortly, over."

"Copy. You bringing Cur. ...uh, Mister Barber in for questioning? Over." Barber nodded back and forth to reveal his own answer to the Deputy's query.

"That's affirmative, Deputy, although I'm meeting with some verbal resistance at the moment. Over."

Smirking loudly, Barber rolled his eyes in disgust.

"Need assistance, Daniel? I'm sure the Lieutenant and Officer Danley wouldn't mind ridin' out there with me. Over."

275

Daniel saw Barber's shoulders slump in defeat, the cockiness of moments before replaced by a somber weariness as his eyes lowered to the graveled driveway. "Not necessary, Deputy. I do believe Curtis just had a change of heart. Be there within fifteen. Over and out."

"Copy, Sheriff. Call me if you need me. Over and out."

Swinging his body around until his lower abdomen rested on the edge of the pickup s hood, Barber cupped his hands behind his back and leaned forward. "Do your duty then, Sheriff Dan. Once a suspect, *always* a suspect, I reckon."

Backing up a step, Daniel started to reach for his cuffs before pausing with a resounding groan. "Like I told you before, Curtis, it's just a few questions. No need for unnecessary hardware."

Looking slightly bemused, Barber turned, his large hands held palms up. "Just climb in the back. I'll chauffeur, if you don't mind," Daniel said with a polite sweeping of his left arm.

"Damn it, Dan, I'm gonna lose my job over this. You gonna find me another? Elm Hill isn't exactly an employment Mecca, y'know," he grumbled, ducking down as Daniel held the cruiser's rear passenger door open.

Pulling from the driveway, which was littered with various sized stacks of lumber, roofing tile, and scattered tools, Daniel shot the man a passing glance through the security mesh that separated them. "I'll talk to Stony for you, okay? He'll understand."

Blankly scanning the passing wilderness as they prepared to turn onto the main highway, Barber witnessed a lightning strike over a distant tree line.

276

"Don't be too sure about that, Sheriff. Sometimes, the things people do ain't so easy to comprehend," he whispered grimly.

As a light rain began to pelt the cruiser's windshield, Daniel felt a jolting sensation run a spastic confidence course through his chest and abdomen. Thunder rocked the cruiser as it neared a steep grade, filling his throat with warm bile that he was forced to gag back down as inconspicuously as possible.

Glancing in the rear-view to ensure secrecy, Daniel watched Curtis Barber's eyes grow wide with panic just as the man's jaws parted to scream out, his left hand pointing straight ahead.

Daniel averted his eyes to the road just as the oncoming vehicle rammed the front of the cruiser, sending the front end skidding hard to the right while the rear end fishtailed wildly. The cruiser's horn sounded off in desperate, wounded cries as it scooted across the dirt shoulder and down into a grassy ravine, its speed hardly altered by the fact that it now traveled sideways instead of horizontally. The side-winding vehicle flipped once before rolling to a stop in the matted weeds it had so roughly blazed a trail through, leaving a smattering of broken metal and fiberglass in its smoking wake.

When Daniel regained consciousness, it was to the smell of warm, sickly sweet breath that reeked of rot gut whiskey pelting his face as he hung upside down from the driver's seat like a snoozing bat.

***

Time: 1103 HOURS
Date: SAME DAY

"Oh my...sweet lord...*where?* He had this laying about his living room for anyone to see?" Kayla asked in shocked disbelief, her mouth agape. The natural slant of her eyes, to which Aaron had oft referred to jokingly as 'floss grooves', had vanished, growing increasingly wider with awestruck amazement.

"Sitting alone on the top of his VCR/DVD player. I could read the label from across the room. It was almost...like he had *left* it there for me to find. Either that or the old bastard figured nobody would ever be the wiser and got careless."

Studying the VHS tape as if it were the rarest of archaeological discoveries, Kayla read the label, the title of which had been scribbled out in dark black marker, aloud for at least the fifth time since had Aaron handed it to her.

"*Exterminator – The Final Cut, Final Volume* – circa 1988. What else could it be but...that night in Conquest? He must have... he somehow must have--"

"Yep. The smarmy son of a bitch snatched the VHS tapes from the cameramen after he cut 'em down, then edited his own 'final version' from what they'd filmed," Aaron finished for her, stopping only to sip the cool champagne they had popped the cork on just moments before.

"How long had we heard of a mythical 'bootleg' version of the Exterminators Last Stand? Remember that clown in St Louis who guaranteed a copy, then tried to pass off that rancid bestiality porn crap instead? Wonder how that greedy bastard got along without benefit of a left knee cap?"

Kayla placed the tape in her lap as she retrieved her

278

own champagne glass, then took a quick sip and smiled happily. "Good stuff, Aaron. I'm impressed. I was expecting nothing more extravagant than Boone's Farm or possibly Ripple."

He bowed playfully before gulping the remainder of his own drink.

"I recall first hearing of a bootleg back in late ninety-one or two. That Hispanic guy in El Paso who wanted five-hundred bucks for what he claimed was the only existing copy in North America," she continued with a dazed, distant look.

Raising a finger airborne, Aaron's face lit up with recognition.

"Ah yes, Juan Rodriguez Gonzales Perez the Third. Man was born of three mothers and countless fathers, if I recall correctly. I hear they do *wonders* with glass eyes these days…all colors and shades, real life-like."

"All this time and there actually *was* a tape. I wonder why he never tried to market it."

Refilling his glass, Aaron took up position directly in front of the low-humming AC unit, allowing the cool air to cascade over his slightly bowed head. "Who's to say he didn't? We didn't delve into the overseas market, other than the Middle East. Might have been a bestseller in South America or Asia. He had enough money to glide on from Conquest, but a man like Parks has to feed his ego on occasion just to announce to the world that he wasn't just some underground legend, that he did indeed exist."

Kayla hugged the tape to her frail chest, pulling her chair next to Aaron, who kneeled to place his arm around her shoulders. "God, I wish we could view it, Aaron."

His frown was comically over-exaggerated "What

the *hell* for, woman? You like watching yourself get skewered on film?"

She punched his arm playfully, her breathing labored from the exertion. "It's not that, you shit. It might actually be...therapeutic in a strange sort of way. Besides, I'd get to see myself the way....it...I *used* to be...at least before it all got so viciously... taken away."

"Didn't see a need to pack a TV and VCR, Dragon Lady. Not to worry, we'll have plenty of time for *movie-time* after the deed is done," he replied, hugging her close, although cautious not to apply undue pressure on her frail frame.

A brief glance of pure admiration passed between two, broken only when Aaron balanced his glass to Kayla's lips and followed with a swallow of his own.

"Go pull the rain gear from the van. I can't wait anymore," she whispered calmly.

He nodded and gave her shoulder a final tug. "Kayla my sweet, let's go fulfill our destiny."

She beamed with joy, her eyes moist with fresh tears. "Let's."

***

Time: 1113 HOURS
Date: SAME DAY

"You sure you ain't *broke* somewhere? I mean, that was one helluva spill, Sheriff. I ain't seen a tumble like that since ol'Caleb Markum nailed that oak tree off Highway 11 a few years back, 'member?"

Daniel waved the other man off, leaning back into the matted grass to escape the overwhelming odor of alcohol caressing his battered face. A small trickle of semi-dried blood hung from the left side of his mustache, the nostril above displaying a crimson ring that looked as if it had been drawn on. Although his left shoulder blade throbbed and the top of his scalp stung from numerous thumps against the cruiser's roof, he felt surprisingly intact otherwise.

"I'm fine, Hoyt, just back off, will you? Jesus, I'm catching a buzz from your breath."

The older man rose from where Daniel sat, holding his hands out in a gesture of surrender even as he surveyed the wrecked cruiser, which sat upside down approximately twenty to twenty-five yards to the north. Misty rain pelted the man's head and shoulders, transforming his light blue *BAMA ATHLETIC DEPT* T-shirt a darker shade of blackish purple.

"Whoa, Sheriff, it wasn't *me* straddling the yellow line. 'Sides, last drink I had was at *least* four hours ago. Had a nip of Bacardi with my eggs, that's all. Doctors are sayin' that one or two belts a day are actually good for a person these days."

Stumbling to his feet, Daniel grabbed Hoyt's extended arms for support. After righting himself somewhat, he was able to walk over a few steps, where Curtis Barber lay flat on his back, a thick forearm covering his eyes from the falling rain. "You able to take inventory yet, Curtis?"

"Just wet and bruised, Sheriff. You trying to kill my ass *before* you convict it?

Ever think of *watching* the road while you drive, Daniel?" he grumbled angrily, eventually leaning up with a loud grunt.

"Sheriff, listen…I called that masculine deputy of

yours 'fore I left the house…she told me where you was. Ain't no coincidence that we, uh, *ran* into each other out here…there's an *emergency* , least ways, there might be anyhow," Hoyt blurted, tightly gripping the crock of Daniel's right elbow.

A Mack semi zoomed by the trio, slowing once it spotted the overturned cruiser, then accelerating even faster as it neared the grade ahead.

"You were…looking for me, Hoyt? What's going on?"

"It's Doug Matson, Sheriff…I saw somebody haul him off. It was a-an insurance man. Knocked Doug out and stuffed 'im in his car. Kidnappin' in broad daylight, can you believe it? Same jackass was up to my place just a half-hour earlier. I'm damn lucky he didn't worry about me bein' a witness to what he did to Doug. I ain't never…"

Daniel placed a hand on Hoyt's chest in a calming gesture just as a maroon Chevy Citation whizzed by in the direction of town, the silver-haired lady behind its wheel seemingly oblivious, or simply indifferent, to their plight.

"Slow down, Hoyt, slow way down. Let me shake a few cobwebs loose."

The older man paced from side to side as Daniel bowed his head to suck in a series of protracted breaths, his body language like that of a man literally dying to urinate.

"Now, what's this about Doug Matson and an insurance man?"

"Yeah, least that's what he told me he was, but come to think of it, he sure as hell didn't try too hard to sell me anything."

"Tell me something, Hoyt,' Daniel asked while gently wiping his nose with a blood-smeared handkerchief, "did you report any of this to Tra...to Deputy Morton before barreling down the road like a bat outta hades to find me?"

His eyes suddenly transformed into twin blank slates, Hoyt's lips quivered as he stared into the misting rain above, scuffling his feet from side to side like a scolded child.

"Well, uh, I...um...naw, I guess I didn't...tell her much, that is."

"Why, Hoyt? She is a trained law enforcement official, equally capable of..."

The man broke in angrily, his cheeks and forehead turning rose red beneath the moistness. " Damn it, Daniel, I wanted the Sheriff, not some muscled up female playin' Jack Webb! My neighbor's in some deep manure, I believe. And stop talkin' at me like I'm some wet behind the ears jackass, will ya? I told ya what I saw, but not *all* of what I know."

Curtis Barber took a few wobbly steps towards the cruiser, shook his head in disbelief, then joined the two men at the shoulder of the road just as the misting rain finally began to dissipate. "Emergency or not, the squad car over there ain't taking us anywhere."

Ignoring the comment, Daniel placed a hand on Hoyt's shoulder, his eyesight still blurred to some extent, although the focus was improving as seconds passed. "Alright, Hoyt, I apologize *unreservedly* . Now, what do you know that you haven't told me?"

"I'll tell you on the way, Sheriff. We've got to go. There ain't no time to-- " Smirking, Barber threw his arms into the air and turned his head back towards the cruiser. " How are we gonna manage that, pal? A three-seated bicycle? Hitchhiking, maybe?"

Glancing over Hoyt's right shoulder, Daniel noticed the older man's late- 80s model Buick parked on the shoulder, facing the opposite direction. Other than a badly crushed left fender, it hardly looked worse for wear.

"Le Sabre still running, Hoyt?"

The older man whirled around as if to ensure the car's continued presence before turning back to Daniel wearing a smile of pure pride. "Purrin' like a kitten a few minutes ago, despite the collusion. By God, you can tell real metal versus fiberglass, can't ya?"

Hoyt continued to nod, his wide smile never wavering, as Daniel and Barber exchanged a fleeting look that was unintentionally comical.

"Well, Hoyt? If it is an emergency, and by God, it had *better* be...I'll need to commandeer your vehicle."

The older man's smile faded a bit, although the annoying nod never even slowed.

"Ready when you are, Hoyt," Daniel blurted, gripping the man's arm and pulling him around roughly, then shoving him in the direction of the car.

"See if it'll actually start while I check the radio in the cruiser. Got to let Tracy know what's happened."

Strolling away in the direction of the overturned unit, Daniel slowed to address Barber, who'd yet to budge from his previous pose . "You'll be going with us, Curtis. Go ahead and load up."

Sighing in obvious disgust, Barber trudged slowly forward just as the Buick's engine whined to life in the foreground. "This shit just keeps getting better and better," he mumbled, although easily loud enough to be

284

heard over the car's low-idling hum.

Daniel joined the other two men a few moments later, motioning for Hoyt to scoot to the passenger side as he slid behind the wheel. "Radio's dead as a hammer. Whole electrical system is fried."

Daniel paused to allow a blue Ford Taurus to pull by, the driver straining to peer over his shoulder at the wrecked cruiser, then started to pull onto the highway before again sliding to an abrupt halt.

"Hoyt?" he asked wearily, adjusting his cap, the bill of which was now slightly warped.

"Yeah?"

"Mind letting me in on our destination, old buddy?"

From the backseat, Curtis Barber howled, slapping his knee in droll disbelief.

***

Time: 1123 HOURS
Date: SAME DAY

"Nothin' but static. I'll give it a few more minutes. Might just be electrical interference from the storm," Deputy Morton said calmly enough, although her facial expression revealed something drastically dissimilar. Her gut felt suddenly bloated with anxiety, her eyes frighteningly bloodshot from a build-up of the same.

The two officers both nodded without responding, each similarly dressed in plain clothes casuals that did little to conceal their chosen profession. Deputy Morton offered them coffee for at least the third time in the half-hour since their arrival, to which they each politely declined. As each of them had scanned the interior of the

285

office upon entering, she had noted their respective expressions. It was a look she'd seen countless times from visiting law enforcement officials, a barely readable smirk that reeked of arrogance and an underlying disdain, especially from those assigned from the state. 'Small town cops incapable of handling their own' was the popular theory. It never ceased to infuriate her, although she never allowed them the pleasure of ever realizing it.

"Um, Deputy…do you have a diner or fast food joint nearby?" the older, although lower-ranking man named Danley asked while stifling a yawn.

"Right around the corner. Best darn burgers in Central 'Bama,'" she replied a bit too enthusiastically and was stricken with immediate regret.

"Give us a half-hour. Maybe the sheriff will have arrived by then," Lieutenant Galvin said, echoing his subordinate's weary tone.

"If something urgent comes up in the meantime, I'll contact you there," Deputy Morton replied as the men began to exit.

That *something* had already happened, she knew, watching the two men saunter casually past the office window. A something that more than likely involved a two-hundred seventy-five pound ex-convict on a premeditated rampage, assaulting her friend and supervisor in a fit of rage. The radio had never failed to transmit or receive, regardless of weather conditions. The static she was hearing was low, weirdly muted, as if the cruiser itself had been disabled and the radio power cut. Glancing at the wall clock to her left, she came to a decision. If contact, radio or otherwise, wasn't established by noon, she would seek Daniel out in her POV. She wouldn't mind having the state boys along if they so desired, but wouldn't insist on their assistance. After all, she was going on gut instinct *alone*. There was nothing tangible to prove her negative vibes as being anything but. Daniel could have accidentally unplugged his mike and be setting inside Barber's home, sipping ice cold lemonade and jawing about old school days, but she seriously doubted it was that simple. Barber had obviously been less than thrilled about the whole interrogation idea, but seemed to have caved in during the brief radio chat, no doubt due to her mentioning the presence of the state officers. She wondered if, once inside the cruiser, Barber had simply blown a fuse, ignoring the consequences of such reckless behavior in a blind panic fueled by his own guilt. What if Daniel was right about him?

If Barber did indeed slay Lance Hendricks, he wasn't exactly the milquetoast type to roll over and willingly take his punishment. Even if he wasn't the guilty party, a recently released felon might easily press the panic button underneath the strain of such acquisitions.

Staring at the console with a look of dazed concern, Deputy Morton pulled the .38 from her holster and passed it from palm to palm, then checked the cylinder to ensure each chamber was filled.

The clock read eleven-thirty-seven. Sighing nervously, she felt as though time had literally stood still within the cramped office space, as she alone occupied her own personal black hole of swirling misery, the everyday surroundings mutating and blurring into a mass of shapes that were both unrecognizable and utterly meaningless in scope. Tracy Morton had never been one to believe in such prehistoric ideals as 'female intuition', nor did she buy into the popular phenomenon of

287

premonition that had become so commonplace in the 21st Century, created and nurtured by such media devices as psychics that 'spoke to the dead' and tarot card reading 'voodoo' priestesses who actually haled from Akron, Ohio. Stubborn to a fault, she prided herself in never buying into anything on face value alone. She was a stout disciple of the 'prove it to me with cold hard facts' crowd, an attitude that the Sheriff's Academy had done little to soften.

That said, as she sipped lukewarm coffee and continued to glare at a radio console that refused to adhere to her mental command to sound off, Tracy Morton realized beyond the shadow of a doubt that the clouds drifting above Elm Hill, Alabama were thick with malevolence. Malevolence sprinkled with just a touch of insanity.

***

Time: 11:32 HOURS
Date: SAME DAY

"Kayla, is it just me or is the self-proclaimed 'toughest hombre on the Planet' sprouting tears?" Aaron blurted sarcastically, holding the man's head upright with the palm of his right hand.

Kayla wheeled herself forward until her propped feet were parked directly beneath the slanted gurney. The clear plastic raingear she sported covered all but the circle of her face, small spatters of crimson visible at the chest and thighs.

Reaching up with a rubber glove - covered hand, she roughly poked the left corner of the man's eye with her right index finger. Studying the glove with mock amazement, her reply was purposely stoic, spoken in the robotic tone of a college professor at the mid-way point of a rather dry, lengthy seminar. "Why, I do believe Mr. Universal *Bad-Ass* is indeed weeping like a six-month old with a rather nasty case of diaper rash."

The man had cringed back at her touch, the duct tape over his mouth carving a square groove around the whole of his mouth with each frantic toss or turn of his head. His eyelids began to droop as the pain at his feet and ankles returned in sweeping, throbbing waves of indescribable agony.

Aaron leaned forward and executed a lightning quick head-butt, thumping the man's forehead with jackhammer force.

"Don't fade on us, Slick. We've got enough juice to light you up for weeks on end if need be, but the last thing we want is for your sorry carcass to conk out prematurely."

Aaron was donned in similar rain-gear, although his attire was camouflage styled and was hoodless. Instead, his headgear of choice was a badly worn baseball cap with the bill pulled around backwards, the word *PUNISHER* spelled out in white over a faded light blue background.

His eyes growing wide and aware once more, the man's jaws strained to expand beneath the constricting binds while whipping his head viciously from side to side.

Low guttural groans caught at the back of his throat as his blurry vision focused just enough to partially identify the objects lying to his left on a rolling metal tray.

Beside a handful of syringes and what looked like a hacksaw and surgical pliers sat two plump, purple tinted lumps of flesh of similar size and shape. Blinking madly as if to dismiss the scene as nothing more than a dope-induced hallucination, the man then attempted to pee r downward, past his bloated belly towards his tightly bound feet, as if to verify the nightmare as more than just a figment of his fractured imagination.

Unable to see past his own heaving mid-section, he reluctantly turned to again focus on the tray. The closest of the objects faced him at just the correct angle to allow for a positive identification, despite his frenzied, yet quickly weakening attempts at denial.

The hangnail he had spent many a recent night digging at with a pair of clippers and a metal nail file had slowly become infected, leaving one side of the toe horribly swollen.

Being cleanly severed from its host hadn't done much in the way of remedying that specific malady. The mad giggle trapped at the base of the man's throat came out muffled, more a garbled cough than a hysterical cackle.

"Recognize 'em, Mason?" Aaron grinned, reaching over to playfully tweak what had been the man's left big toe and subsequently flipping it over like a semi-cooked hot dog.

"Don't lose any sleep over it, old buddy. Losing a couple of rancid smelling toes shouldn't bother a man who'll soon be without *legs*, don't you agree?"

His eyes grew even wider, darting wildly from Aaron to Kayla as if viewing a rapidly moving game of ping-pong.

"Hey, we had to start somewhere. Cheer up, Parks,

Kayla here wanted to clip your testicles first, but I talked her out of it...for *now,* anyhow. Too much blood involved, which of course leads to extensive damage control afterwards."

"Bind his forehead, Aaron," Kayla injected without a hint of humor, the surgical snips held in her good hand laid lazily across the man's tremor-racked lower abdomen.

"I don't want it thrashing about when I start on his fingers. Son of a bitch might get *lucky* and snap his own neck."

After a moment's struggle in holding the man's wriggling head flush against the gurney, Aaron tightened and buckled the wide leather strap, the bottom of which ended just above the man's eyebrows. Backing away, Aaron cocked his head to one side as if trying desperately to comprehend the man's harried grunts, his ear mere inches from the bound man's covered lips.

Backing up a step, Aaron placed a gloved hand on Kayla's shoulder and gently massaged her through the rain gear.

"Why? Is that the question, Mason? *Why?* What did you expect from us once we finally caught up with you...a handful of birthday cards and a six pack of your favorite steroid? A busload of hookers for you to hospitalize maybe? Remember Earl Barron, Parks?"

Unable to even twitch his head in response, the man instead rolled his eyes in apparent indifference.

"No? Let me refresh that horribly inept long-term memory of yours. He signed your paycheck back in Conquest, mister. He allowed for your extravagant, albeit undeniably warped lifestyle, in the year's time that you did his bidding. The man was set to retire to an island

291

paradise, his conscience no longer able to justify the underground empire he had established. Sure, he planned your death, no denial there. The man knew a rabid dog that begged to be put down when he saw one. At least you'd go out the only suitable way for a so-called *warrior* like yourself, in the heat of battle. A man like Earl Barron didn't deserve to die at your soiled hands…"

Removing the scalpel from the tray with blinding quickness, Aaron then pulled the sharp edge of the blade across the man's right biceps with just enough force to draw blood in a pencil thin line.

"That man was almost seventy year's old, asshole. He was also unarmed and completely helpless. I saw him raise his arms in surrender just before you gutted him like a bull in a slaughterhouse. I also saw you smile as you did it, pal."

Pulling the blade from the sliced flesh, Aaron wiped the thin trail of crimson gently across the bound man's left cheekbone. The man's breathing seemed to stop, his eyes squinted shut.

"Better start praying to Satan for your heart to stop or a vessel to blow in your brain, pal. Otherwise, we're all in for the long haul here. Look at the bright side, Mason," Aaron concluded with a grin born from utter insanity just before peering lovingly downward at his equally demented partner. "You're making medical history, old son. The first living being to witness his own autopsy… first hand. And, speaking of hands, and fingers more specifically…heeeeeerrre's Doctor Lee!"

The man felt enormous pressure in the area of his left index finger, followed by a sharp snapping sound not unlike scissors blades clicking together.

"He's gonna be kicked off the bowling team for

292

sure!" screeched the female voice, h er maniacal giggling drowning out the stifled screams that followed.

*****

Time: 11:37 HOURS
Date: SAME DAY

"Old Whitmore Road? You sure they turned off *there*, Hoyt?"

"Well, *hell* yeah. I kept my distance as to not give myself away, but I saw 'em take a right and fade behind that line of young pines there."

Daniel winced, his face a permanent scowl of gnawing doubt. "Nothing down there but Sam Crowell's old horse stables and the Whitmore place, which has probably crumbled into dust by now," he said grimly, nonetheless slowing to execute the turn, the Buick's engine whining weakly as he let off the gas.

"Strange, ain't it? Road don't go nowhere either. Dead ends at the south edge of Mann Lake, right?" Hoyt replied, gripping the passenger door handle in a white-knuckled death grip.

"Sure does. Hoyt, are you absolutely sure that you saw them…"

"Yes, Sheriff, I'm *damned* sure. I thought about followin' them on my lonesome, then thought better of it. I ain't no cop, and never pretended to be the brave sort neither."

"Sheriff, I want you to know I'm not only gonna sue the county for mental duress, but also mental cruelty," Curtis Barber chimed in drolly from the backseat, leaning hard to the left as the car swerved.

293

Daniel slowed the Buick almost to a complete stop once the tires had left asphalt for gravel, a new spattering of rain beginning to pelt the windshield. "Yeah, and why would that be, Curtis?"

Laughing sarcastically, Barber reached over and slapped Hoyt Wilson on the right shoulder, causing the older man to recoil in shock. " A supposedly trained law enforcement officer follows the advice of a man who rammed him into a ditch, not to mention smells like the inside of a Jim Beam bottle, on the *possibility* of a *supposed* kidnapping by a traveling insurance man. He drives the actual vehicle that disabled his cruiser five miles out of town, down a dead-end dirt road without any other source of information or evidence to prove potential wrong doing. Holy *shit on a tar shingle*, Sheriff, what other reasons do I need? This crazy crap is the definition of inefficient police procedure. Who is this guy anyhow, the friggin' Mayor? A visiting Congressman maybe?"

"Pipe down, Curtis. Hoyt's a veteran of two wars, for your information, and I 'd take *his* word over an ex-con's any day of the week," Daniel snapped back through gritted teeth, staring at Barber through the rear view mirror as he braked to a stop.

"How about protecting the good citizen's within your jurisdiction, Sheriff Dan? You seem to not give a *good* damn that you almost got me killed, and now you're dragging me along to witness a possible felony."

"Ya think that bird ain't a real insurance man, Sheriff?" Hoyt asked fretfully while rubbing his hands together like a mad doctor's demented assistant.

Ignoring the question, Daniel instead scanned the thick, overgrown forest engulfing them from both sides of the wide gravel road. Oak, pine, and elm tree limbs, some green and leafy and others bare and rotted, hovered above and around them like a pulsating web.

"My bet is that your neighbor missed a few premium payments, Homer. Those insurance companies can be downright ruthless, y'know," Barber spat sarcastically, folding his hulking arms across his chest.

"That's Hoyt, *boy*. Show a little respect for your elders," the older man replied without turning around.

"Respect? For what exactly? A soused up old coot that has me smack dab at the center of a wild-goose chase that doesn't have shit to do with yours truly? Not likely, *Homer*."

Hoyt Wilson was at least eighty pounds lighter and three inches shorter than Curtis Barber, their respective builds comparable to a retired, slightly gone to seed Lightweight versus the current Heavyweight champ. Those facts aside, Barber couldn't deny the icy fear at the pit of his stomach in the moments following the older man's turning on him like a rabid animal. Hoyt's perfectly straight, albeit slightly yellow shaded teeth were fully bared, his thin, pursed lips curled in a wicked snarl.

"Listen up, asshole…my drinkin' is my business and my business alone. Least I ain't no killer of teenage girls. Drunken bum that I am, what *you* are is a helluva lot worse."

"Both of you stick a cork in it!" Daniel blurted, squinting through the rain pelting the Buick's partially cracked windshield. Hoyt spun back around in a blur, leaving Barber shaken and befuddled at his own skittishness. "I'm gonna cruise on down to the old Whitmore place and check it out. If something strange is going down, it's probably a good thing we're in Hoyt's ride. At least we won't be so obvious to the…um,

295

insurance man or whoever he is. Whatever happens, you two remain in the vehicle at all times, got it?"

"Ain't you gonna call your Deputy for backup?"

"Hoyt, the nearest residence is Barry Foote's place, and that's a good three miles ahead. If this is the emergency you say it is, there's no time to go searching for a phone. Worse comes to worse, I'll send you over to Barry's to ring the station."

Accelerating gradually ahead, Daniel tried to recall the last time he'd frequented the southern edge of Mann Lake, not to mention old Whitmore Road.

As if reading the sheriff's thoughts, Curtis Barber spoke up just as the Buick coughed and sputtered up a steep, rocky stretch of road leading into an even thicker stretch of forest. "Kinda takes you down memory lane, huh Sheriff? Wasn't this the trail we used to call *Hard-On Lane*? Man, I used to bring Lisa Harrison down here regularly on Friday nights. Girl could suck the chrome off a trailer hitch."

Deep within the murky regions of his inner mind's eye, Daniel traveled over the road as it had been almost two decades earlier. The thick foliage vanished, tree limbs no longer reaching into the road but pulled back onto the sparse shoulder and into adjoining ditches, mere saplings as opposed to what they would become as the years ticked past.

A flash of lightning vanquished the illusion as quickly as a light switch being clicked off, raindrops increasing in both size and frequency, despite the ample cover provided by the trees above.

"You sipped a bit of the grape down this particular drag at one time, didn't you, Dan? Boones' Farm maybe? TJ Swan on ice? Mad Dog Twenty-Twenty was my

296

poison of choice in those days. Helped keep my tool cool and my peter metered, if you know what I mean," Barber droned on seemingly to his own amusement.

"I, uh…yeah, seems I do recall this stretch of woods being mighty popular in our time. Looks like it's been left to the squirrels and opossums since."

"You ever take Debbie Rainer down here, boy? She have the same oral talents as that other girl you was talkin' about?" Hoyt asked timidly and without a hint of sarcasm.

"You talking to me or the Sheriff, rummy?" Barber countered grimly.

"Stow it, you two. We're only a few hundred yards away…at least, I think we are."

Steering his way cautiously through a series of wicked, winding curves, the last of which found the road littered with broken, decayed limbs as thick as Louisville Sluggers, Daniel parked to the left of a dilapidated wooden sign that read *DEAD END* in horribly faded letters that might have once been dark brown or possibly even black, with the letters *'FUC '* and *'U'* scribbled in red paint at the bottom.

"Lake's up ahead about a mile or so. Whitmore Farmhouse should be on the right about fifty yards."

"Man your vehicle, Hoyt. I'm taking Curtis with me," he continued, gauging the larger man's reaction through the rear-view. After witnessing nothing more dramatic than a brief scowl and a barely evident nod of the head, Daniel turned back to Hoyt, gesturing to the older man like an adult to a pre-teen child.

"Give us fifteen minutes, Hoyt. If we don't turn that corner up ahead in that time, you peel out and call my deputy, you hear?"

Hoyt glanced down at the ancient Timex Sports-Watch wrapped around his right wrist then back up without speaking. His face was ghostly white, ashen.

"Don't blow a breaker, Hoyt. It's probably nothing. We'll be back in less than ten," Daniel said, reaching to pat the man 's shoulder, which felt as solid as stone from coiled tenseness.

Following Daniel's lead, Barber closed the Buick's passenger door with a gentle series of pushes before lining up directly behind the smaller man as both were pelted by dime-sized raindrops falling from both the sky and the oversaturated trees overhead.

Daniel pulled his revolver free and gestured for Barber to follow his lead with a quick nod.

"Don't I get a gun or something, Sheriff? I mean, you haven't even deputized me yet."

"Only got one, and I'm keeping it. Besides, you ain't no deputy of mine. You can pick up a stick on something if you'd like, just keep within my line of site, *got* it?"

Keeping at least a three-foot distance from the sheriff's boot heels, Barber's tone grew increasingly bitter. The moist smells of the woods assaulted their nostrils as they drew further away from the Buick, the only sounds that of birds chirping and the occasional howling of a faraway dog, more than likely a lost hunting canine in frantic search of its master.

"Aw, *now* I get it Sheriff keeps suspect close at hand in case of possible escape attempt. Think I'll pass on your stick offer, Daniel. Might just give you the excuse you're looking for to point that little pea shooter at me."

"Tick a lock, mister. We're coming to the end of the curve. House should be on the right another thirty feet or so," Daniel whispered harshly, his knees slightly bent as

298

he leaned away from a jagged pine tree trunk that had taken up residence on the corner of the roadway. Daniel secretly thought that its split tip resembled a multi-headed snake in mid-strike. Such musings were less than comforting as he rambled forth, unconsciously tapping the .38's barrel against the right side of his knee.

At initial glance, the Whitmore home looked surprisingly sturdy, despite the obvious neglect. The roof and walls seemed intact, while the front porch appeared no worse for wear other than the expected overgrowth of weeds and piled leaves padding the accompanying lawn.

Tiptoeing past the rusted mailbox like two men trekking through a live minefield; each halted their forward progress at precisely the same moment.

"Somebody's been here, alright," Daniel alleged, balancing on the front half of his boots as he kneeled down to inspect the recently matted grass that had once been a cleared gravel drive.

"Probably *still* here, Sherlock. Damn, maybe Homer Boozehound wasn't imagining things," Barber replied in a barely audible mumble, joining Daniel near the ground as both men carefully scanned the perimeter of the home.

It wasn't until they both arose in unison that the faint sound of not-too -distant voices filled their respective ears. Exchanging a fearful glance, the two men bolted for the porch, their steps mercifully muffled by the wet leaves in their path.

***

"Shoot the bastard up, Aaron. He's starting to fade."

"Doesn't show much of a threshold for pain, does he, sweet-thang? Think we should add a dose of Ritalin to

299

the mix?"

Wheeling over to the metal tray, Kayla scooped up the second in a line of four loaded syringes. Her rain smock was coated in thick smears of blood from her neckline to her thighs, her shiny face drenched in sweat from the overwhelming humidity trapped within the shed's limited confines.

"Possibly later. Let's finish up the Dexedrine injections first. I've got some crushed Cylert prepped for the grand finale."

Backing away as to better survey their work, Aaron resembled a mad sculpture performing a self-critique. "Fess up, honey-buns. After all these years, is it all you dreamt it'd be? It is living up to expectations?"

Recklessly plunging the needle into the incapacitated man's left forearm, Kayla paused with her thumb posed stiffly on edge the plunger. "Hard to say, Aaron. Ask me once we get to stage three. Better yet, ask me once we've completed disposal of the remains. It may take hours or even days of painstakingly deep reflection to properly answer."

She shoved the plunger forward with a single thrust, then pulled the needle free and wheeled backed a few feet, almost backing onto the tip of Aaron's boots.

Both watched in eerie fascination as the remaining fingers on the man's left hand began to tremor and his eyes fluttered spastically.

"What say we take a quick inventory before commencing, my dear?" Aaron quipped, stepping forward to roll the tray between themselves and the gurney.

Kayla reached over and gently cupped the items, rolling them teasingly from one gloved hand to another.

"Think he's hungry? I could fry up a mess of *chicken fingers*...or possibly a human variation of *pig's feet*..."

Aaron shot her an exaggerated grimace...

"Lord, woman, you are one *sick* puppy. I *like* that in a woman."

Pulling the chair to the left of the gurney, Kayla stared hard at the waking man's fevered spasms, seemingly deliberating the next spot of choice for selected mutilation.

The man's left hand was void its thumb and index finger, while the right was similarly ravaged, the pinkie and index fingers jagged, bloody nubs.

The man's eyes grew impossibly wide as a revived consciousness swept through his veins, fed by flowing waves of artificial stimuli. As had been the case countless times since the session had commenced, his frantic, muffled cries began anew, the veins in his neck cable-cord thick.

"Hey, Darlin', what's say we remove the duct tape and let old Mason have his say. We need an unbiased opinion on our work thus far, anyhow. After all, who better to critique than the victim himself?"

Kayla Lee nodded amiably, retrieving a tiny pair of surgical snips from the far right corner of the tray, the only corner remaining that wasn't at least partially blood stained.

" Splendid notion, Doctor Kyle. Who knows? He might even provide us with a useful tip or three. Ensure the tape can be easily re-applied though, Aaron, in case he begins to howl. I know we're isolated out here, but..."

Stepping towards the gurney, Aaron waived her off with one crimson-slick gloved hand. " Understood, my spring fresh cherry blossom. The first sign of wailing

301

from ol' Mister H here, and I'll personally remove both his lips *and* tongue."

A single jerk from one corner, and the tape ripped free with a sickening tearing sound, releasing a veritable torrent of reddish saliva from the man's bottom lip. Aaron let the strip of tape dangle from the right side of the man's mouth, then backed away and folded his arms, casually leaning against the rear of Kayla's chair.

The man spat weakly, the leather bind across his forehead preventing the glutinous fluids from clearing his exposed chest and abdomen, then immediately executed a series of harsh, hacking coughs.

"Damn, son, bet you could use a cold belt of Pepto Bismol right about now," Aaron jibed, watching in mild disgust as a rather chunky blob of rose-color ed phlegm dribbled onto the center of the man's chin. "You heaving up a lung or what? Never figured you for a heavy smoker, Mason. Not *cigarette's* anyhow."

"Bas...c-craz...crazy...basta ...w-why...are ..." the man managed in a weak, haggard tone, his left eye lid temporarily stuck shut.

"Easy, big fella. Take it slow. I know it's difficult to build complete sentences under the circumstances. Take your time. Suck in some of this splendid, country air. After all, it's some of the *last* you'll ever experience."

" My fear of wild screams seems a bit far-fetched at this point, Aaron. Saw off a few digits and Universal Tough Guy here turns to instant pudding. I have to say, I'm more perplexed than disappointed, but it is somewhat of a let-down, nonetheless."

The man's sights switched to Kayla, who instantaneously felt a shock wave of extreme fear grip her gut in a steely vice. The tortured orbs revealed nothing to her that resembled even the faintest recognition. Instead, they screamed desperation and confusion. A confusion that seemed less manufactured than horrifically sincere.

"I…It…you…making…the wr…" he man mumbled before another series of choking coughs cut him off.

"Tell ya what, chuckles, what's say we remove a testicle and see if that assists in clearing the old airways. I've heard a well-placed scream straight from the diaphragm does wonders for asthma. Might do the same for fluid build-up," Aaron practically yelled, scooping the blood-soaked surgical snips from the tray as he moved swiftly forward.

"Aaron…wait."

Ignoring Kayla's low-pitched request, he instead reached for the man's shriveled manhood with one hand while separating the tool's razor-sharp blades with the other.

"Hold it, DAMN IT!"

Frozen into position, Aaron turned to her angrily. "What? You want his balls for yourself? Gonna make a *charm bracelet* out of 'em? Be my guest by all fucking means," he retorted, shoving the snips under her chin, the edge of the blade mere inches from her exposed flesh. Her gaze was piercing, her expression dour to the extreme. Her yellowish tanned skin was as pasty white as he'd ever seen it.

"Jesus, w*hat* is it, woman?"

"Tell me Aaron, does your head still tingle and throb as when you were searching for Parks? You know, that psychic meter of yours?"

"Of course not. I t shut off like a burned out bulb the minute this jackass answered his front door."

303

"Sure it wasn't even before that?"

Cocking his head quizzically to one side, Aaron removed his gloved hand from the man's groin and turned to face his partner, leaving a d ark smear in the outline of his fingers in the process.

"Exactly what is the point, Kayla? Mason's here's gonna expire from old age if we don't..."

"Psychosomatic signal, Aaron Maybe it shut off *only* because your mind convinced itself that you had your man, you ever consider that?"

Bending down until he could meet her stare directly, Aaron briefly paused to release a laborious sigh, all the while displaying a sad, pathetic smile. "Kayla, isn't it a little late in the game for such doubts? I mean, what now? We break out the needle and thread and sew the poor bastard's toes and fingers back *on*? Is it guilt? Is that what's causing y-- "

"No, goddamn it! It's not guilt, Aaron! Take a good, long look," she shrieked, pointing over Aaron's bowed shoulder and to the m an strapped to the gurney, 'wipe away your rage for just a moment and take a *good* look."

"Sh...m...my...g-gi...give..." the man muttered as Aaron started to turn. "*BULLSHIT!* I'm not hearing this now, Kayla! It's too late for this *shit* !" he yelled, reaching up to slap the man across the face, a loud crack filling the air as gobs of congealed blood and bile sprayed airborne in thick waves.

Warm tears sprang from her eyes as she reached up to grab Aaron by the loose folds of his rain gear. "I had my doubts all along, Aaron, I just *wanted* to believe so badly that I ignored all instinct. After all these years, I couldn't... resist the hope. Read his eyes, man. He...does not...recognize...us. He doesn't know...*why* we're...k-killing him."

In the split-second's silence that followed Kayla's final spoken word, the sharp, crisp sound of a revolver's hammer being pulled securely into place filled the structure.

They turned in unison, the front wheels of Kayla's chair barely avoiding running over the tips of Aaron's boots for the second time in five minutes.

"Then what say you *refrain* from killing him altogether?" the man said, pointing the weapon straight out from his chest, the barrel end wavering wildly.

Kayla felt her heart stop as the invaders carefully stepped inside the shed.

Behind her, Aaron Kyle tucked the surgical tool behind his back, like a child hiding an object from an inquisitive parent.

Mercifully, the man on the gurney fell into a black pit of unconsciousness; his last waking thought a sewn tapestry of befuddlement that went eons past being defined as simple confusion.

***

Time: 1149 HOURS
Date: SAME DAY

Slamming the phone down as if discarding a piece of red-hot rod iron, Deputy Morton practically place-kicked the small garbage can out of her way as she bolted for the office door, her car keys curled tightly inside her right fist.

Marge Bellingham's raspy voice still echoed in her mind, the dialogue slightly altered with each rewind and subsequent playback, but the gist of what had been said shockingly coherent and concise, despite the woman's advancing age. Marge was ninety years young if she had been a day and reportedly being treated in a Jasper Hospital twice a month for the early stages of Alzheimer's. Despite these known facts, Tracy still managed to spit a mouthful of coffee onto her computer keyboard once the phoned message had been conveyed.

The cruiser sitting upside down in a ditch without either Daniel or Curtis Barber, or anyone *else* for that matter, anywhere in sight. Bobby Kendrick had called in to confirm Marge's claim just as Tracy had practically leapt from her chair.

Jogging around the east side of the building to reach her Accord, Tracy momentarily considered first stopping by the diner to ask the state boys for assistance, but dismissed it just as rapidly, choosing to grab a portable two-way unit instead. She would call into the station periodically, hoping to catch them once they returned from lunch, where both would more than likely be lounging, waiting for her or Daniel.

Swerving onto Main Street with a loud squeal of smoking tread, she tossed the blue light onto her narrow dash and immediately activated it. She estimated a ten to twelve minute ETA to the crash site, depending on how many of the lunch crowd she'd be forced to dodge and weave through along the route.

It wasn't until she got approximately three miles out of town that she discovered the two-way radio had ceased operations. Irately tossing it into the backseat, she felt the initial pangs of panic flutter through her chest like a thick swarm of butterflies.

Butterflies armed with talon-like claws capable of

306

shredding a psyche already weakening beneath a storm cloud of uncertainty.

Her first gut feeling, the 'danger klaxon' from an hour past, had apparently come true, at least to some degree. She hoped and *prayed* that her second, one involving impending death for someone very close to her, would miss the mark entirely.

***

"Don't move or even twitch. I haven't pointed this thing at anyone in over five years, so let's allow extreme caution to be our byword, folks," Daniel said, attempting to steady the revolver by cupping his left hand beneath his right, which actually held the weapon.

"Jesus Crow, what the...*h-hell*?" Curtis Barber stammered, standing a scant foot or so behind the sheriff, his fists clinched tightly at his sides.

"Sheriff, I...it's not what it seems. There are mitigating circumstances..." Kayla began, stopping only when she felt Aaron's hand press forcefully against her left shoulder.

"Agent Lee, remember protocol. Allow me to brief the good sheriff."

Nudging forward a half-step, Daniel squinted while closely scanning the man's features, most notably the shape of his nose and chin. "Agent...Krane?" he babbled before dropping his gaze to the wheelchair bound Asian beauty, who was busy peeling the hood back from her face and hair.

"Guilty as charged, Sheriff...Wilkins, wasn't it?" Aaron grinned, shifting the snips from one hand to the other behind his back while using Kayla as concealment.

307

"Whitlock. How about producing that badge for me, *Agent*? I require a closer look."

"Certainly, Sheriff. It's in the house, as is Agent Lee's similar credentials. How about I..."

Daniel raised the revolver's barrel until it pointed directly between the man's cool, penetrating eyes. "Don't make me repeat myself, Krane, or whatever your name really is. What's going on here, Mister? Who's that man you're... butchering?"

"Simply an interrogation, Sheriff. The kind the bureau likes to keep on the QT, for obvious reasons involving PR. This man is a known terrorist whose activities we've been monitoring for..."

"Looks more like a *mob* interrogation to me," Daniel interrupted, scooting another half step forward before bowing down for a better look at the bound man's face.

"My...god! That's Douglas Matson! You...you're *torturing* Doug Matson?" Utterly still except for his trembling lips and rapidly blinking eyes, Curtis Barber suddenly realized an urgent need to pee. "Who the hell's Doug Matson?" he barked, his tattered mind unable to process the grisly scene without fear of breaking into a fit of hysterical laughter.

"A local retiree. S-spoke to him just days ago, in fact," Daniel replied, instantly backing away the step he had previously gained Aaron Kyle nodded his head from side to side, the conceded grin he displayed never wavering.

"Afraid not, Sheriff. He's a retiree all right, but the profession he claimed is pure mythology, I'm afraid. His real name is Mason. Mason Parks."

"Better known to us by his codename: Mister Hate," Kayla added shakily. "Oh, cut me some fucking slack,"

308

Barber blurted, feeling his thighs and lower back begin to ache from the constant tension.

Backing up until he stood even with the larger man, Daniel's tone was surprisingly authoritative, despite the growing infestation of butterflies swirling within his gut and the insistent tingling at the base of his skull. "Quiet, Curtis. I need you to walk carefully over and push that metal tray to the far wall."

"Kiss my lily-white ass, Whitlock. I shouldn't even be he--"

"*DO IT NOW!* I'm trying to protect us both, damn it."

Huffing like an enraged bull, Barber walked forward and gripped the relatively light tray by its squared edges, groaning aloud when a select few of the blood-drenched instruments slid to one corner.

Re-joining Daniel a moment later, his cheeks were flushed, a look of pure disgust painted across his rugged visage. "They...there's fingers on that tray, Dan...fingers...*and* toes. FBI interrogation my ass...*those two* are the terrorists," he managed, standing just to the left of the pointed revolver.

"I saw...what was missing," Daniel replied somewhat hesitantly, referring to the man strapped to the gurney. He then took a long stride forward, the barrel now pointed just over Kayla's head at Aaron's chest.

"Hands behind your heads. Mister, you get down on your knees. Lady, I want you to pull whatever plug is necessary to disarm that chair."

Kayla smiled wryly. "Disarm....what do you..."

"Lady, for all I know it's equipped with a heat-seeking missile. I said turn it *off*." Daniel's eyes quickly shifted back to Aaron, who had yet to budge.

"Show me the hands, Mister."

"Sheriff, I realize this must seem barbaric in the extreme, but you've got to understand. "

Raising the barrel until it again pointed in the general area of Aaron's forehead, Daniel bared his teeth and practically whistled his next command. "You've got five seconds, pal."

The movement was so graceful, so fluid, that Daniel would have sworn he'd been temporarily 'blacked out' in some strange time lapse, somehow unable to visualize the actual movements until the aftermath. He heard Curtis gasp at his side, a weirdly feminine release for a man of such enormous statue and machismo demeanor.

Aaron held the tip of the surgical snips twin blades at the left side of Kayla's neck, midway between her shoulder blade and jaw line. The man's face bore no signs of regret nor a semblance of fear. The woman's was a mask of comic shock, her normally slanted eyes as large as coffee saucers.

"Afraid I can't allow that, Sheriff. Not…now, when we're so very, *very* close to mission completion."

"A-Aaron? W-what are…y-you… " Kayla stammered as the blades gently pinched her flesh in a deadly tease.

His reply was stoic, robotic, like a voice mail recording. "No sacrifice too great, K. We both understood that without actually saying it."

"B-but…I…you wo-wouldn't…"

"If Sheriff Dillon over there refuses to drop the peashooter, yes, I *will*, my dear. As my old boss and mentor Earl used to spout; make no *bones* about it."

Kayla's breathing became instantaneously labored, her pulse rate increasing two-fold in a matter of seconds.

310

Her lungs felt as if someone had fired a flare inside her frail chest cavity. She had known Aaron Kyle for almost twenty years, from their initial interview through the living hell of the Conquest, New Mexico debacle, followed by years of painstaking investigation and the accompanying criminal capers that funded the former. She knew exactly one thing about the man that had always held true. A character trait that held little comfort to her at that moment: Aaron Kyle *did not* bluff.

"So, gonna kill your partner just like that? Come on, Krane...don't let the small, southern town surroundings fool you. I had the *idiot* tattoo removed from my forehead at birth," Daniel quipped calmly while holding the revolver steady.

"You drop that gun, Whitlock, you and me are worm dirt," Barber added nervously.

"Ain't going to happen, Curtis. Hold your ground."

"Like I got a choice?" Barber spat nervously.

Aaron shook his head sadly, temporarily staring into the shed's rotted rafters. "Thought I was in Alabama. Isn't Missouri the *Show Me* state?" Without warning, he shoved the blades forward less than a half-inch. Kayla shrieked aloud as her life source spewed forth to coat the snips in thin, dark streams.

"A-Aar-Aaron...don't," she managed weakly, her eyes now shut tight, her working arm held straight out from her body, the hand held palm up. She resembled a crippled blind woman navigating an unfamiliar room.

"Up to the constable, sweetie. The next one will do considerably more damage, Sheriff. What say *you*?"

Daniel removed his left hand from beneath the right and reached back until it made contact with Barber's lower stomach, never allowing the revolver's aim to waver from the general vicinity of Aaron Kyle's face. "Back to the right, Curtis, away from the door. Give 'em a clear path."

Both men side-stepped over approximately seven to eight feet until they were close enough to reach over and touch the partially rotted right interior wall.

Aaron nodded silently, using his legs and lower body in an attempt to push the wheelchair forward. After two laborious tugs that led to very little progress, he stood back, the tips of the surgical tool still braced against Kayla's wounded neck. "Your sense of humanity overwhelms me, Sheriff. Kayla dear, reach down and kick-start this baby, will you? Without power, it's a bit like pushing a square boulder."

The chair hummed to life a second later and lumbered forward at a snail's pace, Aaron using his left hand to control the throttle on the chair's arm rest, his chin resting lightly on Kayla's shoulder.

His hands propped at either side of his waist, Curtis Barber couldn't take his eyes off the bound man, his bloody nude body hanging from the gurney like a modern-day messiah, a small town martyr viscously sacrificed for reasons as yet unknown.

"Might be worth calling his bluff, Sheriff. After all, the chink is equally guilty.

Wouldn't be any great loss to society," he grumbled.

Daniel replied just as the chair whirred painstakingly by their position, mere feet from the open shed entrance. "Don't recall asking y our opinion, Curtis. Nobody's dying if I can help it."

Pulling back on the throttle, Aaron Kyle's expression and body language were a study in the art of indecision. As the chair hummed in idle, he glanced over at the

312

sheriff and then back over his left shoulder at the man previously identified as Douglas Matson.

"What's the deal? Why are you stopping, *Aaron*?" Daniel asked disgustedly, emphasizing the man's name if for no other reason than to let him know he hadn't missed it. Once again, he cradled the revolver in both hands, the sites lined up at the center of his target's skull, just above the left ear.

Apparently ignoring the question, Aaron instead leaned up and turned his gaze directly towards Kayla, temporarily blocking her face from the other two men. "I…can't leave him breathing, Kayla. We've come too far to allow it," he whispered, wearing a sad smile as his eyes instantly filled with fresh moistness.

"I'm…sorry. It wouldn't have worked anyhow, sweet thing. State cops or the f eds would have nabbed us before we crossed the Georgia line."

Leaning forward, Daniel cocked his head to one side in an attempt to tune in on the conversation. " You staying or going, mister?" he queried, feeling his shoulders burn from the constant effort of keeping the gun airborne and precisely aimed.

Kayla blinked several times, attempting to clear her own blurred vision caused by building tears. "A-Aaron…" she began through trembling lips.

Placing his left hand gently over her mouth, he nodded through closed eyes, reopening them just before speaking for the final time. "You're one hell of a warrior, Kayla Lee. Toughest I've ever met, man or woman. *Do not* give up the fight in my absence."

Pushing away from the chair with cheetah speed, Aaron cocked his right arm as he leapt back towards the gurney, the crimson tips of the surgical sheers leading the way like twin lightning bolts.

Daniel jerked the .38 wildly to the left in a feeble attempt to follow the blurred form, realizing instantly that the man on the gurney was about to die.

The deafening retort that follow ed filled the confined space like a close-range artillery blast, the aftermath of which left all present in a state of perplexed shock as to exactly what had transpired.

The sharpened tips of the surgical tool had been mere inches from the unconscious man's exposed throat when the shot had rang out, slinging Aaron Kyle past his intended target as if he'd been shoved violently forward by some mysterious, unseen force. It wasn't until he was splayed out onto the dusty floor to the left of the gurney, the surgical snips sailing from his grip and into a far, darkened corner of the shed, that several dark, circular wounds became evident on Aaron's upper back. His booted feet twitched several times just as the crimson stains began to spread onto his sides and lower back from the gaping holes between his shoulder blades.

His gaze frozen on the revolver he continued to point at the fallen figure a half-dozen feet away, Daniel couldn't recall actually firing, and no smoke was evident from the nozzle.

Kayla Lee's shrieking cries followed, her head bowed with her hand covering her eyes.

Curtis Barber's eyes darted wildly from the fallen man to Daniel, then back again.

"Sheriff, did you...I didn't see you f-fire the..."

Daniel's lips felt shriveled, his tongue and throat suddenly parched. "I...I don't think I..."

Each man's head turned in synchronized harmony as a figured stepped through the shed entrance, an elongated

314

shadow preceding the actual form.

"That's cause it *wasn't* you, Sheriff. Left to your slow as chilled molasses reflexes, ol' Doug over there'd be filleted like a catfish by now," the man announced in a bizarrely humorous tone, the sawed off shotgun he held pointed directly at Daniel's chest.

Though Kayla Lee's reaction was of simple confusion at the man's entrance and/or appearance, Sheriff Daniel Whitlock and Curtis Barber stood with their mouths agape, like two members of the same choir preparing to belt out an opening chorus.

"Drop the revolver, Daniel," the man ordered, his tone suddenly void of both wit and, shockingly, any sign of the deep southern drawl from seconds earlier, "we've got serious matters to discuss."

***

Deputy Morton leaned in through the shattered driver's door of the overturned cruiser, initially searching for evidence of possible blood loss or signs of the struggle that might have caused the accident. After discovering only a single semi-dried spot about the size of a nail head at the center of the front seat, she began to rummage through the scattered paperwork, cassette tapes and broken glass for a clue, possibly a scribbled note or something similar, to Daniel's whereabouts.

Thumbing through a handful of the cassettes, she couldn't refrain from grinning. " John Cougar Mellencamp…Cheap Trick…Genesis…Doobie Brothers? Boss, you are *truly* trapped in a musical time warp."

"Ouch, son of a *gun*," she barked as her knee raked

across a jagged shard of glass.

Nothing. Nada. No trace of a hint, as my Pete is apt to say when he's feelin' particularly comedic. Jesus, what now? Was Barber actually desperate enough to cold-cock Dan as he drove, willing to take his chances on the wreck to follow? If so, where in blazes are they? No report of anyone bein' transported to the nearest med centers from our area. Barber might have flagged someone down after the accident, feigning injury, then kidnapped the lot of 'em.

Deciding that Barber's residence would be the next logical stop, she began to back from the wreckage when the radio console hanging overhead caught her attention. The mike hung from its coiled cord onto the cruiser's dented roof, but the console itself had remained remarkably intact, the metal brackets that held it in place virtually undamaged.

"That ain't right,' she mumbled, reaching up to pinch the severed black wire between her thumb and forefinger, "no wonder all I got was static back at the station." The wire peeked out from what would have been the back rear portion of the radio, and had obviously been sliced in lieu of being torn or accidentally disconnected in any way.

"Now why would the lunatic even bother to cut off communication to a wrecked unit?" she pondered, sliding cautiously from the cab.

A recently waxed, black Ford F-150 pulled onto the shoulder just as Deputy Morton made it back to her Accord, the two-way radio held tightly to the right side of her face.

"Jesus, Tracy, what happened to the patrol car? Is the sheriff okay?" Mayor Will Jenkins asked in a panicky

316

tone, his reddish brown hair, what Deputy Morton liked to refer to as a *Just For Men* experiment gone awry, slicked tightly to his forehead.

"Not sure, Mayor. He was bringin' Curtis Barber in for questioning. I've found neither hide nor hair of either one as of yet."

"I'll call the state and have them send-" he began, checking the rear mirror as he started to back away.

"Don't bother, Mayor. Two state officers came down this mornin'. They're at the station now. My radio's out. Run by the station and assist them in a quick sweep around town."

Rubbing a stubby-fingered hand through his reddish-gray beard, the Mayor stared at the overturned cruiser and shook his head in amazement as Deputy Morton once again tossed the useless two-way into the Honda's back seat. "Will do, Deputy. We'll put together a group to search the surrounding farm roads and such."

The mayor made a quick U-turn and sped back in the same direction as he had come.

"Any other day and I'd find great pleasure in ticketing him for that little maneuver," she grumbled, pulling out onto the damp pavement just as the clouds above her opened, accompanied by muffled thunderclaps that seemed far over the distant horizon.

As she neared the cut-off that would ultimately lead to Curtis Barber's driveway, a streak of lightning lit up the landscape behind her. Tracy suddenly felt like someone of a higher power was playing the 'warm, cold' game with her in the matter of her missing mentor, and that she was presently the ladder the two. Still, her instincts told her to press on despite the powerful urge to second guess.

317

Minutes later, just as she braked to turn left past the man's mailbox, hail stones the size of marbles began to mercilessly pelt her vehicle. Parking directly behind the man's gray pickup, Tracy paused to allow the barrage to subside before exiting.

"Lord, I sincerely hope this ain't an omen."

Chapter Eight
Confessions/Sleeping Dogs Lie

"You just gonna leave that man out there to die? He's lost a lot of blood, and the heat…"

Securing the nylon rope around Daniel's wrists, which were pinned behind his back in the straight back lawn chair, the man snorted sarcastically but refused to speak. He hadn't muttered a single word since forcing them into the farmhouse by gunpoint some ten minutes earlier.

"Damn it, Hoyt, what *is* going on here?"

Kayla, trussed tightly to her chair at the chest, wrists and feet, groaned aloud, her eyes rolling annoyingly.

"Well, for starters, his name isn't *Hoyt,* Sheriff. Are you chronically dense or what?"

"Lady, I don't give a rat's ass if he's Hannibal Fucking Lector, this has nothing to do with me *or* the sheriff, for that matter. You and your former partner are the reason we're trussed up like prize hogs at a Founder's Day roast," Barber injected, his massive upper body entwined in several rows of rope, as were his calves and ankles.

"Wrong place at the wrong time, big boy. What can I say? You two couldn't have had shittier luck," she replied with a sneer, "as for the Hannibal Lector remark…it isn't a terrible stretch…unfortunately for us all."

Watching the man circle around to the center of the room, the shotgun now leaning casually against the recently unloaded video equipment, Daniel felt his hands and wrists grow numb from the constant pressure.

"I get the feeling that luck played no part

whatsoever. Am I right, *Hoyt*? "

"Right as rain, Daniel. Although I have to admit that clippin' your cruiser without breaking my own damn neck in the process was a dangerously dicey maneuver at best," the man replied while bending to hook up the combination TV/DVD/VCR to the small generator parked at the center of the living room. After ordering everyone inside the house, the sheriff's revolver now conspicuously absent, the man known county wide as Elm Hill's town drunkard and little else had, via twelve gauge shotgun, forced Daniel and Curtis Barber to unload the Buick's packed trunk. Kayla was then bound to her wheelchair chair by Barber as the man stood guard a dozen feet away. The two folding lawn chairs were constructed of solid plastic and each locked snugly beneath the seat to prevent slippage. The man instructed Daniel to bind Barber to the first of these before carefully checking the tension of the ropes. He then returned the favor for the sheriff before returning to the car to retrieve the video setup. Kayla and Daniel sat side by side, a mere two feet apart from one another, while Barber was positioned across from them, leaving at least a six-foot space in between.

"What's this crap, rummy? Movie time?" Barber spat hatefully, the relatively narrow ropes cutting a deep wedge into his muscular chest and upper arms.

The man didn't respond while backing away from the equipment to give it an initial test, a small black remote device curled into his right palm.

Feeling a few select droplets of sweat pour into and subsequently burn at the corners of both eyes, Daniel glared across at Barber and nodded vehemently from side to side.

Barber scoffed aloud and turned his attention to the dusty flooring at his feet. "How about a clue, Hoyt? One hint as to *why* we're tied to chairs in the center of this condemned house while your neighbor hangs naked in a shed out back, possibly bleeding to death? Maybe just a small tidbit of info as to exactly why you shot down that other mystery man in what seemed like an act of saving grace but obviously wasn't? How's about it, Hoyt? I mean, you do owe me for all the times I *didn't* bust you for DUI over the past few years."

The small color set blazed to life in a solid blue screen, emitting a smirking grin from the man just as he turned to face Daniel, waving the remote like a conductor's wand.

"All in good time, Sheriff Whitlock. I understand your frustration. Doesn't really mean *shit* to me, but I do understand it. The video entertainment segment of our program is really meant for Ms. Lee only. I do hope yourself and the convict over there can enjoy its sordid contents without fully comprehending its missing prologue. It's kinda like watching a film sequel without first viewing the original, but I'll fill in the blanks later during our question and answer segment."

Stepping over until he faced Kayla directly, the man leaned down until they were perfectly eye-level.

"Persistent little bitch, ain't ya?' he queried cheerily, cocking his head slightly to the left to match her pose, " Aaron I can understand. After all, a portion of his pathetic manhood was stolen, plus the fact that he was unfortunate enough to witness his mentor's untimely death. You, on the other hand…my dear, you are truly an enigma wrapped within a mystery."

"There's an assigned seat in hell waiting on you,

Parks. Got your name stenciled across the back in flaming red letters. I'll look you up once the final roll is called in the Hades *Hall of Fame*. Look you up and piss gasoline onto the eternal fire that slowly seers away your rancid flesh," she retorted calmly, her voice barely above a whisper.

His head flung back like a baying wolf, the man's laughter was smarmy, purposely obnoxious. "Seer away my rancid… oh, pardon me while I shiver and shake uncontrollably. What the hell was that, *Shakespeare*?"

The man lurched forward in a frenzied blur, halting his forward progress only when his face practically pressed again hers. The scent of stale cigarettes and rye whiskey assaulted Kayla's nostrils as his lips parted to speak, revealing the yellow, nicotine stained teeth within. She could barely refrain from openly gagging.

"Why do you insist on dying, woman? Makes me wonder why I *bothered* to spare your chink ass those other times. As you well know, I never was prone to pity. There was just something…so pathetic about you. Never quite found it in me to finish you off. Not to worry, though," he smirked, "ain't no danger of a three-peat."

"Be my guest, dickhead. If I get a last request, please perform the execution *before* the tape rolls. I simply *loathe* old reruns," she replied contemptuously, her lower lip quivering afterwards.

Rising to his feet, the man nodded in mock sympathy.

"Afraid that would be a serious breach of protocol, Kayla. After all, with Aaron permanently down for the count, you're my most stringent critic. I'll need your review for my own peace of mind."

Daniel felt his mind was adrift in a fog bank that

grew ever thicker as the seconds passed. Watching a man he had known, or at least *thought* he had known, for over a decade strut and prance about the room like an under-medicated psychopath, using an accent and vocabulary that were utterly alien in nature only increased the surreal quality of the scenario. He hadn't felt so detached from reality since the night at Mann Lake when Debra Lee Rainer's body had been discovered on the creek bank. It wasn't quite the 'wake me, I'm dreaming' sensation, but it was at *least* a distant, invariably more sinister, cousin of the same.

"Listen, Hoyt, or *Parks,* or whatever your name is...you need *help.* I can promise you'll receive the best care the state can provide. Your mental health will be evaluated before any criminal charges are--"

The man retrieved the remote from his belt and peered over at Daniel, placing a single finger over his own lips in a polite 'shushing' gesture. "*Quiet,* Sheriff. Just watch the film. It's one of my personal favorites, as I'm sure it holds a warm place in Kayla's heart, as well. As you view the opening shots, I'll turn on the AC. Getting a bit muggy in here."

Pressing the play button as he sauntered over to the small AC unit, the man danced an impromptu jig that told Daniel more than he wanted to know concerning the man's current mental state. The man wasn't just dangerous, he was *insanely* dangerous, an individual who had spent countless years or even decades bottled up in a false identity, living for the day when the submerged maniac within would again be given the ignition keys to his rotted soul.

The man Daniel had known as Hoyt Wilson, town drunk and gentle malcontent, was going to kill them all.

As the initial frame faded into view on the small set, a wave of cool air from the nearby AC unit struck Daniel's forehead, instantly turning the perspiration on his brow into icy chilled streams. He thought of Kara first and foremost as the tape's volume was pumped to ear-shattering decibel levels.

He thought of Tracy secondly, a faint glimmer of hope piercing an otherwise hopelessly pessimistic outlook. She would have gotten word on the overturned cruiser at least a half-hour earlier, although clues to her supervisor's actual whereabouts would be pitifully few and far between. As far as his bleary mind could recall, no one had witnessed their departure from the scene of the wreck, nor observed their trek onto Whitmore road some twenty minutes later. Still, Daniel had no choice but believe that his more-than-capable subordinate would indeed find them. After all, Tracy Morton's main strength as a deputy sheriff was her dogged tenacity and unrelenting determination. He could only pray she found them in time to prevent the inevitable.

Averting his full attention to the TV screen, Daniel found himself involuntarily mesmerized from the opening frame.

***

Hurriedly backing out of Curtis Barber's rain-soaked driveway, Deputy Morton inhaled deeply in a feeble attempt to ward off the massive swarm of butterflies flurrying within her chest and gut.

Despite her best efforts to avoid dwelling on the object occupying her passenger's seat, it seemed to mentally beacon her; forcing her weary, bloodshot eyes to ensure its continued presence within the vehicle. The circular end of its wooden handle protruded a few inches from the gallon-sized Zip-Loc she had used for protective wrap. She frowned thinking of the boxes of unused evidence bags stuffed within the cruiser's trunk. Forced to dig through the man's kitchen cabinets, she had stumbled across the Zip-Loc's and carefully encased the object, handling it as cautiously as a biochemist with a vial full of potentially fatal toxins.

She had entered the home (the front door had been unlocked) in hopes of either finding a clue to the two men's whereabouts or to possibly use Barber's phone to call the station. Nixed on both counts (no signs or phone in sight), she had taken a few moments to scan the residence, the majority of which seemed to be under major renovation.

She spotted the claw-hammer tucked haphazardly beneath a wadded up shower curtain, which had been stuffed between the toilet and eastern-most bathroom wall. It hadn't been the hammer itself that had initially piqued her interest, as various tools lay shattered in seemingly every room of the home, but the condition of the clawed end, which had protruded curiously from beneath the curtain like insect feelers. What she had first dismissed as partially dried paint on the curved edges had, in fact, held a sticky texture and a slight coppery odor upon closer inspection.

Moments later, she had lifted the hammer by the edge of its circular wooden handle and placed it carefully into the plastic bag, using a discarded paper towel to cover her own prints.

Pulling onto the main highway back towards town, she decided to stop by the first available homestead in order to borrow a phone. She figured the Mayor had already contacted the state boys, but wanted to pass on her location in case they wanted to meet her halfway. As she sped towards the steep grade where the overturned patrol car still lay, her mind bred many varied, frightening possibilities on the origin of the hammer's grisly condition, most of which involved Daniel. She had taken an extra five minutes before departing Barber's residence to perform a thorough walk-through around the surrounding property and had found nothing out of the ordinary.

The nearest DNA lab was two hours away in Birmingham, and she planned on handing the hammer to one of the state officers for quick transport.

As she passed the downed cruiser and circled through a series of short, sharp curves, she spotted a large, brown-colored metal mailbox with the name R&W SIMS fronting a narrow dirt road to her left. Braking hard in order to make the turn, the vehicle's back wheels spun temporarily on the slick pavement.

Biting her lower lip nervously, Tracy had two quick hopes; that somebody would be home at the Sims' place, and that she could manage to maintain her bowels as the cramps gripping her lower gut became more prevalent.

***

Video Commentary Voice Over: *The first infiltrator I had the displeasure of bumpin' into was a black guy who was later ID'd as T.C Eastmon, a street thug pimp from some inner city who made the fatal mistake of playin' up to the camera instead of properly stalkin' his prey Hence, the outcome you're about to*

326

witness...

(In the background, the music to Nazareth's 'Hair of the Dog' can be heard)

From a rear angle, a large shadow falls from the ceiling. TC Eastmon's head peers upward just as the blade penetrates his skull. He falls back, his arms and legs executing a grisly death-dance as the shadowed form rolls to the opposite side of the small foyer, leaping to its feet in a martial arts pose even as its victim collapses in a heap. The machete blade is buried deep into the black man's face and forehead, the wooden handle protruding from the wound like an oversized oven thermometer.

The camera, although shaking wildly as if caught in the midst of a powerful earthquake, continues to follow the shadow figure as it steps over the victim and proceeds forward, directly towards the lens.

Video Commentary Voice Over: *After I snatched up the porch monkey's rapier, I seriously considered carving up the cameraman, but then figured what the hell? If he had the balls to maintain filming after seein' that, I wasn't about to interfere with a masterpiece in the makin'. I could hear the poor bastard whimpering behind the hood he had draped over his face. Still, he followed me down the hall, keepin' a ten to twelve foot distance between us. I did warn him that if he managed to give away my position during filming, they'd find his head stuffed in an air duct.*

Couple of minutes later, I ducked into one of the large hall closets just outside my sleepin' quarters, dragging the lens-jock inside with me. I figured somebody would eventually be knuckleheaded enough to stick their head inside for a quick peek. That someone turned out to be a familiar face, although at the time I

327

couldn't for the life of me place it.

The camera's narrow beam of light temporarily illuminates the face peering guardedly into the wide closet space from behind the solid oak door. She is Asian, a tightly wound ponytail slung across her shoulder like a thick black snake. The loaded crossbow she grips shoots forward as the thin laser of light rests on her forehead. The camera is temporarily blocked as a large form leaps into its path, the picture clearing somewhat as its operator stumbles out into the hallway.

The crossbow lays on the carpeted floor, the arrow it held having penetrated a nearby wall in an obvious misfire. The lengthy bladed rapier has also been discarded, propped against a hall table some ten feet from the rear of the combatants, as if purposely placed there.

The Asian female implements a series of side and front kicks at her mammoth opponent, followed by combinations of straight jabs, left and right hooks, and uppercuts Her screams are warrior-like, even as her resolve weakens in light of the minimal damage she inflicts.

The onslaught does little to halt the massive form's forward progress, although he grunts in primal rage with each blow endured. He slings a forearm, followed by a vicious left hook that is cobra-quick, barely registering on film as anything more than a misty blur until the follow through. The Asian female thumps from the wall like a human pinball, as if tossed from a medieval catapult.

The camera freezes on a circular splotch of dark crimson where the left side of her head had impacted.

The hulking figure immediately scoops her from the carpet, hoisting her long, trim frame over head with shocking ease. He grunts like a recently de-iced Neanderthal before plunging her limp form downward across his knee with brutal force. The snapping sound comes across the camera's built-in audio in all its grisly

clarity, sounding like a rotted tree branch crunched beneath a heavy work boot. The man lays the woman's grotesquely twisted, broken body on the carpet with great care, ensuring her neck and head aren't accidentally slung backward in the process. The cameraman's childish sniveling can be heard as the victor kneels over the woman and slowly removes his shorts, followed by the black tights of his fallen prey.

As the rape ensures, the camera mercifully finds a home on the ceiling for a full three-minute interval as animalistic grunts and moans fill the dimly lit space.

The next scene follows the predator as he steps over the woman's splayed form, her face a bloodied mess from the open head wound that continues to bleed profusely as the camera lens swims atop her in passing. The man scoops up the crossbow and quickly reloads, pulling a fresh arrow from a small duffel the girl had discarded once the hand to hand combat had commenced. He turns to the cameraman and shoots him a wink before proceeding up the pitch-black hall.

"C'mon, boy….the party's just begun. I'd be damned impolite of me not to formally greet the rest of my guests, now wouldn't it?"

(background music now supplied by Ozzie Osbourne in the form of 'Bark at The Moon')

VIDEO COMMENTARY VOICE OVER: *I had a feeling the remaining assassins would be armed to the teeth, but also knew I only had to waste one of 'em in* *order to even up the odds by acquirin' a pop gun of my own. Hidin' in closets wasn't gonna cut it anymore, since they were more than likely shootin' first and openin' doors second.*

I needed to get back to the workout room to execute the diversionary tactics I had in mind. It was about that time that cameraman number one went off the deep end.

Dude was strictly SOL from there. He was makin' too much noise, and was sure to give me away before I ever reached the gym. At least I was a sport about it and gave his pathetic ass a fair shot. More than he deserved. Poor bastard had about as much chance as a Boy Scout with a slingshot, but I didn't have to give 'im anything. I just thought it would...look better on film if I did. (laughs)

Muffled footsteps fill the darkened hall as the man jogs back towards the camera, stopping short of actually ramming the lens with his charging frame. Smiling broadly, a thin line of crimson clearly visible from his busted lower lip, he tosses the bow underhanded until it falls to the floor at the cameraman's tightly laced black boots. The camera swoops down to the object, then back up the man, who is standing with his arms spread wide in a mock gesture of unconditional surrender.

"I'd advise you to pick it up and use it pal. You've got five seconds before I'm on your puny carcass like white on rice."

The smile fades in the light of the lens, replaced by a predatory sneer that oozes primeval menace. The light bathes the crossbow one last time, a gloved hand visible as it reaches down to retrieve.

The camera drops and instantly focuses on a nearby wall from carpet level.

The scream is high-pitched, ear-splitting, but is quickly cut off, replaced by a low gurgling that soon mutates into stilted silence.

Muffled footsteps can be heard in the distance as the camera is lifted, hoisted towards the tiled ceiling and then waved forward in a single, blurred wave. It focuses on the victim's face for only a split-second as the footsteps grow clearer and whispering voices become apparent. His neck is clearly broken, lolling to one side at an impossible angle, the eyes open and horribly aware.

An oversized hand grasp's the man's collar and drags him into a separate hallway, then into a small room that is empty save for a mini-refrigerator and a mostly empty bookcase. The camera is set atop the waist high fridge, its light turned to the wall as shuffling noises ensue. Something is draped over the lens a second later and the film goes dark.

VIDEO COMMENTARY VOICE OVER: *It was a bush league move, no doubt, and I never figured it would actually work, but hell's bells, it wasn't like there were many other options. The shirt ripped up the back when I tried buttoning it, and the pants were easily two sizes too small, but I managed to get 'em around my waist, barely. Hard to believe, but the guy's size eleven boots fit without cuttin' off blood flow. With my face planted behind the camera, they'd never be able to ID me until it was too late...I hoped. The crossbow tucked easily to my left side, my finger planted on the trigger as I re-entered that hallway. I knew there were two more turns to make before the workout room, one of which passed by the kitchen and living room areas, so there was no way I was gonna go unnoticed. Hey, even an ultra-talented warrior such as myself requires a boost from Lady Luck.*

On this specific night, that old bitch was most definitely smilin' up at me from the Devil's den she'd been occupyin'.

The camera focuses unevenly on the rambling form sprinting from the west end of the hall, the hooded soldier waiving frantically for a clear path through the narrow space, an AK-47 tucked snugly at his chest.

The sound of the crossbow's release follows, a low click followed by a brief hissing noise. The soldier had been only a dozen feet away upon impact. The arrow pierces his throat just underneath where his hood ends-- dead center at the Adam's apple. The camera zooms in as the AK-47 drops to the carpet, the man's hands dancing and jiggling as if he was attempting an 'air guitar' session to a rock tune only he can hear. The arrow has pinned him to the wall like a mounted trophy, his body growing limp as the spasms finally, mercifully cease.

Pointing the camera directly at his own grinning mug, the man's bizarre tone exhumes a good- natured cheer that is remarkably *inhuman* given the repugnant circumstances. " Stupid shit was gonna jog right on by me. Where did the shirts hire these people, *Moron 's R 'Us*? I did this idiot a favor." Reaching down, the man slings the discarded combat rifle over the opposite shoulder of the one the camera occupies, then reaches up to salvage the dead man's night goggles.

The picture shoots ahead to a double-door entrance that is propped open on both sides Static dominates the screen as the operator performs a combat roll of some sort, the lens ultimately landing on one end of a rather large weight bench. The distinct clicking of an ammo clip being pulled free and subsequently popped back into place is heard, followed by short, huffing breaths.

"Come to poppa, you dumb bastards," a husky voice beacons.

As before, the echoes of approaching boot steps can be heard growing ever closer.

(The background music is currently Lynyrd Skynyrd's 'O.R.R'(Outlaws, Renegades, Rebels))

VIDEO COMMENTARY VOICE OVER: *The workout room was stocked with bulky, elongated equipment that was perfect for camouflage. I donned the night goggles, ducked behind a wide squat rack and waited. Predictably, they entered through the front and back of the room simultaneously, both of 'em utilizing combat rolls similar to the one I'd perfected over the years. They began firin' as soon as the rolls ended, one to the south of the room and the other to the north. I felt chunks of ceiling tile and shattered mortar rain down on my head and back, and it became damned obvious that they knew I was there. I couldn't take the chance of risin' from my crouch, but also knew that if they were allowed to complete their line sweep, I'd be chewin' slugs within a matter of minutes.*

I took a couple of deep breaths, set the weapon on auto, and uncoiled, huggin' that AK like a newborn to mama's tit. It wasn't until I had rolled to a stop to line up a shot that I noticed the cameraman. He was turned to the right, pointing the lens right where I figured my initial spray of fire outta go. Imbeciles were allowin' him to place their positions in a neat little spotlight for yours truly. If those so-called 'professional soldiers' were the real deal, they were doin' some serious sleepwalkin' on this mission. They either overestimated their own talent, or underestimated mine. In either case, they were Spam on toast.

The room lights up like a burning fireworks stand, scattered rifle fire echoing from three separate directions. The soldier near the north entrance falls back in a lurch, his arms pin- wheeling madly as his weapon sails from his hands, forcing the nearby cameraman to duck away from its end over end trajectory. The wall to his back is coated in blood spatters that bring to mind abstract artwork on a wide scale canvas.

Rolling behind a set of narrow weight benches, the intended target resets his clip as countless shots continuously ricochet both behind and in front of his limited cover. He winces as a round pelts his breastbone, his Kevlar vest taking the brunt of the impact.

Running the slim barrel through the space provided between the benches wooden incline and metal support bars, a single spray of fire ensues, effectively ending the standoff as the camera then looms over a fallen soldier near the south entry/exit way.

He lays on his back, three dime-sized holes torn into his upper chest and neck. A thick stream of blood coats his lips and chin. The intended prey sprints towards the camera, which instantly whirls toward the north exit, the next few scenes far too murky or jumbled to distinguish. A cackling laugh is heard, followed by a sharp, hideous snapping sound.

The camera zooms in on the same devilish grin as earlier, the night goggles now propped atop his sweat-moistened scalp. "Forgot my damned manners again…really should've thanked the camera jockey for playing 'bird dog'. He pointed 'em out for me perfectly. Ah well, he's in no shape to appreciate my gratitude at this point. 'Sides, I need to check on my other guests."

Hitching the camera to his right shoulder, the man

strolls over to soldier number two's still twitching torso and pulls a fresh clip from the rifle lying a few feet to his left. He sprints through the room's north exit, past a wide kitchen entrance to his right, then pauses after a short jog down a noticeably wider hallway. A dim light illuminates from the area he approaches, the entrance marked by a set of three steps leading down into its apparently spacious confines. Muffled voices whisper in the near distance, low laughter follows the inaudible words.

Backing quietly against a nearby wall, he sucks in three lengthy breaths and slowly blows them out as the camera displays the gloomy hall he has just occupied. He can be heard checking the AK's clip. A small chuckle is barely audible just as the scene begins to dramatically alter.

(The background music switches to The Tubes' rendition of 'Mister Hate') **VIDEO VOICE OVER COMMENTARY:** *Cockiness is one thing, but downright knuckleheaded stupidity is another commodity entirely. These boys were literally ate up with both...in spades. I leapt into that living room expecting nothing less than a small Army , having pretty well accepted my own fate at the time. I was in 'take out as many assholes as you can before goin' down' mode by then, so the lack of firepower that greeted me both pleasantly surprised and, fired up as I was for a good scrape, disappointed me as well.*

It was setup like an interview room on Entertainment Tonight, tri-pod braced cameras from three angles, spotlights as big as tractor-trailer wheels, even a set of high-back chairs sittin' to face one another. You would 'a thought that the 60 Minutes gang had set up shop. I was half-expectin' Mike Wallace to walk up and greet me

335

with a smile.

Jackasses obviously hadn't expected me to be walkin' upright at that point, much less pissin' lava at the very sight of 'em. Aaron Kyle I spotted right away, his eyes as big as dinner saucers upon my entrance, fumblin' around in his jacket for a peashooter, no doubt. Mandrake the shit-eater stood next to him, and I swear by all that's unholy that old crap-breath was the single person in that room actually happy to see me, smilin' like he just struck oil under the livin' room carpet. An older man I later discovered to be the big cheese himself, M r. Head Honcho of World-Wide Video Corporation, one Earl Len Barron, had been standing slightly behind the two others, his arms wrapped around their respective shoulders. They looked like three reminiscing war buddies The old man shoved Aaron and Mandrake ahead a few steps for personal cover once he realized I wasn't one of his hired assassins.

I decided against a combat roll and instead ran directly at 'em like a defensive end with a free shot at a quarterback's blind side.

When my epitaph is written, they may call me many things, from a ruthless cold-bloodied maniac to a conscience-less machine without a shred of human decency. One thing the som' bitches cannot say about me, at least honestly, is that I never gave the other poor bastard a fighting chance.

I dropped the AK and waded into those spineless motherfuckers like a runaway tank.

The tall, thin man wearing wraparound sunglasses shoves the older man further back just before impact is made with the uniformed attacker. The camera posed at the men's back is toppled over as the two combatants flip into and then over it, camera number two clearly revealing the older man being flung over a nearby sectional couch, one of his black casual shoes tossed into the air like a discarded Frisbee.

As the taller man scuffles with the uniformed attacker, who looks to outweigh him by at least one-hundred pounds of pure bulk, the third man pulls a small revolver from his jacket pocket and points it towards the two combatants. The man's hands shake uncontrollably, his face frozen in a contorted grimace. He begins to whine like a frightened child, backing from the scene until he drifts from either of the remaining camera's limited range.

The thin man jumps from the larger man's grasp, his arms spread wide as he strikes a wide pose, each hand wielding similarly sized switch-blade knives. The thin man laughs through purplish lips that, strangely, never seem to part.

The larger man bounds to his feet and instantly takes up the stance of a classically trained boxer. Pulling the night goggles from his face with a swift tug, he casually tosses them aside and resets his arm in a frontal 'blocking stance.'

"Hiya, diarrhea breath. Ready to die?" he asks almost nonchalantly.

"Bring it on, bad a ss. I've counted the hours," the thin man practically screams.

From out of camera range, a series of sharp retorts can be heard. The larger man reels back, attempting to cover the nickel-sized wound that has just appeared on his right thigh. His gloved hand is quickly saturated in blood as he falls back and proceeds to roll between the two high back chairs. More shots ring out, one of the chairs' front legs splintered upon impact.

"Goddamn it, Aaron! Not this way!" the thin man wails, as if he is the target of the unseen shooter.

"Die, you miserable *FUCK*!" an off camera voice shrieks as a final shot ricochets harmlessly off the tile flooring a full foot from its target's booted feet.

The thin man lunges forward, whipping the twin blades back and forth indiscriminately as if slashing an invisible foe.

Kicking out with his right boot, the larger man sends the remains of the battered chair sailing into the thin man's exposed shins. The man yelps in pain, although his grim, determined expressed remains intact. The larger man charges forward, landing a viscous head butt underneath the thin man's bony chin even as one of the blades sinks deep into his left shoulder, just above the clavicle bone. The handle of the knife protrudes from the larger man's punctured flesh like a tent stake as he lands atop the thin man with a resounding thump. Sitting atop the thin man's chest with his tree-trunk sized thighs across his smaller opponent's chest and upper arms, the larger man proceeds to throw several punches, his arms twin blurs as they arc downward with piston-like precision.

An exquisitely dressed young man wearing thin-framed glasses leaps into the fray from the left, climbing on the larger man's back in an apparent attempt to reach the man's eyes with clawed hands. The man in the black suit and tie growls like a mortally wounded animal.

The large man backhands his latest attacker with a closed fist, sending the man flailing backwards as a torrent of blood gushes forth from his crushed nose and lips. "Be patient, preppy. I'll get to you right after I'm done with ol' turd lips here," the large man grunts aloud while placing his massive hands on either side of the thin man's skull. "See ya in hell, Mandrake, where *your* eternal damnation will no doubt involve brushing and flossing for all of infinity."

The thin man gurgles an obscenity just before his head is jerked brutally forward and snapped like dry kindling. The large man releases the dead man's skull, allowing it to drop back with a muffled thud. He stands stiffly, reaching up to pull the submerged blade from his shoulder, all the while eyeing someone off camera that he begins calmly addressing.

"Damn, Aaron, that's a nasty bleeder you got, pal. Tell ya what, I'll give you a few seconds to re-coop. Meanwhile, your boss and I really need to cha t about the bad manners displayed tonight. I mean, *really* ...burst into a man's home in the middle of the night without a courtesy phone call first? I had so little time to prepare."

The man vanishes from sight with the blade held low at his side, the sound of something heavy being dragged roughly across a hard surface soon drowns out the pathetic cries from possibly the same source.

Curled into a fetal position, the older man lays at the large man's boots, a bloody gash clearly visible across his pale forehead. He whimpers unintelligibly, his knees pulled to his chest and his hands draped over his face. "Hey Aaron, check out Mr. CEO, ballin' and simperin' like a five year old with a bee sting. Tell him to rise up and take it like a man, Aaron. Tell him the old adage *'fuck with the bull, get the horns'* was said for a reason. Tell him how fortunate he is to see the Reaper comin', which was more than yours truly was allowed. Tell him he should 'a hired more assassins and less cameramen.

339

Oh, why you're at it, the large man leans down and pulls the older man up by the gnarled collar of his dress shirt, 'tell him I'll plan on paying his surviving family members a little visit in the months to come."

The first jab of the pointed blade penetrates the old man's right eye. The second pops the left pupil like a ripe plum. The third is executed with much greater force, burying it to the handle just below the man's left temple. The old man gasps aloud, his eyes rolling back even as his body goes limp.

Pulling the blade free as he allows the body to slump to the floor, the large man wipes the fresh blood onto the front of his camouflaged shirt as he steps off camera to his right.

"Keep...f-fucking a-around...j-jackass... c-calvary will b-be here a-any s-second," the bespectacled man babbles, dragged by his left ankle next to the most recent victim, the blood from his facial wounds mixing into the wide smear already present from the old man's injuries.

"Appreciate your concern for my welfare, sunshine. Not to worry, *buddy*-boy, this won't take long," the large man replies, turning to ensure coverage from at least one of the cameras.

Pulling the smaller man up by his thick, wavy hair, he points directly into the camera with the crimson stained tip of the blade he loosely clutches. "Now, look into the camera and say *cheese,* pretty boy. Sincerely though, this is gonna sting a bit," the large man sneers, the knife hand dipping low just as he pulls the other man airborne with the other.

"Noooooooo..." the man pleads as the blade tip appears beneath his groin. *"Well here's comes Aaron with his pecker in his hand, he's a one ball man and he's*

340

off to the rodeo..." the voice croons cheerily as the screen fades to black.

(The initial guitar riffs to CCR's 'Bad Moon Rising' ensue)

VIDEO VOICE OVER COMMENTARY: *Can you believe they actually cut the final scene? I considered that particular segment the ultimate coup de grace, but the distributor thought it 'overkill.' Overkill in a snuff flick? Never knew there was such a thing as 'going too far.' They must'a figured a guy getting castrated live on film might turn off a few of the more sensitive buyers in the North American region, I dunno. Sure as hell don't bother the Middle Eastern or South American sickos.*

Anyhow, I sat there for another few seconds and watched Kyle bleed as he tried to tuck his missing balls back into the sac. It was kinda pathetic to watch, come to think of it, and damned uncomfortable for us who still own a pair. I figure he bled to death within five or ten minutes, after the shock from loss of fluids set in. Thought about finishin' the little weasel off, but that would'a been too easy. Too, dare I say it... humane.

I booked it to the bedroom and raided the hidden safe behind the headboard. Had a small duffel full of miscellaneous cash and a few bags of pot stashed away that I figured I could use to soothe my pains. Ran back to the living room, gave Aaron one final kick to the ribs just for the pure joy of it, then shoved three of the camera units into the duffel.

I found the Jeep parked about fifty yards outside the entrance road to the hacienda, all gassed up with a chauffeur already in place. They guy tried to pull a revolver from his jacket just as I shattered his face with a backhand. Like I said, there's cocky and then there's fucking stone-cold stupid.

I heard and then saw the choppers descend on the grounds about ten minutes later. Kyle hadn't been fibbin' after all. The cavalry did arrive, only I'm pretty damn sure it was two separate factions. Must have been one helluva scrap. Kinda wish I had been there to participate.

Well, hope you enjoyed the show, you sick fucks. Just remember…be kind and rewind.

Static envelops the screen.

***

"Okay group, what did ya think? Don't hold back now…my skin's only slightly thicker than toilet paper, but I *can* take it."

Daniel could only shake his head in stunned disbelief, his unblinking eyes frozen on the enigma standing before them, a man he had initially chalked up as simply deranged, trapped within the unrelenting throngs of a complete nervous breakdown. Such a diagnosis was the most logical assumption from the layman point of view, and invariably easier to accept than the alternative, that being that Hoyt Wilson the town drunk was in reality a cold-bloodied assassin for hire named Mason Parks.

Curtis Barber spoke in a deep, sarcastic growl.

"You telling us that bullshit was authentic and you were the *star* of the show? As the midget once said…*Welcome to Fantasy Island* …"

Taking up position directly behind Kayla, the man rested his elbows on either side of the wheelchair's high back seat. "Ah, those who disbelieve in hopes of soothing their inner fears. Tell 'em, Kayla."

342

Her face was void of all expression as the words escaped her cracked, chapped lips.

"It's...it's true. The man standing behind me is...one and the same...Mason...Parks. AKA Mister Hate, although his...current outward appearance, voice, and mannerisms might speak otherwise. The passing of years, along with what I'm certain was extensive reconstruction facial surgery, has created a remarkable disguise, I must admit, although I'm certain the bastard's heart is just as black and poison-filled as in decades past."

Leaning forward, he gently kissed the back of her head. "Thank ya, Darlin'...love you too. Now, for a quick synopsis on my part, just to fill in some blanks for all concerned."

Daniel finally managed to rediscover the use of his vocal cords just as the man again took center stage between the trio, the shotgun slung loosely across his right shoulder. Before speaking, Daniel couldn't help but think the man resembled a hopelessly deranged circus barker. "So you just happened to choose Elm Hill, Alabama as your city of choice to go on the lam, and as the town drunk to boot?"

The man howled like a baying wolf, whipping his head as far back as his stubby neck would allow. He then knelt down with the weapon balanced over his bent right knee, facing the two men. " Sheriff, you are one dim bulb, anybody ever tell ya that?"

Daniel's reply came in the form of angry stare.

"What better way to stay hidden than to become transparent to those around you? Nobody ever took me seriously around here, least of all the *po* -lice force. I was just a pathetic old lush you were forced to run off the streets once a month. Unfortunately, I seemed to delve into my role a bit too well, I'm afraid. Can't live without at least a pint a day of the hard stuff tickling my gullet these days. Ah, the price one pays for anonymity."

Barber glared across at Kayla, who was now silently weeping, her cheeks moist with fresh tears. "This clown really is the same guy as on the tape? Those people weren't…actors?"

Kayla nodded in sheer agony as all eyes had turned to focus on her for a reply.

The man previously known as Hoyt Wilson stood and stretched as if slowly rising from an extended nap, then strolled over to Kayla and extended a hand towards her face. She turned away from his touch with a jerk, groaning aloud as if enduring physical torture.

"Kayla, like the fine investigator she is, hit the old twenty penny right square on the head. The duffel load of cash I'd taken from the Ranch, along with several CDs I'd secretly managed to open in different banks along the East Coast and overseas left me fairly well off to go into immediate hiding. A contact of mine who will remain nameless, same guy who assisted in setting up my bank accounts actually, knew a defrocked plastic surgeon in Washington State Guy had supposedly been on the mob's parole for years. Specialized in 'face altering' techniques, if you get my drift. Needless to say, I was outta commission for several months afterward. Guy did a bang up job, although at the time I'd specifically requested James Garner's nose. Y 'know, the Rockford Files guy. Figured I'd be a regular chick magnet with a Hollywood snout."

The man turned from Kayla and back towards the men, both of whom had struggled mightily with their bonds, to no avail, while his back had been to them. "The

344

change in my physical stature was a long, arduous ordeal. I mean, ya just don't *stop* staying in shape overnight. I still pound the weights, even to this day. Got a set of 'em in my barn, along with a Universal machine. Even so, weaning myself off the muscle enhancers was pure hell for years. Dropped almost seventy-five pounds of pure hardness over that time. I had skin hangin' in places I never knew existed. The booze helped age me, as well. Not exactly the AMA's idea of a healthy way to diet, but as you folks can surely attest, it did the job."

"What about the s-scar on that man's thigh? You were shot in the same exact spot during the ranch massacre. Aaron f-found that damned tape inside his home and...Aaron also told m-me that the place reeked of...d-death," Kayla croak ed, dark streaks of eye shadow making a bee-line down her cheeks and onto her chin and neck.

The man spun back to face her, executing a textbook military about-face. "Ah, the mystery that is my good neighbor Douglas. Ol' Lockjaw I used to call 'im. We'd been living next to each other for almost seven years down the same isolated stretch of road, and I never heard the man string more than one sentence together without looking worn to a frazzle from the effort. 'Bout four years back, Old Lockjaw picked the wrong evening for a neighborly visit. Actually, I think it was the screams that led 'im to my place that night, but he never owned up to such. Needless to say, he walked in on something he wasn't supposed to see. The scar on Doug's leg wasn't my best work, but it sufficed, needless to say."

Kayla managed a strained smile through the frozen scowl she'd been wearing. " So we were right. You were back to your old tricks, right here in *Sleepy Hollow*.

345

Aaron and I followed the trail all the way from East Texas."

Shrugging playfully, the man whirled around upon hearing the sheriff's frustrated groans, training the shotgun's front site at the center of the bound man's chest. "Question, Constable? Comment?"

"Yeah...you two mind translating exactly what you're talking about? I lost *all* telepathic skills in a freak lightning incident a few years back," Daniel retorted irately, large veins visible across his forehead and beneath his throbbing temples.

"His own personal killing ground, Sheriff. He...recruited the homeless from at least three states, forced or, more likely, *enticed* them into his vehicle with baseless promises, then brought them here and murdered them in cold blood. He used his neighbor 's land as a burial ground."

"Ah, ah, ah,' the man interjected, waiving a s ingle finger from side to side, 'I gave each of those men a fighting chance, Miss Lee. I provided 'em with a weapon and a ten-second head start from the center of my backyard. Not once did I stoop to shooting my quarry in the back either. In fact, firearms were never utilized. Hand weapons only. Tell me how I could'a possibly been more sporting."

"How about by letting them be, you fucking loon? Ever think of that? Brother, you got some *serious* issues, mental stability wise," Barber barked, no longer bothering to conceal his continuing struggle with his bonds.

"This coming from a man convicted of slashing a teenage girl and stapling her corpse to a tree? Man, talk about the pot callin' the kettle black," the man replied

346

indifferently, now standing directly in front of the sheriff, the shotgun hanging loosely at his sides.

"The man paid his debt to society, Parks. It's not too late for you to do the right thing here. Cut me loose and I'll see to you get the he-"

The shotgun's barrel clanked loudly against the tip of Daniel's chin before being pressed firmly against the center of his throat. " You mention psychiatric assistance one more time, Whitlock, and there'll be scraping your brain tissue off the nearest wall."

The barrel dropped slowly, and Daniel smiled weakly between nervous swallows as the other man backed away.

"What's the plan then, Mr. Parks? What exactly do you have in mind for us? Charades tournament maybe? Twenty questions on the history of serial killers?" he asked sardonically, a spastic tick forming at the corner of his right eye.

"Calm down, Sheriff, before you blow an artery. I've never seen a lawman more disinterested in the why's of such a juicy potboiler. Allow me to fill in the blanks for dear Kayla, although I'd think at least a *portion* of this ought to pique your own interest. She's *owed* as much, anyhow. I'm kinda sad that Aaron isn't able to be with us, but for some reason I just couldn't allow him to terminate old Lockjaw. Might just be a case of jealousy, I dunno. Blade envy maybe. Guess only Doctor Phil could figure that one out."

Once again, the man turned to face the wheelchair. Kayla Lee had attempted to wipe the trail of tears from her cheeks. Multi-colored streaks lined her face, like that of a craze d sports fan performing a pre-game ritual with water colored paints.

347

"I had been at the edge of the pasture that split our land, zipping my latest conquest into a homemade body bag I'd constructed out of large trash bags. Doug walked up on me with the stealth of a cat. Never even heard a leaf crunch, and my senses are usually pretty damned reliable. Thought the poor guy was gonna keel right then and there after he noticed the guy's hand sticking out of one corner of the bag. Lockjaw tried to run, but he never had a chance. I held 'im hostage in my spare bedroom for a few days, trying to figure exactly what to do with him. Having him conveniently vanish wasn't the answer. Too damned many questions would'a been raised. I knew he had a daughter away at college at UAB, one of the few personal tidbits I'd picked up in our limited conversations. I forced Doug to watch the Conquest tape over and over, 'til he could've narrated that bad boy without benefit of the video footage.

Y'know, I wish I'd had the guts to have *Exterminator: The Final Kill* distributed worldwide…would'a made me a boatload of cash at the time. Just couldn't take the chance, not with human bloodhounds like Kayla and ol' one-ball Kyle around. Ah well, no guts, no glory."

Anyhow, I told Doug about the other…combatants I had brought to the house in the previous few months since my…urge to terminate had returned. Basically, I made Doug understand what I am… what I…*do.*"

They say everybody is given a talent at birth. Mine is to eradicate, plain and simple.

I let him go not long after, once the ground rules had been laid out and thoroughly understood. He would keep my little secret. He would construct a twenty feet wide by forty feet long shelter for the sole purpose of housing the bodies of the fallen. He would maintain the upkeep of said shelter, to include providing adequate lime to cover the effects of decomposition, thus eliminating a portion of the accompanying odor. A copy of the Conquest tape would be kept in plain sight within his home at all times. He would agree to these conditions without question. If not, his daughter would disappear without a trace, as would her captor. After several months or possibly years, he would begin receiving parts of her in the mail. Ol' Lockjaw really loved that kid, to that I can personally attest to. Never understood the whole concept of unconditional love myself. Then again, the whole family thing is warped in the extreme. Whole lotta sick crap executed in the name of *devotion* these days."

"He actually caved in on those ludicrous conditions? Four years and the man never attempted to turn you in?" Daniel asked curtly, feeling the rope around his left wrist loosen a bit as he continued to twist and curl his wrist in a clockwise motion.

Mason Parks replied without turning around as he again knelt before Kayla. The two seemed engaged in a 'stare down', their eyes locked and utterly unblinking.

"I can be *very* persuasive, Sheriff Dan. Oh, I'm sure Douglas considered many varied plans to do just that over the years. I guess it simply came down to the stark fear that he'd drop the ball somewhere along the line and his only child would suffer a slow, horrible death. A death he could have prevented by cooperating. To answer the scar question, he kindly allowed me to invoke that particular wound myself, at my insistence, of course."

"Jesus, didn't he know you were slowly pinning your crimes, old and new, onto him? The bodies, the tape, identifiable marks," Kayla finally blurted, her good hand

349

gnarled like a hawk's talon.

"There's that 'love' factor I harped on earlier, Kayla. Weird, wild shit that it is the man would've done anything…and just about did Poor SOB got filleted like a prize sea-bass, all in the name of family."

"So you called our office, complaining of strange screams in the night, just to set up Matson? Why draw the undue attention?" Daniel queried as his left wrist squirmed free from the bonds and immediately began the task of freeing the right.

"*Somebody* was closing in I could feel it like a bad bout of arthritis on a January morning At first I chalked it up to paranoia, but knew better as time passed. So yeah, I had planned on sneaking out the back way while Old Lockjaw took the fall."

Parks stood at the center of the circle like a lounge performer, leaning to one side while using the shotgun's frame as an oversized cane. "So why didn't you, jackass?" Barber chimed in rudely.

"Pride, I guess. Sounds crazy, but when I opened my front door and Aaron stood there in that pathetic disguise, something inside me clicked. Suddenly, I knew running and hiding again wasn't in the cards this time around. Nineteen years of playing war criminal was more than enough. A man has to face his ghosts in order to dismiss 'em. It wasn't like I had smoked the Pope that night in New Mexico. It was kill or be killed and I chose the former. Why should *I* be the one to suffer in paranoid isolation for the rest of my days? True, the competitive urge has driven me to extremes in the past few years, but every person has vices. Mine are just a bit…eccentric."

"Competitive ur… You make it sound like a retired football player coming out of retirement! You're a

350

sadistic, blood-thirsty freak of nature, Mason. Haven't you ever considered the dementia that hangs around your neck like a charm bracelet? You're a grade-A nut ball with a penchant for inflicting fatal injury; a festering, raging boil to humanity. Think of the countless generations of souls that were never born because of your savagery. The suffering you 've caused is infinite in its soulless brutality. *You sick, sadistic FUCK!"* Kayla screamed, spittle flying from her mouth in thick layers, her arm and hand shaking uncontrollably as the entire chair seemed to roll forward without benefit of a power source.

"Sorry, sweet thing. Such compliments are a waste at this point, I'm afraid," he grinned, leveling the shotgun at her frail, concave chest.

"I do apologize for the delay, Kayla. Saddest part is, you really died over twenty years ago, in that queer-boy Markum's mansion. I will say this for ya, not many seek revenge on someone for *not* taking their life at an earlier opportunity. Well, like they say…third time's the charm…"

Kayla raised her arm and positioned her hand directly into the shotgun's path. Her middle finger arose just as the room ignited in an explosion of thunder and smoke.

Daniel screamed aloud, a resounding *NO* that was drowned out by the blast as he leaned hard to the left, tipping the chair over on its side.

Curtis Barber refused to flinch, his entire body slumping within the restrictive bonds.

Kayla Lee's head vanished above the eyebrows, wiped away in a wave of splintered bone, shredded flesh, and blood-matted strands of billowy black hair. Her good hand had fallen into her lap, the fingers twitching madly, as if resting atop an invisible computer keyboard, attempting to type out a final, desperate message as the steely grasp of death gripped her fading soul.

Backing away a half step as if to survey his handy work, Mason Parks nodded solemnly. Discarding the weapon, he folded his arms casually across his chest. "That was a first. Mercy killings ain't exactly my specialty," he whispered in a low mumble, as if speaking only to himself.

Wriggling wildly in an attempt to further loosen the binds across his chest, Daniel released a frustrated groan as the left side of his head thumped forcefully against the tile flooring. A moment later he was being hoisted back into an upright position and the ropes subsequently tightened at his back, including the previously freed left hand.

"You murdering, heartless bastard...how could you...she was crippled for god's sake..."

"I did her a *favor* , Sheriff, despite what you or anybody else thinks. Don't you *get* it? She despised the ground I walked on, tracked me like a coon dog for almost nineteen years, solely because I *refused* to take her life on two earlier occasions. The only person she hated worse than me was *herself,* Sheriff Dan. Every detail of Kayla's existence, from joining the FBI to playing 'Ironside' the past two decades was done out of self-pity and self-loathing. I could'a saved her a lifetime of misery by slitting her throat back in Sperryville, after that sick fuck Scott Markum had raped and tortured her. See what you get for showing pity? I'll never that mistake again, not on purpose anyhow."

"Real angel of mercy, you are, you twisted shit,"

352

Barber said with a snarl.

Parks quickly sidestepped over until he loomed over the larger man, who cringed back involuntarily, his eyes wide with shock.

"Had enough of your mouthy crap, big fella. I think its ample time we switched formats on this little to-do, now that the Asian bitch is beyond interrupting.

"Jesus," Daniel cried, lowering his chin to his still - heaving chest as Parks again positioned himself behind his chair.

"Damn, Constable, don't despair. I guarantee this will be worth our whiles. Actually, the drama to come is the single reason I haven't already reloaded old faithful and turned you and King Kong over there into country fried puree."

Shoved forward in a lurch, the chair's front legs threatened to tip forward as they screeched across the tile. Daniel felt his gorge rise at the sudden movement. He was spun violently around and thrust forward once again until the space between his own knee caps and those of Barber's was mere inches.

"What the h-hell are y-you... " Daniel croaked weakly, his breath escaping in short gasps. He deduced in silent terror that he was only moments from a full blown, chest imploding heart attack. A part of him pleaded for it to be so, figuring the alternative wasn't likely to be near as peaceful a passing.

Barber glowered across at him, his lips pursed like a man sworn to absolute secrecy but aching to divulge a Pandora's box full of confidential information.

Parks leaned between the two men from the right, placing a firm, callused hand on each of their shoulders. " Sorry 'bout the rough treatment, Sheriff Dan, but I'm too

353

damn old and worn out to drag the Jolly Green Giant here around the room. You ain't exactly full of feathers yourself, Sunshine."

Leaning back up, Parks clapped his hands enthusiastically and then rubbed his palms together in gleeful anticipation. Daniel turned his head from the man's wide, toothy, gruesomely warped smile and instead concentrated on Barber, whose face had gone frighteningly blank, thick, circular beads of sweat rolling down his cheeks like moist tumbleweeds. "Okay, hombres. Here's the scenario: as a citizen in good standing, if not always sober and not quite law abiding, of the Elm Hill community for a full decade, I found myself enthralled by one specific incident in the town's less than sordid past. It wasn't like I didn't have time to discover a hobby or two while hidin' out in Mayberry, USA, y'know? Other than the occasional extermination, that is.

People spoke of this specific item in low whispers, I noticed, like they were discussing a horribly disfigured relative. I mean, you would'a thought Reverend Collins from the Baptist church had been nabbed running a kiddie porn ring or something. It's a taboo subject here in these here parts, and one near and dear to both you chap's hearts. I speak of course…'he leaned back down, his hands balanced atop his own knees, '… of the murder of one Debra Lee Rainer."

Daniel instantly choked on the minute amount of spit his parched mouth held.

Chapter Nine
Coming Clean/Aftermath

"Damn, Dan, didn't mean to make ya spit up a lung," Mason Parks smirked, gently patting Daniel on the left shoulder, 'it's just that this particular case fascinates me no end. A&E material, 'Grisly, small-town homicide shocks community', that sort of happy crap. I've collected every tidbit through the years. Took quite a few trips to Birmingham just to research microfiche and old press clippings. Of course, in the last few years the Internet has made such legwork a thing of the past."

His expression remaining a blank slate, Barber seemed to be staring past Daniel to the mutilated body slumped in the background.

Retrieving the shotgun from the wall he had leaned it against following Kayla's sudden, shocking demise, Parks began to nonchalantly reload, like a man replacing the batteries in his TV remote. "Look at it from my perspective, gents. A case I've obsessed over for years, and here I sat with the two *prime* involved parties. No way I'm vacating the premises without a suitable interrogation and possible resolution. You can understand my position, can't ya? This is once in a lifetime type shit, boys."

His coughing spell finally having subsided, Daniel's expression was as scornful as the words that accompanied it. "Possible resolution? Hate to burst your bubble, Parks, but a jury of twelve decided that particular detail a long time back, or didn't you bother to *research* the trial?"

Parks' eyes darted from Daniel to Barber and then back again, as if carefully gauging their every response.

"Textbook kangaroo court, Sheriff. A 'Pasty'
trail--I've heard such travesties of justice referred to in the past--with ol' Curtis the menace playing the part of Pasty. Ya see, I'm of the unique opinion that old muscles here was set up like a bowling pin by the local authorities, both of whom are presently pushin' up daisies, I might add."

Barber broke from his trance as if physically slapped, his brow creased with curiosity. "Oh, so you 're on *my* side? Damn, don't I feel secure now. Fucking *homicidal maniac support* at it's very finest. Where were ya eighteen years ago, Sparky? Whoops, that's right...you were a tad busy with your *other* hobby, cold-blooded murder."

Parks shoved the shotgun barrel flush against the left side of the larger man's skull and held it there. The good cheer of moments earlier had vanished in a blink, replaced by a growling sneer. "New rule: speak when spoken to. That's gratitude for ya."

Parks backed away shaking his head, dropping the weapon's barrel to the floor, then ambled over to the horribly disfigured corpse of Kayla Lee and seemed to size it up, like a boxer studying his opposition before the opening bell. "A judge needs a throne, I say. What better than a mobile one?"

Leaning the shotgun next to the nearby TV unit, he reached over and cupped Kayla beneath each arm and pulled her from the chair with the ease of a man scooping up a feathered pillow. The gaping crater that had been her forehead and scalp continued to bleed profusely as he tossed the carcass to the side like a dismembered slap of beef, coating his neck, shirt and lap in the process. The room was suddenly engulfed in a sharp, coppery scent.

"What a freakin' mess. For a shriveled up crip, the chink sure packed away a shit-load of juice," he said indifferently while mounting the chair. After taking a moment to reposition the arm and leg rests to suit his larger frame, he powered it up with the joyful enthusiasm of a young boy with his first motorized toy then spun it forward until it sat a few feet to the left of his prisoners.

As the overwhelming stench of the woman's fluids assaulted his flaring nostrils, Daniel bent as far to the right as his binds would allow and vomited, the majority of the oatmeal textured glut landing atop his own shoulder and upper chest.

"Now, now, none of that, Sheriff. You're gonna ruin my appetite, and I had my heart set on a double Whopper with cheese after the trial."

"Sick motherf..." Barber began, though quickly falling silent upon viewing Parks' contemptuous look.

Daniel spat weakly until his mouth was emptied, although several mushy clumps hung from the corners of his mustache. "What's the...purpose of this, Parks?"

"Like I said, Constable, I simply wish to re-examine the facts, to which I'm certain were purposely misrepresented in the original case, and basic ally set the record straight in my own mind. I just...*have* to know for certain, that's all. Call me stubbornly inquisitive."

Backing the chair a foot or so with a single backwards thrust, Parks snatched the shotgun from its leaning position and sat it across his lap, then pulled ahead and parked, cutting the chair 's power. "Ho-kay. Here's the plan, guys. Pretty simple, actually. I query; you answer. My advice is to answer honestly, as if your very life depends on it, which coincidentally, it does. If Judge Parks deems purposeful deceit on the witness's part, I will subtract a mental demerit. At the conclusion of said trial, said demerits will be tallied and a suitable punishment carried out. In other words, lie and you *die horribly,* regardless of my final decision on the Rainer case. Look at it this way, if you're innocent, you've got nothin' to fib about anyhow, am I right?"

"If...*we're* innocent? Who's we, you cracked son of a bitch? Somebody in the room with us besides Curtis?" Daniel whispered between coughs, eyeing the 'Judge' with weary contempt.

Parks cocked his head slightly to the left. His tone was openly mocking; the words slow and deliberate, as if he was addressing a deaf foreigner.

"Why, Daniel, don't you get it? The man on trial here today...is *you.*"

Although his face remained stony and unmoving, Daniel's upper body visibly tensed.

"You're nuts, Parks. Certifiably so. Why don't you...just do...what you do best and get done with it?"

"Heard Lance Hendricks bought the farm last night. Sheriff, wasn't he the man with the shiny silver badge in Elm Hill when Debra Rainer was murdered?"

"Yeah, he was. Not much of a revelation there, Parks"

"What was his deputy's name? Detmire? Dagwood?"

Daniel grinned in exasperated disgust. "Detmer, Bill Detmer."

"Passed away a few years back, correct? Lung cancer or some such inner-body cannibalism?"

"Cirrhosis of the liver back in two-thousand..."

Leaning back, Parks rested his chin atop his clinched right fist. His eyebrows were cocked, his forehead crinkled, like an inquisitive reporter grilling a deceitful politician. " Drank himself to death more than likely. Hmm…happens to a lot of former law enforcement types, I hear. Mostly stress, the experts say. In some cases, it's the stress of keeping dark, evil secrets for too many years. Eats away at their guts like a starvin' wolverine on a deer's shinbone. Bet ol' Bill was keeping a real corker bottled up. Lance too, for that matter, though in his case , somebody else made damn sure the secret was gonna stay bottled up, *permanently*. You had a date with lovely Miss Rainer that evening, didn't you, Sheriff?"

"Listen, you psychotic pile of dog tu-" Daniel began, the veins on his forehead becoming more pronounced even as the flesh on his face grew a dark shade of maroon.

"Buckin' for a demerit, Constable," Parks replied sternly. "Just answer the question."

Sighing deeply, Daniel's head fell back just as he seemed to resign himself to cooperate with the madman's folly. Curtis Barber locked his sights on the sheriff, his head slumped slightly forward. He resembled a man sentenced to life in a hospital waiting room, the recesses of his inner mind entangled in cobweb netting that was slowly evaporating his very soul. Daniel half-expected the man to soon begin drooling.

The next few moments passed like a dementia-laced episode of *Matlock* filmed in the deepest recesses of hell, the back and forth banter executed with machine-gun quickness and with virtually no hesitation in between. Daniel felt strangely adrift in a swirling, angry sea of unreality, surfing a surrealistic dreamscape with waters stocked with ravenous predators.

Predators desiring a taste of his flesh and his flesh

Daniel :

"We had a date, yeah. We'd been seeing each other for a month or…two, maybe."

Parks:

"You stated at the trial that you ran into some pals down at Mann Lake and got separated from her."

Daniel:

"Yeah. Starting sipping a few brews and jawing with the guys. Some of Debbie's friends were down there. I figured she went off with some of them. Turned out… I was…wrong."

Parks:

"Curtis Barber was Elm Hill's designated juvenile delinquent, wasn't he? A real bad ass with a penchant for fightin', stealin', and dopin', isn't that a fair description?"

Daniel:

"He.. .I guess…yeah."

Parks:

"You spot him at Mann Lake that evening while 'jawing' with the gang?"

Daniel:

"Yeah. He drove up with Billy Wheeler in Curtis' beat up old Ford pickup ."

Parks:

"You do any 'jawing 'with Curtis yourself that particular night?"

Daniel:

"No. Curtis and I rarely spoke. We…uh, hung in different circles."

Parks:

"You see 'em depart the scene?"

Daniel:

"No, I didn't exactly keep up with 'em. There were at least twenty or thirty of us milling about that night."

Parks:

"Funny thing, nobody reported seeing your girl and Curtis leaving the scene together either. Seems such an event would'a stood out, considering Miss Rainer came from a different side of the tracks than bad boy Curt. You'd think some tongues would 've wagged. Billy Wheeler testified that he didn't recall much after he and Curt got to the lake, just woke up in his own bed the next morning, hung over as a sailor after an overnight port pass. Couldn't remember when or how he even got there. Weird that no one 'fessed up to giving that boy a ride from the lake. You think he walked the four-plus miles back to his mama's house?"

Daniel:

"No idea. Like I said, I didn't hang with Billy Wheeler or his crowd. They were just down there as part of the cruising and boozing crowd, we figured."

Parks:

"You didn't look for Debbie after you noticed her missing?"

Daniel:

"We weren't married, damn it. Besides, I was buzzing pretty good by the time I left the lake. Only thing on my mind was finding a nice, soft bed to pass out onto."

Parks:

"Nobody rode from the lake back to town with you?"

Daniel :

"Nope. Most were still partying. I was never an all-

361

night drinking kind of guy."

Parks:

"How'd you feel the next day when you found out about Debbie?"

Daniel:

"Shocked. Disgusted. Just...pained."

Parks:

"Guilty, maybe?"

Daniel:

"That...well, yeah...maybe. After all...she was with me earlier that night. Her parents, they ..uh...looked at me like...well, like it was my fault."

Parks:

"No, let me rephrase. I mean guilty over *killing* the girl, Daniel? Guilty over slicing her open like a Thanksgiving roast and then practically nailing her ass to that tree with barbed wire. *That* kind of guilt..."

Daniel:

"You're full of sh- -"

Parks:

" Sheriff Hendricks, rest his lying, deceitful soul, testified that mere moments after his deputy had discovered the girl's body at the east side of Mann Lake, that he just happened to run across Curtis passed out in his pickup on the west side. Yeah, Curtis was coated in the girl's blood; the back of his shirt was supposedly drenched in it. Yeah, Curtis had a handful of Debbie's matted hair clutched in his right fist like a trophy scalp. And yeah, after two days of non-stop interrogation, he did admit to visibly seeing her sometime that evening. Not murdering her, mind you, just *seeing* her. He'd been toasted on rum, tequila , and gin since around four that afternoon, so specifics in his story were damn hard to

362

come by.

"Then again, why the hell was the majority of the blood found on the *back* of his shirt? Did he somehow stab her while walking backwards? Damn, didn't know one of Curtis's many talents included contortionist. Also, not much was said about the golf-ball sized lump found on the back of his head upon examination that night. The prosecution chalked it up to either Debbie getting in a lucky blow or a drunken fall on Curtis' part.

"Bottom line was this: Curtis was an easy fall guy for all involved. Tenth-grade dropout, in and out of trouble since he was twelve. Doper, drunk, why not a *murderer*, right? On the other hand, Daniel Whitlock had a father on the city council and a mom who organized bake sales for the local church. Daniel Whitlock was the starting wing-back slash tight end for the football team and a power-hitting third baseman on the baseball team. Daniel Whitlock had a future. Curtis Barber was a drunken, brawling malcontent bred from white trash whose future eventually lay within the Alabama penal system. This starting to make sense to you, Daniel? Am I boring you to tears with these made-up facts?"

Daniel:

"You're starting to froth at the mouth, Parks. You behind on your shots?"

Parks:

"What happened, Dan? She refuse d to surrender the pink to ya that night?

You have a boner that just wouldn't take no for an answer? It's no sin, brother…been there myself many times. "

Daniel:

Kiss my…ass, you sick son of a--"

Parks:

"Or maybe she wanted it and you couldn't deliver. Maybe you made a horrific discovery that night concerning young Dan Whitlock's sexual preference? You a closet butt-bandit, Sheriff? You enjoy slidin' down the Hershey Highway?"

Daniel:

"...man, you are *fried*..."

Parks:

"How extensive was the interview session between yourself and Sheriff Hendricks, Dan? I'd wager my left nut it didn't last more than a few minutes. 'Sides, they had their man in custody already. Why question such a fine, upstanding young man with such a bright future lying ahead of 'im? Man, you must have been sweating cannon balls driving around the back roads with that mangled corpse stashed in your trunk, huh? Wasn't it like a miracle from above to discover old Curtis here, passed out in his truck and just waiting to be set up?"

Daniel:

"Over and out, asshole. You're nuts."

Parks:

"Really? Then why is it your face speaks otherwise, Sheriff? Why the fresh coat of *pers-pi-ra-tion* ? Looks like an old ghost just rose up and bit you squarely on the ol' nut-bag. I ain't seen skin that damn pasty on anything other than a day old corpse."

Daniel:

"Maybe it's because I'm strapped to this chair in a room that smells like a slaughterhouse, waiting for you to decide exactly when you're gonna *kill* me. Situations like that just might make a *normal* man nervous, you think?"

Parks:

364

"They say confession is good for the soul, Daniel. Cleanse yours while you have the chance. Like you said, time is fast runnin 'out."

Daniel:

"I don't have to play your game. I *won't* play it."

Parks:

"When did you decide to off Hendricks? Man was half-dead already. Couldn't wait for 'natural causes', I guess. You must'a been scared shitless he was finally gonna spill, especially when word got out that Barber was paroled. Why the panic, Constable? Barber's lawyer had the DNA checked back in '99. No traces of any bodily fluids other than Debbie's and Curt's. They couldn't place ya at the scene. I guess with Hendricks all doped up and in pain the way he was the last few months, there was always the chance his lips might start flappin' unconsciously, huh?"

Daniel:

"He was a good man, Lance. Deserved…better."

Parks:

"Better than a claw hammer to the skull, you mean? Yeah, wouldn't exactly be the way I'd wanna go out, either."

Daniel (gasping aloud):

"C-claw…how do…you…did you?"

Parks:

"You're babbling, Constable Dan. Your face gets much whiter, I'm gonna check your pulse."

Daniel:

It's not l-like that, I…uh…"

Parks:

"Oh, but it *is* like that, Sheriff. That was you planting the murder weapon at Barber's home, wasn't it? I swear,

365

I could hear your knees knockin' from fifty feet away. Saw your hands shaking too. You really ain't cut out for murder, Daniel. Performing the deed a few times in one's lifetime hardly makes them an expert in such matters."

Daniel (shaking his head vigorously from side to side):

"Wh-what do you mean, s-saw me? Why bother to fr... why frame me for a murder right before...you...kill me anyway? Lord, you are *not* to be believed..." *Parks:*

"Might as well drop the act, Dan. I got'cha on film, boy. Crouched in the weeds like I was, I damn near got chewed into gristle by mosquitoes, chiggers, and ticks, but the camcorder caught ya in all your nervous glory. If you look close enough and freeze the tape, you can just make out the hammer's handle sticking out as you walked it towards the house."

Daniel:

"I...you're so full of..."

Parks:

"Good for the soul, Daniel."

Daniel (voice cracking):

"There's... n-no way anybody will...b-elieve..."

Parks:

"Confess now and it goes no further than this room, Daniel. I just have to know for *myself,* that's all."

Daniel (sobbing):

"B-but...it's not r-right. It's n-not..."

Parks (leaning over, placing a hand on the crying man's left shoulder in a consoling gesture):

"You really want to greet your maker as a liar *and* a murderer, Daniel? What would little Kara think of her father if she knew?"

Daniel (long pause. Raises his head slowly, his face

glowing red): (His voice is robotic, void of emotion)

"Hendricks had c-called me at home…several times over the past few weeks. His doctors had him on morphine. He was talking…out of his head. I…had t-to. The man was…in misery anyway. I did him a f-favor, really. Like I said…he was a good man, Lance. A…good m-man."

Parks:

"What about Debbie Lee? *Why,* Daniel?"

Daniel (eyes vacant, unblinking):

I-it just got…it got…way out of hand. We left the lake and found a nice, deserted spot off the beaten path, away from all the roving drunks. It started out…kissing and fondling, like always. That night she seemed more…aggressive, I guess you'd say. I saw that as a green light to test the waters, so to speak.

Debbie stopped me cold when I began…feeling her up. Lousy tease got me rock hard and then backed off, like she had planned it that way. Desperate as I was, I told her I was a virgin, which I was, in hopes of maybe tantalizing her into finishing what she started."

(Long pause)

Parks:

"And? Got'cha so far. Been there, done that."

Daniel (voice again cracking somewhat):

"She…l-laughed at me. I'm talking the howls of a hyena, man (*laughing nervously*). Think if she'd had a bullhorn and a spotlight, she would've put me on center stage. Said she was gonna 'spread it around' that I was a cherry. Big, bad football player, she always called me. Debbie hated jocks as a rule, you know. She had a real mean, c-cruel…streak. Some folks say her mother was the same. I'd never really seen that side of her 'til…that night. She'd had a...five or six beers I guess. Turned her into a real...bitch. A real...*hateful* bitch.

"Maybe it was... the booze, I dunno, but after about the third chorus of that irritating chatter of hers, I completely l-lost it. The punch was nothing more than a jab, you know? A straight left jab that should've just...stunned her at worst. I'd meant... to use the flat of my hand...not a fist. Guess I just...lost it...big time. Next thing I know, she's just lying there in the back seat, her head sit all crooked, her mouth and forehead bleeding like I'd used a Louisville slugger...repeatedly. I *swear* to all that's holy... I o-only remember hitting her once, and even that's a blur. Like I didn't really do it, you know? Like maybe I saw it happen, but it...wasn't me.

"Needless to say, she had no pulse. As I was...t-tucking her deeper into the floorboard, I noticed the back of her head was bleeding as well. The window handle on her side was soaked with it. Sad to say, but I was just happy to be rid of the laughing . That don't sound right, does it?"

Parks:

"Women, Dan. Cold-hearted leeches who live to suck dry the souls of good men like you and I."

Daniel:

"Y-yeah. My ex had s-some of the same traits. Anyhow, I recall driving around the lake like a madman, debating what to...do with her. Talk about sobering up quick ; it was like I had never popped a single beer tab by the time I ran across Curtis lying half-out of his pickup. I used my tire iron to make sure he didn't wake up, then smeared some of his blood on Debbie and vice versa Thought about... leaving her body in his truck, but figured he'd just wake up and dispose of it himself,

368

leaving me as the prime suspect in her disappearance. So I drove her up the road a mile or so and found just the right spot...o ff the beaten path but just accessible enough to be discovered within a matter of days.

"That old, barbed wire fence provided the last detail. I...t-turned my head as it ran across her throat. I swear, I didn't even look at her, even when I was...binding her...to that tree."

Parks:

"Hendricks and Detmer ever really consider you a suspect?"

Daniel (his eyes clamped shut):

"They c-checked my car a few days later, but I could tell their hearts just weren't into it. By that time, I had cleaned, re-cleaned, and re-cleaned again. I had to dirty up the back seat just to keep *down* suspicion."

Parks:

"They knew though, didn't they, Daniel? Deep down, they knew."

Daniel (smiling wearily):

"They had to suspect more than they let on. But Curtis Barber was the perfect fall guy. He had been a pimple on Elm Hill's rear end for years. They saw their chance to pop the zit... and they didn't hesitate."

Parks:

"Tell the truth, Sheriff Daniel Whitlock, hasn't a cargo-plane full of bricks just departed those slumped shoulder of yours?"

Daniel (eyes still closed, head bowed):

"It...ate, eats at me every day of my life. Every minute, every d-damned second. A minute's repentance don't make up for what I did, Parks. I'm...not like you. I was born with human feelings...with...compassion. I

369

think...that's why I became a cop...why I came back to Elm Hill . I've been trying to make up for...what I did...what I became that night."

Parks (sneering):

"Made up for it by murdering the former sheriff, a man practically on life-support, with a claw hammer? Son, that ain't exactly the definition of human compassion, 'cept maybe in the *satanic* version of Webster's."

Daniel (screaming):

"I've got a daughter, *SHIT FOR BRAINS!* She ain't about to spend her entire life paying for her father's *FUCK UPS!*"

Parks (leaning over until the two men are nose to nose):

"Go ahead and justify it any way you want, Dan. Bottom line is this: whether you want to admit it or not... me and you are two peas in a pod, son. The psycho line is a fine one, and you crossed it decades ago. Welcome to *my* world, Whitlock."

***

Parks wheeled the chair back at top speed, braked hard, then whizzed around in a circle, parking just to the right of Curtis Barber, whose bland, lifeless expression had remained amazingly unchanged throughout Daniel's shocking testimony. Pushing himself from the chair like an Olympian dismounting the parallel bars, Parks leaned over and placed his left hand on the back of the larger man's scalp, as if to apply a gentle massage.

"Well, Curtis, you've heard the good sheriff's tear-jerkin' admission of guilt in the case of state vs. Dan

Whitlock. Anything to say in light of this ground-shakin' evidence, my boy?"

Barber glanced up at the other man, then slowly back over to Daniel, whose entire body shook uncontrollably beneath his binds. The smile emerged in tiny increments, taking a full thirty seconds to reach its wide, toothy crescendo. "I ain't one to cry easy, Mason, but I gotta admit," he said, winking playfully, "I might just need a hanky. Nineteen years I waited to hear those words, man. Sweet as fresh spun honey, they were."

Daniel wheezed like a man emerging from an icy lake, staring at the two men through wide, moistened eyes.

Parks giggled madly as he stood behind Barber's chair and began methodically slicing through the man's binds with a large butcher knife seemingly pulled from thin air. "You see ol' Dan's expression, Curtis? Damned if that alone didn't make the whole shebang worthwhile."

"I see the whimpering bastard. Pathetic, ain't he?" Barber replied sourly as the severed rope fell free from his chest and arms. He stood upright a moment later, stretching his massively pumped arms high into the air as if awakening from a lengthy nap.

"I d-don't get...a... setup? All...a setup? " Daniel babbled, peering up at the giant figure that loomed over him, casting a wall-sized shadow over his badly shaking frame.

"Damn, he's a bright one, alright. This town is gonna lose a fine, stalwart lawman, Mason. Ya just can't replace such quality without enduring some hard times," Barber beamed while leaning down until the two men were perfectly eye to eye.

"Yeah, the locals won't ever understand how such an

371

upstanding member of the community could turn out to be, in reality, a bloodthirsty murderer. A soulless killer hiding behind that shiny silver badge like a force field he thought would never be penetrated by past evil doings," Parks ranted in the background, altering his voice to emphasize false drama.

Daniel could smell the large man's pungent body odor, coupled with the sour breath that accompanied it. He shuttered openly, although refusing to break the man's stony stare.

"You got that right, partner. Sheriff Whitlock had it all mapped out from day one of my parole release, didn't ya, Dan? Who better to seek revenge on the sheriff who put him away but a recently released convict with a past history of random violence? I no sooner had the lights turned on at the old homestead before he makes a bee - line over to Hendricks' place and hammers the man's face into ground chuck. Swings by my place to stash the hammer and then picks me up for questioning. I get the feeling a warrant to search my place was in order next, right Dan?"

Daniel said nothing, his lips pursed together like a man holding his breath in toxin-laced waters. Curtis Barber stood and crossed his massive arms across his chest, backing away until he stood beside Mason Parks, the two men posing stiffly together as if awaiting a camera's flash.

"Be sure and stop me if I say something that don't ring true, Dan, you hear?"

"Go, man, GO!" Parks bellowed, clapping the larger man between the shoulder blades.

"Eighteen years, man…eighteen years of my life flushed down a shit-stained sewer 'cause it was convenient for you to do so. I saw you at the trail, man. You, Hendricks and Detmer all wore the same look, the same guilty mask. I had almost two decades to mull it over, Dan. There was no *other* suspect You have any idea how it feels to read hometown news clippings from Elm Hill and see that 'Dan Whitlock joins the Army' or 'Dan Whitlock Returns Home to Seek Office.' The day I read you got elected sheriff, I performed my first jailhouse rape. Held out for almost eight years, Constable, but I had to release some steam that night or I was eventually gonna kill somebody for real."

"Don't forget to tell 'im about me, partner," Parks chimed in, casually picking his teeth with a bloodstained pinkie.

"Enter Hoyt…um…Mason Parks,' Barber said, side-stepping over as if introducing a stage act, "my truest believer. Mason began writing me at the unit about seven years back, just to let me know he supported my innocence, and that he'd began to study the case a year or so earlier. Mason agreed wholeheartedly that Elm Hill's current sheriff in good standing was, in reality, the community's only experienced murderer at large. 'Course, he couldn't make such a bold statement in writing, being that our mail was monitored pretty close. This man actually started driving up to the unit on visiting days to share his opinion face to face."

Daniel coughed harshly, the words hanging in his throat like hot phlegm. The two men waiting patiently for him to recover, each with an arm wrapped around the other like drinking buddies standing around a beer-filled cooler. "Y-you knew…w-what this man… w-was…what he…d-*did*…and you continued a…r-relationship?" he finally croaked in a sick, weary tone.

"What he was, Daniel? What *he* was? What the hell are you, son? Drop the holier than thou act, Sheriff...it don't wash," Barber raved, the flesh of his cheeks and forehead suddenly glowing red.

"I'm not l-like.. that. What happened was...tragic, got outta control...but I n-never meant to-- "

"Whatever. Cut the whiny babbling, will ya, Sheriff? I'm starting to get embarrassed for you," Parks injected with a smirk.

"Thanks, Mason I was about to discipline the good sheriff on how rude it is to interrupt, especially a man he attempted to frame twice in less than a twenty year span."

Barber began pacing the room, waving his arms like a Baptist preacher delivering the final evening sermon in a packed tent revival. "Mason and I made a pact, Constable. Upon my parole, he would assist in proving my innocence, as well as a certain sheriff's guilt. In turn, I'd help him cover his tracks as he departed Elm Hill for good. He felt his time running out that whoever was trailing him was nearing the end of the trail. We never counted on that certain whoever arriving during phase one of the pact. Sure as hell complicated matters, but as it turned out, as I'm sure my partner will agree, things couldn't have turned out better.

"Ya see, Daniel, seeing you convicted of a nineteen year old homicide is just the tip of the fucking iceberg, pal,' Barber chanted joyously, stepping over and planting his size thirteen work boot on the stiffening corpse that had been Kayla Lee, 'now we've got three other bodies to pin on your cowardly ass. Let's see you bullshit your way outta this one, buddy boy. Death row is just a gavel thumpin' away.

"By the way Dan, there never was a video of you

374

planting the hammer. I found the damned thing, completely by accident mind you, right where you stashed it, all neatly wrapped and crusted over with dried blood. After we add your prints back to the handle, that 'll be body number four on our 'Sheriff turns serial killer' checklist. We do, however, now own a taped recording of your recent confession, ain't that right, partner?"

Kneeling in front of Daniel like a man bowing at an altar, Parks' expression was decidedly grim, displaying none of the good humor or sarcastic wit from just moments earlier. "Yep. Got it right here in my back pocket. Too bad it's a moot point, Curtis." Either by choice or accident, the words went unheeded as Barber continued to ramble and rave unabashedly in the background. "Ain't gonna tell ya when we'll turn that little jewel over to state authorities. Might be a week…might be months…hell, might even be *years.* You'll have to sweat it out, Daniel, sweat it out like I was forced to sweat out the *6,671* days spent in a ten by twelve cell upstate for the murder *you* committed. 'Course, once they find you wading around in the middle of this blood bath, it might not even matter in the grand scheme of things, sentencing wise Right, Mason?"

Sighing loudly as he stood, Parks then walked over and retrieved the shotgun. "I said forget it."

Barber froze in mid-tirade before whirling around at lightning speed. "Forget *what*?"

"Forget the frame-job. Wasn't expecting the outside interference. Supposed to be just you, me and Sheriff D. We could clean this sty for days, and they'd still find traces of us all over it. Only one that'll get pinned for these killings is yours truly. Can't allow that, no siree, Bob. Not at this late stage in the game."

375

His face displaying a pained grimace sculpted in granite, Barber stepped between Daniel and Parks, again frantically waving his huge arms as he bellowed. "Fuck that horseshit, Parks. Shit happens. You just disappear as planned, dude. I'll take care of the rest. No way this asshole is skatin' away from this without a conviction and some serious time behind bars. I ain't even *hearing* this…"

The smaller man stepped forward until the space between the two men was less than six inches. Despite his forehead barely reaching the other man's chin, it was Barber who backed off a half-step, clearly shaken by Park's aggressive stance. "He dies here and now, '*dude.*' No way I'm leaving behind a functional witness, especially a cop. Sheriff Dan here might'a played ball if it was just him, prayin' that we never turned over the tape. Too many bodies to account for now. The state police would have us both caged in a matter of hours. Sorry to wreck the party, but at least *some* measure of revenge is better 'n nothin', am I right?"

"Damn it, Mason, it *ain't* right. I've waited too long for this day, man. I'm risking my own ass here too. I say it's a risk worth taking."

"Ain't living in a cage again, pal…ever. Not for you or anybody else. My curiosity in this matter's been taken care of. The good sheriff don't leave here breathin', and that's *that,*" Parks whispered angrily, visibly hugging the shotgun a bit tighter across his upper chest.

Backing away a few feet, Barber's eyes fell on Daniel's slumped form, whose chin seemed permanently glued to his chest. "This jackass deserves to suffer like I did…*worse* than I did! Just killing him ain't enough."

"Momento, Slick. Be back in a sec. Keep your pal

376

company in the meantime," Parks said, practically sprinting out of the room, through the kitchen, and out the back door.

Daniel's head arose at the sound of the back door slamming shut, like a man shaken from the darkened catacombs of a horrific nightmare.

"How's it feel, you lying prick?' Barber whispered, his lips just inches from Daniel's left ear . "Is that pig shit I smell? You crap your drawers already? Man, we ain't even started yet."

"S-sorry, Curtis. Wish I could get those y-years back for you. I'm…truly sor…" Daniel muttered, his face so pasty it looked to have been dipped in flour.

The larger man grunted before whispering his harsh reply. "Oh, you're gonna be sorry, shit-heel. Sorry your worthless carcass ever crawled from between your mama's legs."

Barber leaned upright as he heard the back door swing open, taking an additional moment to slap Daniel across the back of his skull with an open palm.

"You two jawing 'bout old times? Well, I'm sure you've got a lot to catch up on,' Parks quipped, tossing something across the room in Barber's direction as he quick-stepped into the living room. " Here, have some cutlery."

The ivory-handled machete slapped the larger man's palm upon its flat descent. Barber 's eyes grew huge, as if he had just willingly reached out and snatched a live hand grenade. "I ain't using this on him, man. One swing from this flesh-clever and the ballgames over in ten ticks flat."

Holding out his right hand, Parks displayed the small surgical scalpel as if it were the keys to a kingdom overflowing with infinite riches.

"Small blade, big blade, it's all the same, Parks. I should have the final say in this, damn it, and I say we cold-cock 'im, place the shotgun in one of his hands and a bone saw from the shed in the other, smear just a smidgen of his blood on and around each body, then h--"

"Tell ya what, Curt. Let's cut to the chase here, so to speak. I say he dies, you say he lives. We seem to be at an impasse with no mediator in sight. Only one way to settle this, as I see it."

Barber cocked his head quizzically as Parks backed away a step and pointed the scalpel straight ahead like a fencing sword. "Simplicity, knucklehead, simplicity in itself. I waste you, the sheriff is well-burnt toast. You waste me, your blackmail scheme goes ahead full throttle."

Groaning aloud, Barber shook his head from side to side, dropping the machete to his side.

"Damn, Mason, this ain't no time for fucking around. We *have* to decide, damn it!"

The smaller man's pose never wavered, nor did his steely gaze. "Who's fuckin' around, Barber? Pardon the pun, son, but I'm *deadly* serious."

"Shit, man, that's crazy I'm not about to kill you...why would I want to?" Barber whined, staring down at the machete like it was an alien pod attached to his hand.

Parks grinned like a ravenous predator preparing to initiate the killing blow on a badly wounded prey. " Damn right you ain't about to kill me, muscles. I 'm the *pro* here, remember? You're the rookie. Gotta tell ya, I've always wanted to take you on, partner. All I needed was a reason. Thought about just shooting you, but what fun would that be?"

378

Barber wiped his brow wearily, the machete still hanging loosely at his side. "I can't believe we're even talking about this, man."

"Then, by all means, let's stop talkin' and start the dance," Parks spat sarcastically as he began pacing cat-like a few feet behind Daniel's chair.

The larger man held his free hand straight out with the palm out, nodding his head stiffly from side to side. " Mason, listen…dude, there has to be another way, a compromise we can reach. Listen …let's take Whitlock with us. If we 're gonna off him anyway, hell, let's at least take our time and enjoy it. A few days…a week maybe. I've got a cousin who's got a secluded cabin in West Virginia. We could…"

Parks lunged ahead a step, grinning devilishly. "No dice, Curtis . Quit stalling and start scrapin'. 'Sides, I'm *all* talked out."

Although the effort to lift his head and maintain an upright position drained what little energy remained within his tattered frame, Daniel managed to do so, drawn to the impromptu duel between two separate but distinct evils whose argument centered solely on details of his own demise. The demarcation line between reality and fantasy had long since vanished, replaced by a grisly middle ground that was a peculiar hodgepodge of both worlds. He felt both sweet relief at his own admission of guilt and terrified at the eventual ramifications to his battered soul. A final, pathetic struggle with his bonds had been accomplished sorely on fumes, the effort in keeping his eyelids from slamming shut a Herculean one.

He realized he wasn't making it out alive, and wept silently for his beloved daughter. Kara was strong, he knew, stronger than most adults he'd known. Still, she would struggle mightily with his death, and even mightier with the murder allegations that would surely follow. The stain placed on her name would follow her until her own passing. This was the single thought that pained Daniel the most, like an ice pick to his already decompressing heart. He dwelled briefly on the reaction of his former partner and friend, Tracy Morton, a young woman he had grown to both admire and respect. He hoped that she, if no one else, could look past the deed at the young, naïve young man behind it. A split-second of uncontrolled rage; a single punch that had ended one person's life and basically ruined two others. The Hendrick's scenario he had no logical explanation for, even for his own tattered conscience. As hard as he tried to pawn it off as a 'mercy killing', it simply didn't wash. Pre-meditated murder; simple as that. Whether fueled by insanity or fear, his soul was eternally damned regardless. He could only hope, mostly for Kara 's sake, that it would never be tied back to him, although he was obviously hapless to retrieve the cassette tape that supplied his confession of the deed.

Curtis Barber's bitterness was typical of someone robbed of a large majority of their life, the prime years whittled away like bark from an aged pine. Daniel bore no grudge, despite the situation. More than likely, he realized, he would have exacted a similar revenge or something at least on par with but not quite equal to actual homicide. For Daniel's part, not a single day had passed during those years that could erase the guilt or anxiety he wore like an invisible shroud. The military stint had provided a physical escape, but the deed followed along to each and every stop like a stray dog trailing raw meat.

380

As the men who were to decide his fate congregated at the center of the room, Daniel discovered his mind had spiraled into two separate and distinct factions in regard to a possible outcome. One portion selfishly rooted for Curtis Barber and his 'blackmail scheme' to come out victorious; the other siding with Mason Parks in hoping for a quick, merciful, mostly painless death.

Bubbly drool oozed from the corners of his mouth as he waited for the aftermath, a hapless spectator to his own execution. It wasn't until he watched Mason Parks sail by his chair in a spastic blur that Daniel initially noticed the solid object curled within his own left hand. Strain as he might, he couldn't recall when it had been placed there, though the supplier of the cold steel blade was easily enough deduced. Smiling like a man passing gas after hours of intense strain, Daniel began to meticulously work the sharp edge of the straight razor across the binds that secured his wrists, being careful not to open a fatal wound across the same in the process.

"You got a death wish, you little shit? Back the hell off, Mason, I d-don't want to have to waste you!" Barber yelled, backing almost into a far wall as Parks stormed forward like a charging bull, slowing only when the larger man began swinging the machete from side to side like a mini-pendulum.

"Gotta be honest with ya, Curt, now that the love's left our relationship…I never was gonna let you live, at least, not for very long anyhow."

The other man paused, the machete held shoulder high and cocked like a baseball bat, then threw his head back in an animalistic wail, the veins in his bulging neck resembling special effects bladders at the bursting point.

The smaller man's eyes widened with maniacal glee.

381

"That's it, big fella! Bring it the hell *ON* !"

A few feet from where the battle ensued, Daniel felt the rope over his right wrist begin to unravel and fall away, the warm stickiness of his own blood washing over his limp fingers creating an oddly comforting sensation. It was as if he were being spiritually cleansed by his own sinful fluids while experiencing a miraculous liberation. A preordained liberation that he prayed would eventually lead to sweet retribution for a hopelessly damned soul.

***

Peering cautiously into the driver's side front seat of Hoyt's badly dented Buick, Deputy Morton noticed several small, circular, maroon spatters on the seat and floorboard and felt her pulse rate intensify almost instantly. "This can't be good," she muttered, leaning over the front seat to inspect the back while being careful not to smudge any possible evidence, " …cannot…be…good at all."

She spotted a single streak of semi-dried crimson at the center point of the back seat, a three to four inch long smear pressed into the cloth which looked to have been wiped in a rushed attempt to clear it away. "Probably from the wreck, that's all. No reason to believe anything else, Trace. Reel in the paranoia, girl, 'fore you run outta line."

Looking through the slightly cracked windshield to the winding curve ahead, the sigh she exhaled was laced with anxiety, and her teeth clicked together nervously. "What the hell are you doin' down *here*, Daniel ?"

She'd departed Randall Sim's place over forty minutes earlier, having called both the station and the mayor's office. Jeff Greene, a local farmer, had spoken to the mayor upon his arrival back into town and mentioned seeing Daniel driving down near Mann Lake in Hoyt Wilson's old beat up Buick, with at least two passengers inside. Tracy had asked the Major to ride along with Lt. Galvin and Sergeant Danley in a quick search of the numerous back roads on the north end of the lake while she patrolled a similar maze of one-lanes and narrow pathways on the south end. In her haste, she hadn't mentioned the hammer found at Barber's residence. Besides, finding her supervisor was priority number one, especially if the owner of the aforementioned hammer was behind his disappearance.

She had parked her Accord a few feet behind Hoyt's beater, her heart having sunk like a le ad pipe in quicksand upon first viewing the vehicle from a distance. Finding it abandoned hadn't exactly calmed her nerves, although such a discovery had been preferable to several decidedly *grisly* alternatives that had raced through her mind while nearing the car with revolver in hand.

After checking the .38's fully loaded cylinders for at least the fifth time since leaving Curtis Barber's place, Tracy turned to give her own car a final, forlorn glance before trudging forward towards the old Whitmore place. If she recalled correctly, the homestead was no more than a few hundred yards past the sharp curve ahead. The soggy gravel crunched loudly beneath her boots, and she quickly departed the main road for the overgrown, leaf-coated shoulder in order to muffle her steps. Tracy wasn't exactly sure why she was bothering to be so cat-like in her approach. She could cover the same distance in a matter of seconds via auto, dismissing the fear in her gut as nothing more than the overzealous pining of a woefully under-experienced cop facing the unknown. Somehow, such a trite, oversimplified dismissal wouldn't take. Deputy Morton sincerely hoped that a case of slight embarrassment at her own cautiousness would turn out to be the worst-case scenario when all was said and done.

"Well, better safe than sorry, I've heard it said," she whispered, ducking a series of low-hanging oak limbs as she neared the crest of the curve.

***

Parks dived ahead, whipping the scalpel from left to right in a turbulent blur, cursing as the larger man ducked effortlessly away.

"Damn, ain't you quick for a walkin' mountain? Prison time served you well, big boy."

Barber attempted a wild sprint in the direction of the kitchen, but was quickly cut off by a sweeping right leg that caught him just above the ankles. He somehow managed to hang onto the machete even as his own momentum sent him sprawling into the center of the room, rolling over the TV/VCR/DVD combo in the process.

Just as he sprang to his feet, the back of Park's left fist landed solidly at the back of his left ear, followed by a hard kick to his solar plexus that emptied both lungs in a single huff. A closed fist to his left eye completed the fatal trilogy of blows, and sent his massive frame pin-wheeling back like a puppet with severed strings.

Barber landed just to the left of Daniel's chair, the machete sailing from his grip upon landing. The smaller man landed atop his heaving chest with a resounding thump, and Barber felt the scalpel's edge bite gently into

384

the soft flesh beneath his chin. "Son, I am truly disheartened. And here I thought a big toned som' bitch like yourself would provide at least *some* competition for my worn out old ass."

"It...don't h-have to b-be like...d-don't... d-do it, M-M-Mason..." Barber gurgled as the blade slid across his throat and pierced several layers of skin. "K-k-kill t-the b-b-bastard...I d-don 't c-c-care..."

A moment later, Barber was forced to inhale the smaller man's warm, soured breath as he leaned down until the two were practically kissing. "Put your mind at ease, big fella. Soon as I 'm done carvin' you a permanent necktie, that's exactly what I plan to do. Say hey to Aaron and Kayla for me, Curt. Tell 'em to keep my seat warm down there. Reckon I'll join y'all soon enough." Mason Park's right arm, the one gripping the scalpel, tensed as he prepared to apply fatal pressure.

He paused at the sensation of cold steel pressing firmly against the nape of his neck.

"D-drop the weapon, Parks. Drop it *now* or occupy that assigned seat in hell you were just talking about a bit sooner than expected."

Parks winced as Daniel shoved the shotgun barrel forward, landing with a muffled thud at the base of his skull.

"I said...drop the carving tool, asshole...now."

"Well, I'll be...never thought you'd cut yourself loose that quick, Sheriff. I should'a known better. Never pays to be fair."

The three men were posed like a museum piece in a murderer's row gallery, a statue created solely to display man's casual penchant for eliminating his fellow man. Curtis Barber's thick, sweat-greased arms were splayed out on either side of him, his eyes closed and face clinched in agony. Mason Parks sat atop the large man's colossal chest, leaning forward with his left hand pinned across his victim's forehead and his right tucked beneath the man's pointy chin, cocked and primed for the kill. Daniel Whitlock stood with unbending knees less than a foot behind Parks, the arms which held the weapon tucked evenly against his rib cage, his haggard expression revealing a man who has crossed over into a dimension of misery few ever emerge from with their sanity intact.

"Just wanted to give ya a sporting chance, and look at the knee-deep shit I find myself in," Parks spat without a hint of fear.

Similarly, Daniel's tone was equally collected, although more stilted, like a man speaking from the darkest recesses of a deep trance. "Ten seconds, Parks. Ten seconds to remove the knife from Barber's throat and toss it away or I apply a few added pounds of pressure to this bad boy's trigger mechanism."

"W-Whitl-lock, p-p-pull the t-t-trig…ger, y-y-you a-a-ass…h-h-hole," Barber mumbled, his lips never actually parting.

Snickering aloud as blood from Barber's throat wound began to coat his fingers, Mason Parks leaned back as to shove the barrel tighter against his own flesh. "Well, it ain't like he ain't got the testicular fortitude to do just that, Curt. We both know the man has killed before, right? Question is, does he consider your worthless hide worth saving or just his own?"

"Five seconds."

"You'll never find the cassette, Sheriff. You know… the one containin' your tearful, heart-string tuggin'

386

confession of the murder of Debbie Rainer. I hid that little jewel away a few minutes back when you and Curt here were cruisin' down memory lane. You won't find it without me, but someone *else* might when the crime scene is investigated."

"B-b-blow him a -away or h-he'll....w-w-waste us both," Barber said in a moaning whisper, his right hand slowly rising from the floor and towards the leaking wound just above his Adam's apple.

The semi-frozen trio grew eerily silent for a full ten seconds, the bizarre lull broken by Parks 'sarcastic giggling. " Countdown seems to have passed, Dan. Was it possibly somethin' I said?"

Moving as if in virtual slow-motion, Daniel pulled the shotgun's barrel away from Parks' neck, leaving two circular indentions on the man's pasty flesh.

"That's what I thought you'd say, Sheriff. Now, let's all take a deep breath and discuss this situation intelligently, what do ya s--"

Twirling the shotgun's wooden stock around with the quickness and grace of a well-trained member of a military rifle brigade, Daniel drove the blunt end straight down with all the force he could muster. The crack resounded like a thick piece of kindling being struck with the heavy end of a sledgehammer, sending Parks tumbling to the left in a curled heap, the bloodied scalpel dropping harmlessly onto Barber's upper chest.

Barber rolled first onto his side and then upright on his knees, clutching his injured throat and coughing harshly.

Taking a few cautious steps over, Daniel kept the shotgun's sites pointed at the back of Parks' head that lay face down, the finger of his left hand twitching slightly.

Daniel could see a narrow trail of blood rolling onto the man's neck from behind his right ear.

"Y-you cr-crazy jackass…he c-could've sliced my damn head off with a r-reflex…w-why didn't you scatter his fucking brains?" Barber shrieked, glaring disgustingly at his own blood-stained hands as he rose shakily to his feet. His nose now bled profusely from the earlier punch, although the neck cut's leakage had apparently ceased.

Taking a step forward, Daniel reached out with his right boot and nudged the fallen man's left thigh, gently at first and then with increased force. Backing away until he cleared the man's shoe heels, his shoulders slumping in relief, Daniel never got completely turned around before being hammered across the chest with a telephone-pole sized forearm. The shotgun sailed from his grasping fingers as he reeled back, his backward momentum halted only when his upper back slammed into the home's solid oak front door , thick chunks of dislodged ceiling tile and insulation raining down into his eyes and open mouth.

Even as he attempted to rise, his vision filled with images of bright, sparking light in various sizes and shapes, Daniel could hear Barber's mocking tone as if the man were speaking from *inside* his ear canal.

"Dan, you ain't the sharpest tack in the bag, are you, son? *Never* turn your back on the enemy…didn't the military teach you anything that stuck?"

As his eyesight gradually cleared, Daniel could make out the man's enormously pumped outline, as well as that of the machete he yielded.

"No, I ain't gonna kill you, but their ain't nothing in the plan that says I can't inflict a little pain."

Daniel used the door to push himself up, spitting the

388

dust from his lips as he tried desperately to refill his
battered lungs.

"Think I'll take a couple of fingers, just for old
time's sake," he heard Barber crack just as the man's
extra-wide shadow covered Daniel's face and upper
body.

He waited for just a split-second more, until he could
smell the man's rancid body odor lingering beneath his
flaring nostrils, then shoved himself forward by using his
left boot to push off the door's lower section, while
simultaneously ducking his head into battering position.
Skull met jawbone with a thunderous crack, and Daniel
found himself reeling back once again, feeling as if he
had just head-butted a bulldozer. Once again, the front
door served as his braking mechanism, his teeth
chattering forcefully together upon impact, slicing into
the very tip of his protruding tongue in the process. A
coppery taste filled his mouth as he kneeled in a dire
attempt to catch his breath, his vision still badly
unfocused due to both the ceiling dust and the constant
traumas.

Still, Daniel could hear Barber groaning from
somewhere nearby, a few scattered curse words
whispered harshly between low, shrill cries. Rising just
enough to place his hands atop his shaky kneecaps,
Daniel lifted his head and blinked rapidly as he stared
straight ahead, the swirling, misty fog coating his senses
slowly beginning to lift. He could hear shuffling from at
least two separate sections of the room, but was still
unable to distinguish specific shapes or movements.

"Miserable murderin' fucks, both of you...'he heard
Barber shriek from what seemed like another room
entirely, the large man's normally deep voice now

389

nothing more than a shrill, nasal whine, 'my nose is mangled all to hell... no thanks to both you assholes...goddamned thing must look like a mashed turd bleeding like a stuck fucking pig."

Scrambling blindly forward, Daniel used the finger of one hand to rub his debris-littered eyes while holding the other straight out from his body like the rudder of a ship sailing through stormy, treacherous waters. His left boot struck something solid, and he glanced down to see the overturned TV blocking his path. Upon side-stepping to the left, as he finally began to regain the majority of his vision, he bumped in to something as solid as a rock wall, grinding his teeth together for at least the fifth time in the previous half hour.

"Going somewhere, Sheriff?"

Daniel executed an instinctive duck a moment too late, as the fist originally targeted for the center of his face (possibly a fatal blow, considering the force administered) instead bounced off the center of his forehead, snapping his neck back viciously. He wobbled backwards, miraculously managing to stay upright despite the overwhelming urge to topple over and remain prone, allowing the sweet relief of unconsciousness to soothe his battered psyche.

"Both you jackasses are gonna pay for the nose, Dan old buddy, like I needed *another* reason to thump your carcass."

Despite the piercing, throbbing pains that assault ed every nerve ending in his shell-shocked frame, Daniel barely refrained from laughing aloud at the man's squeaky, whiny tone. Barber sounded as if he'd just inhaled a giant bottle of helium. Either that or someone had attached a clothespin to his nostrils.

390

Watching the huge individual approach him with all the speed of a three-toed sloth, Daniel realized without a small degree of pent up anger that he was being taken lightly; woefully underestimated for no other reason than the other man's admittedly intimidating size. He had duly trained to take advantage of such overconfidence in an opponent, although actually having the occasion to test such measures had never arisen in his decade-plus law enforcement career.

Holding out his left hand palms up, Dani el ducked away like a whipped pup, his pleads delivered in a passive, defeated tone that instantly brought a wide smile to his opponents bloodied visage. "E-enough...Curtis p-please, man...I-I've g-got a daughter..."

"I know all about Kara, Dan. Saw her be-boppin' down Main Street the other day," he smirked. "Nice ass for jail bait. Give 'er a few years and I'll be on that like flies on shit. 'Sides, she's gonna need some serious consoling after her dad's revealed as a vicious killer, am I right?"

Barber waded in chin first, his left fist flung back in a ridiculously telegraphed manner. With unexpected speed and preciseness, Daniel uncoiled from his semi-crouch and threw a series of short, potent jabs, the first of which caught the other man square in the throat, following up the barrage with a front kick that landed just below the man's breastbone.

Barber tipped back on his heels, then fell forward just as Daniel swung his left elbow around at a downward arc, crushing the man's already damaged nose and ripping an inch-long tear into his right cheek. Despite the beating, Barber lumbered forward and wrapped his enormously pumped arms around Daniel's upper body in a vice-like grip. The two men's heads banged together violently, Barber's nose once again catching the brunt of the impact. Spitting out thick wads of blood that had leaked into his opened mouth, Barber then laced his thick fingers together at the pit of

Daniel's back and began to squeeze. Feeling as if his chest cavity was mere seconds from imploding, Daniel attempted another head butt, but discovered that his inner battery had been drained hopelessly dry.

Barber's animalistic grunts increased in volume the more pressure he applied, cocking his head sharply to the right as to avoid Daniel's weakened blows.

Feeling as though his heart had literally been squeezed to a halt, Daniel realized he was just seconds from passing out. In an act of pure survival instinct, he stretched his neck out as far as it would reach, opening his mouth grotesquely wide, like a dental patient prepping for a root canal. His probing lips found an exposed earlobe a moment later, followed by teeth that clamped down like jagged, twin vices.

The larger man's nasal screams were accompanied by a final crushing reflex, his arms tightening like steel bands just before an abrupt release that flung Daniel across the room like balsa wood in a funnel cloud. Spitting free a large, rubbery chunk of Barber's ear, Daniel had felt something inside him give just as he'd went airborne; something undeniably *vital* to his inner workings.

His limp form had barely cleared the top of Kayla's wheelchair, landing in an awkward sprawl with the majority of the impact centered on his left hip and shoulder. Daniel could hear Curtis Barber's echoed curses, but they were strangely muffled and utterly incomprehensible. The burning sensation at Daniel's upper chest and the left side of his rib cage was excruciating, as if both had been coated with battery acid. With each mouthful of air that entered his lungs, the pain increased ten-fold, like a knife blade was being driven fatally deep. In attempting to turn onto his back, he felt his consciousness severely wane. He heard a muted popping sound from somewhere in the vicinity of his lower back as he completed the roll. He managed to raise his head just enough to see Barber wobble back into his sights, the left side of the man's neck drenched in crimson as he cradled his mutilated ear.

"Where's that damned machete? To hell with the *slow* burn, Whitlock, I'm carving you up like Thanksgiving yard bird, motherfucker."

Daniel's head lolled to the right as his vision grew increasingly shaded, the realization that he could no longer feel his legs or practically *anything* below the waist becoming dreadfully apparent He watched Barber's boots shuffle by, then peered upward and saw the ruin of the man's face. Everything below the eyes was smeared in blood, the coveralls he wore merely blood-spattered on the right side but shockingly saturated on the left, where the remainder of his ear hung like a torn sail.

"Where the hell is that thing? I had it a sec--"

"Psst. Right here, muscles. "

If asked under oath, Daniel would have answered that if given the opportunity, he might have yelled out a suitable warning, although at that particular moment it time, such a noble, heroic act would have been hopelessly moot. From Daniel's limited perspective, Curtis Barber had been standing a scant three to four feet away, backing on his heels while frantically searching for the machete or some similarly sharp-edged weapon. He watched the large man whirl to his right, the head and shoulders whipping around so quickly that the lower torso and legs had little opportunity to follow suit.

A trio of noises ensued, all of which were equally gruesome in terms of what they defined. The 'whooshing' of the blade precluded the impact of honed steel into soft flesh, leading to the reverberation of a moderately heavy, severed body part bouncing onto a hard tile surface. Daniel had blinked just as Barber's head was in the process of detachment, leaving a split-second gap until his eyes reopened to the skull-less torso shuddering backward towards his own fallen frame. A crimson geyser erupted from the neck's stump, a seemingly endless gusher that spewed forth in all directions simultaneously. After veering sharply to the left, the body finally collapsed in a heap to Daniel's right, saturating his thighs and calves with a final spray that shot forth in a fine mist as if released from a pressurized paint can. The fingers of Curtis Barber's left hand coiled and relaxed several times before performing a conclusive twitch, the connecting forearm visibly tensing and subsequently relaxing with the thick muscles of the bicep soon following suit.

"Well, he *did* ask for it," Mason Parks quipped, suddenly looming over Daniel as if he had been beamed into position. His hair was matted from fluids released by the earlier blow Daniel had administered with the shotgun's butt, though he looked positively luminous otherwise, the maniacal grin and cocked eyebrows stubbornly intact. Discarding the machete n a quick flip of his wrist, Parks leaned down and gripped Daniel firmly by his disheveled bangs, lifting his head roughly.

Daniel shut his eyes and felt something large, round, and decidedly moist being tucked behind his neck.

"There ya go, partner. No need to strain your neck. That was one helluva beatin' old Curt put on ya. You look a little...*bent,* dude. Don't think you'll be tryin' out for the gymnastics team anytime soon."

Although hesitant to do so, Daniel reopened his bleary, bloodshot orbs to the sight of Parks standing a few feet ahead, pointing a revolver that looked frighteningly familiar.

"Hate to kill a man with his own weapon, Dan, but hey...it'll certainly add mystique to the overall mystery, huh? Just think, Sheriff, decades from now, school kids to senior citizens all over the great state of Alabama will whisper your name, some in awe and others in fear. You're gonna be the Halloween story told around the campfire, the boogey-*law* man that shattered nature's laws while upholding man's. Sheriff Whitlock, the devil behind the shiny, silver badge. Ain't it a hoot? Hell, do believe I'm actually jealous."

Staring down the blue steel barrel of a weapon he had never before fired in the line of duty, the coppery scent of Curtis Barber's leaking life-source filling his nostrils in thick, stout waves, Daniel felt the paralysis shoot up his spine like an electric current as the simple act of maintaining consciousness became increasingly difficult.

A large portion of his tattered physique welcomed the forthcoming bullet, desired it like he had craved nothing else before; lusted after its brutal finality infinitely more than any woman he had ever known. The small minority that clung desperately to life was the father within him; Kara Whitlock's provider, advisor, and dare he ponder, *role model* ? His eyes darted from side to side as his arms spread from his sides, grasping blindly for anything he might possible utilize for defense.

"Sorry, Dan. I'm all done being a good sport. The last hour has been as exhilaratin' as I've spent since that night in the New Mexico desert , but alas, all good things do come to an end."

Daniel stubbornly refused to even wince as the man stepped forward and took direct aim at the center of his forehead. He glared defiantly into Mason Park's leering eyes, bravely fighting the urge to turn away from the inevitable.

"Any last words, Constable?"

Daniel's weak whisper was precluded by a hacking cough and a series of garbling swallows "A-a-a t...l-least...I...w-was...n-n...n-never like...y-you..."

Barber winked as he cocked the .38's hammer back.

"The lesser of two evils is still evil, son...your horns are just a *bit* less pronounced, that's all."

A shrieking scream filled the room like a detonated mine, as if the originator were utilizing a bullhorn set at the highest possible volume.

"*FREEZE!* Drop the weapon, Hoyt...and I mean *NOW!*"

Deputy Morton stood at the kitchen entrance, her knees slightly bent; both hands gripping her revolver in the classic shooter's pose. Her eyes were huge, her mouth twitching slightly at the corners.

St raining like a man attempting to move a mountain in order to simply turn his head towards her, Daniel envisioned his subordinate and friend as two separate and distinct entities; one the avenging angel, her billowy white wings tucked in at the sides as she prepared to do

396

battle with evil personified for the fate of his very soul. The second manifestation equally surreal but vastly different; a ghastly image of death encircled his partner like a shadowy cloak, the corners of her mouth turned down in a grisly upside down grin, her eyes dark, hollow sockets from which crimson tears sprang forth. As a tidal wave of anguish gripped his chest in an iron vice, Daniel realized that it was the second of the two images which held less fantasy than cold, stark reality.

"Well, well, well...if it ain't Deputy Dyke, come to the rescue ," Barber blurted, the position of the revolver he held unchanged despite the new threat.

Tracy Morton could feel every fiber of her body tingle as if she were suffering from a horrendous case of poison oak from the *underside* of her flesh. She had heard the commotion within the front room while passing the aged, badly rusted mailbox at the end of the drive. The decision to enter the home through the backdoor had been based on access availability only. If she'd found the back entrance closed and/or locked, she would have immediately retraced back to the front. Instead, it had been standing wide open, even the torn screen that fronted it unlatched and partially agape.

"Dammit, I ain't one to repeat myself when pointin' a firearm at somebody, Hoyt. Drop the sheriff's weapon immediately and back away with your hands behind your head."

"T-T-Trace...g-get... o-out... get... h-help," Daniel stammered, the message being relayed in both his tone and expression one that his deputy mistook to mean imminent danger *other* than what she could already visualize.

"Now ain't that the sweetest thing? You sure you

397

two weren't bumpin' uglies at the station house when no one was looking?" Barber spat indifferently, not budging an iota except to glance quickly over at Daniel and then back to Tracy. "Nice gesture, Dan, but a bit foolish in the overall scheme of things, don'cha think? Deputy Morton has stepped into a considerably deep pile of cow excrement, and there ain't no backin' out now. She understood the possible consequences, could've run like a rabbit with its bushy little tail ablaze, but instead showed more balls than most men I've encountered and waded in with both boots just to save her dear mentor, co-worker, and I still suspect, *lover*. I'll give credit where credit is due, y'know? Brass balls, missy."

Despite her best efforts to avoid focusing on the carnage all around them, Tracy couldn't help but take a mental inventory of the horrific scene, one she could have never imagined in a thousand collective nightmares. The small, obviously female body laying to her far right, void of *most* of its head. The massive, obviously male body also to her right, minus the *entirety* of same. The entire room literally drenched in various shades and textures of human blood, a grisly red tapestry which emitted a sharp, metallic smell she could only imagine compared to a livestock slaughterhouse during peak working hours. Her boss, his legs splayed out like a discarded puppet as his head rested crookedly on an object she initially refused to identify in fear of screaming aloud. A pumpkin-shaped object she was eventually forced to accept as indeed being the severed head of one Curtis Lee Barber, his face frozen in comical shock with each eye stretched wide and his mouth trapped in a wide, perpetual grin.

In stark contrast, Mason Parks' practically gleamed

398

with boyish enthusiasm as he remained eerily calm. "You missed a helluva party, Deputy Dyke. All-Star cast, to boot. Allow me to go over the guest list briefly. We had a vengeful ex-FBI agent and her lunatic, one-ball partner; a vengeful ex-convict out for blood; my ex-neighbor playing the pivotal role of the living cadaver with the mistaken identity; and Sheriff Daniel 'skeletons in the closet' Whitlock in a co-starring role with yours truly, Hoyt Wilson, town drunk, AKA Mason Parks, assassin for hire. Any questions 'fore we wrap for the day?"

Taking a single step forward, Tracy felt her boot slide on the sticky moistness, her trigger finger tightening to the edge of release. "I'll worry about details later, Hoy...uh, um...whoever you are. Right now I simply want you to drop the gun and back...the ...hell...up."

Parks' finally broke the stare just long enough to peer over at his intended target.

"She's a brave one, Dan, no doubt. But she really should've heeded your advice and scampered away."

"T-Tracy...j-just go...I-I 'm...not...w-worth..." Daniel pleaded, weakly raising his right arm a few inches in a feeble attempt to waive her away.

Mason turned back towards Tracy, his cheery grin having vanished in lieu of an animalistic sneer. " Oh, just in case the unthinkable happens and I depart this hovel in a plastic bag, there's a cassette tape stuck in the mailbox out front, darlin'. Let's just say it sheds a whole new light on beloved Sheriff W there, one you ain't apt to believe."

"Last chance, Mister. I ain't asking agai..."

Tracy pulled the trigger just as her left shoulder exploded as if struck by lightning.

Staring up at the water-stained ceiling that split the living room and kitchen areas, her vision fading in and out in sporadic waves, she realized in shocked amazement that Elm Hill's resident lush had actually whirled his weapon around and fired within the same blip in time it had taken her to simply pull the trigger. Darkness overcame her just as she reached to caress the gaping wound just below her badly shattered collarbone.

Less than six feet away from Deputy Morton's sprawled feet, Daniel wriggled his head until he was again facing front, the strain of the effort forcing him to suck in several deep breaths in order to refrain from passing out. His arms and shoulders seemed to be slowly recharging, although his lower body was a hopeless mishmash of numb, tingling parts that had long since grown utterly useless. If his lungs had been willing and able to do so, he would have screamed with unrestrained delight, applauding like the lone witness to a biblical event of universal proportions.

Mason Parks lay on his right side, his left leg wriggling in spastic shock. Daniel couldn't quite make out the man's face from his severely limited angle, but Parks' labored groans were clearly audible in the otherwise tranquil setting.

Inhaling as if preparing to dive into deep waters, Daniel used his left arm to push himself onto his right side. His initial motivation was to be able to better survey the damage done to Parks while somehow managing to drag himself closer to Tracy. As his half-roll ended, Daniel's right shoulder landed atop the still smoking barrel of his own revolver In reaching around his body to retrieve it, he lurched onto his stomach, unable to halt or even slow his momentum. It took two full minutes of frantic struggle to haul himself over onto his back; his legs and lower back nothing more than dead weight.

Daniel felt like a beached fish as he laid his head back and huffed like an exhausted marathon runner passing the finish line. In turning his head to the right a moment later, he was greeted by the severed head he'd been unwittingly using as a neck prop. The pent-up scream hung in his raw, ragged throat just as movement caught his eye from the vicinity of his splayed feet.

A few feet away, near the same time that her boss was grasping for his long-lost .38 , Tracy Morton reawakened with rapidly blinking eyes, the constant throbbing sensation at her left shoulder not unlike an aggravated wisdom tooth being stabbed repeatedly with an ice pick. Although unable to respond in any manner other than a low whimper, Tracy felt a mysterious presence tugging at her scalp just as a fairly stout breeze of outside air massaged her face. She heard the screen door gently close behind her as a whispering voice broke the silence from the living room.

Daniel gagged as a boot heel dug into his throat. His right hand tugged at the man's ankle in a pathetic attempt to pull the leg away even as the revolver was being jerked roughly from his left.

"Now, now, Sheriff Dan, you ain't the sort to plug a man while he's down, are ya?" Parks scowled through bloodied teeth, a perfectly circular hole drilled into his left cheek, the ensuing leakage literally pouring into his open mouth as he spoke. "Actually, you probably ain't at that, but unfortunately for you, I am *just* that sort."

Daniel shut his eyes as Parks lowered the .38 until the front site was parked less than six inches from the center of his forehead.

"Adios, Constable."

A low click ensued, then another, followed by

Daniel's exasperated sigh and Mason Park's muted curses. "Som' Bitch! Ya had only one bullet in this mother? Well, Jesus crow, Sheriff *Fife*. Don't tell me...the others are stuffed down your left *shirt* pocket, right?" Parks bellowed before tossing the revolver aside and backing away.

Given a temporary respite, Daniel's severely battered and fatigued psyche acknowledged the fact that mounting any type defense was laughably out of the question. Teetering on the outer edges of unconsciousness, he found only enough strength to turn in the direction of his fallen partner, silently praying as he checked for even the slightest of movements from her still frame. A few feet into the foreground, as Mason Parks reached down to retrieve the machete that was obviously targeted to end his suffering, Daniel clearly saw the sign of life he'd sought, though from a completely unexpected source.

"Ho-kay, I hear the bell tollin', Sheriff Dan. Now we can finally end this here dance," Parks spewed, stepping forward with the weapon coiled back for a final, fatal strike.

Daniel's head whirled back around just as a single word pierced the air like a ballistic missile, freezing his attacker in mid-stride... *"PARKS!"*

Looking away from Daniel as if his movements were being controlled via joystick, Mason couldn't help but break into a loud, raucous guffaw at the high-pitched shriek's originator.

Positioned on his knees, his entire torso a virtual roadmap of blood and gore from the gaping exit wounds at his chest and upper abdomen, Aaron Kyle nonetheless pointed the shotgun with such cocky casualness that Daniel momentarily deduced that he was witnessing one brain-twister of an illusion.

"Aaron my boy, I surrender to your greatness," Parks muttered, bowing just slightly while dropping the machete and twisting about to better expose his frontal torso.

"H-hope…this…h-hurts… y-you…miserable… f-fuck," Kyle replied through lips chapped with his own caked-on bodily fluids.

The shotgun's retort sent both shooter and target sailing in opposite directions like puppets pulled from separate sets of strings.

Mason Parks landed in a spattered pile of his own bone and tissue, blown out his upper back in ragged, moist chunks, while Aaron Kyle skidded across the kitchen floor like an iced skater shot from a cannon across a frozen rink.

Bowing his head as if witnessing a moment of silence for those befallen, Daniel heard two distinct sounds before everything around him fell jarringly quiet. A brief, shrill giggle coming from the far corner of the kitchen, one easily defined with the joy of ultimate satisfaction and sweet retribution. This was followed by a low, pained groan near the final resting spot of one Mason Parks, a deep, harsh moan that eventually transformed into a whispered gasp.

As he began the arduous task of crawling in the direction of his fallen friend and partner, Daniel had a harder time defining such an indignant whimper. He finally resigned himself to the possibility that Mason Parks might've been allowed a quick glimpse into his own bleak, damnable future, and had been far *less* than thrilled.

Daniel passed out several times within the five

minutes it took him to reach Tracy. Her breathing was harsh but stabilized, and he managed to pack her wound with an unsoiled portion of his uniform shirt. She regained consciousness momentarily, as he tucked his arm beneath her neck for support. Her smile was radiant despite the situation, and Daniel felt her warmness flood his chest.

Before being swept away by cloaking waves of darkness, Daniel wondered if he would ever witness such a smile again, considering the contents of a certain cassette tape that would soon be discovered amidst all the carnage.

The state police arrived a half-hour later to find the two officers passed out in each other's arms like slumbering lovers.

Within the short span of a few hours, state and federal authorities, a s well as media types from four states descended on the small burg of Elm Hill, Alabama like swarming locusts.

It would be almost two calendar years before a sense of normalcy would re-emerge.

EPILOGUE:

Tracy Morto n glares into the small compact one last time then stuffs it deep into the large brown Dooney Burke purse at her side. Begrudgingly satisfied that her short, coifed hair can look no better, she sigh s heavily, leaning back to place her recently polished boots atop the desk.

Pete had just phoned to tell her he wouldn't be off work until after five, and for her to go ahead without him. Checking her watch for at least the fourth time in the previous ten minutes, she saw it was just a quarter past noon. Daniel wouldn't be expecting her until two-thirty at the earliest, since kick-off was at three-fifteen. She hadn't spoken to him in a week, not since he'd called to gloat about the Crimson Tide's 43 to 17 trouncing of LSU in Baton Rouge, the same night Auburn had smacked Arkansas 23 to 0 on the plains. The annual Iron Bowl was going to be extra special this time around, due to both teams lurking near the AP top five with identical 10-1 records. The very atmosphere of small Alabama towns such as Elm Hill changed dramatically during Iron Bowl week, becoming thick with anticipation as families and friends stubbornly chose sides and prepared for psychological battle, SEC football style.

She felt strange wearing civilian clothes while on duty, but allowed herself the privilege without a twinge of guilt. It was only once a year, after all, and the badge above her right breast hung just as straight from plain cotton as from a polyester mix.

Staring at the lit monitor to her right, she saw no

emails calling to her other than the usual midday surge of 'get rich' offers and 'DVD and CD' sales pitches that seemed endless. Dale was set to return from a morning fishing trip in less than an hour to take the post, giving her plenty of time for reflection.

Barely twenty-three and less than twelve months out of the Academy, Dale Watts had slowly become a fine, dependable deputy; a bright, organized overachiever with a glowing future in law enforcement if he so desired.

Placing her hands tightly behind her neck and securely locking the fingers in place, Tracy felt a familiar twinge at her left shoulder. It was faint but obvious, and never failed to flood her mind with memories best left forgotten, although chances of permanent dismissal were pure fairy tale.

As with the pain (phantom or otherwise authentic) near her collarbone and deltoid region, Sheriff Morton felt her eyes begin to glaze as the hypnotic effect ensued. As was normally the case, no matter how hard she fought to quell the surge, the inner movie projector clicked into play mode as images flooded forth with tidal wave force.

She had awoken in a Birmingham hospital a day after the shooting, the bullet that shattered her collarbone having passed through and exiting just beneath her left shoulder blade. Although in her heavily sedated state she would never recall doing so, she had instructed Pete to drive immediately back to Elm Hill and retrieve a certain object from the Whitmore mailbox, cautioning him on the seriousness of being caught tampering with a crime scene. Pete had later told her that he'd never seen her so shaken, so completely rattled. Beyond all hopes, he had found the tape exactly where Mason Parks had hinted. Crime scene investigators had apparently drawn an invisible line of demarcation around the dilapidated home that *hadn't* included the driveway. Pete said that his heavily sedated better-half had been grimly adamant about his *not* listening to the cassette 's content, the tone of her voice possessing a threatening edge he had hadn't detected before or since.

To this day, Tracy was certain Pete had indeed adhered to that particular command. If not, the man was a better actor than she could've ever imagined.

It was a full year before federal and state agencies were able to completely sew together the tapestry of deceit, mistaken identities, and cold-blooded murder into a neatly organized package for the whole world to see, marvel at, and obsess over.

Three non-fiction novels, two television (one cable, one network) movies, and an episode of *City Confidential* later, the public and media's interest in the case's grisliest details finally, mercifully, began to wane. There was always a fresh murder mystery to avert their ever-scanning eyes, always a new string of tragic deaths to ponder and discuss over the workplace water cooler.

The bodies of seven homeless men were found in the storm cellar of Douglas Matson's house , a retired pharmacist who had been unfortunate enough to have Mason Parks, hired killer and all-around mass *and* serial murderer, as a neighbor. The man had died strapped to a gurney, having slowly bled to death from numerous cuts and involuntary amputations.

Parks had obviously set up Matson as his personal fall guy in case the authorities or an old enemy were to somehow unmask his cover as Elm Hill's mostly harmless town drunk. Aaron Kyle and Kayla Lee had sniffed it out first, murdering the wrong man in a torture

407

session right out of the Spanish Inquisition. No one could understand why Parks hadn't departed town upon initially discovering his cover blown. After all, his enemies had clearly fallen for the guise. There had been no logical reason for his appearance at the Whitmore home other than simple bloodlust. He was a species of animal, *fortunately* rare in nature that was unable to resist the opportunity to watch others suffer, even at the expense of his own life.

Locals were more amazed at his decade long 'town drunk' stint as *Hoyt Wilson* than the gruesome acts that followed, although none could actually come forth and claim to 'know' Hoyt other than in polite passing. Even his regular drinking buddies stated that Parks had been strangely 'aloof 'and the 'loner' type, though they could recall no outwardly violent tendencies in the man. Sympathy for Curtis Barber's fate was hard pressed to find within the community, the overwhelming consensus being along the lines of 'lay with snakes and expect to be bitten.'

Tracy had hardly escaped the media onslaught, having turning down several offers for 'true-life' crime novels based upon her experience within the bloody massacre at the Whitmore home.

The town council had voted her into office just days after the incident, an offer she found impossible to refuse in light of the circumstances Pete had backed her decision, albeit a bit wearily. In the twenty-six months since she had taken the helm, she hadn't found cause to remove the revolver from her holster once, except to fire into the air at the annual Founder's Day sack race. She prayed the remainder of her tenure remain as tranquil.

Daniel had remained hospitalized for fifteen months,

the state sheriff's association picking up the tabs on medical bills that had reached astronomical levels, before being returned to Elm Hill as its first paraplegic citizen. The town had held a 'Welcome Home' event at the town-square, an idea co-authored by both Tracy and the mayor. Although openly uneasy at the start, Daniel seemed to warm up to the notion after being handed a 'key to the city' by his daughter, along with a passel of heartfelt, sincere wishes from at least a thousand of the town's citizens.

Daniel was provided a permanent 'home care nurse' to assist with his daily care, another perk provided free of charge by the sheriff's association. This allowed Kara to pursue her school activities with limited interruption. She planned on attending the University of Alabama in less than two years, hoping to major in journalism and eventually ply her trade as a published novelist. Her father proclaimed to be her number one supporter in backing such lofty aspirations, vowing in secret to his former deputy that he would indeed survive to see his daughter graduate college and become a success in whatever endeavor she chose.

As for the cassette, it had taken Elm Hill's newly christened sheriff a full month to work up enough courage to punch the play button on her and Pete's home stereo. Her husband had been at work, getting in some much-needed overtime. Tracy's hands had shaken like an alcoholic suffering from the latter stages of the DTs while fitting the cassette into place. The voices of two dead men reverberating within the walls of her living room sent chills up her spine, true, but it was the shocking, shrieking confession of her former mentor that had sent Tracy sprinting into a nearby bathroom, barely avoiding throwing up onto the hallway carpet along the way.

For three excruciatingly long days afterward, a wrestling match of sorts took place within her subconscious. A mental battle royal involving such complicated matters as legalities versus loyalty, friendship versus moral obligation, and of course, the old stress-inducing standby of simply 'doing the right thing.' On day three of the struggle, conscience was soundly defeated in a landslide of epic proportions, taken to the psychological woodshed due to three distinct factors that overrode all else.

The man might possibly have saved her life by packing her wound with his shirt, accomplishing this while already suffering the effects of a life-threatening paralysis. The man had been more than a superior. He had been a true and tried friend to both herself and her husband. In the span of a lifetime, only a few such individuals every truly cross one's path.

Most importantly, Tracy decided that the man had already been punished enough, both from a mental and physical standpoint. Whether behind thick prison walls or those of his own home, Daniel would be forced to live with the decisions he'd made until the day came when he breathed his last, upon which his *maker* would pass a suitable sentence to match his earthly crimes. For now, he resided within the severely limited confines of his own purgatory, a dark, depression-filled landscape Tracy realized she could never even begin to truly visualize.

The cassette tape had melted and burned within a pile of dry leaves that very afternoon as yellow-tinted flames filled Tracy's moistening eyes. The claw hammer found within Curtis Barber's residence now hung in

410

Pete's woodshed out back, the handle sufficiently waxed and the metal head polished almost to the point of gleaming.

***

The phone's intrusive ring snapped Tracy from her self-imposed daze. Daniel asked if she'd come by around two, since TVLand was showing a special 'boxed set' of *Andy Griffith* episodes an hour before the Tide-Tigers kick-off on ESPN. She promised to be there as soon as her deputy reported in for afternoon duty. Tracy thoroughly enjoyed visiting Mayberry in Daniel's presence. Besides the company of his only child, it was the one thing he truly seemed to derive joy from as his health slowly deteriorated.

Besides, it was something they could share together while avoiding certain aspects of the past, certain…details better left locked away in dark, misty catacombs, never to be spoken of or dwelled upon. Details that faded over time, at least for Tracy, like childhood memories and the faces that accompanied them. Details better forgotten amongst close friends, wherein personal trust, loyalty and dependability were placed above all else.

Tracy rose from her seat, flinching slightly as the aching in her shoulder seemed to temporarily intensify. As she turned to peer out onto the sparse traffic cruising along Main Street, the sidewalks of which were littered with falling elm leaves, she began to unconsciously whistle an old TV theme song. A theme song entitled 'the fishing hole', usually accompanied by a tall, brown haired man wearing a sheriff's uniform, walking a country trail with his young, bare-footed son.

Real life could indeed be that good, Tracy deduced, if one simply *allowed* it to be.

www.ingramcontent.com/pod-product-compliance
Lightning Source LLC
Chambersburg PA
CBHW011652010726
47499CB00010B/3228